MUST LOVE

War

A SISTERS OF THE APOCALYPSE NOVEL

SHELLY CHALMERS

Dedicated to all the librarian-superheroes getting books into the hands of readers, keeping local libraries thriving, and helping to form central nodes of community – thank you. Thank you especially to my local librarians, Lana and Sandra – you both rock!

ACKNOWLEDGMENTS

As ever and always, I have a lot of people to thank in the creation of this book.

Thank you first to all of you who've enjoyed and read the series, coming to know the sisters of the apocalypse as I have. I hope you enjoy the conclusion of the series as much as I do.

This was a first for me, getting input on some setting and character names from my lovely friends over on Facebook, and boy was it fun, spoiling me for choice! First, a big thank you to Lucia Roe for suggesting the winning name selected for Rojo – Spanish for War's color, "red," in case you were wondering. Additional thanks to Melonie and Kris for suggesting Maximus or Max, which I also liked, and which kept coming up in random selection, meaning Anna's horse got to have two names (being Rojo, he'd of course insist on two names.) Thank you to everyone who enthusiastically chimed in.

Lana, thank you for your suggestions of top crime cities – while I didn't use them as settings, you might notice they do appear. And yes, you may need to get used to being acknowledged and thanked in books as you continue to be so enthusiastic and supportive. Likewise, a big thank you to Denny B for your help selecting Chicago (and even the neighborhood!) somewhere I now very much want to visit.

By now, with the messed-up relationships my characters all seem to have with their parents, it seems like I ought to mention again that I'm blessed to experience just the opposite with my wonderful parents and family. Thank you, guys, for being so fantastic that the trauma experienced by my characters is only a figment of my imagination, whereas the support you've given me is wonderfully real.

If you've read the books and live in or around my local small town, I suspect you may recognize some of the landmarks I've fictionalized and the general layout I've used for Beckwell. Please know that while I use the general geographical layout and aspects of the local history, all other aspects are complete fiction. I'm very fortunate to have found a warm, welcoming community in which to raise my family – and I hope you've enjoyed seeing my version of rural Canada, and the journey of the Beckwell residents. And don't worry – it's not over yet! You'll get to meet more in the "Shades of Beckwell" series where we get to head back to the Senior Center and meet some more fun town heroes.

Thank you as always to my amazing editor, Tera Cuskaden, for keeping track of all the details, catching my dumb mistakes, and helping to make my books stronger. You are the Queen of Details! The gorgeous covers are all thanks to Christa Holland of Paper & Sage.

Likewise thank you to my patient critique partner, Shelly A. for encouraging me when I'm down, and kicking my butt when I need it – my writing gets better because of you.

Thank you to Neelam for quietly supporting my books from day one, long before anyone else ever saw them. I likely never would have made it this far without you. Big hugs, lady!

And last (but never least) thank you to my girls for understanding sometimes I need to work, but it never means I love you less. Then to Matt: my very own superhero, Mr. Right, and the best support and husband I could ever dream up. Thank you, and lots of love.

CHAPTER 1

The knitting club had set her house on fire. At this point, she shouldn't have been surprised. Although almost being roasted alive in her bed had been an unpleasant way to wake up.

Anna Fray, War clan, stood barefoot in the cool grass, wearing only the pair of flannel pink-and-gray bunny pajamas she'd escaped the house in. She watched the flames consume her garage, her house, everything she'd owned. Everything that should have mattered.

She cocked her head, watching the flames, peculiarly detached. She wrapped her arms around herself, shivering despite the fact it was hardly cold, the pre-dawn a small respite from what would undoubtedly be another hot July day. Then again, she hadn't felt warm in months. Not since January. Not since she'd died while helping her friends face down a god and some hideous soul-sucking beasts before being resurrected. Evidently, that sort of thing had unexpected side effects.

Adolebitque illud.

Let it burn.

Perhaps if she stared at it hard enough, focused on what she'd lost, maybe it would break through the numbness. Maybe…she'd care.

The flames shot higher into the early dawn gray sky, the tall poplars whispering and shivering as if they were watching, gossiping while the house burned.

Oh, Gaia, but the gossip this would fuel. Among the rest of the townspeople, some of whom might feel a bit bad for their part in it—or so one could hope. Among her friends, three of the horsewomen of the apocalypse—Pestilence, Famine, and Death respectfully, even if they had risen hopelessly out of order. They'd all think this was "A Sign." That finally, Anna would rise with them, become War, and they would officially become The Four.

She narrowed her eyes and dug her fingernails into her forearms through the flannel.

One of the beams supporting the roof gave way in a massive explosion of sparks.

Yes, well, there was a reason War had been last since it was a more corrupting influence that threatened the safety of everyone around her. She would not become that destructive force. Even if it did appear that she'd inherited more of the dangerous abilities inherent to her clan.

Her voice, especially if emotions were involved, had long had the ability to incite people to violence. Yesterday, just before closing at the library, she'd oh-so-mildly whispered the word "overdue" to one of the knitting club members. The knitting club still met in the library Wednesday nights, even with the rumors whirling about her; use of the library for club events was free. She certainly hadn't expected that mild whisper would incite the whole bunch of them—half of them over the age of seventy—to come back and torch her house. And her with it if she hadn't heard them and woken up in time.

She stared at the flames, let them call to her, to the answering flame of War deep inside. Let herself think of how long she'd scraped and saved for this damned little house, how every bedraggled inch of it hadn't been much, but it had been hers. The house had never been about the four walls, but autonomy at eighteen from anyone else's custody, rules, and expectations. It had been freedom...of a sort.

The heat of War, of her abilities, flared inside. Nothing else. No sudden attack of sentiment. No damp eyes missing her few paltry possessions.

The small, single-car garage had almost burned out, only the lump of twisted metal that used to be her car in the middle of it.

Another wall of the house collapsed inward. That one used to be part of her bedroom. The wall fell where her bed used to be. Where until she'd heard their voices, heard the crackle of flames, she'd been sleeping.

Summer had been dry thus far. It would take so little for a spark to reach the surrounding trees and brush—or perhaps the long, tangled grass she'd been meaning to cut when she had time...or ran out of books to read. The loss of the house might not elicit significant emotion in her, but her neighbors might not feel the same for their properties. In a town as small as Beckwell, there was only a volunteer fire department, and half of them were on summer vacation. She might as well do what she could to stop the flames before they ruined someone else's day.

She closed her eyes. Inhaling deeply, she sucked in a breath of smoky air that burned a path down into her lungs. When she dug deep enough, there were answering flames within her. War ability, scorching and blistering. She grabbed hold of that ability tight until it connected with the flames devouring her house.

Besides a tendency for alarmingly short lifespans, high incidences of homicide, and lives that were for the most part brutal and violent, affinity for fire was just one of the gifts War clan was known for. All descendants of the original four horsemen were divided into large, international clans. Well, large except for War, with their tendency to kill or be killed.

The flames writhing through the house, hungrily devouring what had been her home, fought her as she and War's flame connected to them. The wild flames urged her to join them. Let them do more harm, spread and consume…or be consumed if she preferred. Fire was irritatingly rebellious that way. Like every other aspect of War ability, dangerous.

That was the corrupting and most dangerous part of War, the way it lured you in, made you want to be devoured by its flames and its power rather than controlling them. It'd been like that all her life, that temptation, that promise of power and fearlessness when so often she'd been powerless and afraid. But she hadn't given in then, and she damn well wouldn't start today.

She closed her eyes and focused on the flames, beat them back, grasped them tight in a stranglehold and held, squeezed until they couldn't breathe. Until there was no more fight, no more life.

She opened her eyes to see the last of the flames sizzle out amid thick black smoke, the charcoal skeleton of what had been her little house still smoking. Breathing in the smoky air, she let the furor of War ability drain out of her, sink into oblivion in some dark part of her. Where it could stay for good, thank you very much. The house, like the rest of her life, wasn't much. She'd started at the library when she was sixteen to afford said house. She loved the library and books…but if the previous librarian hadn't passed away and Anna inherited the position of head librarian, perhaps she would have done something else. Or perhaps not. It'd been quiet, with plenty of books and few patrons, so it wasn't too bad. It just…was.

Six months ago, she'd still wondered if maybe there was more. As she watched the three of her friends ascend to power and find love, she'd wondered what that felt like, if a happy ending could ever be possible for a War.

Six months ago, she might have cried to see her house burn. All those books destroyed—undoubtedly her most valuable property. To lose the one place other than the library where she was safe, where she couldn't hurt anyone else.

Then one of her friends had risen. The idiot gods had attacked, afraid of the horsewomen. Inconveniently, Anna had gotten herself killed. Her friend, Nia, who'd risen as Death was able to bring her back, and yet... A certain coldness had settled over her that left everything numbed, a detachment that dulled her emotions, settled a sameness over all aspects of her life. Even her friends had noticed, kept asking how she was, exchanged significant looks with one another that she pretended not to notice.

Six months ago, she'd died. Despite the steadiness of her pulse and the warmth of her blood, perhaps not all of her had come back.

If that wasn't further reason she shouldn't rise as War—among the three million and forty-seven others—then someone wasn't listening.

An engine roared behind her, and she turned and watched as a stylish, low-slung luxury car tore into her yard. The car bumped over the unevenness of her grassy driveway. The color appeared black in the pale light, the car all sleek lines and aerodynamics, though this one was dark green, the brand the one named after the cat, something expensive. Cars held little interest for her, other than their ability to convey her from one place to another.

This one, though, this one she recognized.

He didn't drive it often, a car like this too flamboyant in a small town like Beckwell. Sometimes she suspected he disguised it so no one saw it.

She always saw it. Always saw the truth.

Warmth sputtered to life inside her. The only real heat she'd felt since dying. Not War's fire—she'd smothered that as effectively as the flames on her house. Damnable, inconvenient, illogical, dangerous heat. Because of *him*.

She crossed her arms over her chest and straightened to her full height. Attempted to look nonplussed. Which was mostly true, despite the small part of her that said really, she should be upset. She wouldn't give him a weakness to use against her. He held too much power over her as it was.

The engine was still running as the door opened and he unfolded his large, muscular body from the low seat. Jogged over to her, his clothing as dark as the car. Dark hair slicked back in waves, face square and overtly masculine, perfectly symmetrical, dark brows, strong jaw shadowed with whiskers, equally dark eyes. Masculine beauty at its pinnacle.

He slowed as he approached, close enough she could see flecks of amber in his pewter eyes, the color changeable like a stormy summer sky.

The heat that spread over her because of him was more potent than the fire that had devoured her house and the singeing heat of War's flames combined. Something she should have grown out of yet never seemed to. Yes, he was attractive and the subject of her juvenile fantasies, but that had nothing to do with *him*. Now, on top of the fire and having her possessions reduced to one pair of second-hand gray flannel bunny pajamas, she'd have to deal with his interrogation.

Anna whispered a quick prayer to Gaia, primordial mother Goddess and only deity worth worshiping. *Faex*.

"Anna, are you all right?" Concern etched his features. Amber sparked in that pewter gaze, his voice molten chocolate flowing over her, tinged with the slightest hint of an accent she'd never been able to place.

"Why are you here?" If she kept her voice cold, perhaps it would remind her to stay objective. To not be stupid enough to ever forget who and what he was. The danger he'd placed she and her friends in time after time.

The fact that Wars didn't get happy endings. Ever.

Just like her parents, they were more likely to die horrible and brutal deaths.

He raised a dark brow and glanced at the blackened remains of her house, most of the smoke dissipated, illuminated by the rising sun. "I thought, perhaps, you could use assistance."

Assistance. Ha. More likely he was spying on her. He spied on everyone, and her most of all it seemed. Always there when she might need him, if she was in trouble. It was unacceptable and very unhelpful in crushing any childish infatuations some people might have held.

She nodded, then spun on her heel. "Yes. I could use a ride." She marched over to his car, his presence at her back making awareness tingle up and down her spine, making the pajama bottoms seem ridiculously thin and worn, almost indecent, though they likely covered her better than most daytime wear.

The car's engine still purred like a crouching mountain lion.

She reached the passenger door. Her lips tightened. Of course, *his* car wouldn't have a blasted standard door handle. It was just like him, to have a car that wanted to make an already challenging morning worse because now she looked like an idiot who couldn't open a door.

A dark shadow and warmth crowded her, forced her to look up and suck in a deep breath.

"How did your house burn down, Anna?" He said it as though somehow it was *her* fault.

She was tall, but he easily towered over her, the breadth of him enough to cause a small trill to shiver

7

through her, slide straight to her womb. He was broad across the shoulders, and undoubtedly there was a rugged, muscular chest under that dark gray dress-shirt.

He was temptation incarnate from the sharp edge of his jawline and high cheekbones darkened with black-brown whiskers to the often sardonic twist of those supple lips, the hint of an almost-mustache accentuating his expressions. Then there were those piercing eyes, changeable and deep gray, shot with amber when he grew angry. No actors, no models, none of the gods she'd seen could compare with the perfection of his face.

Nor the startling way it made her want to lift her fingers, trace the line of that jaw, feel the tickle of whiskers against her fingertips.

Taste those lips.

Oh, for pity's sake. She was in shock. That was it. Her house burned down, and she reacted coldly because she was in shock, and for the same reason, she was thinking about touching his face, tasting his lips. She dropped her gaze, clenched her teeth, and squeezed her hands, which were trembling in a small, obnoxious way she couldn't stop. "Your car doesn't have door handles."

He touched some spot on the side of the car where a normal vehicle might have had handles, and with a soft hiss, the door popped open. "It doesn't need them. Who started the fire? Are you hurt?"

"I. Am. Fine," she bit out. "And it wasn't me if that's what you're implying."

"You're not fine, and I implied nothing. Who started the fire?" An edge of impatience had crept into his voice, into the small tic at the side of his jaw.

Good. Enough interrogation.

The sooner she got in the car, the sooner he could take her to the library and, and…

Her usually reliable brain stuttered. Couldn't provide the requisite next step. There was always a next step.

She squeezed her hands harder until her nails bit into her palms. Glared at him, as though it was his fault. For all she knew, it was. She was calm. She was in control. She would figure it out just as she always did.

Being the obstinate creature he was, always demanding answers and giving none, he stood in her way. Waited for her answer before he'd give her what she wanted.

To hell with that. She wouldn't tell him who it was. It was hardly Lucille Kyles's fault. Although it might have helped if she'd returned her book on time. Nor was it the knitting clubs' fault for overhearing Anna speak to Ms. Kyle. Her voice—thanks to War—tended to put people into a rage. One that, this time, had cost her a house.

"It doesn't matter," she said and moved to slide past him into the car.

Where another man might have stepped out of the way, he wouldn't cede the battlefield and stood his ground. Which meant her bottom brushed his front, the hardness of his body setting heat ricocheting through her body like sparks in a library.

By the time she slid into the chair and allowed the seat belt to come around her automatically, her breath had roughened, and she experienced unsuitable thoughts about him again. Most of them having to do with turning in his arms and pressing her lips to his to see what he'd do.

He closed the door behind her.

Anna squeezed her hands in her lap—the foolish things still insisted on shaking—and closed her eyes for a moment. Control. She was in control. Emotions didn't control her. Even and especially around him. It was entirely possible he'd used one of his tricks on her, as she didn't react this way to other people. She didn't particularly like them, but she could hold her temper.

Most of the time. If they weren't damaging books or threatening her friends, she was reasonable, logical, controlled.

Except around him.

The car shifted as he folded his tall, lean, muscular bulk into the car. His shoulder bumped hers as he leaned over to close the door.

Her eyes flew open, and she jerked away, pressed herself against the passenger door. Her flannel bunny pajamas, which had seemed a little unseasonable last night, now seemed threadbare and transparent as fine silk. She pressed her lips together and her knees even more tightly together. They'd caught the same ridiculous tremble her hands suffered. How could he possibly take up 60 percent of the car's capacity? He hadn't seemed that large outside, nor the car that small.

"The library, please," she said primly.

He rested his hands, large, long-fingers dusted with dark hair, over the ultra-modern steering wheel. "Who started the fire?"

That undercurrent of suppressed fury or violence remained in his voice.

Called to that deep place inside her. Called to War's fire.

She tamped it down, dumping metaphorical ice water all over any calling or heat—especially if it had to do with him. She lifted her chin, stared straight out the windshield. "Perhaps I started it."

One could hardly tell it'd been a house. Only black skeletal remains stood forlornly in the spot where her house had been, one wall partially standing, most of it blackened lumps and rubble.

Her brow furrowed. She focused on the destruction, testing herself again. She'd lost everything. All her belongings. Her clothing. Her furniture. Her books.

She waited a moment.

The books caused a small pang, deep down. But it passed like a bird flitting overhead, with no lasting impact.

This was concerning. She should care something for what she'd lost. Logic alone said it would be a nuisance to replace. She hadn't allowed herself the frivolity of impassioned purchases; everything was frugal, only what she needed. Emotional detachment, emotional control, had to start somewhere. If there were even the slightest chance she might rise as War, she would control her emotions, and not they her.

He grumbled something beneath his breath, put the car in reverse, backed up, then swung the car around, aiming them back out her driveway. "You could try to be reasonable. I want to help you."

"You want your way, as you always do," she said as the car rolled and bumped over the driveway.

"Fine. I want my way," he ground out. "I'll take you to see Daniel." He pulled out onto the two-lane highway that ran outside her property.

"You don't have to lie to me, and you most certainly will not," she said, heat flaring again as she turned to glare at him. Daniel was not only her friend Piper's fiancé but also the town doctor. Another War ability, the ability to know the truth, had chilled the back of her neck when he'd agreed he wanted his way, which meant he was lying. Peculiar. Didn't he?

She tried for a more conciliatory tone to keep him on his toes. "The library will be fine. Thank you."

A rumbling chuckle rolled out of his throat, curled over her, and sent heat spiraling all sorts of places it had no business going.

Her breasts tightened beneath the flannel shirt, the pilled fabric only brushing against them, making the feeling more intense. She swallowed, crossed her arms, and hoped it hid his effect on her, damn him anyway.

"Ah, but that concession must have been difficult for you. Fine. Provided you show no further symptoms, I'll take you to the apartment above the bar. You can get cleaned up, and I'll call your friends. After which I'll see you to the library."

Her face warmed and her neck tightened. "You'll take me to the library now."

One dark brow rose. "You're sweaty and pale. There's soot on your face and clothing, and you reek of smoke. You just lost your house, along with everything you own. You are many things, but you're not fine."

She surreptitiously examined her clothing for soot. Damn him. There were black smears on her pajama bottoms and top. "I'm naturally pasty, and I was standing near a fire. Soot happens, and it washes off. I lost my house, not my home. It was the place I kept my books and clothes, cooked my food, and occasionally slept. I'll be perfectly safe at the library."

A low growl rumbled in his throat, and he adjusted his grip on the steering wheel. "Whoever burned down your house could just as well attack you there."

"Not with the wards you placed on it."

There was a small pause. "What wards?"

The back of her neck chilled. Unfortunately, when it came to him, she could tell if he was lying, but not what the truth was. This time, though, it didn't matter. She'd tricked him. "The ones you just confirmed. I saw you prancing around out there a few weeks after Nia got back from Braelyn."

Braelyn was the home of the gods, gods who'd arrested and imprisoned her friend Nia on trumped-up charges of breaking the laws of nature when she brought someone back from death. It hadn't ended well for the gods. Nia had risen as Death, and then the four women had stolen one of the god's immortality when he'd attacked Beckwell in vengeance. The same battle that had gotten Anna killed.

"I don't prance," the large man beside her rumbled.

No, he didn't. He strode with power and self-assurance, command in every inch of him as he entered a room or just walked across the street. Anna shivered.

"Sashayed then." She could almost hear his teeth grinding. Served him right. He called everyone by their full names mostly, she suspected, because it irritated them.

"Hadrianna…" he said warningly.

Right on schedule. Sometimes she pretended to be bothered by it since even he deserved his small pleasures, but if she was rising—her stomach clenched—she didn't have that luxury. "It doesn't bother me, you know. I like the historical reference. Hadrian was a brilliant emperor, considered one of the Five Good Emperors, and known more for building than killing. My parents probably didn't know that when they selected the name. Not nearly bloodthirsty enough for the War clan."

He just shook his head, a small smile playing at his lips. "I am utterly transparent to you, am I?"

"Of course."

Not at all. Other people's secrets whispered themselves to her, from their infidelities to their dark pasts. Not his. She only knew whether he lied, which was most of the time, or spoke the truth. They'd also known each other most of her life, though all she really knew of him was what he chose to reveal.

She scowled out the passenger side window at the passing trees that hemmed in either side of the road. "Library. Please."

"How many books did you lose?" he asked quietly.

Her shoulders tightened. The house was just a building. The car a means of transport. The books though… They were treasures, her only escape since people were dishonest and complicated, with their silly social rules, and their truths insisting on revealing themselves to her whether she wanted them or not.

Except the books had started to do the same. Words rearranging themselves on the page to correct untruths and mistakes. It was like her dearest, most-trusted companions had stabbed her in the back.

"A few. Nothing precious. I moved most of them to the library after your prancing and my suspicions."

"Setting wards, not prancing." His voice roughened. "I'm sorry, Anna. I should have been more careful. I suspected the gods would come after you next. They've come after all your friends, and you're the most vulnerable without your full abilities. I didn't consider the danger any of the residents could pose. I should have."

"I can take care of myself," she said, her voice tight. Ahead, the trees thinned with Beckwell proper, the small clutch of buildings that made up the central town.

"Of course, you can. It doesn't mean I don't want to help."

Help. All everyone seemed to want to do lately was help. She massaged her forehead, foolish hands still shaking. Could they make her dinner? Did she want to talk about it? Was everything okay?

Didn't they understand that asking only made it worse, only made it harder to ignore?

His fingers tapped along the top of the steering wheel. "Fine. If you won't see Daniel, what about the others? Ginny? Piper? Nia?"

"Piper's very pregnant; she doesn't need additional stress. Ginny is slammed with cupcake orders and the complications of the new business. Nia's house is full enough, what with all the kids. I told you. I lost my house. The library is my home."

"A library is not a home," he said, shooting her a sideways look that dared question her logic.

She pretended to ignore it, shifting in her seat. "Not

to you maybe."

"I mean it isn't a proper home. Wards can protect the structure, but it's a public building. It can't receive the same protection and wards that a private residence can." He hesitated a moment. "Come home with me."

Her pulse jumped into her throat, heat flared through her, and for a second, her throat squeezed so tight she couldn't breathe. Go home. With *him*. When she'd been small, she'd lived with him for just over a week before he sent her away, and he still reserved that same room for her on the rare occasion—twice in the last decade—that she'd stayed there. She eased in one small breath after another, looking down to find her fingers dug into her pink-and-gray bunny pajamas.

It should have been fear that made her want to avoid his house.

It wasn't.

At least, not fear of him. But fear of herself. Of desire too long held, too damned difficult to ignore, especially in this close a proximity. Dear Gaia, what if he found out?

"No, the library," she managed to wheeze out.

"Are you okay? You're not breathing properly. Probably smoke inhalation. We're going—" He gunned the engine toward the empty four-way.

"I'm fine!" she bellowed. "Library. And watch your driving. You know what a stickler for rules Mal's become."

Mal, or rather, Malcolm Quilan, used to be the town bad boy, but since moving in with Nia, he'd become not only the local police chief but also very particular when it came to things like rolling stops and speeding through the four-way.

Trees thinned on either side of the road and gave way to the few buildings that made up central Beckwell, with the school to the left, gas station and bar to the right, and across the four-way stop, the emergency station's blocky blue metal building. Across from that, her library, a log structure with a welcoming front porch.

He turned into the parking lot of the bar before pulling around back, the tires crunching through the gravel. He shut off the car, the headlights still illuminating the backside of the old house that had been converted into the bar. *His* bar.

Silence crept in, making the dim, quiet morning surrounding them more intimate and velvety.

"This *isn't* the library. Very well. I'll walk." She reached for the door handle. She had to get out of here. Away from temptation.

One minute he was in the car. The next, he opened her door and stood blocking her way. He'd either moved lightning fast...or he'd used some of his other abilities.

He leaned down, meeting her glare. "Come inside. At least have a shower, get changed. The apartment above the bar is empty."

She narrowed her eyes. "Then I can get rid of you?" She couldn't afford to spend more time with him, not with the irrational responses he triggered within her. Emotion: hot, strong, and dangerous. Rather like the man himself.

He raised a brow but said nothing.

She growled before rolling her eyes. "Fine. Move and let me past." *Please don't make me get too close again. Please save me from myself and my idiotic libido.*

He moved aside to let her climb out.

He was, without a doubt, the most irritatingly gorgeous man she'd ever met.

No, not man. Demigod. Loki. Trouble spelled with an "L." And the last person a woman about to rise as War could risk getting entangled with.

CHAPTER 2

The thing about beginnings was that, inevitably, they demand endings. Creation begets destruction.

That was where he, Loki Laufeyjarson, came in. And why Anna Fray became an alluring complication he hadn't anticipated. He needed War, which meant he needed Anna alive and strong—and he'd use whatever means necessary to keep her that way. Including—and especially—summoning the wrath of her friends and picking fights.

Loki pressed send on the 9-1-1 text he'd sent her friends, pocketed the phone, then leaned back against the wall outside the closed bathroom door in the apartment above the bar, listening to the rushing water of the shower inside. Warm mist scented with floral shampoo rose from beneath the door as Anna washed off the aftereffects of the fire. Images of water and bubbles sluicing over shining, wet female flesh and between generous breasts frolicked through his head. His body stirred.

He opened his eyes. Frowned.

Anna was both essential to his plan and a most unexpected distraction.

She was supposed to be his former ward who would rise as War and help him achieve his ultimate destiny. Ragnarök. The end of the world, but a new beginning for humanity. Hope.

Of course, being Anna, she'd happily smashed the elegant simplicity of those plans to smithereens. Worse, not even with intentionality, simply just by being. Just as she'd remained his ward when the Lacks had taken her in but were too reluctant to take full responsibility for a War heir, she remained always on the periphery of his thoughts. She saw through all his best illusions—even the exceptionally good ones, which was galling. She was the one person whose thoughts he couldn't enter. She analyzed his behavior like Freud, saw through every lie. She appeared oblivious to her physical attributes, the arresting woman she'd grown into these past few years. She was reckless, blunt, and stubborn. He and her friends had been telling her for months the gods would come after her, but she seemed to have taken no added precautions, had almost been burned alive in her house, for Ymir's sake. He ground his teeth. She even had him evoking the names of the old gods.

The one person he needed most for the plan, and he was rendered virtually powerless around her. It was as though the Norns laughed at him. Typical for Fates, all of them sadistic.

"Are you standing outside the door?" Anna called out over the rush of the water and through the door, suspicion lacing her voice.

"I'm keeping watch."

"Go away."

"That would make it harder to keep watch."

Grumbles and— He cocked an ear. Yes, that sounded like Latin. She was swearing and cursing him out in Latin.

His lips twitched despite himself.

She was smart as hell, too, something he both admired and dreaded. He pictured her standing there, fully bared and dripping when he opened the door. Another woman, and he'd have opened that door, indulged them both, and sated their bodies.

Not Anna. She had an innate talent for foiling his plans. Ymir help him if she tried to do so intentionally.

The rush of water shut off. Shower curtains slid against the metal rod inside the bathroom. Fabric flapped, and this time he imagined her stroking the soft fluffy towel over her body, down those long legs, over her—

He rubbed at his forehead. His imagination proved especially unhelpful today. This was Anna, who would flay him alive if she had any inkling of half the thoughts he had about her, Beckwell's very own suppressed and delicious librarian. There was a reason sexy librarians were a thing.

A fantasy he, sadly, couldn't indulge. He had to protect Anna, ideally with less lust involved. The gods, jealous of her power and that of her friends, the other horsewomen of the apocalypse, were looking for any vulnerability, and Anna was a lot easier to kill before she rose. Now he had his Beckwellians to worry about, too, starting fires and making a nuisance of themselves.

The bathroom door clicked open.

He was slow to move, as though it didn't matter to him whether she was dressed…or if somehow his wildest fantasy came true, and she stood there, naked, wet, and wanting.

She hesitated in the bathroom doorway, steam erupting around her. Unfortunately, clothed. Long dark hair hung in wet curls around her shoulders, making her skin look even paler, highlighting the blue of her eyes, as clear as the rivers of Jötunheim, Norse land of giants and his birthplace. Her hair wet the dark green silk shirt that gaped at the top and clung to her body, to the damp, bare peaks of her breasts beneath.

His shirt. On her.

He shifted, lust rolling through him, hardening his shaft. A new fantasy that involved the removal of that shirt, or her only ever being allowed to wear that shirt was quick to spring to mind.

It was official. She'd been created to drive him mad.

He should have gone with the plaid, the other spare clothes he kept downstairs for when he was more often in Lou form. The flannel was the softest he could source— he would never wear rags again as he had at the lowest point in his life, at the times he'd hated himself—but choosing between flannel and silk to touch her skin, it had to be silk.

She frowned at her outfit, pulled at the shirt, which only made him harder. His silk shirt didn't conceal the fact that she was braless, and the tight pair of black leggings a former employee had left behind hugged her slim, muscular legs.

"Are you sure…this is all right?" That blue gaze met his.

He should have let her stay in those ridiculous pajamas. Forget her washing the smoke off, being more comfortable. Pink bunnies were, overall, slightly less alluring than clinging silk. Even on Anna.

"The alternative is red flannel." Red would suit the War clan. But in Lou form, he was broader, heavier. A high chance it would gape even more than the silk did, reveal creamy flesh. "Silk is more professional."

She rolled her eyes, then stepped out into the hall. "You know how I feel about lies." Then she shrugged. "Well, it's Thursday. Thursdays are quiet."

Just as he reconsidered his position on seducing Anna to get her to go along with his plan—an idea which he'd considered and discarded numerous times in the past year—she turned on her heel and headed toward the stairs.

"Where are you going?" It chafed, following rather than leading. Though when it came to her, he seemed to forever be chasing.

"To the library," she said, rushing down the stairs.

"It's…" He glanced at his watch. "Just after six in the morning. Have you considered perhaps *not* going in to work the day you nearly died?" His tone was heavy with sarcasm.

She sniffed. "If I did that, the library would barely be open most days."

Concerningly, there wasn't sarcasm in her tone.

He caught up to her just after she stepped through the door, and he blocked her path with his body.

"Let me pass," she ground out, trying to move around him while he mirrored her movements.

He did a quick check of the area, using his eyes and other senses to look for threats. Only trees, a few deer out behind the bar and restaurant, and his car.

"You were almost roasted alive this morning. That's enough attempts on your life for at least an hour. Be careful."

He stepped aside, and Anna grumbled at him some more, marching quickly around the building. He easily kept pace with her, continuing to look for threats.

"Don't tell me what to do." Her footsteps crunched through the gravel of the parking lot.

"I wouldn't dream of it," he murmured. Telling Anna what to do was an almost sure way to get her to the opposite. Convincing her it was her idea in the first place, though, that could work. He'd learned that the moment he entered her parents' burning house and tried to coax the frightened child to abandon her refuge in the closet. Grown-up Anna was no less stubborn. The alluring aspect just made the characteristic more troubling.

The parking lot up front, shared between his bar and

the neighboring minimart and gas station, was deserted this early. As was the school parking lot across the way, a veritable ghost town now that it was summer. Yet he'd foiled two assassin attempts on Anna in as many weeks by the gods' version of the CIA—USELESS. The idiots had never been much for thinking things like that acronym through.

He'd sent the USELESS agents back alive, but bruised and confused enough to make his message clear: Anna was under his protection.

"I'm quite sure I can make it the short distance to the library alone," she said acidly.

Indeed. While she'd be close to unstoppable when she rose, he'd missed the potential threat from the town itself—*his* Beckwellians, *his* town, damn it. He wouldn't miss another.

"I don't mind."

Another grumble and, from the sounds of it, she'd called him an idiot in Latin.

They marched diagonally across the empty four-way stop, her long-gait matched with his. Ymir, those leggings revealed curves he hadn't been certain were there under the dowdy clothing she usually wore. Though dowdy had been better for his peace of mind.

Still keeping watch for threats, he glanced at his watch. His texted 911 should have had the necessary effect. Reinforcements should be arriving just in time to give Anna her space but keep her protected.

He could reposition his hired guard to keep watch at the library, but she would be safer in a residence. Ginny and James were tight in their small house and with the burgeoning cupcake business. Piper and Daniel were out, what with the impending arrival of their twins. Mal and Nia were the best bet, with their rambling house. And considering they were the town Police Chief and the personification of Death.

She'd be safest under his roof. Under his protection. The very idea was risky, letting another War into his home, who could potentially wreak intense emotional damage as the last one had. It was that or see her killed before she could reach her potential. Before she could fulfill his plan.

The trick would be convincing her.

They'd just stepped across the asphalt road and onto the clipped scrub-grass in front of the library when the rumble of a motorcycle growled down the road from the west.

Anna turned a flashing glare on him. "You didn't."

The gray chopper stopped carefully at the four-way, its driver a diminutive, black-clad rider. An even smaller rider, this one dressed in pink, rode in a child's seat behind the black-clad rider. With another rumble, the chopper drove past them and turned into the library parking lot, bringing with it the Death horsewoman, Nia Amort, and her daughter.

Right on time. Nia had become significantly more prompt since rising as Death.

"I told you. I'm. Fine," Anna said.

He let his gaze travel over her, studying her still damp hair, her face with dark slashing brows and full, dark lips, complexion too pale by half. She shivered beneath his silk shirt, a slight chill in the early morning air, those leggings providing little coverage. His librarian fantasy once more firmly in place, his gaze met hers, found the color staining her high cheekbones.

"You are many things. But you are not 'fine.' You need them."

She might have snapped back with something if not for the sound of show tunes and a deafening rendition of "I've Got Rhythm" came from the large, black ice-cream truck with no serving windows as it came barreling down the road from the south.

It barely slowed enough to make the turn into the driveway for the library and community center and heralded the arrival of the Famine horsewoman, Ginny Derth, formerly Lack. She'd been born into the Lack household where Anna had grown up after he'd brought her to Beckwell and was certainly Anna's closest friend.

Anna massaged her forehead.

He looked north for the snot-green Porta Potty service truck. Ah, yes. There it was. Barely a pause at the four-way before it pulled into the parking lot. Piper Bane, Pestilence clan, must have been driving.

"There was no reason to wake them," Anna said stubbornly.

Nia shook her curly hair out as she removed the helmet, then lifted the smaller, pink mini-her off the chopper. She'd brought her daughter, Asha, and once they stepped off the chopper, it transformed into Nia's horse, a large gray owl, which swooped toward the fence and settled there.

The tall, redheaded Ginny had barely climbed out of the ice-cream truck before it transformed into a portly black pig who scrambled toward the fence and started telling the owl something. The owl turned its head and stared at the black pig with something between patience and distaste. The three apocalypse horses had, in recent months, developed a friendship of sorts.

The snot-green Porta Potty truck rolled to a stop. The driver's side door opened, a dainty foot popping out as petite, blonde Piper Bane, currently heavily pregnant, began to step out. The passenger door opened, and a large, bronze-skinned man climbed out in a hurry, rushing around the truck to help her.

Loki's shoulders tightened.

The man was Daniel Quilan. Piper's fiancé. The town doctor. And, formerly, his closest friend. Or perhaps more accurately, his alter ego Lou's friend.

Ymir knew, no one ever trusted Loki enough to call him a friend.

The three women, accompanied by Nia's daughter and Daniel, headed down the sidewalk toward him and Anna.

Loki tucked his hands in his pockets and glanced toward the bar. She'd be with her friends. Better he headed back to the bar. Not interfere or wait for them to ask him to leave.

"I told you I was fine. I don't need a doctor," Anna said, her gaze on Daniel.

"If he's here anyway..." He'd communicated his concern via text. Daniel didn't respond to the texts, but nor could he glower his disappointment via text over what he saw as Loki's betrayal.

Anna turned her glare on him. "You should go."

Her friends came up beside her. Daniel's glare was the fiercest, but the others looked only a little friendlier. There was his cue.

He gave Anna a short nod, then offered her friends the same before he turned and strode back toward the bar.

She was safe for now. He just needed to convince her to see his plan through.

To trigger Ragnarök by rising as War and killing him.

CHAPTER 3

Her hand on the library door, Anna ground her teeth as she watched Loki's powerful form make his escape. He cut across the lawn in front of the library, then diagonally through the four-way toward his bar. He'd brought her friends down on her head, and now she'd have to find some way to convince them all was well, damn him.

"So, the fire. Was that sexcapades gone wrong? You're wearing Loki's shirt." Nia, the petite Death horsewoman, was first up the sidewalk to reach Anna. The breeze blew Nia's short, curly black hair in her face, and she shoved it aside, a smartass smile quirking her eyebrow and curving her lips.

"What's 'sexcapades,' Mama?" Her four-year-old daughter and mini-me, Asha, said, yawning as she stepped out from behind Nia. Pink pajama bottoms stuck out from beneath her coat. She waved at Anna. "Hi, Auntie Anna."

"Grown-up stuff. Auntie Anna is in denial," Nia said.

"Hello, Asha," Anna said almost pleasantly before

she turned her back on the two of them and punched in the code for the door lock.

The idea that she and Loki would... Heat curled through her. She frowned, shaking off the inappropriate reaction. He was Loki. She wasn't foolish enough to believe a stable, loving relationship was possible for any War heir, especially not with someone like him. Emotion and love were dangerous for Wars. Had killed her parents.

Then there was the entire "Loki" element. Admittedly, he was hotter than sin, making any of the men she'd met since pale in dull comparison. Known troublemaker. Liar and trickster extraordinaire. She would never have been foolish enough to trust her heart in guiding her actions, particularly if it led to him. Even if there was the remotest possibility he could be interested.

Although, that look he'd given her before he'd left... So heated, so hungry...

"Is denial because she died?" Asha whispered in the non-whispers four-year-olds did best.

The door popped open, and Anna turned toward Nia. "Really?"

Nia shrugged. "She's only kind of four. She may as well understand the world sooner rather than later. And this isn't cool, Anna, almost getting yourself killed for the second time in six months."

Now they both just looked at her, Nia and her mini-me, who saw far more than a child should be able to. Ha. Just wait until Nia found out Asha's truth. That was no ordinary child.

Anna ignored them both, stepping into the library and disarming the security system. "Why don't you take Asha home. She's tired. I'm fine."

"You know, if you're going to keep lying about it, the least you could do is come up with a different line," petite, blonde, and heavily pregnant Piper Bane, Pestilence clan said, huffing a little. "Your house burned down. You can't be okay."

Piper came through the door flanked by Ginny and Daniel. Piper was pregnant with twins, and Daniel had developed acute paranoia, hardly letting his fiancée out of his sight.

Daniel finished helping Piper take a seat at the scarred conference table near the front of the library, the scene of many such meetings—though fortunately, few had been about Anna. This past year they'd had to pull up extra chairs, but the core always remained her and her three closest friends since kindergarten. The only people she trusted.

The ones she had to protect from some truths.

She may have trained them, she may have prepared them to rise, but she was woefully unprepared herself. She wasn't as strong as them. She couldn't become one of the Four, because she couldn't control the abilities. The abilities controlled her, would destroy her if they could.

Anna busied herself with the usual tasks getting the library open for the day: turn on the lights, boot the computer, check for returns.

Daniel cleared his throat, straightened his muscular frame that was almost as large as Loki's, and turned his caramel gaze on her. "I understand there was a fire. Possible smoke inhalation, burns."

You're not winning this, Loki. She fisted her hands, straightening in front of the computer. "No. You heard wrong. I'm fine."

"Bullshit." Nia pretended to cough as she returned from the children's section where she'd settled Asha down in one of the new beanbag chairs. She then perched on the edge of the table. It was possible the Death horsewoman was allergic to sitting in chairs like a normal human being. She shucked off her boots and put one foot on the chair, letting the other swing, her gaze steady and too perceptive.

Anna looked away. The slightly smoky, musty scent of Special Collections, most of which was stored behind her circulation desk, was comfortingly familiar. She hadn't lied to Loki; this was more home than her house had ever been. She'd escaped here from the Lacks' benevolent negligence. Here, among the pages of books she'd found escape, then when it had turned into a job at sixteen, that money had provided a different escape.

Seemingly as though the library woke with her presence, the books began their whispering, but not their shouting, the maddening habit they seemed to have acquired in the past six months. Whispers from the stacks, from the non-fiction and biographies telling her every fallacy they held. From the fiction section, whispering every historical inaccuracy, every scientific impossibility. They were like the rustle of pages, whispers between the shelves, but impossible to ignore. Thankfully, the truths weren't yet deafening – which meant she couldn't be that tired. War revealed the truths in a constant, sanity-challenging avalanche. She was still able to block them out partially, which also still made books better than people. Ergo, she was up to convincing her friends she was fine. Then she'd have a normal day at the library and, well, the plan wasn't much more than that yet. For now, it would do.

The ghosts, though, they were almost as bad as people. Another unfortunate side effect of dying: now Anna could see the blasted things, and perhaps worse, she'd had to concede that Nia was right. The library did have too many ghosts, most of them lined up for Nia's ghost therapy sessions in the children's section, and almost as loud as the living with their truths, the sins that haunted them in life and held them here in death. As if potentially rising as the War horsewoman wasn't bad enough, she had to contend with Death gifts too? Grossly unfair.

"Come on, Anna. Take a seat over here. We're not going away until you talk to us, tell us what happened," Ginny said, settling at the table with a steaming pail of her delectable muffins. Research and time had yet to prove the heir to Famine's cooking was harmful, though it was impossible to resist, even for her fellow horsewomen, who were supposed to be immune to each other's abilities.

Anna shot Ginny a baleful glare.

The redhead just raised an eyebrow, pulled out Anna's usual chair at the head of the table, and patted it. She'd gotten much bossier since marriage. Happier, too, which was wonderful. She was the closest thing Anna had to a sister, and Ginny had always gone out of her way to make up for her parents' cool reception growing up.

"If you sit, I'll give you coffee," the Famine heir bribed.

Gaia, she could use the caffeine. Shoulders back, head held high, Anna came around the circulation desk and sat under the obnoxiously watchful gazes of her friends.

Ginny quickly returned with coffee mugs for everyone else, and Anna's extra-large librarian mug which read: "Rearrange my shelves, I'll rearrange your face." Nia had given it to her for Christmas, and besides being charmingly accurate, it held nearly half a liter.

Anna barely resisted tearing it from Ginny's hands, wrapped her cold fingers around the mug, and leaned over to inhale the sacred brew's heavenly scent. Gaia, that was good.

"Geezus, no wonder you never have sex," Nia said. "Okay, enough making out with the coffee. Spill. The fire and Loki being there this morning. Why, what happened, who started the fire, where are you going to stay tonight?"

A small jolt slid through Anna. Where *would* she stay tonight? How peculiar, not to go home to her lumpy bed and the second-hand quilt someone had lovingly stitched before it ended up in the thrift store. Well, there was still the sleeping bag beneath the circulation desk. She'd slept here before. She could again.

Come home with me. Loki's ridiculous offer whispered through her head. He hadn't really meant it, had he? She shivered.

Daniel cleared his throat, sounding potentially as uncomfortable as her. "Ladies, Anna is far too intelligent to get involved with Loki."

"I said fucking, not involved. Totally different," Nia said, then snorted. "Gee, Daniel, your face turns red fast."

"Be nice. He's not as used to ignoring you as we are," Piper said. "If anything, Loki's probably the one who started the fire." Her tone darkened. "Whatever he needed for one of his plans, why let a little thing like morals stop him."

Daniel and Piper both tended to believe the worst of Loki. Understandable due to how he'd manipulated them both. Perhaps she should have told Daniel that the fat friendly bartender he'd called a friend was also Loki in the guise of Lou. She'd always seen through his disguises; they were just another form of a lie. Besides, at the time, the friendship that had started in Daniel's teens hadn't seemed dangerous to either of them. Everyone's certainty that Loki was to blame for all things seemed a bit unfair. He'd also defended and helped them when he could.

Faex. Anna cursed in Latin as she frowned down into her mug. Clearly, the caffeine hadn't kicked in if she was considering defending Loki.

Ginny bumped Anna's elbow. "Hey. That's enough coffee. Even you can't down that whole cup without taking a breath. You could try talking to us. That's what people do—talk to their friends, let them help."

"People who aren't me, perhaps. I can handle my own affairs," Anna said, voice chilly.

"Sweetie, your house burned down this morning.

That has to mean something. To me, at the very least, it means you could use some help," Ginny said gently.

Oh, for pity's sake. Anna's lips tightened. Here they went again. Soon they'd try wrapping her in a blanket, take away her coffee, and give her cocoa.

Ginny grimaced. "You know I love you, that we all love you, right?"

Tingling started at the base of Anna's back, and an ache grew behind her eyes. "I'm not going to like what you have to say, am I?"

Ginny was the only good thing about coming to Beckwell, the sister she'd always dreamed of, and the only warmth that existed in the Lack household. She was as easy to read as a dictionary.

Ginny and the others exchanged a look.

"Spit it out," Anna said.

Piper became intensely interested in her coffee cup.

Daniel stuffed a muffin—the entire muffin—in his mouth.

Nia raised her brows and sipped her coffee, watching.

Ginny scowled at the others, then settled herself and reached for Anna's hand. "The gods and their agents from USELESS have come down hard on Beckwell after the small rebellion when Nia rose. They're threatening families, imposing unreasonable laws about magic usage within all the paranormal communities. They're particularly afraid of us, and they're pissed. They came after me, and they came after Nia…and we've been expecting they'd come after you. With our abilities, we're not as vulnerable to them anymore. You are. We're worried about you."

Anna focused on each of her friends, letting them see just how she felt about them talking about her behind her back. Piper's face was bright pink.

Nia stared right back and lowered her coffee. "Anna,

we know you haven't been 'fine' for a while," she said quietly. "Not since January. When that god killed you."

Anna grabbed her mug and strode away from the table, away from the worry and pity in her friends' faces. She topped up her coffee from the machine. "Would you please make up your mind why you're worried today? Is it the fire, the gods, or my having died? I'm alive now, it was just a house, and we've dealt with the gods once. We'll deal with them again." Her hands trembled as she tried to pour herself more coffee. She clenched her teeth against it and squeezed the coffee pot tighter.

Uncomfortable, tense silence stretched behind her from the conference table.

She squeezed her eyes shut, took one breath, two. *She* was supposed to be the one who took care of them. She was the one who made the plans, always had a plan.

You don't have a plan now, a small voice whispered inside.

She'd spent all this time preparing them for when they rose and hadn't really thought what she'd do when—or if—she rose herself. Now here she was, inciting old women to burn her house down, not a hint of any of the positive companion abilities like her friends had experienced. She wasn't a healer like Piper was, a baker and plant-whisperer like Ginny, nor able to reverse death itself like Nia. War's companion ability should have been peace, but she hadn't seen a hint of it in herself or barely anything about it in her research.

Woodenly, she forced herself back to the table, back into her chair. They were trying to help her. They were being kind, something they were much better at than her, especially when it came to the receiving end. She turned her mug on the table until it was perfectly square in front of her.

"I...I'm sorry," she said, a burning ache in the back of her throat. "Yes, today has been stressful. I appreciate your concern I just…I need to deal with this on my own."

"You don't have to," Piper said softly. "You've always been there for us."

"The gods will come after you because just like us, they know you're War. You will rise," Ginny said. "And they're going to have one honey of a fight on their hands when they do."

Gaia, please don't let it be true. Please let there be some chance, however small, that this wasn't it, and she wasn't already doomed to rise as War. The worst of the horsemen clans, it was all about destruction and violence.

"Maybe…you should consider finding somewhere safe. Loki invited us to stay with him when the gods came after me. I suspect he'd be willing to extend that invitation to you too," Ginny said slowly.

Her throat squeezed. He already had.

"You don't…think I can take care of myself?" She lifted her gaze to her friends.

Nia snorted. "Dude, if anyone could take of themselves, it'd be you. But—"

She was cut off by a knock on the door.

They all shared a look. This was a private party, and it was still too early for anyone to even dream the library was open.

Daniel went to peer through the curtain, then unlocked and opened the door.

His identical twin brother, Mal Quilan, his dark brown hair ruffled and a scowl on his handsome face, stepped in, carrying a small animal cage. "Chief Quilan" was stitched on the breast pocket of his dark green police uniform, and there were dark shadows under his eyes. He clanked the cage down on the table. "Sorry I'm late. Got Loki's 911, but had this to handle."

Anna glanced at the cage, her lips thinning. There was a bird in there, medium-sized, gray with lighter tones around the head and tops of the wings above the black tips. A pigeon. Flying vermin. On her library table.

"Daddy?" A sleepy Asha stumbled from the back of the library, rubbing her eyes then running from the children's section when she spotted Mal.

Mal scooped her up into his arms. "Hey, Peanut. Sorry I was late. How 'bout I take you home and we have pancakes, then a nap?"

Anna crossed her arms and nodded toward the cage. "You'll be taking your bird with you, I hope."

Mal sent a dark look toward the cage and snorted. "Nope. Pretty sure he's your problem now, not mine."

Everyone leaned in for a closer look, even Asha from Mal's arms.

Everyone except Anna.

Her throat squeezed too tight for words, held that way until she had to gasp for breath, spots dancing in front of her eyes. Her hands shook harder now. *No, no, no, it couldn't be...*

"What? You've never seen a pigeon before?" the pigeon said, clear as day, the voice masculine, entitled, and pissed off.

Everyone but Asha and Anna leaned back from the cage.

Anna struggled not to hyperventilate. The pigeon could *talk*. She backed up until she collided with the circulation desk. Yes, fine, she may have started watching for talking animals recently—because she wanted to avoid them.

"Each horseman shall be granted a horse, suitable to their ability, clan, and milieu." The words of the horseman clans mocked her.

Horseman horses were rarely actual horses these days. Her friends' had started as a toad, a grasshopper, and a moth respectively.

"It's a talking bird! Can I keep it?" Asha cried.

"I am not a thing. You may not keep me," the bird

said, growing ever more irritated. It hopped closer to the cage door, its head twitching as it blinked those black beady eyes. "You. Officer Yokel. I demand you let me out of here and issue a formal apology."

Mal leaned closer, glowering, his voice a growl. "Yeah, good luck with that. If I knew how to charge a pigeon with assaulting an officer or with any of the charges you racked up last night it'd be years before you flew free, buddy." He massaged an angry red scratch on the side of his muscular neck. Then he scrubbed a hand down over his face. "I'm arguing with a winged rat. I need to go home. Get some sleep. Ready to go, Peanut?"

Daniel leaned closer. "What exactly did it do?" He studied the bird like the unusual specimen it was.

The pigeon grunted, hopping around the cage again, ruffling his wings. "Sure, Officer Dufus. Why don't you tell them some of the lies you cooked up?"

"Careful. It bites. And lies. *You* started a bar fight over at Loki's Place," Mal said, referring to Loki's bar and restaurant, formerly known as Lou's Place...until they'd all figured out the truth.

It'd always been Loki's place to her. His territory. Necessary to avoid for her sanity.

"A bird started a bar fight?" Nia hopped off the table and whistled, studying the bird. "Damn, Mal. You should have called me. I would have liked to see that." She snuggled into his side, kissing him on his jaw.

He wrapped his free arm around her.

"I did not start the fight," the bird said indignantly. "That bartender refused to serve me. That's specism. She broke the law. Not me. You arrested me."

Anna frowned. Actually...that did sound like specism. She gave herself an internal shake. It was a talking bird. Trouble with wings. She'd had quite enough trouble for this decade today already.

"Maybe. That didn't mean you had to attack the

bartender or pick up that bottle with your talons that you swung at her. Ditto with the three people who tried to stop you amid your nonstop swears and insults. Never mind all the bottles you broke and threw after that," Mal said.

The pigeon preened, spreading his wings and shaking them out before settling the feathers once more. "Amateurs didn't know what hit them." There was a note of pride in its voice.

Her friends looked from her to the pigeon, then back again, finally landing back on her.

Anna crossed her arms. "There's hardly need to jump to conclusions."

Her friends looked doubtful.

She turned on Mal. "You don't know it's my…that it has anything to do with me. It could be a shapeshifter. A pixie in animal form. Enchanted that way. Someone's familiar."

Mal stifled a yawn, his gaze intentionally bland as he adjusted his grip on Asha in one arm, his other still around Nia, hand sliding up and down her bare arm. His gaze, though, never left Anna as he spoke. "Tell her your name, bird."

"Maximus Rojo," the pigeon said. "I realize identifying specific species might be difficult for someone with such limited intellect, but I'm a pigeon. Should I just go around calling you 'man'?" It barked out a laugh. "Then again, guess you'd have to *be* a man for that."

A tic started in Mal's jaw. He leaned over, pressed a kiss to Nia's head, then curled both arms around Asha. "I'm beat. Esther good giving you a ride? I saw her and the others outside," he said, referring to Nia's horse.

Nia grabbed his collar and tugged him closer, pressing an open-mouthed kiss to his lips. Short, but hot.

Anna looked away, her face burning.

"She can stay with me if you're that tired," Nia said

softly, bringing Anna's gaze up again.

"Nah. Peanut and I need some daddy-daughter time." Mal rubbed his hand through Nia's curls before he gave Asha a wink.

The emotion curling between them was so pure, so true it almost hurt to look at. The same thing she saw with Ginny and James, and Piper and Daniel.

There was that tiny twinge inside Anna again, shifting the icy blanket, the hint of a foggy memory with her parents. The thought made her stomach hurt, the faint memory of Daddy's arms around her, him swinging her around and around in the garden while she and Mommy laughed. A moment when life was perfect.

She shifted her gaze away again, blinking away the memory.

"No stomach for the saccharine? Me neither," the pigeon, or rather Maximus Rojo said.

Carrier pigeons had a long history with battle. Maximus, meaning greatest or largest, was also associated with Magnus Maximus, a legendary Roman usurper, distinguished general, and popular emperor. Then there was Rojo. Spanish for red.

War's color.

Faex. Her stomach quivered, the coffee sloshing uneasily.

The pigeon hopped closer within the cage, peered belligerently out at her. "What? You got a problem with me?"

"You're him, aren't you? The War horse," Anna whispered.

She was vaguely aware of her friends watching her, Mal and Asha near the door. Ginny, Nia, and Piper stood, flanked her like defensive warriors.

"What's it to you if I am?" the bird demanded.

Anna took a deep, shuddering breath that didn't quiet the nausea whirling in her stomach. Her hands trembled again, and her knees were in little better a state. Goddess, did this mean it was impossible to forestall the possibility any longer? Was her rising inevitable?

No, please, please, there had to be a way to escape it. Any way.

"I…" Her voice stuck in her throat. She tried again. "I'm War."

CHAPTER 4

Maximus Rojo, the gray talking pigeon, poked his beak through the bars of the animal cage, as though to get a better look at Anna.

Gaia, if only she'd never set eyes on him. A faint flutter of panic rippled through her. She needed time alone. She needed to *plan*. Now more than ever.

"Oh, hell no," the pigeon said, voice rough.

"She really is," Ginny said, clearing her throat from where she stood to Anna's left. "We're the horsewomen. The Four. I'm Famine." She pointed to Nia, on Anna's right. "She's Death." Then pointed to Piper next to her. "Pestilence. Anna is War."

"Maybe…maybe I'm not?" Anna said hopefully.

No one seemed to hear her. They were all focused on the pigeon. Who was focused on her.

The bird shook its head. "It's horse*men*. The four horse*men* of the apocalypse. Which means she can't be War. War clan, maybe. Not *the* War."

"Why not?" Anna said, stepping closer for the first

time. "You came here because I'm rising, didn't you?"

What was she doing? She shouldn't be getting closer to it. She didn't want to be War. It probably had fleas.

It could ruin what little she had left of her life. Her stomach quivered again.

"Then someone made a mistake." The pigeon's claws clicked across the cage bottom as it approached her, leaning more of its head through the bars. "War is men's work." It twitched its head toward Mal and Daniel. "Even Idiot One or Two over there would be better at it than you."

"Yeah…he's not growing on me," Daniel murmured to his brother. He turned to Piper. "I'm sorry for every mean thing I ever said about Queenie," he said, referring to Piper's horse that'd started as a temperamental skunk. Stink intact.

Mal snorted. "Try spending the night with it. I swear it's lucky I didn't break its neck."

"Daddy, that's not nice," Asha scolded.

"It's a very bad bird, Peanut," Mal said.

Anna listened to them with half a mind, too focused on the dratted bird. All the horses started in smaller form, and they grew as their horsewoman's ability grew.

Her gaze narrowed on the vermin. "Clearly, you're popular with women," she said caustically. "Who says you're really the War horse? All the others have been intelligent and helpful."

Ginny coughed, her face coloring. "Well…" Her horse, Roger, was gutter-minded with a thing for show tunes, and he'd been that way from the day he arrived, usually offering less than useful advice.

"Oh, sweetheart, I am definitely the War horse. You see? This is why so much power should never be granted to a woman. Women are too emotional, too fragile for War," the pigeon said. "Every War has always been male. Every horse, too, and always will be. It's a partnership

41

that works."

At least Roger's heart was in the right place, compared to this chauvinistic, ignorant pest.

"You're bluffing," Anna said. "*Statum tuo neque testimonio*. State your evidence." She'd done exhaustive research on all the clans, especially War, and while indeed, previous War horsemen had been male, there'd been nothing to indicate the gender of the horses.

The pigeon lifted a claw and gripped the cage. "Nearly one thousand years of history and memory. From the first horse, Bellator the Brave, followed by Mardane, Ajax, Cadmar, and Reginald."

She recognized half of the names, not all...but she hadn't been able to find all of them. Blast.

The pigeon cocked his head. "That good enough, Princess?"

Anna's teeth clicked together, and she glared at the beast. "Don't call me that." Once, she'd been Daddy's Princess, and Mommy his Queen. Look how that had ended. A royal massacre. "Don't listen to him. He's making it up."

But her neck wasn't cold with any hint of a lie. The bird was an arrogant ass, but he wasn't a liar.

As usual, no one listened to her. They never did. Didn't matter what truth she told them. How dangerous she knew Piper's boyfriend had been. Piper said Anna just didn't understand boys. How predatory Ginny's first husband had been. Ginny hugged Anna and promised she wasn't losing her, that she didn't have to be afraid.

"You mean...you remember the history and have the intact memories of the previous horses?" Ginny leaned forward. "All of the others had no memory from before they arrived in Beckwell. You guys, this is *huge*."

Anna glared sourly at the pigeon. "If the knowledge is real."

Knowledge that might tell her how and why the

others rose, perhaps how to avoid rising herself. She shifted uncomfortably, Loki's silk shirt shushing against her, the fabric hot, reminding her of the way he'd looked at her.

"Queenie mostly hopped up and down and sent useless images," Piper mused about her horse. "Words would have been *so* much easier."

Nia sniffed. "No kidding. That's way ahead of where Esther and I were when we met, her trying to communicate like a friggin' ghost. Even Daniel and Mal can hear him."

"Everyone he insulted last night could hear and understand him really well too." Mal stifled another yawn. "Look, while sorting out psycho-chicken sounds fascinating, I can't charge him with anything, which sucks balls, and I'm tired. Asha and I are out of here," Mal said, giving Nia another quick kiss before he and his daughter headed out the door, Asha waving at her mother from over his shoulder.

Daniel glanced at his watch. "I should get back to the Senior Center and prep for today's surgery." Beckwell's Senior Center also held Daniel's medical offices and acted as a hospital for the town. He hesitated and glanced at Piper, then her belly. Twins did make her bigger, but it also made her higher risk…plus the paranormal aspect of the pregnancy left another huge unknown. "Willing to head over with me?"

Piper glanced at the others, rubbing her belly again. She bit her lip, glanced at the girls. "I should stay here…"

Anna forced a smile, gave her a gentle push toward Daniel. "You should go with Daniel. For the last time, I'm *fine*."

Piper still hesitated, until she found reassurance in the gazes of the other two horsewomen. She sighed. "I'll let them argue with you. Loki's is the safest place right now. You'll only have to stay there a little while." She glanced at the bird.

Anna's stomach flipped. Piper didn't have to say the rest. She meant until Anna rose. The arrival of the horse meant the rising had begun.

Having her house burned down by the knitting club likely signaled something significant too. War had begun to settle in her life. Razing it all down in flames, leaving destruction and pain in its wake, because that was what War did.

"You take care of her, Daniel Do-Right," Nia said warningly. She pointed at her eyes, then back to him. "I've got my eye on you."

Once, Daniel might have been wary of the comment, maybe even irritated at the nickname referring to his former status as town Golden Boy.

Now, though, a small grin pulled at his lips as he helped Piper out the door. "Likewise. You be sure to let me know if you need anything." Another glance at Anna before he and Piper left.

The whisper of the books moved in to fill the quiet left by the departure of the four living. The volume was increasing. Whispers from outside, human secrets began to creep through her thoughts too. Anna massaged her forehead.

The pigeon snorted. "Exactly my point. Too emotional. Someone really messed up, giving women power."

Anna barely glanced at the bird. It might be right about too much emotion being dangerous for War. War didn't do happy endings like the romance novels she secretly adored. Wars were more frequently associated with violence, prison sentences, and early graves. It was that corruptive element about War, terrible even in its infancy; it would only be worse if she rose. Magnified exponentially, it could destroy everything and everyone she cared about, taking over more and more of her until all that had been Anna was gone, and it was only War, only the violence, the murder, the rage remained.

Not every War could claim they'd killed their parents the first time they spoke. Just the sound of their voice throwing her parents into such a rage, her father had murdered her mother, torched the house, and turned the weapon on himself.

She'd been vigilant to keep her emotions in check since. To ensure she never hurt anyone else again.

She turned to Nia and Ginny, both still looking at her like they harbored threats involving blankets and cocoa. Loki's was probably the safest...if not for the temptation of Loki. She couldn't stay with her friends, couldn't risk involving them in the danger that surrounded her. They undoubtedly preferred their homes weren't charbroiled.

"Weren't you all just insisting we can't trust Loki? Besides, he has crazy Daphne in his home. If I'm there, I may make her even more violent." Daphne Spinner was one of the Fates who'd tried to force the Four to help them end the world, not someone who needed encouragement to be violent. "I'll spend the day in the library. Broad daylight, center of town, I'll be safe."

"Someone could burn it down like they did your house," Nia said. "You never have said who did that."

"Books are a fire hazard," the pigeon said. "Bookshelves could fall on you, crushing you. The roof could lose structural integrity. Although"—the pigeon glanced at the windows, hopping closer and peering toward them, his quick motions jerky—"my move would be to shoot in through the window. Bullet, arrow, grenade even."

Anna, Nia, and Ginny all glanced at the windows. Collectively took a few steps back into the children's section.

"Hey! What about me?" the pigeon called.

"Why don't you wait for that grenade?" Nia

suggested.

Images of all the ways they could be attacked in the library flashed through Anna's mind. Along with how vulnerable the bird was sitting there on the table. Plus, the longer he stayed there, the higher the likelihood he might defile her table. She shuddered and headed back toward the table and the cage.

"Anna, windows," Ginny said significantly, pointing at the closed blinds over the front windows, the only ones with any real view into the building.

A sense of unease tickled over Anna's shoulders like a scratchy sweater, centered in the small of her back. She paused near the edge of the circulation desk and the coffee pot.

The sensation was itchy, like that gray sweater she'd gotten in a five-dollar bag at the thrift store and never taken to.

Burned up like the rest of her wardrobe. Most of it from five-dollar bags, the things no one else wanted. Getting attached to clothes or letting them influence your emotions was just a distraction—and against the rules in remaining logical. Cheap, serviceable, utilitarian was all she needed.

"Although, shooting you does seem a tad modern for the gods," Ginny mused.

"I'm Death. Any killing around here is in my jurisdiction. I say no, so we're good." Nia flopped into one of the beanbag chairs in the children's section, looking like a kid herself.

"Ahem. Princess? You were letting me out?" the pigeon prompted.

For pity's sake, now both her friends were thinking more logically than she was. And of all nicknames, why did the horrid creature have to call her that? The name brought an image of Dad's face to mind, those moments when he whirled her in the air, and she thought she could fly…and then that last day. His face contorted with rage, spittle at the corner of his lips, the rage her voice had prompted destroying both her parents. Burning away her future.

The bird needed to go. The notion propelled Anna to move. The itchiness in her lower back was only getting worse. She reached the table and the cage, the pigeon's beady eyes watching as she fiddled with the latch. The sooner it left, the sooner it could find the real War heir. Find anyone but her.

The pigeon moved toward the latch.

Anna paused, leaned down to look it in the beady eyes. "I may not be *the* War, that's yet to be determined, but if you bite me or defecate in my library, I will batter you with a broom until you look like a plucked chicken."

The pigeon considered her. "Duly noted."

She opened the cage door, and the pigeon stepped out carefully before it flew up and landed on the top of the cage where it could more evenly meet her gaze.

"You may be *a* War, but you'll never be *the* War, Princess. War will never be a woman, isn't weak enough to need protection. You might have brought me here somehow, but you're not my true partner."

Anna's smile was tight. "I hope you're right. And that we never meet again." She headed for the library door.

"Anna don't—" Ginny said.

She glanced back, gave them a dark look. The itching was unbearable now. She rubbed her back. "Please. It's the library. I'm safe."

She opened the door.

The pigeon flew out the door.

A man dressed in a balaclava in the middle of summer and camouflage clothing dove inside. He somersaulted, coming up on his knees and raising a small thing like looked like a wand.

Anna froze. The itching sensation covered her entire body. For a moment, she couldn't move.

Ginny and Nia shouted from the back of the library and raced toward her.

Then, curiously, time seemed to move in slow motion.

The stranger began to move his lips. She couldn't move. Couldn't look away from that wand. No, not a wand. A weapon.

Her mind supplied the name—a "Verdict" because the gods were irritating—and full directions for how it worked, how it killed, and that this Verdict was set to kill. Huh. Another War ability. Knowledge of all weapons. Predictably related to violence. Not that useful as she stared at the man as he pulled the weapon backward, aimed it.

He started to whisper the killing words to activate.

This had been a terrible day. The fire. Loki. The pigeon. Now this.

A bright light flashed from the weapon. Zinged toward her.

She dove to one side, clear of the weapon's fire.

Unfortunately, not clear of her two friends who crashed into her, flattened her into the stale-smelling carpet. Time slammed back into her, left her dizzy and wheezing on the ground. What in the name of Gaia had just happened?

With a furious snarl, Loki lunged through the front door, wearing jeans and a large plaid shirt. For a second, it looked as though two Lokis tackled the stranger to the ground.

"Down!" he shouted, grappling with the stranger.

Another flash of light as the weapon discharged again.

The two large men rolled across the floor.

"Sic him, guys," Nia growled, tangled up with Anna

and Ginny on the floor. "No, not Loki. The other one. Get the weapon," Nia said.

Anna tried to look up from between the red curls draped over her vision. Saw the wispy figures emerging through the walls and up through the floor that grabbed onto the stranger and held him tight. Ghosts. Attacking at Nia's order.

Loki sat back on his haunches, his teeth still barred. He had the weapon in his hand and snapped it in two.

The stranger continued to struggle against the grip, cursing and snarling at Loki and the girls.

Ginny scrambled off Anna, an elbow accidentally whooshing the air from Anna's lungs.

"You, stay down," growled the usually sweet Ginny, before she rose to her feet and walked toward the immobile man. She pulled the balaclava off his head, revealing a blond man with a deep scar across his one cheek. She touched his forehead, and he quieted, stared up at her like an obedient dog.

Famine could control all desires.

Loki wrestled the man upright, then turned the full scorching heat of his amber glare on Anna. "By Ymir, what were you thinking of opening the door and standing out in the open like that?"

Her vision was still faintly blurred, and it felt like she'd run a mile. Her voice was faint. "I...was letting the pigeon out." Not, perhaps her smartest move—nor response. She blinked, tried to shake her head while not appearing to do so. She already looked the fool. No sense compounding it.

Blast. Were her hands shaking? Again?

Loki stared at her, an incredulous look on his face. His shirt was askew, tight only in the shoulders and made for someone twice his girth. Perhaps this was his Lou disguise. His dark hair was uncharacteristically ruffled, and he had a scratch above his eyebrow. Then he growled

to himself and turned away from her to Nia and Ginny.
Dismissing her.

"Petunia, stay here, keep her safe. Genevieve, if you
would accompany me and our...guest to the town border,
let's make sure he can't return, shall we?"

Anna clenched her hands into fists. "How dare you—
"

Loki turned that scorching glare back on her, drying
up her words. He shook his head before he, Ginny, and
the stranger slipped out the library door. A briefer pause
as, from the light turning red on the door, he locked them
both in.

The cold that had become her companion slid over
her, doused her anger, numbed. She climbed wearily to
her feet. She was too tired to be angry. The day was not
off to a promising start. She glanced at the clock above
the door. It wasn't even eight thirty yet.

She leaned on the conference table, dragged her cup
toward her, and drained the remainder of the coffee. If the
gods were after her, she'd only carry that danger with her
to any of her friends' houses. Piper was due any day, their
house small as it was. Ginny and James were similarly
tight in their house, his brother visiting and the other room
converted to an office for their business. Nia and Mal had
Asha to protect, along with all their ghosts already.

If she had any chance of avoiding rising as War—or
hurting all the people War could devastate—she had to
depend on logic, not emotion. Today's developments
proved rising could be unavoidable. It was little use
denying her dangerous attraction to the demigod, but
she'd resisted those sentiments since she was a teenager.
Indeed, as her friends pointed out, Loki's offer, to go to
his house, was the most logical solution.

A shiver, part chill, part something she refused to
investigate, slid through her.

"You can't go on like this," Nia said quietly, at

Anna's side.

Anna started, surprised to find the Death horsewoman at her elbow. "Haven't we gone over this enough already?"

"Coming back from the dead isn't easy," Nia said quietly, unreasonably sober and sympathetic.

Better she was sarcastic and cutting.

Anna scrubbed her foot on the carpet, frowned. If anyone might know, it would be Nia. "Will it get better?" She'd asked herself that for months now. Maybe longer. Would her career at the library be enough to satisfy that deep emptiness inside? Would celebrating her friends' success and happiness rub off enough to light the dark corners of her world?

Nia shrugged. "That's up to you, not me. I'm Death, not your therapist. But ignoring it? That's *not* going to help. Neither is pretending you're invincible. You're not."

"No, she's not," Loki said, stepping back into the library, Ginny at his side.

Ginny twisted her hands together and refused to meet Anna's gaze. A pink stain tinted her cheekbones.

Loki waited until she looked at him again. Until their gazes met. His eyes were back to gray, mesmerizing and whirling like a stormy sky, shot with amber lightning.

"We tried it your way," he said, his tone brooking no argument. "You almost died. For the second time today. Now we do it my way. You'll come home with me."

CHAPTER 5

For Ymir's sake. Insane. The woman was going to drive him insane. He needed to keep her safe, and she seemed determined to place herself in harm's path. Damn the risk. She was coming to his house.

While he was still picturing her limp, lifeless body, she gave him an inscrutable look. Just looked at him. As though she hadn't just almost died—again.

Loki's heart still pounded, and the image of the USELESS agent, his weapon trained on Anna, the killing trigger on his lips would remain permanently acid-etched behind his eyes. He'd spotted the agent, hadn't been too concerned…until Anna opened the door.

He scrubbed a hand over his face and tried to remember he was usually known for his charm and easy temper. Or at least, he was usually better at maintaining the appearance of them.

What had she and Nia been saying just before he'd come in?

"Anna. Get your things," he said, trying to gentle his

voice, but he wanted no doubt it was a command, not a request.

Another oblique look, cool assessment in her blue gaze.

She said nothing, but turned and walked behind the reception desk, started picking through books.

His temper flared again. Stubborn creature. He forced himself to take a steadying breath, to consider his strategy. Ordering Anna around was sure to get her back up. Yet right now, he didn't seem able to stop himself. "The horse. Is it coming?" The words came out no more conciliatory.

"That isn't my horse," Anna said with a frown, still sorting through books, not even bothering to look up.

Nia snorted. "The talking, hot-tempered, know-it-all pigeon? Yeah, I don't see any resemblance at all," she said dryly.

Anna flinched.

His hands clenched, all his awareness focused in on that reaction. Anna didn't flinch. Not when he'd pulled her from her parents' burning home, or in the nights after. Not when she'd faced down bullies on the school ground, some of them twice her age and size. Nor when he was called into the principal's office with her, and she faced down the principal too. Little wonder the Lacks had insisted he remain her official guardian. Anna didn't flinch. She fought. She was War.

She'd also lost her home this morning, then been attacked.

He tamped down the temper out of his voice. Logic. He'd appeal to her logic. "This isn't the first assassination attempt," he said bluntly. "There have been others, and more will come."

She'd finished sorting books. Now she rummaged around in a drawer beneath the desk, the top of her dark head barely visible.

He ground his teeth. She was ignoring him and his reason. As though the argument wasn't worth her effort. He inhaled deeply and tried to recapture some semblance of calm. He'd dealt with stubborn blockheads before, from his parents to the gods of Asgard. He was usually better at finding the right words and didn't lose his calm.

Except with Anna.

"We just want you to be safe," Ginny added softly.

"You don't have to worry about the library," Nia added, her tone grudging. "I'll even, you know, take shifts. So it's open."

Yes, because keeping the library open on the day she'd almost died—twice—was the priority.

He smothered a growl, then closed his eyes a moment. No calm reason there either. "My home is safer. Well protected with wards and protection spells." He'd also be there…though reminding her of that fact and their proximity was unlikely to make her more amenable to the plan.

It was not, perhaps, the wisest plan installing the next War in his house just now. Never mind his history with the clan and the Four, there was Daphne Spinner to consider. Imprisoned in his home, Daphne was one of the former Fates with a death wish and a dangerous chaos goddess currently trapped within her, itching to escape and destroy the world. Anna's presence would undoubtedly agitate the already unstable woman. As well as potentially create a point of vulnerability, since this particular Fate saw and knew all that was present.

He tapped his hand against his thigh. Of course, that was nothing compared to the temptation of Anna in his home. This Anna. Without the protection of her friends' presence, nor her dowdy clothing.

Though if she continued to aggravate him as she had today, willfully ignoring him, it would help control any attraction.

He massaged his forehead again. "Hadrianna, please just gather your things."

"I already have," she said, her voice coming from directly in front of him.

Ymir save him from revealing any more weaknesses than he already had. The thought slowed his reaction as he dropped his hand and let his gaze slowly drift over her until he sank into those crystalline blue eyes. The color was changeable, and lovelier than all the lakes in Asgard. Her brown hair was drying, leaving unruly tendrils to curl around her cheekbones and at her forehead. His silk shirt slid over her curves, making her flesh seem even softer, more touchable.

She had a scruffy looking blue knapsack over one shoulder, the strap cutting into her shoulder suggesting it was heavy. Likely stuffed with books.

Packed and ready to go.

But...she'd been arguing with him.

Why wasn't she arguing with him?

Almost two decades had passed since he'd invited her into his life and brought her here, to Beckwell. A child then, the same mix of wariness, curiosity, and vulnerability warring in her blue gaze. She'd always seen too deeply inside him, right through every lie, no matter how kindly intended. Ymir knew the dark beasts she'd see in him.

Not a child any longer. The past few years had awakened an uncomfortable desire within him, a need to involve himself more in his life than simply protect her. Which complicated matters.

"Are we going?" she said.

He cleared his throat, forced himself to look away. "Of course."

"Here. Take my cell. So we can get ahold of you. And you us." Ginny leaped forward and pressed a smartphone with a pink sparkly case into Anna's hand before embracing the War horsewoman, despite Anna's stiff response.

In case she needed to be free of him, they meant. He suppressed a sigh. It was always the same. It didn't matter what he did. They never trusted him. Certainly not as much as they trusted each other.

"Esther and I can bust right through the door if necessary," Nia said, coming forward and giving Anna's elbow a squeeze. She winked. "Don't suppose that's the Bigass Book of Boring in there, huh?"

She referred to the collected notes on the horsemen clans that Anna had amassed over years of research.

"More like Bigass Book of Scary," Ginny said with a sniff. "It's okay, right?"

Anna caressed the strap of her knapsack, a certain reverence in her touch as though she touched the book itself. A small smile pulled at her lips, the first hint of relief he'd seen since he found her. "It was just as well I didn't take it home last night."

A small knot in his neck eased, watching the way she tightened her grip on the strap of her knapsack.

She hadn't lost everything. He'd find a way to replace the rest, perhaps secret donations to the library if necessary. Though definitely not the hideous clothes she'd favored. She'd never accept his charity. His gaze skimmed over her again. Silk suited her.

The women completed their farewells, and then he and Anna moved together out the door and across the road toward his bar and vehicle.

Curious thing. Leaving with one of the women, when usually it was just he who left. Or was forced out.

She paused at the four-way stop, and he almost bumped into her. The hint of lavender tickled his nose, the thin barrier of silk so easily pulled back to reveal her.

His shirt draped over her, *his* colors. Anna would be as fiery and forthright in bed as she was otherwise. Ymir, the way his body hardened one would think it'd been years since he'd availed himself of a willing body—always discreetly in the city or far from here. With someone who didn't know his face, didn't know his identity, was willing to enjoy their time as he did but had no expectation it would continue beyond the morning.

There would be no disguises between him and Anna. It would just be his face she saw.

Too many repercussions, complications, attachments to confront the next morning. All three of which were elements he'd attempted to eradicate from his life for his protection. Further reason to keep his hands and lust to himself.

The moment passed, seemingly unnoticed by Anna, and she stepped forward across the four-way, their strides again equally matched.

So many others in this town, anywhere he went where they knew him, recognized his name, associated the myths, and looked at him a particular way. A hint of wariness in their gaze, a distance they kept. A touch of fear in their countenance.

Never Anna. She would always meet him word for word, fight for fight, kiss for kiss.

Oh, Ymir help him. She was about to enter his home. Alone. He was so close to achieving his plan and starting Ragnarök. Convincing Anna to rise was the last step. All he had to do was remember why he needed her—and that it wasn't in his bed.

ᏰᏅ

A few minutes later, for the second time that day, Anna was alone with Loki in the small confines of his car.

House charbroiled? Check.

Interrogated by her friends? Check.

Chauvinistic pigeon foretelling the doom of all things? Check.

Assassin? Check.

Gaia, this really had been a day. Best of all, according to the glowing digital display in the high-tech console, it wasn't even noon yet. Lovely.

She stared pointedly out the windshield, clutching her knapsack with white fingers. It bulged with her massive book of research notes that the girls uncharitably called the Bigass Book of Boring or Scary, depending on the day. Loki's scent, something like patchouli, or maybe cedar, softly wafted toward her, the warmth of his body near her. Every time he shifted, his knuckles almost brushed her thigh.

Logical. Be logical. She was headed to his home because it was safest, because it was logical. She helped no one if she was dead. Considering the direction today had thus far taken, better to take precautions.

The town was waking. Cars pulled up to the gas station and mini-mart next to Loki's restaurant and bar. A few turned into the school parking lot across the road, perhaps for some sports activity or summer camp. She and Loki quickly passed through town, out into the isolated, tree-lined highway. His flashy car and their route took them away from town, her friends, her library. Distractions.

It'd been strange, leaving the library with him. The way her friends left with their significant others. For a moment, when she'd paused at the four-way, and he'd stopped behind her, so close, his warmth had caressed her back, his breath ruffled her neck, and she'd been intensely aware of him as not merely the often-irritating presence who manipulated her and her friends, but as a man. A large, beautiful, inherently masculine presence, one who'd featured too strongly in her fantasies for, well, forever. The moment passing so quickly she wondered if she'd imagined it, his fingers had grazed her waist through the silk.

She'd sucked in a breath. She'd wondered, too often,

what it would be like to touch him. How it might feel for him to look at her and see not just plain old Anna the librarian, but as a woman, with sexual longing and desires, long removed from the child she'd been.

The moment had passed. Likely he hadn't noticed.

Unfortunately, seated in his car next to him, her nerve endings still tingled with awareness that flowed from her fingertips to her toes and all the parts in between. Awareness that reminded her DIY was not always the best option, and sometimes, she ached for relief from the solitude.

He flexed his fingers against the wheel. Long, capable fingers dusted with dark hair. His jaw was hard and square, something between a hint of whiskers and almost a mustache darkening his jaw and above his lips, making her fingers prickle with the desire to know if they were soft or prickly beneath her fingertips, beneath her lips. The skin at the corner of his eyes creased, brows lowering as he carefully slowed them around the curves, perfectly in control of the powerful car, seemingly always in control of everything, including now as he shifted the purring engine. That aspect was both irritating...and toe-curling sexy. He accelerated as they reached long, open stretches of road, the vibration of the car rippling through her.

"Is the beast particularly fearsome?" he asked.

She jumped. "The...what?" She zapped her gaze forward again, but blast, her face grew hot. Caught staring. Gaia help her. Figured, the way today was going.

"A spider perhaps?"

Research indicated the name Loki meant spinner of plots or spider. So...technically true. Though no eight-legged beast had ever had quite the same effect on her. She'd still been a child when she realized other people didn't see him the way she did. She'd questioned him about it, inadvertently revealing her ability to see through his magic.

She cleared her throat. "Not at all. I was simply scrutinizing your disguise. You're wearing plaid; ergo, you must be in your Lou disguise."

One corner of those beautiful lips curled, though fortunately, he didn't turn the power of that gaze on her. "Ah. Searching for failings. Of course."

If only that's what she'd been doing. Thank the Goddess some small, functioning part of her brain had noticed he wore plaid...instead of just dreaming about what lay beneath. His disguises may have fooled everyone else, but she only ever saw Loki in his true form.

"Not always." Was she so terrible to him? Well...possibly. Only for her own sanity. "It seemed a useful skill to develop. I've always seen through your disguises, which means perhaps I could see through others."

Practically plausible.

Though she'd long thought he'd be far less distracting as the overweight, bald bartender, Lou, her friends had described.

"Ah." His focus returned to the road.

She forced her fingers to loosen where they ached around the edges of the book in the bag. As though "ah" meant anything. She frowned. Even staring out the window, she pictured his hard, square jaw, the slight curl to his black-brown hair, the slightly crooked profile of his nose.

This was the Loki she'd always seen. Little wonder the boys at school had always seemed, well, boys. Why every hero in every romance she read was dark haired and swarthy, damn him.

She tapped her foot impatiently in her borrowed runners. Such thoughts were foolish, immature, *emotional*. He wasn't even a man, but a being. What if that horrid bird was her horse? War couldn't afford the luxury of fantasizing about Loki.

Vinait qui se vincit. The only way she could survive War rising, or somehow escaping its clutches, was if she kept herself in tight control. And that meant all Loki-related nonsense needed to stop. She was neither a child nor a teenager. She knew him. Or at least, what he chose to show her.

A glance his direction showed his fingers were tight on the wheel, and a small tic had started in his jaw. Sign of a vulnerability. Perhaps it bothered him how easily she saw through his disguises. Well, considering how essentially everything about him "bothered" her it seemed fair.

"I appreciate your sacrifice inviting me into your home, but we both know it's a short-term solution at best," she said, again looking out the windshield.

"I see," he said mildly.

They turned down the long, winding driveway toward his house. His was paved, compared to most of the others in the area, and trees lined the long, curving driveway, deep purple pin cherry that rippled in the breeze beneath the towering poplars.

"You didn't want me there as a child. I can't see my being there would be better now that I'm an adult."

He'd rescued her from the fire, taken her first into his car, then his home and she'd thought a prince from one of her fairy-tales had come to rescue her. Until just as quickly he'd dumped her unceremoniously into the cold discomfort of the Lacks' household, their fear of him and her heritage likely the only reason they'd put up with her presence at all.

A small frown creased his forehead, though he didn't look at her. "It wasn't that I didn't want you there——"

She sniffed, as the whisper of the lie breathed icy breath on the nape of her neck. "Please don't waste either of our time with lies. You didn't want me there. You were relieved to leave me at the Lacks'.'"

He hadn't even looked back when he'd driven away. Though she'd run to the door and run out after him, unable to shout after him, unwilling to risk speaking and sending this new family into a downward spiral. She'd barely spoken at all for more than a year afterward.

His lips were tight, but he said nothing. Perhaps annoyed by her calling his lie.

With anyone else, the truth would have whispered itself to her. With him, she could only tell he had lied. Some relief, true, to not have to continue to stare at him placidly while his darkest truths revealed themselves to her. Though on occasion, with this man, it could be handy. To leave him a smidgen off-centered. As he left her.

"It also seems ill-advised, my being in your house while Daphne is still there," she continued.

If he wouldn't budge, they could play twenty-thousand questions.

"What would I do without you to question my every action," he murmured.

"She is still at your house then? It's been months. I thought you'd have turned her over."

"Turned her over to who? The gods want to kill you and don't believe she's dangerous. I'm dealing with it."

Her neck grew cold, the sign she'd learned to recognize as a lie for as long as she could remember. "Lie. Interesting."

Amber flashed in his gaze, and his fingers twisted on the wheel. "Hadrianna, what game are you playing?"

A rather intriguing one, as it turned out. "I told you. I like my name. Why do you feel the need to push me away? To push everyone away?" The formality appeared to be his method of distancing himself. Perhaps it concealed a weakness she could use against him.

They came around a curve in the road, and his large, Gothic-revival house came into view. The building was imposing and grand, the many windows glinting like watchful eyes in the morning light. An intriguing mass of imposing cupolas, archways, and ornate trim on the deep burgundy and black-trimmed building.

At five, still reeling and not entirely comprehending her parents' deaths, she'd thought he'd brought her back to his castle. A place she'd finally be safe.

Twenty-three years later, despite all she knew about him, about the architectural styles and the history of the house and the area, it still looked like a fairy-tale castle. The safety element remained unclear.

The purr of the engine stopped as he pulled up near the front door, the covered porch, and tall, imposing wood doors leading inside. To his world, his territory.

She turned. Swallowed as she found his gaze, deep, gray and stormy, on her.

"Perhaps I'm trying to keep my distance for your safety, Anna," he said, saying her name like a lingering purr.

The sound sent reverberations of the foolish emotional kind ricocheting through her, setting heated fires deep within.

He crossed his hands over the wheel and leaned back in the seat, his gaze never leaving hers. "Or perhaps I merely need to keep my favorite chess piece safe."

Cool air ruffled her neck, but only a light spring breeze, not the arctic breath of winter. It meant a partial lie.

Which part was true?

Her throat was too thick to ask.

His gaze grew heavy-lidded, almost lazy before he freed her, glancing out the windshield. "Of course, I could just be worried about you. As your friends are. Something happened six months ago, during the battle at Nia's house. Didn't it?"

Warmth settled in her chest with certainty. With the

truth. He was worried about her. The foolishness was becoming an epidemic. Goddess help the next person to suggest hot cocoa.

She located and reached for the door handle, clutching her knapsack with her book against her chest like a shield. The door popped open with a quiet hush. "Well. Neither you nor my friends should worry. I died once. I can't see that the second time would be as bad." She unfolded herself and stepped out of the door, hurrying toward the stairs.

He caught her elbow before she reached the first step, his hand slipping to her hand, bare skin brushing bare skin. His eyes flared amber. "You *what*?"

Fiery heat flowed through their connection, his fingers twined with hers.

The flash of images rippled behind her eyes, namely she and Loki, naked and tangled together. Her breath stuttered. Need, want, desire, broken dreams, pain, all of it surged within her at his touch.

At the truth. Though *what* truth remained the question.

She jerked away. No. She might have to depend on him for the short term, but he—and War—wouldn't break her. She wouldn't fall for the lure of emotion. *Vinait qui se vincit*—to conquer, conquer oneself—would become her motto to live by. To survive by.

Two steps up toward the front door, she twisted to look at him, to toss the words back casually before she stormed inside. Around him, the usual numbness didn't seem to apply, the one time it might have come in handy. Her words came out raw, torn from the back of her throat. "I died." She swallowed, tossed her head and straightened. Stupid hands shook again around her knapsack. Her voice, though, when she spoke again was steadier. "If anything, it proves I needn't be afraid of death. So perhaps if worst comes to worst, there is one way I can guarantee I won't rise as War."

CHAPTER 6

Anna left him standing there like a fool as she strode briskly toward the front doors and pulled one open before someone could answer it. Then shut it quietly behind her. Shut him out.

Loki blew out a breath and tucked his hands in his pockets before he turned and strode back to the car, gave himself time to think while he parked it in the garage around back. He'd gone about this all wrong. He needed to do better if he was going to convince her to see reason.

Anna had died, and he hadn't even known it. Ymir. Worse, she claimed she'd be willing to die again if it meant avoiding rising as War.

He pulled into the long, multi-car garage, then stepped back out into the sun and strode for the house, his mind whirring faster than the garage door as it closed behind him.

This new development could be a problem. More of a problem than Anna being so desperate to avoid rising. If she'd died before, it meant should one of the USELESS agents be successful, or should she somehow be harmed otherwise, even Nia, Death herself, couldn't bring Anna back. Once, maybe. Twice, and the soul traveled straight and fast toward the doors to the afterlife and beyond. No stopping at go, no lingering glances, just...gone.

Lips tight, there was still a frown on his face as he stepped quickly onto the back porch and through the rear entrance, in through the kitchen.

"Good morning, Mr. Laufeyjarson. You're up and about early this morning," his cook and housekeeper, Mrs. Greaves, called, kneading bread in the elegant, dark wood kitchen on one of the cream marble countertops.

"It is a day for early activity, Mrs. Greaves," he responded, offering a distracted smile as he headed toward the foyer.

More dark wood surrounded him in the paneling and floors, the elegant and tasteful antiques. Well, most hadn't been antiques when he'd bought them. They were comfortable, high quality, a reminder of the good parts of his life in Asgard, and a symbol of the quality of life he was determined to live. Proof he was far from the desperate, ruined state he'd lived in for too many decades. This was his domain, his sanctuary.

A scuffed pair of running shoes sat near the front door. The pair he'd lent her. Her faint lavender fragrance lingered in the air, though she was long gone. His lips thinned, and he glared at the shoes, hesitating a moment before he slipped off his Italian-leather loafers. Setting his beside hers, the shining black leather a stark contrast to the running shoes. They weren't even really hers, just something he'd found in the lost and found, as he didn't keep shoes of different sizes around. No matter his human form, it'd never occurred to him to change his foot size.

He should have known she'd died. He should have been more careful to protect her.

He'd done no better with her than he had Peter.

Trevor, his manservant, appeared soundlessly at Loki's elbow, emerging from whatever hidey-hole he secreted himself in. As ever, his tall, slim form was immaculately attired in a suit, despite it being July. His dark hair, medium-toned skin, and light gray eyes suggested mixed ancestry, and the man was infallible.

He did, however, take obsequious to whole new levels, despite Loki's encouragement to the contrary since his hiring in January. Just as well his term, as with Mrs. Greaves and Mr. Holkom, the gardener and odd-job man, would be done by December. New servants at the beginning of each year. No attachments, no more pain of losing them when he outlived them as he had others. Too many others.

"Sir," Trevor said, ducking his dark head.

"Loki or Mr. Laufeyjarson works well enough," Loki said, narrowly refraining from rolling his eyes. It was an improvement over the 'milord' and other nonsense the man had started with. "Where is Ms. Fray?"

One attachment he'd already let get too close.

"She's headed up to 'her room,' as she put it. Though her bag hardly looked sufficient for her stay."

Her room. The room he'd given her that first night he brought her here as a child. The room across the hall from his, in case she'd cried out. She hadn't. But it meant now desirable, adult Anna was installed with convenient access to his bed. This could be a problem.

"There was a fire this morning. She's lost everything. Please see she has whatever she needs – clothing, books, anything other than leaving the house."

To his credit, Trevor didn't even bat an eye. "Is she a 'guest' like Ms. Spinner?"

"No. Ms. Fray is not a prisoner, nor is she dangerous." Other than to his sanity. He rubbed his eyebrow, and glanced upward, as though somehow he could see through the floors up to the top, one of the upper suites that had been altered for the imprisonment of Daphne Spinner. "Although, speaking of Ms. Spinner, how is she today?"

"Agitated. A touch more manic than usual. The nurse suggested we may need to call in Dr. Quilan again, to adjust her medication."

"I should check on her myself. You'll see to Ms. Fray's needs?" At Trevor's nod, Loki headed toward the staircase, taking them quickly, two stairs at a time. Best to get this over with quickly.

Up the first staircase to the second floor with its lush carpet and more wood. His and Anna's suites were close by. Close enough he paused, wondered if he should check on her, but quickly discarded the thought and continued up the second flight of stairs. Anna needed her space. Besides which, he'd been negligent not checking on Daphne earlier.

Up the stairs, then down the hall. This one with a runner over the planked floor. The last time anyone had been up here, Peter had decided as a teenager he needed more space, more distance. At other times, it used to be for servants' quarters. Once, the halls and his house had bustled with activity and life. Servants, friends, visitors from Beckwell. But he'd been reminded that humans were all too fragile. There'd been so many funerals in such a short span. Too many. The one-year term and no-attachments policy had become a means of survival.

Now his footsteps seemed to echo in the quiet hall. At the end was the table and chair for Daphne's nurse and two chairs outside the door for the two guards.

He gave them both a polite nod before one of the guards stood and unlocked the door, then stepped inside the dim room.

Some of the furniture had been removed from the suite, to ensure Daphne couldn't harm herself. The chaos goddess trapped inside her demanded a painful, violent death to be free – one Daphne, driven insane by the creature, was determined to give her, and Loki just as determined she not find. Therefore the room was still comfortable, with a four-poster bed, dresser secured to the wall, television, books. There were lights, but Daphne seemed to prefer the darkness.

Honestly, at times it was like he'd accidentally stumbled into a Gothic novel. Never his favorite genre.

He stepped cautiously into the room. She'd have known he was coming as soon as he'd decided it downstairs in the foyer, and she'd attacked him before. She knew everything that was at present. Which also likely hadn't helped her sanity. "Ms. Spinner. How are you today?"

There was a cackle from one of the far corners. "Better than she is. Whoosh go the flames! Barbeque War horsewoman. I'll have mine with honey-garlic." She cackled again.

His hands fisted, and he forced his fingers straight, approached the corner of the room carefully.

Most of the time, she seemed to prefer curling up and rocking, babbling to herself—or perhaps to the goddess. She'd been here for six months, but he needed to figure out a better, long-term solution. After finding the goddess in the vessel she'd been contained in, the goddess had convinced Daphne to let her possess her with the usual promises of power. The goddess couldn't form a body without her vessel—human or otherwise—being destroyed in a violent act of rage. Which meant he had to figure out either how to extend Daphne's natural lifespan or find someone capable of removing the goddess without setting it free.

Thus far, the search had been fruitless. Thanks to the war between the humanoid species—Magicals and Normals all involved—the demons were unwilling to get involved in an affair they considered the gods' problem.

The gods were ignorant enough they might just execute Daphne—their usual solution to anyone who aggravated them—and potentially release the goddess. Perhaps a human mental hospital for the criminally insane, though he and Trevor had found nothing suitable yet.

The primary warring factions of the great magical wars were divided by Veils that kept them apart. Particularly, kept humans away from the dominant magical species. The mortal realm was mirrored by Braelyn, home of the gods, and Daimoleigh, home of the demons, but no one in any of the three worlds wanted anything to do with Daphne. Prison warden wasn't a role he relished, but it was one he appeared temporarily stuck with. If he didn't find another solution, if Daphne died of natural causes, he'd have to find someone else to allow the goddess to possess them, or risk her escaping…and the inevitable destruction that would follow.

Daphne knelt near one of the windows that had been carefully barred from the inside and out. She was smart and resourceful. She'd already tried digging through the plaster and lathe with a plastic spoon.

He crouched down beside her despite the smell.

Her eyes gleamed out of the paleness of her face, beneath the wild tangle of dark hair. They had to call in the extra nurses to help bathe her; she'd tried to drown herself otherwise. She had been pretty once, but now scratches scoured deep gouges on her arms, no matter how short they kept her nails. As though she was trying to pull open her skin for the goddess to emerge.

A green light shone briefly in her eyes. The goddess looking out at him. He could feel her, the dangerous power of her, her urge to kill and maim and destroy. There was a reason she'd been imprisoned for hundreds of years. Why they didn't dare let her free. Daphne and the goddess had already murdered a young family and almost succeeded in dying. Would have, without Nia's intervention. The insanity was not Daphne's fault. The cruelty was, and something he couldn't abide.

"Is there anything I can get you, Miss Spinner?" he asked, ignoring her comment about Anna.

The madwoman's lips curled upward. "I will be free, you know. She will be free. You can't keep us here forever. Then we're going to destroy everything you care about. Starting with her. Anna. We will flay her alive before she burns, flesh curling from her limbs as she dies."

"The food is fine? Should I see if the nurses can assist you with a bath?" He knew better than to respond to her goads, no matter the way it tightened the muscles in his neck, the images it provoked.

That manic smile never slipped. "You've brought everything we need to the house today. She sees your secrets. She will dig up every one. She will see you for what you really are. She will die, and you will fail."

"Ah, but Ms. Spinner, you see the present, not the future." He stood smoothly, then turned his back and headed toward the door. "Let the nurse know if there's anything else you require. You might try reading. Or the television."

He sensed the movement, the surge of power that made the lights flicker before she raged toward him with an animal snarl. "Nurse," he called, turning easily to encounter Daphne before she reached him. She wasn't as fast as him, still human, but wiry and strong. He caught her arms, helped hold her as the nurse and the guards rushed in. Helped him get her to the bed, where the nurse administered a sedative.

Daphne secured and quieted, Loki, the nurse, and the guards exited the room. This was the usual course of a visit to her. He promised he'd contact Daniel and the psychiatrist again before he headed back down the hall, feeling old.

She wanted someone to kill her. When he told Anna what he needed, would she think him as mad as Ms. Spinner?

He paused near the door that had been Peter's, barely a moment this time. He didn't need to go in. It was all boxed up, nothing left to see. Besides which, he wasn't feeling especially masochistic today.

Sometimes he imagined he could still hear them: the servants, the friends who'd once called this their home too. And of course, Peter and his friends. Peter had been so young, orphaned by the Spanish Flu and his father's fevered madness, a War heir, right here in Beckwell, as though the Fates smiled on Loki. It took so little effort to find three others from the horsemen clans: John, Michael, and Matthew. Even as tensions rose in Europe, rumors whirled through Beckwell that these would be *the* Four, and as though fulfilling that belief – or because they believed the rumors themselves – Peter and the others began to rise.

Just in time for the outbreak of yet another war. Peter remained too young, too rash, too unprepared. The Four were powerful, able to convince so many—too many—to enlist with them, but without full understanding of their abilities, they remained mortal and vulnerable.

Old pain knifed through Loki. Ymir, he'd made so many mistakes.

The memory of the telegraph operator's arrival with those four hated telegrams remained far too fresh. The first four of many. For a while, it had hurt to even breathe.

He strode briskly down the hall and away from the past that stung with pain even all these years.

Daphne was right. The longer Anna stayed here, the more likely it was she'd uncover his secrets. Some of them at any rate. Which was why he'd sent her to the Lacks' household shortly after he'd brought her to Beckwell. He wouldn't make the same mistakes as he had with Peter, despite the letters she'd written him those first weeks, well-reasoned even for a child so young. All the benefits she could provide living in his house. The letters had stopped after the first month. She'd formed a friendship with Ginny. Then Nia and Piper after they all started school. They'd started to form the bonds of the Four they were only beginning to understand now. He knew better than to try and get between again.

Down the first staircase, he barely glanced down the hall toward his suite and Anna's before he continued down the second staircase, back to the foyer.

Once more, Trevor met him there. "Sir. There are…visitors." The man's lip quivered slightly. "From the town."

Evidently, the day was not destined to become easier.

ॐ

Faex. Anna was in full retreat. It wasn't yet noon, and *now* she was trapped in Loki's house. She needed a plan, and she needed one fast. She'd swept into the house ahead of him, seeing as the only other option was turning and running back toward town. Toward her library, which was neither assassin-proof nor the sanctuary she'd hoped. Or toward her friends, who were just waiting for her to rise, for War to consume what little life she had. She brushed past Loki's minion, someone new she didn't recognize, but he was always changing them. She muttered something about her room and headed upstairs.

Toward the room he'd given her as a child. Toward the only sanctuary she had left. In Loki's house. Beautiful as it was, stepping into it was like one more cage, too small as she paced across. The massive four-poster bed dominated the room and was hung in cream embroidered bedclothes with touches of green, Loki's color. The rest of the furniture was tasteful and elegant, mahogany pieces with deceptively delicate looking legs.

The silence of the room, of the house, thudded in her

ears, sped her step. The world was spiraling out of control, and she didn't even have a proper plan to get it back in order again. She dropped her knapsack on the bed. Tried sitting down. Got up again. Paced some more.

She massaged her forehead. Alone wasn't any better. Possibly worse.

She closed her eyes and could see the crackle of the flames, taste the smoke in her mouth, watch as everything burned away. Or see her friends' identical worried expressions, worried about eccentric Anna, evidently close to diving off the deep end. Now *he'd* think the same thing. Gah! She shouldn't have been so rash. Shouldn't have implied she'd kill herself to escape War.

Thinking of him only spurred images of him. The amber fury in his gaze he'd barely been able to contain when he'd arrived at her house. The intensity in his eyes when she'd stepped out of the shower. That disturbing read she'd gotten off him, their bodies twined together. She'd never gotten anything so strong from him before. What she felt around him was too intense, too consuming.

Too dangerous.

She clutched her head. Clenched her teeth against the threatening wildfire that threatened to sweep up through her and incinerate everything in its path. That was War. It burned away everything she'd worked for, everything she dreamed of, everything she'd struggled to become all to reform her into something else. A soldier, a tool of the universe, a killer. When she rose and completed the Four, who was to say they didn't bring about the apocalypse?

She sucked in one shaking breath after another. Her vision wavered. Her knees trembled. She squeezed her hands together, finally crouching down on the floor, head touching her knees.

Control, control, control.

Get yourself under control. You cannot fall apart. Get it together, Anna.

Control, control, control.
You are in charge, not the emotions. You.

She chanted the words again and again until the panicked flutter of her heart began to slow. Until she could finally lift her head and take a slow, shuddering breath. Air. Maybe she just needed fresh air.

She climbed to her feet and headed for the large window. After shoving back the heavy drapes, she slid aside the sheer panels beneath to reveal the window.

Anna jumped at the pigeon perched outside, its beady gaze on her, head quirked this way and that, movements jerky. It tapped its beak on the glass.

Gaia, what had she done to deserve today? She gave the bird a flat look, then reluctantly undid the latch and pushed one side of the screenless window open. The faint hope existed that she'd lost her mind and was letting a random bird into Loki's house.

"What do you want?"

The pigeon stepped inside, poked its head in, and looked around. "Nice place."

So much for hope. "I thought you decided I wasn't War."

The bird stopped in front of her, shook out its wings. "I came here because you're rising as War, but you shouldn't be. So, I was thinking. Maybe we could partner up. Figure out who is."

Today had been so terrible, and there was something tempting to the offer, even the faint idea of good news on a day like this. "Partner? With you? I pity whoever does rise as War, and I know nothing about finding them. There are no others in Beckwell."

The bird lifted into the air and flew over to the bed before he perched on her knapsack. "You have research."

Her eyes narrowed. It couldn't know what it stood on. She flapped her hand at him. "Off the bed. I don't want feces all over it. It's mine for now. The knitting club burned down my house this morning."

The bird slowly turned, stuck its wings out partially as though they were hands on hips. "Look, Princess, I might look like a pigeon, but don't mistake me for a normal bird. Knitting club, huh? Sorry to hear that." It tapped a foot on the knapsack. "I thought the research in here would be a good start to find the real War."

Her throat and mouth went dry. "How could you know about the book?"

The bird looked away, pacing the length of the knapsack, then hopping off to poke at the delicately embroidered quilt, then back onto the knapsack. Almost as though he avoided her gaze. "We might have a…connection of some variety."

She could barely breathe. Connection. Like her friends were connected to their horses. Like the first step toward inexorable doom. "Explain."

The bird cleared its throat. "I know what the other War horses knew…and what you know."

"None of the others could do that."

"War is about history and memory. Who insulted who, who killed who. Memory of the truth. War is the second horse, 'and the power was granted to him' Revelations says. We are the memory of the Four and their commander."

Her stomach lurched. It was as she'd feared: War was worse than the others. The pigeon was worse than all the other horses combined. "What power exactly?"

"Knowledge. Like the book. Like memory."

Anna sat heavily on the edge of the bed, stomach queasy, but also a faint lightness daring to come to life inside. The buoyancy of hope. Her friends' horses had recognized them as horsewomen. If this one didn't, perhaps she really wasn't War. "We could figure out who the real War is…"

"And break the connection between us." The bird

finished her sentence. "Precisely. I saw how you reacted at the library to that attack. First, no real War would have let anyone sneak up on them. You should have sensed the attack. Second, no War would let someone else protect them; they'd do it themselves."

"What should I have done? Karate-chopped the assassin?" Although…that itchy feeling she'd had. It'd gotten worse right before the attack. Was that the sense telling her she was in danger? There'd also been the strange way she'd identified and understood the weapon's usage and everything moving in slow-motion. She might have done something if she hadn't been tackled by her friends first.

"Karate-chopping is optional. You just stood there, useless," the bird said. "Not that I'm surprised." He looked her up and down. "Not War."

"Fine. You have a plan? How do we find the real one? The sooner I'm rid of you, the better." Likewise, the sooner she could get out of Loki's house. Logical or not, staying with him for an extended period was untenable. He made her feel too much; never mind her friends were already talking. What would the town think? If she could avoid becoming War, she needed a normal life to return to.

The bird hopped closer. "We're in Loki's house. King of lies and secrets. The horsemen have been part of his plan for some time. If anyone knows where the true War is, he does."

The idea had merit.

And provided hope there was some way she didn't have to rise as War.

"Bird—"

"Maximus Rojo. See? A man would have remembered that."

She narrowed her eyes. "The sooner you're gone, the better. Fine. Maximus—"

"Rojo." A brief pause. "I think. It's the first time anyone has ever used the name. Rojo seems right though."

"I don't care. Fine, we find the information, I point you in the right direction, and you're gone while I'm free to live my life without you and War."

"Sounds about right."

"Well. Then we have an agreement, Rojo. We just need to be sure Lo—"

The knock on the door cut off the rest of her words. "Ms. Fray, Mr. Laufeyjarson requires your presence downstairs."

CHAPTER 7

Loki didn't have the patience for playing town lord these days. He had War heiresses to manage, gods' assassins to foil, crazed Fates to contain, and an apocalypse to plan. Yes, he'd founded the town. Yes, he was more than willing to help. But they had a town council, even a police chief now. Yet, here they were. He steepled his fingers on his desk, the study surrounding him more dark polished woods and loaded bookshelves. Before him sat two men in the club chairs opposite his desk. The younger of the two was going on about his duties to the town, his benevolence.

Both had known him for years, yet they treated him as an outsider still, the company CEO who never went into the lunchroom. This was why it was easier being his alter ego, Lou. Lou owned and ran the town's communal lunchroom, the bar, where he could share easy laughs with everyone. Lou went places, was welcomed in ways Loki never would be.

He massaged his eyes. Now he was referring to

himself and Lou as two different people. He'd spent too much time with Daphne.

Wearily, he regarded the other occupants filling the room. A group of women who ranged in age from early teens to late nineties, including the one middle-aged woman with white hair, pulled back in a ponytail, who sobbed. Loudly. She was Miss Lucille Kyles. The others made up the Beckwell knitting club. Who held their meetings in the library.

Who may have recently switched from knitting to arson and destroyed Anna's home, almost killing her in the process. His eyes narrowed, and anger sizzled inside him.

He leaned back in his chair, the old leather and wood creaking beneath his bulk. He crossed his arms over his chest.

This only made the mayor stutter—a spineless tit who usually asked for Daniel's help when it came to anything important. Ah, now they'd reached kindness, protection, and leniency. It would seem in the intervening hours, the effect of Anna's voice had worn off, and now the knitting club wanted to apologize for their actions, as though the speed of their apology somehow alleviated their guilt.

The other man, tall, white-haired, and lean, was known to everyone as Old Henry, though it didn't seem so long ago he'd been in his short-pants hiding behind his mother's skirts. He'd become a good mayor in his own right until his retirement, though he remained on the town council.

Fortunately, Daniel, evidently otherwise occupied, was absent. Today had been trying enough without facing the bitter resentment in Daniel's eyes, burning with anger at every memory of their shattered friendship.

Loki ignored the stuttering words of the mayor, his gaze tracing over the other occupants. The arsonists. All of them unable to meet his gaze. Miss Kyles's sobbing began to create an ache behind his eyes.

This was the modern age. There was no reason they had to have this imbecile and Old Henry speak for him. Even the legend of Loki wasn't so terrifying. He'd known many women ten times as fierce as most men. They needed no shield from him.

"Miss Kyles, could we offer you some tea?" he said, interrupting the mayor's drivel. Offering a sedative was undoubtedly uncharitable. Trevor had said he was fetching tea.

"Sir," Trevor said from the doorway, clearing his throat, drawing Loki's and everyone else's attention.

Trevor had not fetched tea.

He'd brought Anna. Who stood in the doorway, still in those tight leggings, still in his shirt. Still no bra, either, from the looks of it. Hot color stained her cheekbones.

Speaking of fierce women…

He should have thought of involving her himself, exercising her authority.

Though…peculiarly, she had a pigeon on her shoulder.

He stood, gesturing her in, careful not to stare at the pigeon, though the others were less able to resist the urge. "A chair for An— Ms. Fray," he said, frowning at the slip of informality in public.

"I'm fine." She waved Trevor away. She stepped into the room, the rosy color in her face darkening, but then lifted her chin.

Several gazes fell away from her, and his floor became the subject of acute focus.

Regal as a goddess, Anna gave him only a glance before she came to stand at his side.

The room was more silent than Thor at a spelling bee.

He barely resisted the smile that tugged at his lips.

She stood at his side. Made it obvious to all she was under his protection, under his roof, and the consequences of attempting to harm her would be dire.

It was Old Henry who had the courage to clear his throat and speak. "Look, Loki, Ms. Fray, let's forget all this jabbering and get to it. Ms. Fray, the town is stronger because of you and your friends, but your presence also puts us at greater risk. From your collective abilities, and the attention of the gods. We've come as intermediaries for the accused."

"The cowards who burned her house down you mean," the pigeon said, gliding down from Anna's shoulder and strutting back and forth across the surface of his desk.

While speaking. Aloud.

Hopefully, it didn't have fleas.

Everyone stared at the bird.

Praise Ymir. Even the sobbing Miss Kyles was shocked into silence.

"Rojo," Anna said warningly.

The pigeon stopped, did an abrupt face until it glared at the crying woman directly, its tail feathers twitching. "I should have known it'd be a woman behind it, having a hysterical fit and burning down another woman's house. What about a good old-fashioned boxing match? A duel. Face-to-face. Honest. None of this sneaking around in the dark."

Miss Kyles started sobbing again.

Loki sighed, massaging the pounding in his temples. The winged vermin wasn't helping. "Miss Fray. What Old Henry is likely getting to is talk of reparation."

"Reparation, indeed," Old Henry said gruffly, clearing his throat and looking up nervously from beneath his bushy white eyebrows. "We're none of us fools. We know what you and your friends could do to us and this town, Ms. Fray. I hope you'll also remember the support we showed your Death friend, Miss Amort, when the coward gods came after her. The same support we'd be willing to extend to you, should the need arise, and if we aren't all pounded flat or imprisoned by the gods first."

The gods had been making threatening noises again. Other than the assassination attempts. He'd have to do something about it.

"Excuses and whining. What are you willing to offer?" the pigeon demanded.

Hmm. Perhaps the vermin had some redeeming qualities.

At Old Henry's incredulous look—evidently he was unused to negotiating with birds—Loki gestured that he continue.

The white-haired man cleared his throat. "Well...we have funds. We could replace the house and contents. Could build a new one, though that would take a while..."

"No," Anna said, her voice quiet but firm above the sound of sobbing.

Loki couldn't help but turn enough to see her, to admire— Er, watch her, as they all did.

The color in her cheeks only emphasized the strong bone structure, the soft tendrils of dark hair escaping her braid softening her face. Those eyes though. Such a pure, crystalline blue, the likes of which he'd never seen before. Her power gleamed through her eyes, the power of her abilities, her personality, her soul.

Ymir help him, now he was waxing poetic. Between Anna's allure and Daphne's psychosis, he was screwed.

"Miss Kyles," Anna said quietly. Then a little less quietly, when she didn't seem to be overheard above the sobs.

The collected group stirred, shifted, and frowned. Tension gathered like storm clouds, the electrical crackle of Anna's ability sparking through the room.

As though realizing what was happening—stirring

the same unintentional rage that had caused them to burn down her house in the first place—she pressed her lips closed, her brows coming down.

He worked his jaw. She couldn't even tell them not to burn down her house again or demand an apology without getting them riled again.

He reached for her hand. The crackle of power and energy between them, the violent undercurrent flowing out into the room was like grabbing a livewire. He drew it into him, like letting lightning course through his body. He clenched his teeth against the jolt and burn. It lasted barely a moment, barely stole his breath, and Anna wasn't even stirred into a fury.

Eyes wide, lips slightly parted, she stared into his eyes.

He nodded, not sure his voice would work for a moment or two, hopeful she understood. He'd absorbed enough ability for her to be able to speak without causing violence.

She flicked her gaze back to their audience, attentive and wide-eyed.

"I want a favor. No expiry date, no strings," she said hurriedly, as though afraid the effect of his energy dampening would wear off.

This was hardly anything to the last time he'd done it, at Ginny's wedding when Anna was in full temper. But even this minute energy felt stronger than it had, caused conflict more quickly.

She felt stronger.

The pigeon watched the audience expectantly. Nia was right. The opinionated bird was Anna's apocalypse horse.

Old Henry appeared puzzled, leaning forward. "I don't understand, Miss. A favor from Miss Kyles? The knitting club? They're very sorry for the whole–"

"A favor from the whole town. If or when I ask, you

all listen," Anna said.

Loki leaned back in his seat.

Old Henry did the same, his white brows raised.

Miss Kyles made louder sobbing sounds by some twisted miracle of nature.

The mayor—the cowardly mouse—leaned toward Old Henry. "We can't promise everyone's agreement," he whispered loudly enough they could all hear.

Old Henry had already stood and extended a hand to Anna. "Done. One favor, owed at the will of Miss Fray, by the town of Beckwell."

Anna took the older man's hand, and new energy crackled in the room. The energy of something significant, recorded and noted in the fabric of time and the universe.

Anna paled, as though she sensed it too. Still, she squared her shoulders again, even as Henry and the mayor gathered the knitting club and Miss Kyles, then said their hurried goodbyes.

Loki barely noticed. He couldn't look away from Anna, from the sharp cleverness in her blue eyes, the slim but strong physique of a warrior. Her request was pure strategy, something he might have asked for or suggested.

It was all War. All she had to do was recognize it, and that she would and should rise. Then the Four would rise, she could kill him, and he could save the world.

CHAPTER 8

Sneaking through Loki's house and unearthing his secrets did seem a tad uncouth, considering his generosity in taking her in, Anna considered the next morning as she waited for Rojo's signal. A soft whistle came from a little farther down the wood-paneled hall, and she hurried to the next concealment point. What choice did she have? She had to find an alternate War, someone who wouldn't be so easily corrupted by War, who wouldn't be as dangerous to the world, and who possessed more of the companion abilities to offset War's destructiveness. That meant raiding Loki's house and uncovering what he knew, discovering if there was any possibility of avoiding rising.

Yesterday as the town council and knitting club departed, Anna had looked up and seen amber heat flickering in Loki's gaze. Her request from Old Henry had been strategic. If the gods did come after Beckwell or she and her friends, they'd need all the allies they could find. In Loki's eyes, his admiration was clear. He was looking at her, as though maybe he really saw *her*. The very idea warmed her like the glow from a fire. Perhaps the way condemned witches had felt before it caught their feet and bodies on fire.

Retreat had been the only sensible solution, returning to her room to pace, caged again. To plan. Though every thought circled back to the fact she was in the company of a talking pigeon who was almost certainly War's horse, and that she was in Loki's house. The fantasy only continued when his minion wheeled in a rack of beautiful vintage clothing, outfits already arranged on the hangers. The bubble had popped when dinner last night was delivered to her room on a tray, then breakfast the same. She should have been grateful. Loki was giving her space, no quiet intimacy of dinner, no pretending their lives could ever truly intersect.

Another whistle. Focus. The mission. Operation Escape War.

"Clear," Rojo said, after swooping ahead to clear their position down the stairs into the front foyer, with its gleaming floor and stunning woodwork. Old-school luxury, refined as an old-fashioned men's club, every inch of the house was stamped with Loki's taste.

Anna quickly made her way down the stairs. No sign of Loki nor any of his three minions yet. The first two—the cook, and the odd-job man who primarily seemed to work outside—those didn't concern her much. It was the primary minion who'd wheeled the rack of clothing into her room last night, who spoke to her with peculiar familiarity, as though he knew her...he was a concern. Slight, well-put-together, he was unassuming and appeared friendly. Yet a slight tickle in her lower back said there was more to Mr. Minion than met the eyes.

She strode across the front hall. Pulled on the sliding door to the study where they'd met the contingent from Beckwell yesterday. It wouldn't budge. Her lips thinned.

Loki might not be around, but they didn't have free rein.

"Pick it?" Rojo said quietly, landing on her shoulder.

"No. It'd be just like Loki to lock it, just keep us occupied trying to get inside." Anna bit her lip. There was also a dangerous prisoner locked in one of these rooms. They didn't need to release Daphne accidentally. "Unlocked rooms first." She gestured across the hall to the parlor.

They stepped into the room she was perhaps most familiar with. The large, spacious front parlor where she and her friends had collected when Ginny was under threat. Like most of the house, it was old-world luxury, tasteful and warm with wood paneling, dark curtains, leather club chairs, and a small chaise near the large white stone fireplace. All it needed was some gentlemen with their cigars and brandy.

This was the room he'd first brought her to as a child, where he'd wrapped a blanket around her narrow shoulders, promised that he would always protect her. She'd lost part of herself to that pewter gaze, the sincerity in his voice.

Before he'd packed her off to the Lacks like stale leftovers.

She shook off the thought. "Don't overlook the obvious. It might be hidden in plain sight." She started for the sideboard. "You take the higher shelves."

Rojo snorted. "Like a folder labeled 'secret info' here? That seems unlikely." Nonetheless, he poked his beak around on the upper bookshelves that flanked the fireplace, wiggling between undoubtedly expensive art pieces.

Fifteen minutes later, and nothing.

Anna frowned at the room, hands on her hips.

"Now we pick the lock?" Rojo said hopefully.

"Now we find another unlocked room," she said, heading back into the foyer, then down the hall from the study. The search would be easier if they knew exactly what they were looking for.

Loki, like his house, was old-world luxury. A lord mingling with the plebs. While he wasn't averse to technology—she'd seen him with his smartphone—something important like research he might go old school.

A bit like her.

She frowned at the thought, tried the next door. A shallow closet this time, loaded with cleaning supplies.

Where was he anyway? It would be like him to be watching her, amused by her efforts.

The idea of that pewter gaze on her sent a small curl of heat whirling through her.

Faex.

She'd heard him last night, the sure footsteps striding down the hall outside her bedroom suite definitely his. The odd-job minion who worked outside wouldn't have ventured inside, so it couldn't have been his footsteps. Nor did it sound like the softer, feminine footfalls of the cook/housekeeper, and the head minion walked quickly, stealthily.

Loki's reason for being there was perfectly sound: his bedroom was directly across from hers. His sure footsteps outside her door had paused a moment. She'd lain in bed, clutching the covers like some Victorian heroine, listening, breathless, biting her lip. Too many foolish fantasies flitting through her head. Not that Loki was anything other than the consummate gentleman. Sadly.

"Try this one," Rojo said, stopping at the next set of doors, his voice making her start.

She firmed her lips. Enough daydreaming; she'd given Loki far too many hours of that already in her life.

Placing her hand on the pull of another set of sliding doors, this one rolled easily, opening a gap between the doors. Faint light shone inside, sunlight from the looks.

"I vote we should start with the locked rooms. You're giving him too much credit," Rojo grouched.

"*Puto vos esse molestissimos,*" Anna muttered beneath her breath.

"I find you annoying too, Princess," Rojo said, not missing a beat as he leaned forward, peering into the room. His claws bit into her shoulder. "Come on. Enough lollygagging."

Anna grabbed him by the feet just before he shook to the air, glared into his beady little eyes. "You speak Latin, and you use the term lollygagging?"

He flapped his wings to escape. "I'm not the one who has to be such a know-it-all she swears in Latin." He jabbed her hard in the hand with his beak.

She gasped, her fingers opening as a small red droplet of blood formed where he'd pecked her. "*Faex!*"

He flew well above her head and out of reach. "I told you. We have a connection. You may be rising as War, but it's a mistake. We need to find the real War," he said, zero remorse in his tone. "Don't you listen to anything?" He dove through the partially opened doorway.

"I hate you."

"If I had weaknesses, like feelings, I'd say right back at you, Princess," Rojo said, but there was little heat in his words.

Anna ground her teeth, ensuring the doors were perfectly closed. No sense the minions spotting the open doors. Now the feathered rat mocked her lack of emotional control.

"Think we may have found the place," Rojo said, awe in his voice.

She turned. And beheld heaven.

Her breath caught, and she walked forward a few steps, head swiveling to take it all in, surrounding her, and up…and up.

Light streamed through two windows that soared

nearly thirty feet high, the height of the room, a soaring two stories at least. The windows flanked a massive fireplace with ornate Victorian overmantel, above which was a framed painting of a young man she'd never seen before. Her gaze paused on it, his brown hair, soft face, slightly old-fashioned clothes. Who was he that he'd been important enough for Loki to keep this reminder of him?

Deep green leather chairs flanked the fireplace. But it was the books... Oh, the books! Those stole her breath.

Shelves covered every wall other than the windows. A second-story catwalk and gallery surrounded the room that was easily the size of the entire Beckwell library and then half again. A winding metalwork staircase led up to the second story. Books weighed down the shelves, were stacked against the shelves. Ancient tomes, modern paperbacks, mysterious leather tomes she itched to explore.

The whispers of the words scratched at her ears, whispering their stories, their truths.

"What are you waiting for? Get searching, Princess," Rojo said, flapping and gliding up to the second story.

Anna blinked, pushed the whispering voices to the back of her mind and forced herself to turn. To face exquisitely carved shelves and their contents. It took only a glance to see how carefully organized the books were. Divided by fiction and nonfiction, then by topic and alphabetized. She leaned forward. It might have been the newer Library of Congress Classification system rather than the Dewey Decimal system most people and most libraries were more familiar with. How interesting.

"It's mostly fiction up here," Rojo called down.

"You can read?" Well, the damned bird spoke Latin. Being literate wasn't beyond possibility.

"Of course, I can read." The flying rat sounded offended as he flew down to the main floor, perching on a nearby shelve. "All carrier pigeons can. How else could we carry out our noble calling?"

She raised a brow. "It doesn't work that way." She contemplated explaining normal pigeons and quickly discarded the idea. "Keep searching, even in the fiction. It'd be like Loki to secret something away with misfiling." Though it did seem sinful to disrupt such a carefully cataloged collection.

"Women. So clueless," Rojo scoffed, flying back up to the gallery walk. "As though pigeons can't read."

"Carries eons of history in his head, speaks Latin, has my knowledge and research…still thinks pigeons can read," she muttered, carefully scanning the shelf. She pulled out a book or two, sometimes checking for hidden spaces, sometimes out of curiosity.

"I heard that," Rojo shouted down.

"You were supposed to," she said. "Be sure to check for voids and secret hiding places."

They continued to hunt the shelves for the next hour, the whispers of the books growing in volume as her weariness grew.

Rojo's whistle broke her focus. "Better get up here, Princess."

Anna stood, stretching her back before heading to the staircase and up to the gallery walk.

He was down near the far wall, not far from one of the windows.

She knelt beside him.

He tapped on a book spine with his beak, then gave another tap on the book next to it.

The tap elicited a peculiarly hollow sound.

False fronts. Her pulse picked up.

She groped around the top and sides to find the edge of the false book front. Finally, her fingers grazed a cool metal piece. She pressed, and with a soft *click*, the front of six books fell forward into her hand.

She drew in a soft breath before she leaned forward

and peered inside. There were what looked like some scrolls, neatly tied with red thread. Some envelopes and folders, yellowed with age. Then down near the bottom, a large, leather-bound book.

The tiniest twinge of guilt waggled in her stomach. Loki had saved her life yesterday. He'd invited her into his home for her protection. She repaid him by sneaking around his house and invading his privacy.

"These papers might have nothing to do with the War clan. We could just…ask Loki what he knows."

The bird stared at her a second, those beady eyes unblinking, unnerving. "Ask him? As though we could believe anything the Prince of Lies tells us?"

"Quite certain the Prince of Lies is Satan. Besides, I'd know if Loki lied."

Rojo scoffed. "You're suckered by the pretty face and going gooey over his eyes. Step aside then. See? This is why you can't be War. Too soft. Too emotional for the job." He poked his beak through the papers.

Anna growled low in her throat. "Feather-brained idiot. Move. If you make a mess of them, he'll know we were here."

Not waiting for Rojo to comply, she elbowed him aside and carefully lifted the papers and other scrolls to free the book. If in doubt, always start with the book.

She barely had to flip through the opening pages to know they'd found Loki's version of her Bigass Book of Awesome. The girls said Boring, but they were just jealous.

His, though, was far older than her. The pages were thick linen paper, shushing as she turned them.

Rojo fluttered up onto her shoulder and leaned over to get a better view. "Bastard was holding out on us."

Indeed. More than a century of notes about the horseman clans, their history, notes on the original Four. She'd been extensive in her research, but she'd never found such a complete source on all four of the clans.

There were finger tabs cut into the pages to indicate the primary topics—more elegant than her rainbow-hued Post-It notes. Despite the urge to read through from cover-to-cover in detail, she flipped to the section on War.

First, there was a section on general history and known abilities. The section was started in black ink, occasional blotches possibly indicating a fountain pen or even quill. More notes had been added in other ink, occasionally pencil, always in the same bold script that marched across the page.

The red horse, associated with fire and the sword Hildebrand. Anna shook her head. Trust a man to think a sword needed naming. Hildebrand was different than the other horseman weapons, with the ability to end all life, even immortals and other paranormal species, and never missed its mark. Figured that the War weapon was exceptionally deadly.

She scanned over the rest. *Voice causes violence. Ability to detect lies. Understands and reads all languages...* Well, she didn't have that one yet. *Ability to create illusions and false-truths. Super strength and battle prowess, fight sense...* Curious. The notes didn't mention the danger itch.

"He's missing the always battle-ready part," Rojo said, poking his head around her arm.

"The what?"

Rojo shrugged, still reading. "Can't be drunk in a fight. Wars can drink as long and as much as they like, but come even a hint of battle? Bam! Stone-sober, able to lay out anyone."

"I...didn't know that."

The bird sniffed. "Yeah. I'll pretend I'm surprised."

She rolled her eyes and continued reading.

Next came the family trees, tracing the original War and his — Oh my, four different wives and twenty-five children. These twenty-five children became the basis for the next level of descendants, always linking back to these original twenty-five families.

Fray was one of the first listed.

The next section was names. Reams and reams of names were listed on each page including the family branch they descended from, known abilities, date of birth and death, spouse and children if applicable. There was rarely more than one child, and many more lacked either spouse or children. No wonder there weren't as many Wars as there were, say, Famines, who'd been prolific as rabbits.

Her finger paused, trembling, as it traced over her parents' name on the Fray page. The penciled circle around her name. Hadrianna. Her brows rose. Mom was descendant from another of the original twenty-five. She'd been a Wiebe.

"Have to give it to you, Princess," Rojo said. "With your breeding, you might have been a contender. If not for your—"

Her eyes narrowed. "Being female. You've said it."

"I was going to say tits, but yeah, same idea."

"My friends have risen, and they're women."

"They're not War. War is different. Requires a particular type of character to carry that power. Even lesser men have been driven mad with it."

Not surprising, with the way it corrupted everything with ugliness, violence, and blood. She shook her head, then opened the book flat on the floor, staring at the list of names. Hundreds on both sides of the page. "You take the left page, I'll take the right. Look for any where both parents are descendant from the original twenty-five. Make sure they're not dead."

"Not dead. Affirmative."

They were quiet, scanning through first one page, then the next. She wasn't the only one with parents both from the original twenty-five. A voice kept screaming in her head, so why me? Was this still the influence of the Fates who wanted her friends and her to rise? Surely one of these people had greater control over their abilities than she did.

She scratched at the back of her neck, which had started to itch, along with a spot low on her back. It only seemed to get worse.

She tried to focus on the names. Granted, there weren't many that fit the criteria. Unlike the other clans, War numbers were small and dwindling. Not surprising considering a penchant for fighting, making people angry, and never marrying. A disheartening number were marked deceased. Most had never married; even fewer had children, especially in recent years.

There had to be someone else. There only needed to be one…

The masculine cough froze both Anna and Rojo.

"I trust you've found what you were looking for," Loki said, words dripping icicles.

Anna gritted her teeth, grasped the book carefully with both hands, supporting the spine, and came to her feet. She turned, startled to find him directly behind her. The gallery walk was so narrow, she'd have to flatten herself against the railing to pass him.

Not that there was any chance she'd run. The time for retreat was over.

His arms were crossed over his chest, his silk shirt pulled taut over muscle. Amber flickered in the whirling silver-gray of his gaze, and a tic started in his clenched jaw. He stood a full head taller than her. He was a warrior, a demigod, and pissed.

Good. So was she.

She held up the book, her finger marking their spot. Advanced on him. "You kept this from me. The information I've hunted for years. All this time you had it."

He didn't budge, the book between them, her toes almost bumping his, heat radiating off his big body. His gaze, hot and warming with more amber, flicked over her. He scowled. "What the hell are you wearing?"

CHAPTER 9

He'd told Trevor to find Anna clothes, not make her even more of a distraction. Yet now here he was, blurting out the first thing that came to mind like a simpleton. Loki's gaze roved over the knee-length soft cream dress with brown polka-dots that skimmed over Anna's curves, came away at the hip to hint at softer curves ahead. It was feminine and demure. Yet he'd never seen Anna wear something that fit and flattered her body. Made her temptation incarnate when he found her snooping around what had been he and Peter's sanctuary.

What in the name of Ymir was he supposed to do with the woman?

His mind quickly supplied a ready and erotically hot list, many of which involved pressing his lips to hers, lifting her skirt, and pressing her against the bookshelves and burying himself inside her.

His body tightened. His breath grew raspy.

Anna's lips thinned. At least one of them was showing some sense.

She glanced down at her dress, as though noticing it for the first time. Her glare came up, along with her chin. "They're clothes. Your head minion found them for me. Unless you'd prefer I traipse around naked?"

Now there was an image. Her slim form, naked and pale against the backdrop of his house, sending him come-hither looks over one shoulder, dark hair flowing free, the curve of her buttocks ripe for his hand. Leading him to bed.

He cleared his throat and shifted. The gods take him if she noticed his state of arousal. He'd be lucky if all she did was throw him over the balcony.

He kept a carefully neutral expression on his face. He'd been disturbed to find her in here. Now he was more disturbed...though for different reasons.

"Of course, I'd rather you were clothed." Naked would be far better. "But these—" He waved his hand at the dress, the pretty way it hugged her curves, softened her. He hadn't considered what a tragedy it was that all those hideous, body-concealing garments she used to wear had been consumed by fire. "These are old, frumpy, out of date."

These were not only immensely flattering, they dated back to another time. Back to when the house was still full of people and life and echoed with the sound of Peter and his friends, their raucous antics. Servants had bustled in the halls, families he'd known for generations who called him by name, knew and almost accepted him as one of them.

Before the second, even deadlier war called too many to serve. Before the arrival of telegrams and four burial urns, too many funerals. Before the silence and the grief.

A lifetime ago.

Anna scowled. "They're clothes. I'm covered. I hardly need to be a fashion plate." She touched the dress collar.

Dragging his gaze to the slim column of her neck, the silken skin there that plunged toward her breasts.

He shifted his gaze resolutely to her face, clenching his hands against temptation. The same temptation that'd made him avoid the intimacy of dinner with her last night. He'd imagined her lavender scent on the air when he came to bed last night, drew impossible fantasies in his mind of her just across the hall from him, but centuries too far.

"Besides, I like it," she said, as though intentionally being obstinate. "From the forties, isn't it?" She touched the collar again.

He tightened his jaw, returned to the other problem. "You were snooping through my belongings when I entered."

"Yeah. If you two are done ogling each other, I'd like to know where the real War heir is," the mongrel on wings said, strutting along the edge of a bookshelf, glaring at Loki through beady eyes.

Loki kept his tone mild but directed his comment to Anna. He was helpless to look away. "Does the beast have a vision impairment that it can't see you?"

"Ha! No. He means I'm not the only War heir." She pointed at the book.

He kept his gaze locked on her, the effect causing color to stain her cheekbones. Good.

She cleared her throat. "There are other War heirs. Others with similar ancestry, multiple ancestors from the original twenty-five families." She frowned down at the book, vulnerability creeping into her expression.

A weight similar to Yggdrasil, the world tree that held all the Norse worlds, settled on his shoulders with her look. Ah, hell.

"I don't understand why I would rise instead of one of them," she said softly, as though almost speaking to herself.

Because she was the best candidate. Because she was a known quantity. Because there was no one else he'd trust with that much power, that much responsibility. He couldn't control who rose, but telling someone they were "chosen" made them believe it, too. Supposed 'destiny' overrode choice.

Yet the way she opened the book, scanned the page with something akin to desperation tightened the back of his neck. His chest squeezed.

War had taken her parents, left her orphaned, often made her nearly as much of an outsider as he. He'd kept his distance, determined to see her as just another Beckwellian he needed to keep safe but had no connection with.

He'd failed.

"The War horse came to you. You're the best heir," he said, the words raw, the truth practically torn from his throat. He'd said those same words to Peter. Words that had led to Peter's rising...and death.

Her blue gaze shot up to meet his, demanded more.

He smothered a sigh. "I tried to find an alternative."

He'd seen too clearly how much it pained her, the mere possibility of rising as War, so he'd sent people out to all the corners of the globe, on every wild goose chase.

The flying infestation hopped closer, cocked its head. "Sure it's not you who's blind?" It pointed a wing at the book. "There are other names in there. Other options."

Loki shook his head. "There is no one."

"Lie," Anna whispered, staring down at the book, her fingers turning white as she gripped it harder.

His throat tightened. "You should rise."

She slowly raised her gaze to his. The inner glow of the flame glowed hot inner blue eyes. Color stained her cheekbones. "Lie," she repeated, louder.

"Anna, please—"

"Don't lie to me!" she roared, advancing on him.

He held his ground. By Ymir, she was glorious in a rage, strength emanating from her, more ferocious than an avenging angel.

He lowered his gaze to hers, kept his voice firm. "There is no one else suitable."

"I said, stop lying to me," she said, her voice pitched low as she shoved the book into his chest. "They're written down in here. All of them. If you lied about there being no one..." Her voice caught, the small hint at fear only seeming to intensify her fury.

She looked up at him, and the sheen of moisture in her eyes made his innards flip.

"You know I don't want to rise. I never have. Why me? Why am I rising?"

He wouldn't let himself look away, forced himself to stare into her pain.

Pain he'd knowingly caused.

He could say nothing, and there'd be no lie for her to sense. She already had her horse. The process of rising had begun. She would rise.

She would despise him for his part—whether true or the product of her imagination. He would have the safe distance he needed from her. The distance to keep him from the pain of losing her, as he had Peter, as he had too many others. They always left. And she could hurt him so much more than even Peter had.

Besides, pushing her this way nearly guaranteed the success of his plan. She'd undoubtedly be gleeful when she plunged her blade into his heart and ended his life.

She still glared, waiting, that hint of moisture shimmering in her gaze.

He rubbed a hand over his eyes.

She would hate what she became. Her resentment could make her not only more dangerous and volatile, but doomed to a lifetime of misery. Or longer, according to some of the Fates he'd consulted throughout the world.

He couldn't do that to her.

"It's a choice," he said quietly.

She blinked. "It's what?"

"A choice. He said it's a choice. You're going to decide *not* to be War, because the idea is ridiculous," the idiot bird piped up.

Anna barely seemed to notice it. She swallowed, studied a spot on the ground a moment.

One breath passed. Then another, the ticking of the clock on the mantel below loud.

Finally, she looked up at him. "I can…choose not to be War?"

"Potentially. If someone else chooses to rise."

"Who? How do we do that?" she said, words jumbling together in her rush.

Loki hesitated. He'd already said too much. Telling her the rest could mean the failure of his plan. There was no guarantee another War would agree to help him, might even wish to start the apocalypse themselves. He'd worked too long trying to get all the players into the right positions. He was so close.

She stepped closer. Reached out a hand, hesitated a moment, then placed it on his chest. "Please," she whispered.

His heart pounded beneath her hand. He could only stare at her lush lips, feel the heat of her touch leaching through the silk of his shirt to his skin. Then soaking deeper, to some cold place inside of him.

At that moment she might well have asked for anything, and he'd have been helpless to do anything but comply. Even this.

Ymir help him if she ever discovered the depth of her power over him.

"There are four," he said, voice gravelly. "Four other potential heirs we haven't yet fully investigated. I doubt they're as well suited as you—"

"They could rise? Instead of me?" Hope burbled in her eyes, lightened her entire expression.

Damn, me.

"Yes."

"No," the feathered cretin destined for pigeon pot pie said, strutting forward. It pointed a wing at the book again. "There are more than four other War heirs. Demigods can't count?"

Loki shot the winged pest a look that should have incinerated, although that could be unfortunate if it flopped around and set his library aflame before it died.

He turned back to Anna, held out a hand. "My book, if you will."

She gave the book a reluctant look before placing it in his hand, dropping her hand from his chest.

He ignored the cold sense of loss and flipped quickly to the War section, the largest and most perused of them all. He found the appropriate page listing living Wars and ran his finger down the list. Tried to ignore Peter's name.

Anna leaned closer, her lavender scent weaving around him, fuzzing his brain.

Making him appreciate the view offered by the low-cut bodice of the dress. Evidently, someone had located her a new bra too. Or perhaps she'd had a spare at the library. A pity.

She looked up. Colored as she caught the heated nature of his gaze.

He cleared his throat, focused back on the page, the names beneath his fingertip. "This one is ninety-seven. These three are imprisoned for killing this one here. This one is a drug kingpin in Kingston, Jamaica. This one is an assassin, arms dealer, and mafioso in Cape Town, South Africa. He's had a busy year."

He continued to flip pages, identifying the ones he had researched and dismissed. "This one leads a murder ring in Tijuana, Mexico. Leader of a drug gang in Natal, Brazil. This one is trying to start another toddler fight club in St. Louis." He glanced up, raised a brow. "Need I go on? I said there are four potential candidates. Because, of the perhaps two hundred living Wars, my research indicates only those four might not already be homicidal maniacs or criminally dangerous."

Anna stared at him a while before her shoulders sagged. "He's telling the truth, Rojo." She blew out a breath. "Fine. So, what's the next step? Have a meeting to determine who should rise?"

"Bringing War clan members together is always risky," he said slowly. A new plan had started to take shape behind his eyes. A better plan. An opportunity to convince Anna she was the only viable heir. Then she'd rise, his plan would succeed, but she wouldn't be miserable. None of the other candidates could possibly be as promising as her.

"We vet them," he said, meeting her gaze evenly.

"How do we do that? 'Cause I think a cage fight has real potential," the rat-bird said.

Loki tried to tune it out as easily as Anna seemed to. "We need to visit them in person. Be certain they're worthy of the power and responsibility. Remember, too, whoever rises will gain a significant connection to your friends."

Anna's hopeful expression dimmed somewhat. "So...you evaluate them in person?"

"No, Anna. *We*. Only you can identify the lies. You may also have some sense of their ability I don't have, and you'll know whether they'll be compatible with your friends."

She licked her lips, a singularly distracting movement. "I can't leave Beckwell," she whispered, that vulnerable echo of fear in her voice.

"You haven't left Beckwell. You can," he said

gently. This plan continued to prove itself advantageous in more aspects as they went. "You need to."

"But Normals, all those people without paranormal ability... My voice made the knitting club burn down my house. It will be so much worse out there, with Normals. I'm so much more dangerous."

He dared stroke a hand down her arm, the flesh warm, silken, and supple beneath his touch, caught her hand with his. "You won't be alone. I doused the effect at Ginny's wedding and yesterday. I can again."

She caught her breath, her gaze snagging on his. "It hurts you."

Goose bumps pebbled on her skin, and he changed the touch to only his fingertips.

He looked at her. As though a little pain mattered.

Fire and lust flashed between them. Her ability, his, something more.

Perhaps she wasn't as immune and opposed to him as he thought.

"We were making a plan," the pigeon said. Loudly.

Anna jumped back, out of Loki's reach. Lifted her chin and stood her ground.

"So, we scope out these four candidates, then offer them the power?" the brainless wonder bird said.

"We determine their suitability before we reveal any chance of their rising," he said. "For now, the process has begun for Anna. Without interruption, it will reach fruition." He was counting on it.

He paused, studied that blue gaze. Here was the real gambit, the coup de grace. "There is no guarantee any of the candidates will be suitable." No chance of it, if he had his druthers. "I will collude on this plan if I have your word that, should none of the candidates prove suitable, you will rise, Anna." If he was getting her word on one aspect, he might as well see how far luck took him today. "Additionally, once we return to Beckwell you will wield the War sword, Hildebrand, and kill me."

The room was quiet enough to hear the tick of the mantel clock down on the main floor.

Anna just stared, as though he'd gone mad, sprouted horns, or both.

"Huh. Wasn't the direction I expected," the devil bird said.

It took Anna a few more moments before she found her voice. She swallowed and looked him straight in the eye. "You want me to rise and...and kill you? Does it have to be me, or will another War do?"

"Only War can wield all weapons, in particular, the War sword, Hildebrand."

Her eyes narrowed. "Why that sword? Why not another?"

Ymir, it was irritating, all this truth nonsense.

He ground his teeth a moment. "Hildebrand is especially powerful, deadly to even the most powerful creatures. That, and I...made a deal. With the original Four." A drunken mistake more like. "If I die by War's hand and stabbed through by Hildebrand, as per my agreement, I—we—can give humanity another chance. A chance to survive, a new beginning."

The Four had promised him Ragnarök without the endless winter, the battle, the death, the suffering. The world would rise anew and refreshed, shifting humanity's focus from war, pollution, and selfishness. Their eyes would be open, and the new world ready to embrace them.

"You made a deal with the original Four?" Her quirked brow and tone indicated her doubt.

He sighed. "I was drunk."

That she seemed to accept. Of course, she did. It put him in the worst possible light.

She considered a few moments longer, twisting her hands together. "This end. There's no eternal torment? The Four don't have to spread strife and suffering?"

"None." He couldn't resist baiting the trap. "This is the chance you've looked for. Are you going to let my death and your reluctance to leave Beckwell stop you?"

She bit her lip, and he tried not to stare.

Interminable moments crawled past.

At last, she stuck out her hand, lifted her gaze, and her gaze locked with his.

Even before she spoke, he could see victory within his grasp. The success of his plan.

His fingers closed over hers.

"You have my word," she said. "We investigate the candidates, and if none of them are suitable—which seems highly improbable—then I will rise…and kill you." The last was more hesitant.

He wouldn't let himself worry about that. Now he knew he could convince her. Of everything.

CHAPTER 10

By all that was known and written, what in the name of the Goddess had she been thinking when she'd agreed to this harebrained scheme?

Seated once more in Loki's car, Anna squeezed her hands between her knees, massaging the palm of her left hand with her thumb. *Don't panic, don't panic, don't panic. Emotion is dangerous, now more than ever.*

The next morning, following a sleepless night, what little breakfast she could stomach, and a panicked phone call to Ginny to borrow a suitcase, Anna was once more off on one of his plans. Well, a plan she'd agreed to. This time with him, a suitcase of borrowed clothes, and the chauvinistic pigeon from hell.

Last night it had seemed almost sane, this plan to find the other candidates, get one of them to rise instead of her. An escape. At least, she'd tried to make it sound that way to Ginny. The Famine horsewoman had seemed less convinced, kept asking if something had happened between Anna and Loki, if Anna knew what she was getting into. Other things that might have involved a discussion of condoms and the promise to call if Anna got scared.

Got scared. Ha. Her friends seemed to have this deluded idea she was brave, when instead, most of her life was spent planning and counter-planning to minimize risk and threat. To outrun the fears that plagued her like a million little papercuts.

Loki drove them through the quiet section of highway outside his property, houses playing peek-a-boo between the dense green leaves, sun flickering like a disco ball.

Too quickly they reached the four-way stop. Beckwell already bustled despite the early summer hour. Cars pulled in and out of the parking lot of Loki's bar and the minimart. There was a lot of traffic across the road and up the slight rise at the school. All that was familiar and safe.

"Your bar will be fine without you?" she asked.

"I have good staff," he said without looking at her as he pulled to the stop, people staring at his stylish car. He kept his gaze straight ahead, that small tic back in his jaw.

Peculiar, really, to have a car like this but rarely drive it. The black pickup that belonged to his alter ego, Lou—and fit into Beckwell much less conspicuously—was the one she usually saw.

It was their turn to pull through the four-way. Not far beyond that lay Beckwell's borders, then open highway, the world of Normals. So many people even more sensitive to her abilities, more vulnerable to War. Her stomach churned, and she twisted her hands together.

"Daphne. What about Daphne? She's still imprisoned and dangerous in your house, isn't she? It seems risky leaving her care to anyone else."

Loki put his foot back on the brake and this time shot her a look, one dark brow raised. "Again, I have excellent staff. Mal is also going to look in. Anna, leaving Beckwell won't hurt you."

She scoffed and turned to stare out the right window, rubbing her arms. "I just thought we might want to avoid a suicidal Fate running around causing trouble."

"Ah, of course," he said, driving through the four-way.

Too quickly they rolled past the rustic cabin-like exterior of her library on the corner, with its logs and broad front porch. No lights on inside. Empty for who knew how long.

She reached down beside her ankle, checked that her borrowed purse was there, and Ginny's pink sparkly phone. Set it down, rubbed her hands again.

The beastly car ate up the road, her library gone in barely a moment. The Cow Palace raced up next to them, squatting in fuchsia glory amid the quiet agricultural grounds.

"We may miss Beckwell Days," she said, noticing the sign and the freshly cut grass. "Aren't you expected to attend?"

Beckwell Days, the annual celebration of the town's founding and all their weirdness. Usually attended by the town founder, Loki. Although more often in recent years, his alter ego, Lou. She remembered his presence there including plaid for years now.

"I'm certain it will be more than successful without me." Loki reached for the gearshift. His knuckles brushed her thigh through the thin fabric of the skirt.

Awareness tingled through her, joining the unrest whirling in her stomach. Controlling herself was all well and good when she was in town, mere minutes from her friends, plenty of Loki-free territory. Out here, she was dependent on him to help control her abilities. She had no money, no resources, no experience. Was this how Stockholm syndrome began?

Most kidnap victims were likely smart enough not to start out with very mixed emotions about their kidnapper.

"Perhaps our mission will be complete, and we'll be home by that point," he said, as though he hadn't noticed the brief touch.

The car accelerated.

Anna's breath roughened.

There went the ragged town sign. Then out onto a two-lane secondary highway.

She sank into the seat. This was officially as far out of town as she'd been since Loki brought her here twenty-three years ago.

Rojo hopped around on Ginny's pink suitcase in the back seat. He cleared his throat. "Uh, head's up: Princess looks ready to ruin your upholstery."

She stared straight ahead and focused on not making a fool of herself. She was just leaving town. People did it every day. It was worth the risk. They'd find another War. She'd be free. She would *not* be sick.

"Anna? Should I stop?" The deep rumble of Loki's voice with a hint of concern rolled over her, a slight tingle over her skin suggesting he'd turned again to look at her.

Not puking was taking a good deal of focus and shallow breathing. "I'm fine."

"Damn. You say that a *lot*, Princess," the idiot pigeon said.

She tried to ignore him, focused on small, shallow breaths. She'd find someone like her friends, someone who could access all of War's abilities, including the more positive companion abilities. She'd be free. Free to travel, to attend university in person, to see the world.

The thought thickened her throat, filled her inside. Her effect on Normals had made attending University too risky. The internet was amazing but wasn't the same as seeing something up close, experiencing it. If she were free, she'd travel the world like Piper had, be as fearless as Nia, uncover the way she was special like Ginny had. Maybe she'd even finally experience dating.

They whisked along, farther and farther from home, from familiarity, from relative safety. She shifted, the leather seats somehow not quite comfortable.

She scraped her nail along the fleshy part of her hand. She would not let War control and corrupt her; she wouldn't let it hurt anyone else. *Vinait qui se vincit*. She was in control. Of her life. Of whether she puked or not.

"Anna…" Loki said, more softly, his voice caressing the syllables of her name.

Oh Goddess, she'd cracked, attributing his voice with physical abilities.

"I'm fine," she said through gritted teeth.

"Come on, Princess, don't barf. Don't shame the Fray name," Rojo said, flying over and perching on the shoulder of her seat.

"Back seat or trunk. Those are your options, bird," Loki said tightly.

"Name's Rojo, you pencil-necked girl," the bird retorted.

She was traveling away from home and safety with Loki *and* the idiot War horse. Anna dug her nails into her thighs and tried to slow her breathing.

Rojo's words only made her study Loki's neck, which was muscular and perfectly proportioned with his physique. Perfect, even, the way his hair ended in a soft curl at the base of his neck. Too damned perfect, like the way pewter flickered with amber annoyance at the bird.

"He's an apocalypse horse. Even if you did kill him, he'd likely regenerate," she said.

Loki smiled.

Rojo fluttered back to the back seat and his place on her suitcase with a grumble.

It was enough to almost make her smile. That brief allegiance with Loki against the bird.

She frowned at herself. As though they needed any further connection. She needed to find the real War, not let her head get muddled by Loki. He'd try to trick her, to lie and cheat. Deception was coded into his DNA.

"If you two are feeling less homicidal and halfway intelligent, we should discuss the candidates," Rojo said from the back seat, flicking through a notebook. He humphed. "First one is some police chief. Police are quasi-military. I could deal with that. Then there's the businessman. Doesn't sound like War material. Plus, god of small dicks, you realize one of these is a woman. War will *not* be a woman. Too erratic, too emotional, no stomach for the necessary."

"Two of them are women," Loki said mildly. "A female War is likely to be strong, if not stronger than her male counterpart in all areas." Loki squeezed the wheel as if he'd rather his hands were around a feathery neck.

Still more they had in common. As though they needed anything else.

The only thing that could matter was this mission. She needed to focus on the candidates. On controlling herself and her emotions. On *not* rising as War. So that just maybe, someday it wouldn't be so dangerous for her to feel. To love.

§

Two hours later, he, Anna, and the winged rodent—temporarily caged in Anna's large vintage purse—walked out onto the tarmac toward the sleek private jet awaiting them. The one Trevor had been able to arrange on short notice, along with landing rights at each of the necessary airports, clearances for the bird, and accommodations.

Loki slid a glance toward Anna. If he was going to convince her to rise, he needed his wits about him. To focus on her abilities, not the way today's dress flattered as well, if not more, than yesterday's. This one a fitted burgundy number with a pencil skirt that made Anna's legs look even longer, her ass even sexier.

He slipped a pair of aviator sunglasses from his pocket, shielding his eyes as they headed toward the gleaming silver jet. The pilot and copilot welcomed them aboard, the plane too small for a stewardess.

He let Anna precede him, all the better to watch the sway of her progress. She'd stared at him on the car ride, reacted to his small touch in a way that said she wasn't as immune to his charms as she claimed. He could make use of it—were he able to control his reactions to her.

They stepped into the cabin, which was bright and light, pairs of swiveling leather chairs on the left near the front, a banquette sofa and television near the rear, and a door that led to the small bedroom and bathroom. The copilot briefed them on the usual safety requirements and facilities, including a small fridge equipped with snacks and drinks, before they took their seats and prepared for takeoff. He pocketed his sunglasses again in his breast pocket.

Anna freed the winged vermin from the purse, who settled down in one of the seats to sleep.

She took the seat across from him, frowning and fiddling with her seat belt a moment or two, as though puzzled. Being Anna, she figured it out before he could assist. Or bring his hands close to her again.

She peered curiously through the porthole window, her long dark braid brushing her breast.

The jet engines started, and they began to taxi toward the runway with a small jolt, nothing out of the ordinary.

Anna clutched the arms of her seat with white-knuckled fingers.

She'd never been out of Beckwell. Nor aboard a plane.

He unbuckled, switching to the seat next to hers and re-buckling. "They are quite good at this," he said, leaning forward to see if she faked a smile.

Her lips were almost white, pressed together tightly. Too much of the whites of her eyes were visible. She tightened her grip on the chair, and the lights flickered overhead.

The ripple of her power played over his skin. Paranormal ability always played hell on electronics. The kind of electronics that kept planes in the air.

He linked his hands lightly in his lap and leaned back, half-closing his eyes, as though he prepared to sleep rather than prepared to absorb her energy if necessary. "Jets truly are a modern wonder. Especially compared to flying with Freyja's feathered cloak and transforming into a falcon. Flapping your wings any distance does become tiresome." Trap set and baited. *Come on, Anna. Let me distract you.*

They were cleared for takeoff, and the jet taxied to the designated runway. It picked up speed as it prepared for takeoff.

"Freyja's cloak. It was real?" Anna's voice was soft, her breathing so rough he might not have heard her if he hadn't been paying such close attention.

"Many of the legends of the inhabitants of Asgard contain a thread of truth at least. Some are wildly exaggerated, of course." His past wasn't something he usually cared to talk about, but between the jet crashing or Anna's panic, it was worth it.

She slowly turned toward him, as though loath to move. "The ones about you. True or exaggerated?"

The nose of the jet began to rise.

He lifted a hand, placed it on the armrest between them. He shifted his hand forward until he could feel the tingle of Anna's aura, entered her energy space but didn't quite touch her.

"Both," he said, watching as Anna gulped for air, her death grip on the armrests unrelenting. "Let's say my reputation was earned, rightly or wrongly."

"Your monstrous children?" She paused a moment before adding, "Your wives?"

"Fenrir, the great serpent Jormungandr, and Hel, they're real. Any attribution to me is false." He paused. It'd been so long since he'd spoken of them, let himself think of them, his time in Asgard. Of what it'd been like losing that family, too.

Anna's fingers weren't as white. Hints of color returned to her cheeks.

For her, he continued. "Sigyn was my only wife. She and I... It was wishful thinking on my part to believe marrying and settling like the Aesir would ever make me one of them. She was—is—a good woman. But it was clear early on we weren't suited, and we parted as friends. She deserved much better than me, and eventually, she found it."

She studied him. Color returned to her complexion, her hands resting on the armrest. Her fingers, her silken skin, so close to his. The urge to reach for her hand, to tangle his fingers with hers and let her rest her head on his shoulder exploded inside him. The wish to just be at rest together.

Now it was he having trouble breathing. Ymir, what was wrong with him? Rule one: Don't get close. Rule two: Don't get close. Rule three: Don't be an idiot. Here he went breaking all three at once.

"You didn't lie. Didn't even try to," she said. "Your name. It means spider, spinner of plots, doesn't it?"

Her blue gaze saw too much, looked too deeply. Coupled with that absurd desire to hold her hand, she was more dangerous than he'd thought.

He unbuckled, abruptly stood. "The seat reclines. Get some sleep. We'll arrive late, and we need to be on guard." He strode back to the long banquette seating and the small luggage storage beside it.

"What about you?"

He retrieved his chocolate-brown satchel, the leather supple beneath his fingers as he sat on the banquette, unfolded a side table. "Research. Field prep. Sleep, Hadrianna."

While he planned and reminded himself his plot was more important than anything. More important than anyone.

CHAPTER 11

Darkness had fallen by the time they landed in Three Points, Manitoba. Though they'd flown over the small clutch of buildings that glowed in the darkness, it was a dark drive through dense boreal forest into a town that was, Anna decided, a little like Beckwell on steroids. They did have the airport, traffic lights, and plentiful buildings, but small, cozy houses still gave it a small-town feel despite the chain restaurants and lights. The street and traffic lights cast shadows through the car, deepened the hollows of Loki's cheekbones. He focused on the road behind the wheel of their rental car, a creature of dreams and shadows.

On the plane, he'd been so patient with her irrational fears, answered questions she was quite certain he wouldn't have otherwise. It could be his strategy, a way to put her at ease, earn her trust and turn her to his way of thinking.

Or perhaps she was just lonelier and more susceptible than she'd realized.

She pressed her lips tightly together. She needed to focus on the plan. Find and assess the first candidate to see if he was better suited as War. It needed to be someone who could control the destructive War abilities, wouldn't be corrupted by them, and hopefully demonstrated more positive attributes as her friends had.

Rojo poked his head over the center console. "I agree going in covertly to start, but why do I have to ride in the purse? Do I get beer? It's a bar. I think that means I get beer."

"Because talking pigeons are alarming, that's why you're in the purse," Anna said.

"You say alarming, I say icebreaker. I mean, this is my War we're talking about. He's going to be glad to see me," Rojo said.

"We don't know who this Chief Donovan Wiebe is, other than potentially dangerous. No beer, no bar fights, no flying rodents in the front seat." Loki shifted his elbow onto the console, forcing Rojo back.

"Listen, you dickless wonder, one of these days I'm going to be a lot bigger, and then you're going to be sorry," Rojo grumbled, fluttering back up onto the back seat.

Anna tried to smooth the wrinkles out of the slim-fitting burgundy dress—another vintage pick from Loki's minion—and undid her braid, attempted to redo and smooth its frayed state. Her fingers trembled. Other than her parents, whose faces had become faded, she'd never met another War. This could be the one to rise, the one to save her.

Or they'd meet, and there'd be catastrophic results. The reason Wars didn't socialize. They were like pit bulls bred to fight: they didn't get along with normal people, and with each other... Well, only one of them was likely to survive the encounter. At least, that's what she'd heard.

They pulled in front of a low, two-story boxy

building with a flickering neon sign that read "Three Points Hotel and Bar."

Anna blew out a breath. Loki was here, and if nothing else he could diffuse her abilities if they got out of control. That physique of his meant he might come in handy should the need arise. She reached down, opened her purse, and put it on the console. "In you go, Rojo."

The pigeon grumbled but hopped in before she zipped it shut.

Loki shut off the car. "Ready?"

She swore she could feel the weight of his gaze on her. "Chief Donovan Wiebe. Only child, mother born a Viggo, still surviving, father deceased. Police Chief in Three Points for five years, and two years after his arrival, Three Points has been named the most dangerous city to live in Canada three years running. Unmarried, no known romantic interest. No known criminal history, from all appearances an exemplary citizen." She finally turned, met Loki's gaze, black in the dim light, almost managed to give him a haughty look. Doing it without the small quiver that went through her at being the focus of his gaze would have been better. "You're not the only one who can do research."

"I would expect nothing less of you," he murmured, the flicker of almost a smile touching his lips.

She turned away abruptly, groped for the door handle. Gaia, she couldn't keep staring at him. Had to stop thinking how he'd been there for so many of her firsts. First time to Beckwell. First rescue. First flight. First trip outside Alberta.

There was one first he wouldn't be part of. If she found the true War heir, maybe it might be worth the risk of seeing if she could find what her friends had found, experience love in all its forms.

He was standing next to the door as she opened it, offered her his hand as she stepped out of the car.

She glared up at him, but avoiding his touch would be showing weakness. She placed her fingers in his. His touch was strong, his fingers surprisingly work-roughened and warm.

He locked the car, then they turned, and he placed his large hand lightly in the small of her back, his fingers burning through the fine fabric of her dress, shortening her breath, jumbling her thoughts as he guided her forward.

"Keep walking, Hadrianna. I know you've been in a bar before," he teased, his breath ruffling the loose curls near her ear as he held the door and they entered the bar together.

Of course, she had. Although that had been his bar, in Beckwell, where she knew most everyone and could anticipate their actions and reactions.

Scarred, round, faux-wood tables surrounded by chrome and vinyl chairs with cigarette burns were scattered throughout the dim interior. The bar took up the opposite wall, long and dated, smoky mirrors behind the line of bottles, the taps getting the biggest workout. Pool balls clicked over to the right, where four or five pool tables were seeing steady business.

Conversation in the small local watering hole didn't entirely stop as Anna and Loki stepped inside. Three Points was larger than Beckwell, large enough for visitors, chain restaurants and stores, even four hotels. Still, gazes slid toward them, assessed her dress, his expensive dress pants and shirt that stood out among the jeans and T-shirts of the crowd. The whispers of their truths, their infidelities, frauds, petty and violent crimes whispered over her.

"We should have changed at the hotel. We stand out," Anna whispered, glancing around through the dim, yellow-hued interior.

"We were going to in any case. They'll assume we're

just more business travelers. Here, this table," Loki said, pulling out her chair, leaning closer as he gently pressed her down into the chair. His breath whispered over her, the ripple of his voice sending shockwaves through her. "Sit. I'll get us beer. That's our target, over near the pool tables."

At his departure, the whispers of truth seemed to beat louder inside her skull, rousing the flames of War deep inside, heat scouring through her belly. She perched on the edge of the chair, set her purse on the tabletop, and shifted her chair so she could see the pool tables without turning.

"Don't suppose he'll get me one," Rojo muttered from the purse. "Turn me two degrees clockwise, would you? I want to see who I'll be working with."

She shifted the purse on the table, a beak momentarily peeking through the small gap beneath the zipper before vanishing.

"We don't know he'll be the right one," she murmured, her gaze drawn to the large man, their target. He seemed to be the center of attention at the pool tables.

Close to as broad as Loki across the shoulders, the auburn-haired man had a pleasant enough round face, hair cropped short, and a neatly clipped mustache. He wasn't as muscular or trim as Loki, girth spilling over his large bronze belt buckle and jeans.

The pigeon snorted softly. "Don't fool yourself, Princess. That man? He moves like a War. Look at the way the others defer to him? They jump out of his way before he has to say a word. This is his court, his kingdom."

Which meant they'd wandered right into it. Like Alice and the Queen of Hearts.

Anna swallowed, played with her purse strap as she studied him.

There was a way about the man. Even as he laughed

and joked with the other men playing pool—all men, no women—there was a small tightness to his posture, around his eyes. An awareness of them all, but no fear. While everyone else's truths whispered to her—many of his entourage owed him favors and debts—irritatingly she picked up nothing from him.

He glanced up, his blue gaze meeting hers.

Something rippled between them, a heightened awareness. The silky fabric of her dress turned scratchy against her lower back, and heat stung her neck. Her muscles tightened, sounds sharpened, and she could have closed her eyes and pinpointed the position of everyone in the room, including the two people making out in the corner table behind her.

The man turned away and took his shot with the pool cue.

Chills chased up and down her spine, her stomach queasy, cold soaking through her. War abilities flickered to life, flames licking through her with painful intensity. Yet outwardly, she was cool and collected.

Loki brushed her arm, bumped her knee as he returned with two foamy mugs of beer. He sat next to her, his knee bumping hers, his hand resting close to hers on the scarred faux-wood tabletop. His energy—maybe his ability, maybe just him—hummed through her, liquid warmth pooling inside her, soothing the edge of War's flames and dulling the whispers.

He was too precise with his actions. He had to be making the contact intentionally.

His warmth soaked through her. Steadied her, her ultra-sensitivity picking up the spiciness of his scent.

He pushed one of the beers toward her. "Observations?" he asked quietly. "Can you read him?"

The sound of the mug against the tabletop was like fingernails on a chalkboard. He shifted his chair, angled it as she had hers, though this only better aligned them, put him slightly at her back, his hand on the tabletop mere inches from hers.

She tried to hide her grimace, directed it at the mug. "I don't drink beer."

"Nor do I." He casually draped an arm around the back of her chair, and the hairs on her arms rose.

She couldn't look away as he lifted his beer to his lips but never actually took a sip. His pewter gaze remained steady on hers, that one hand almost touching hers.

Point taken. They'd blend. She mimicked his actions. "Won't people notice it never goes down?"

He shrugged, his gaze shifting from her to their target. "I'll make it look like it does. Almost everyone in here is a Normal. From what the bartender says, I'd surmise most of the town is. He was happy to regale me with how Wiebe is often present just as crimes are committed and thus conveniently able to make the arrest."

She glanced at Donovan Wiebe again with his friends, his laughter deep and rolling, though it only made her shoulders tighter. "If most of them are Normals, they'd be more susceptible to his abilities."

"And his manipulation," Loki said quietly, pretending to take another sip. "It also seems suspicious that crime rates have risen under his leadership. Which makes him either clueless or complicit."

"A true War is always in control of his men," Rojo piped up from the purse. "Don't go crossing this guy off our list just because of some coincidences."

Faex. The bird was right. It also meant Wiebe could control his War abilities. Anna turned on Loki. "A War might be attracted to the inherent violence of a place like Three Points. It doesn't mean he caused it." The itch on her lower back intensified. Donovan Wiebe was watching her again, and her body tensed for attack.

Loki shifted next to her. New, darker whiskers

shadowed his square jaw, thickened above his lip, but his gaze wasn't on her. Those supple lips tightened by small increments, the skin around his eyes creasing. He shifted his arm, brought it more closely around her shoulders, his fingers brushing her shoulder. "That may be. If so, he certainly hasn't improved the situation. Here we go," he murmured.

The itch on her back intensified, forced her to turn. Her hands tightened to fists, her nails biting into her palms.

"Good evening, folks. Now, I know this is going to sound strange, ma'am, but you are a dead ringer for old photos of my grandma," a man said from beside her. It was coarse, folksy even, compared to Loki. "Now, why do you think that is?"

Loki's fingers slid down her arm, grazed bare skin, and made goose bumps rise.

She glanced up, met Loki's gaze for a moment, his polite smile already in place. She mimicked his expression and approval glowed in his eyes.

She shifted closer to Loki's warmth, protecting her back, then turned to meet Donovan Wiebe, War clan.

He stood directly next to her. Big, invading her personal space; seated, she was practically at crotch-level. She had to crane her neck back to meet his eyes. The itch on her back was painful, but when she met his eyes her heart hiccoughed.

He had Mom's eyes.

Images of Mom crashed over her, along with the accompanying emotion. The rage, the loss, the hollow ache. Her breath roughened. That night, the smoke burning her throat, the raging heat of the fire, that last look at her home, that little white house as she clung to Loki, peered over his shoulder at the orange-blue flames licked up through the windows, over the roof. Devoured her parents and her future all at once.

Because she was a War. Because she'd spoken and stoked the fight that set her parents off.

Mom had been a Wiebe before she'd married. If Loki hadn't taken Anna to Beckwell, this might have been her closest relative. This might have been a man she knew.

Loki's fingers stroked her bare upper arm, sent tingling and life through her, rushed her back to the present. To the burning on her back, the tightness in her shoulders and muscles, the whispers of truths in her head.

"My wife just said the same of you," Loki said smoothly, the timber of his voice altered, the usual roll of his slight accent replaced with an almost country drawl.

Wait…*wife*?

She couldn't afford the distraction. Focused her attention on Wiebe. The slightly sour smell of sweat and body odor wafted from him. Perhaps he wasn't good with people; Wars weren't known for their popularity.

"Yes, I definitely see the resemblance in your eyes," she said.

"Now isn't that interesting," he murmured. He leaned closer, his beer-sour breath wafting over her, his gaze flickering over her chest then back to her eyes. "It does seem a shame if someone as pretty as you were related to me."

Her smile turned sickly. If this was how he crowded and lewdly looked over would-be relatives, pity to any woman he *wasn't* related to. Plus, she knew better than to ignore the warning itch on her back. Wiebe had a cold sharpness in that blue-gray gaze, accompanied with icy calculation.

Something she'd glimpsed in her reflection.

That didn't mean he'd make a bad War. It could be their innate reaction to each other, that competitive need to outdo each other. He was male. Ergo, more prone to giving into that kind of idiocy.

Loki's warmth, his large, muscular presence next to

her, the sparks firing from where he stroked her skin gave an evenness to her voice. Let her settle her muscles, relax her hands on the table and calculate likely speed with Wiebe's size, check for weapons…nothing visible, but his hands were like meaty hammers.

She gestured at the other chair across the table, even forced her lips into something resembling a smile. Ginny always insisted smiling and polite wording encouraged compliance more than sharply worded commands. Sometimes she was right.

"Please, sit." *Stop leering down my dress and let me interrogate you.* "I believe we're related on my mother's side." As much as admitting she was a War, but it was a calculated risk.

He reached for the chair but pulled it close, practically straddled it as he sat, his knee pressed against hers, the position of his chair locking legs with hers, trapping her in place. Invading her space, perhaps testing her as she did him.

"Well, would you imagine that." He hitched up his belt buckle, further displaying his crotch, then stuck his meaty hand out. A predatory gleam glinted in his eyes. "I'm Donovan Wiebe, Chief of Police around these parts. And you are?"

Loki's large warm hand covered hers on the tabletop, and he leaned forward, bringing her closer to him, surrounding her in his spicy cedar-like scent. "Lou Farbautisson. My wife, Anna." His tone was un-Loki-like—light, open, friendly.

"Nice to meet you, Lou," Wiebe said, something in his gaze suggesting just the opposite. He glanced at their beer, pointed at it. "Say, I am parched. Would you mind getting me one of those?" He pulled out a five-dollar bill and held it out to Loki, but his smile turned back on Anna. "I'm just so tickled meeting family I didn't know."

Maybe he'd never met another War either.

She bared her teeth right back at him. Glanced back at Loki. Gave him the smallest nod.

His pewter gaze flickered over her, his lips almost turned up in a smile. "Of course, but it's on me. You two chat," he said, standing, then squeezing Anna's shoulder and leaning down to whisper in her ear, the whiskers on his jaw tickling her cheek. It was his usual voice, that edge of darkness and sardonic humor, just a hint of an accent that curled her toes in his words. "I'll let the pilot know to be on standby if we need to make a hasty exit. Have fun." He gave Wiebe another un-Loki open smile before he strode away toward the busy bar.

There was a cold spot with Loki's absence, fluttering heat still trickling through her at his touch, at his confidence in her. He didn't question her ability to question Wiebe herself.

Speaking of whom, she turned her attention back to Wiebe.

He was waiting with a predatory look in his eyes. Shifted his seat closer, leaned closer to her. "Does he know you're a War?"

"Is everyone in town a Normal?"

They both paused, gave each other tight looks.

"An answer for an answer," she proposed.

He gave her a short nod. "Most of them. A couple of paras near the edges of town."

"Yes, he knows. Do they know what you are?"

"They know what's good for them. Why did you come here looking for me?"

"You're another War. Someone is going to rise as War. I want to know who. Is the crime rate your doing, or are you just terrible at your job?"

He leaned closer, placed a hand on her knee beneath the table. "Why? Does it turn you on, sweetheart?"

She pushed his hand off. Disgusting. He wouldn't do around her friends. "No. Don't touch me, and you owe me an answer."

He set his elbows on his thighs, let his fingers rest a hairsbreadth from touching her, but still on his own legs. Barely. "This is my town. Nothing happens here that I don't know about, that I don't control. Lots of opportunities for advancement. Who is rising? I hear there's three women in some town out West. War is next." His fingers slipped closer to her knees. He stared at her chest again. "Do you have any real power, or are you just a fan?"

Culus. Her smile tightened. How lovely for him to remind her why she'd had no interest in dating for years now. Too many men like him. Thinking they had the right to touch, to look, to demand whatever they wanted. She'd tried to give him the opportunity to prove he wasn't an ass. He'd failed.

He returned her scrutiny, a small smile playing at his lips as if he really were the Queen of Hearts and she Alice.

He must not have read how that ended.

The itch now burned like insect bites. Flames licked through her, demanded she win. War hungered for a fight.

"That's two questions. No, I'm definitely not a fan of ignorance, despotism, or toxic masculinity."

Wiebe's gaze narrowed, sharpened with a hint of menace. "You should know we get your kind in here from time to time. Sometimes they find themselves in trouble before they find their way home. Sometimes they get lost in those deep, dark woods around here. Such a shame."

Enough of this.

She straightened her shoulders, let the smile drop from her lips, and stuck out her hand. He'd try to squeeze too hard or get inappropriate. She'd get a read on him and learn everything she needed to. "How terrible. It's a good thing we know how to handle trouble, and we live in our own woods. I think we'll be just fine."

"Damn, you're cocky," he said. "But I always know

the truth. I *am* the truth."

She raised a brow. "You think *I'm* arrogant?"

"They say the Four are rising, that the end of the world is coming. Time to pick your allies and choose your battles."

With a dark smile, he gripped his sweaty, sausage fingers around hers.

Fire poured through her, two wildfires colliding, raging hotter, fighting for dominance. Flames burned away the itch in her back, the tightness in her muscles, stole her breath for a moment. The sound of Wiebe's rough breathing, the slight tremor in his knee against hers said he felt it too.

A brief flicker, and images flashed through her. Wiebe, a manic light in his eyes, hair mussed, spittle gathering at the side of his lips while he kicked and beat another man. His satisfied smile. Truths shouted at her, so many of them, so fast, the words blurred. Embezzlement, prostitution, fraud, trickery, extortion, collusion. All ugliness, nothing redeeming.

He dropped her hand first, his broad grin slipping, eyes dilated.

As though maybe he'd seen some truth in their connection too.

She'd seen enough to know Wiebe wasn't a suitable partner for her friends. Especially with that good ol' boy BS.

He leaned closer, fake charm one onionskin away from peeled away. "Who the fuck are you? What was your mother's name again?"

She hadn't said, because she didn't want this man knowing any more about her than necessary. Smoothly, she selected a probable name. "Martha Stryfe."

His eyes narrowed. "You're lying. You've got the look of a Wiebe. And you don't belong here, in my territory, my town." His lip curled. "You're nothing."

The flames seemed to flare once more, burning over her, tempering her body, preparing her muscles, her thoughts. The heat no longer burned. The warning itch was still there, but only a mild reminder. *She* was the fire.

She stood smoothly.

Awareness registered Loki's large presence somewhere nearby. Whispering truths, angry murmurs gathered closer, rising above the country-twang of the song playing over the speaker system. A sickly-sweet taste rose to her tongue, and the hairs on her arms rose in reaction to the rising electrical energy of the coming violence.

The crowd of locals from the bar were gathering closer. Close enough to hear her voice and Wiebe's. To be infected by it.

The faintest hint of unease trickled through her.

She and Loki were the outsiders. They were outnumbered in unfamiliar territory. Potentially innocent people could be drawn into the fight.

"Let's agree to disagree," she said, trying to calm the edge in her voice. "Let us pass. We've gotten what we came for."

Wiebe climbed to his feet, the movement clumsier, slow. He curled his lip at Loki over her shoulder. "You bring him to fight your battles?"

"The lady is more than capable of winning her own wars. Perhaps if you apologize, this night can still end peacefully," Loki said, his voice back to sounding like Loki, that edge of darkness and sardonic humor that made her toes curl. Especially when he was generous with his compliments.

Wiebe sneered. "Apologize? For what?

She raised a brow at Wiebe. "You're running out of opportunities. This is your out."

"No, honey, it was yours." Wiebe whistled, but it was already too late.

Faex. The first shouts and punches came from behind them. A body crashed into one of the tables near them. The sickly-sweet taste grew stronger on her tongue.

Wiebe's lips curled upward. Madness glowed in that gaze so like Mom's. War's corruption already had him.

All the other occupants seemed to slip into slow-motion while she was left at full-speed. Awareness tingled, told her to step out of the way as two men lunged at her at Wiebe's command. Their actions were comically slow. Leaving her plenty of time to duck left, trip the one, clothesline the second, leaving him grabbing his throat. A bit peculiar, fighting like an action hero she'd only ever read about, the actions as simple to her as walking, written out like a script in her head.

The two men were still falling when she lifted and brought her chair down on the one, before flinging him into his partner.

Wiebe and Loki grappled, but while Wiebe was red-faced, Loki looked merely irritated as he avoided the man's clumsy punches while kicking out the feet from beneath three others who tried to attack him, knocking another back over a neighboring table.

Meanwhile, an enraged ball of gray feathers flung beer bottles and hooted and hollered from over near the bar, while others ducked and tried to get closer.

A balding, wild-eyed man came at her with a broken beer bottle. He snarled and twisted for her.

She executed a move where she partially tripped him, then flipped him over her shoulder.

She stepped forward to twist in a roundhouse kick and felled another one. That move at least she knew the name for from books, though she'd certainly never attempted it before.

The idea drifted through her mind without raising concern.

Real-time slammed into her with the force of a wall,

walloping out her breath, leaving her gasping amongst the moans and groans from the bodies littered on the floor. Sucking in a breath, she straightened and smoothed her skirt, looking up to find herself with a heaving, red-faced Donovan Wiebe.

"Why the hell should it be you?" he snarled. "You haven't worked for the power, haven't made use of it like I have." Spittle gathered in the corner of his lips.

Most of the occupants of the bar—all men, none of the women had been stupid enough to stick around—lay in crumpled heaps amid the toppled tables and tangled chairs. Loki's large bulk loomed behind Wiebe, and Rojo strutted toward the War candidate on the other side, settling his wings back into place.

"I've made this town mine. I've made a difference, and this is only the beginning." Wiebe said, chortling on a half-manic laugh.

Anna held up a hand, forestalling Loki from reaching to stop Wiebe. Instead, she stepped closer, War's fire burning through her, tempering her limbs to steel. "I think you've just adequately answered for all of us why you shouldn't be War. I don't know that it will be me, but War is rising. When that happens, when you lose what abilities you have, I hope you have a plan or retreat in mind. Because this—" She indicated the fallen men surrounding them, those who'd followed him without question into stupidity. "This will all go away."

She turned to Rojo. "Are you satisfied?"

The bird nodded. "Yeah, this was fun, but he's an asshole. He doesn't even fight as well as you." He pecked the side of Wiebe's meaty ankle.

Wiebe cried out, glared down incredulously at the bird.

"War is honorable, knows the truth. You're just a thug." Rojo flew up and perched on her shoulder.

If Wiebe found a talking pigeon either concerning or

surprising, Anna missed his reaction as she found herself caught in Loki's pewter gaze, once more shot with amber. A small, satisfied smile curved his lips, his hair was tousled, and his shirt was torn.

He leaned closer to Wiebe. "If you even think of coming after her..." Loki paused then glanced at her. "Well, if you're that stupid, she'll be happy to rectify your mistake." He held out his hand to Anna. "Come. Surely, you've seen enough."

She sighed, the calm assurance she'd felt draining away with every moment. She'd let War take over her, and worse, enjoyed it. Her glance tracked over the destruction of the room, the moans of pain still audible over the latest country song. Piper might make people cough, Ginny could spoil the food, and Nia would talk to the ghosts... None of them would leave a place destroyed like Anna did. She closed trembling fingers over Loki's. "Make your peace now, Wiebe. While you can."

"War will rise, but it won't be you. Doesn't mean I can't still come after you then," he said.

She shrugged. "You can try. But unlike you, I don't have to threaten my friends to know they've got my back. Can you say the same?" She scooped up her purse from the floor where it'd fallen, then she, Loki, and Rojo headed out to the car and out of Three Points.

One candidate down. One less chance to be free of War.

CHAPTER 12

Anna disappeared into the bedroom of the small jet with a bottle of wine shortly before takeoff from Three Points. Despite the temptation to assure himself she was all right, Loki seated himself in a chair facing the bedroom door, his notes on their next candidate in Chicago on his side table, but his thoughts on the woman in the bedroom. The jet taxied and took to the air with the barest shudder. Not a sound from the bedroom, no flicker of lights indicating Anna's paranormal abilities interfered with the electricity.

Wiebe had been more brutish than anticipated. Better to have spared Anna that. Yet the objective had been achieved. Anna had been forced to admit Wiebe was unsuitable and to utilize her abilities, each time bringing her slightly closer to fully rising.

Loki frowned. Again, the heaviness of Yggdrasil settled over him. This should have been the part where he anticipated his coming victory. Anna had been glorious during the fight. He hadn't seen a more powerful female goddess since Freyja.

Yet after, in the car, her shoulders had slumped, her gaze distant as she'd stared out into the passing darkness, her body too still, a brittleness about her.

Now the wine. Ymir knew he'd given into the tempting oblivion of alcohol too often before. To see her do it though…

He unbuttoned his cuffs, frowning as he rolled them up his forearms. She was intelligent. Eventually, she'd see reason. She was War.

"Did you know he'd be such a dick, or was that just a happy coincidence?" the flying rat said, fluttering up onto the chair opposite and cocking his head.

Loki's neck tightened. Anna likely suspected the same thing. He picked up his notebook and pencil, looking over his notes on the next candidate, Matilda Cadman. "I suspected there might be a personality conflict." The circumstances alone were suspicious. He could have turned out to be a good cop in a difficult circumstance, as Mal Quilan was with the gods circling Beckwell like hyenas. Conveniently, Wiebe had quickly proved himself brutish and typical.

The rat bird snorted. "You set her up."

"I thought you didn't care? You should get some sleep."

"Not tired. And she's not War material, that's all. Might have made a decent War if she was a man. Handled herself well in the fight. How many of these Wars have you checked out for yourself? Still hiding the real alternatives?"

"These are the only possible alternatives. I've investigated enough of them." Too many. Too many broken lives, looming like a dark shadow over Anna. She was strong, but rising would change her. As it had Peter.

Unfortunately, there was nothing to indicate any obvious failings with the next candidate. She had a steady career, married, two kids…all unusual for her clan.

Perhaps that was part of why he hadn't investigated too deeply. If he'd discovered a viable alternative, he wasn't certain whether he could keep it from Anna.

Many nights he'd stayed late at the bar, just to keep an eye on Anna while she worked, usually on that bloody book of hers, researching any possibility so she wouldn't rise. Enough to compel him to search too.

The foil bag rattled across from him as the pigeon shoved his head in a bag of chips, crunching loudly. "She'll find out about the other one, you know. Peter. For a woman, she's damned sharp."

Loki's vision dimmed a minute, the words on the page blurring. He forced one steady breath, then another, refused to show any weakness. Pausing, as though mildly curious, he turned to glance at the pigeon. "I'm sorry?"

The pigeon pulled its head out from the bag. "The other War. I remember them, the other War horses, their Wars. Reginald remembers Peter. Remembers you, tangled up in War's life and trying to plot it the way you see fit. Trying to choose who rises, just like you're trying to do now. Like you're trying to do with her."

If Anna found out about Peter—about the others— there was every chance she'd do all she could to foil any hope he had of success. She was touchy about being a "pawn," as she put it. She'd never understand or believe his reasoning. No one ever did.

Sometimes even he wondered if he'd made a mistake. If Peter and his friends wouldn't have been better off if they'd never met him.

Fortunately, she didn't trust the pigeon yet. He'd decide how to frame the truth about Peter, if or when it became necessary. She wouldn't take it well if she discovered he'd attempted to ensure the right horsemen rose before, the right people gained power, as he'd done with her and her friends. As he'd done with Peter and his friends.

Peter was not Anna. They'd both been his wards, but he'd learned from his mistakes with Peter. All the arguments, all the history between them hadn't been enough to stop Peter and the others from walking out of the house and down to the recruitment office. They'd accused him of using them, of being inhuman, with all the emotion of an abacus. Teaching Peter to ride a bike, bandaging his knees, giving him access to all the world's knowledge, all of it was thrown back in his face as manipulation, artificial. The next time, he knew better than to let his emotions get involved. Knew to keep his distance, that as ever and always, no one would ever trust him anyway.

He turned his attention back to his book. "You're seeing conspiracy where there is none."

The pigeon snorted. "Bullshit. Guess we'll see how fast you think on your feet when she figures it all out."

His fingers tightened around the pages of his notebook. He'd just have to be sure she rose before she did. Then, if nothing else, her rage could ensure the success of his plan.

He shoved down that pang deep inside, the one that knew he hadn't been as successful at keeping his distance as hoped.

The soft click of the door froze his muscles, shortened his breath. He raised his gaze slowly.

Anna swayed in the bedroom door, held out the bottle of wine. The light had dimmed in those beautiful blue eyes.

Shit. Hopefully, she hadn't heard them.

"Is there more of this?" she said.

This was not the right path for her. Ymir help him, but he wouldn't let her follow his darkness. "No."

Her lips twisted, and she tossed the bottle. "Liar."

He caught it, unbuckling and moving toward her even as she swayed in the doorway. Yet he stopped a few steps from her. Touching her wouldn't be wise. Was too much temptation as he'd learned at the bar, touching her like he had the right to, his hand possessively in the small of her back, touching her shoulder, her arm. As though she belonged to him.

She glared up at him. Her braid was frayed and undone, dark hair whirling around her shoulders, tempting his fingers to test its softness, to free it from its confines, free her from her inhibition.

He stuffed his hands in his pockets.

She narrowed her eyes, swaying more as she looked between him and Rojo. "What were you two talking about?"

Which theoretically implied she didn't know.

His mind, though, was too focused on the fit of the burgundy dress that hugged her curves, only partially concealing lithe muscle.

"Loki's past," the flying vermin volunteered, or possibly threatened.

Loki's jaw tightened. "Old myths."

Rojo snorted. "Yeah, like that one with the horse. I've been meaning to ask you, god of losers, what was it like, transforming into a female horse and letting another horse fuck you just to wiggle out of a fight?"

Loki's jaw squeezed. Of all the legends and lies about him, that bloody myth with the wall, the giant, and the damned horse was his least favorite.

Anna's gaze settled on him, calculated, concealed. He'd made it a practice to read others, but he'd never been able to see into her thoughts, no matter how he tried.

Denial would only make it seem there was more to deny. Yet the way she looked at him... It'd never mattered before what stories were spread about him. Some he'd spread himself, fueled the rumors when they'd served a purpose. But to have Anna think lowly of him...mattered. Shouldn't have. Didn't aid his plan.

"I never—"

"I know. They're myths, only partial truths," she said, her voice raspy, like she'd spent the night screaming out her pleasure in bed. She never moved her gaze from his, even as she addressed her remarks to the bird. "You should know better by now, Rojo, to think Loki would let anyone use him without a clear purpose. Or to think he'd run from a fight."

His body tightened. The temptation to reach for her was overwhelming. Yet there was also faint accusation in her words. Perhaps she believed as Rojo did that he'd manipulated the situation in Three Points.

Rojo snorted. "You mean he does the fucking, and everyone else is fucked?"

There was the smallest flicker in Anna's gaze, a hint of color that climbed her regal cheekbones.

Unfortunately, probably not because of the vivid imagery the word fucking sparked, especially with that bed behind her. That was probably just him.

She cleared her throat, slid backward in the room. Stepped wrong. She lost her balance.

He caught her hand. Pulled her closer.

Her breath froze, eyes widening. She licked her lips. *Ymir...*

Dark shadows from sleepless nights leant her eyes a bruised quality. There was the smallest tremble in her hand, rippling through her body.

She wasn't his. She was War. She belonged to the plan.

He reached for the nearby bottle of water, pressed it into her hand, and turned her gently. "Drink the water. Get some sleep." *Go enjoy that bed. Alone.* "Tomorrow will bring its own challenges." And likely more temptation. This attraction was getting out of hand.

She turned, her hand on the door as she stepped away. "Another chance tomorrow that I can be free." She closed the door.

Or one step closer to rising as War. And his death.

CHAPTER 13

Loki got little sleep on the long flight from Three Points, spending most of his time pretending to research and check his email. Only bad news from home. Daphne remained agitated and more trouble than usual. The gods were threatening his Beckwellians, and, best of all, USELESS had upped their game against Anna. Instead of their usual assassins, four of whom he'd foiled so far, they'd recruited an old enemy—or family member—depending on one's perspective. Heimdall. Norse watchman of the gods, who'd been born with a stick up his ass and Loki on his shit list.

Plotting how they could stay ahead of Heimdall and wondering about Anna, alone and quiet in the bedroom, kept his thoughts occupied. The echo and consideration of fucked and fucking kept him awake.

Indeed, all of them seemed tired and bleary-eyed by the time they touched down at Chicago's O'Hare Airport and made the roughly half-hour drive to their hotel in picturesque Oak Park. Anna was too pale, that flowing black dress paired with a ruby sweater distractingly feminine. Rojo didn't even complain when he had to duck down into Anna's purse as they checked into the historic brick hotel Trevor had pre-booked for them. No pets allowed, and there was unlikely to be an exception for apocalyptic pigeons.

Still no complaints when he checked them into the king suite. It made Loki's neck twitch, this unusual placidity in his two companions.

They padded quietly through the hotel's stately interior, the luxury reminding him somewhat of home.

He glanced at Anna, who barely seemed to notice.

He'd had a ready cause to explain the king suite was all that was available with wedding season. Or, if he'd had to, counter with the truth that he wanted to be close to her in the event things went as badly as they had in Manitoba.

Instead, as they stepped into the suite, she glanced vaguely at the earthy browns, reds, and burgundies of the furnishings, contemporary meeting classic against light-colored walls. Depositing her pink suitcase near the wall, she headed directly for the writing desk, pulling the pad of paper and a pen toward her.

Her face was pale, but when she glanced up, fire sparked in her gaze again. "I need information. We need to go over everything about this next candidate. We go in with a clear plan this time. We give them a fair assessment, but we know ahead what we're getting into." Her voice was firm, but there was a tremble in her hands, not completely gone when she tightened her grip on the pen until her fingertips turned white.

Loki studied the movement a moment or two, tightness settling in around his lips. Anna was the best candidate. The only one worthy and safe with War's powers. It shouldn't matter how she felt about it, especially not to him. Hell, this entire errand of investigating the other candidates was only to prove the unassailable truth to her, get her to see reason.

Yet...here they were.

Rojo climbed out of the purse and perched on the corner of the desk. "A plan is good." Even the flying rat seemed somewhat shaken by their experience with Wiebe. Though he, too, still needed convincing.

Loki suppressed a sigh as he relaxed on the leather sofa next to the desk, folded his hands behind his head, and leaned back. "First, there's something else we need to consider. The gods have brought in a new man to hunt you down. His name is Heimdall."

"Wait. He's one of you Norse gods, isn't he?" Rojo said.

"Which means he should be a friend?" Anna said.

His lips twitched. "No. Definitely not a friend. Heimdall is indeed the watchman of the Norse gods—or was. Many of them modernized, have moved forward. Some of them, like Odin and Heimdall, prefer the old ways." When gods ruled and man worshiped.

"How is he associated with the USELESS agents?" Anna asked.

Loki frowned. "He founded USELESS. I mention this only so you're aware." Then she couldn't accuse him of hiding it later. "It means the gods are getting desperate if they've called Heimdall in out of retirement."

Heimdall's potential involvement was...troubling. They'd never been on the best terms. Heimdall was said to be destined to kill Loki and had always seemed rather pleased about the idea. He was also intelligent, ruthless, and as relentless as a shark after blood.

"You mean he's dangerous." Anna's voice had grown raspy, concerned.

He needed Anna to focus on the candidates and rising with her own power, at which point, Odin himself was no threat. "Let me worry about Heimdall. We're like...family."

If by family one meant perhaps a cancerous growth. Ymir help him if any of the other Asgardians got involved. Fortunately, the veils that separated Braelyn and the gods from the mortal world also slowed the passage of news from the mortal world. He didn't need their interference, and he was fond enough of some of them—mostly the goddesses—that it would be a shame to kill any of them. Though he couldn't let anything get in the way of his plan.

His turned his head and his gaze met Anna's. A jolt of lust, protectiveness, and something he couldn't define speared through him. Didn't matter what it was specifically, the entire thing read "dangerous." He struggled to keep his words even and leaned back as though bored, closed his eyes.

"Now, our candidate. Her name is Matilda Cadman, though she goes by Tildy. Thirty-four, mother of two, married, employed as a real estate agent."

Even with his eyes closed, he could still picture the way Anna would purse her lips, consider before speaking, maybe put the pen between her lips, the dart of her tongue—

"Cadman is definitely a War name. But she's the War, not her husband?"

"She kept her maiden name. The husband may be unaware of her ancestry. Moreover, don't get overexcited. She has a parole officer."

"It's still a woman—not War. But at least she sounds almost interesting now," Rojo said.

"What did she do?" Anna asked.

"That's the peculiar part; the records are sealed. Either she was underage, or some deal was made. I advise we approach with caution." He could have gotten into the record if he'd cared to, but seeing the parole officer had been enough to eliminate any need to investigate further. Until Anna's demands.

"Crap. This means purse duty again, doesn't it?" Rojo's tone was almost resigned.

Neither Loki nor Anna dignified him with a response.

Instead, Loki couldn't help but crack open his eyes, steal a glance at Anna.

She tapped the butt of the pen on those gorgeous lips before leaning over the paper and writing quickly, brow furrowed, lips tight as she scrawled.

They needed to approach Tildy Cadman with caution...and he needed to proceed with caution, lest he fall even further under Anna's spell.

※

It was fortunate Loki drove the rental, which was some kind of silver luxury car, though not too flashy. His driving left Anna free to stare out the window at the different sights. Here the trees arched gracefully over the sidewalks, elegant houses set back from the street like proper estates. Some were low, modern; others were regal ladies saved from history.

Hemingway's birthplace was somewhere around here, as were several Frank Lloyd Wright houses. Places she'd seen only in photos. She opened the window, inhaled the scent of oak and elm sweating beneath the July sun. Children laughed in a passing playground. There was a peacefulness here, a whole other world outside of her experience. Imagine living where you could walk to work along tree-lined sidewalks straight out of Hollywood.

She frowned at herself, the lightness inside. This wasn't a holiday; this was a mission, her freedom at stake. She needed to focus on the next candidate—and hopefully not end up in a brawl. Again.

"We reached Chicago earlier than expected. We could explore," Loki said, his voice rumbling over her, making warmth slide through her, pool deep inside, temptation incarnate.

"We're not here to play tourist," she said, tone crisper than intended, and directed more at herself than him. Honestly, it was harder and harder to maintain cool logic around him. It was as though he burned it away with every heated glance he threw her, like the way he'd caught her on the plane after her ill-conceived wine binge. The way his gaze raked over her, amber flickering.

Uncharitably, maybe he'd simply been pleased with himself over the way she'd acted in Three Points. Like a typical War. Violent, manipulative, dangerous.

Faex.

"You could return someday. Travel wherever you wish." He paused. "You haven't touched the funds I set aside for you, a small portion of which could allow you to travel freely and for as long as you wished. You also inherit the bulk of my estate and my home upon my death."

A low growl rumbled in her throat. As though it were so simple. As though she could kill another person. "I didn't want your money when I finished school, and I certainly won't take it now. After, if you have your way, I kill you."

"I've lived a long time—"

"As though that makes any difference. I don't want to kill you. Or anyone."

"It won't be like that."

"Oh. Of course. Because plunging a sword into your chest is, what, assisted suicide? How is that any better?"

This time it was he grumbling, as he readjusted his hands on the wheel of the rental. "I'm not suicidal," he ground out.

"We're on the hunt for someone to be the next War, the person you want to kill you. No, wait. The *only* person who *can* kill you. How is that not suicidal?"

"We're here because you don't want to rise. It's more a matter of choosing the best overall option. The horsemen only rise when the world is ripe for apocalypse. I'd rather ensure it's the right apocalypse."

"Ahh. It's an altruistic suicide," she said.

He said nothing, but a glance revealed a muscle worked in his jaw, and he glowered out the front window, pewter gaze once more shot with amber.

Anna pressed her lips tight together. Clearly, it wouldn't matter what she said. He'd made up his mind.

Well, fine. *She* wouldn't kill him. She wasn't going to be War. He had likely lived a lengthy life, even if she wasn't entirely certain how long that was. What did it matter to her what he did, if he didn't harm anyone? Perhaps this pseudo-noble sacrifice was best for him, for everyone. No indication of cold on her neck to indicate lying; he believed he needed to die.

That sick feeling in the pit of her stomach, a fear-irritation combo, couldn't be about him. Nothing personal. Perhaps it was more about her concern for the repercussions of his actions.

She slid another glance at his profile.

Gaia help her, this would all be easier if he wasn't so deliciously gorgeous. Hardly her fault she found him distracting. Most women, and probably some men, would.

"Are you going in as you? Or in some other form?"

He pulled the car over to the side of a sycamore-lined residential street, the houses historic and stately on either side. Frowned a little. "I look as I do now. Is that a problem?"

Only to her state of mind. "No. I just wanted to know." If she was the only one who got to see him like this. Or if other women, this Tildy Cadman, could similarly drool.

He stared a moment at the wheel before turning to her, most of the amber gone from his gaze. "You remember the story?"

He might have forgotten his annoyance, but she

hadn't forgotten hers.

She scowled at him and reached for the door handle. "We're Mr. and Mrs. Farbautisson, looking to relocate to the Oak Park area for business and pleasure. We've been married six years, you want to start a family, I'm still not certain, so, for now, it's just us."

A dark brow rose. "The children are new."

"My suggestion," Rojo piped up from the back seat with a yawn. "Or I suggested the more likely scenario. Your career is moving, she's ready to pop out babies."

She shot a glare at the pigeon. "But I don't live in the dark ages. So, *my* career is on the upswing, and it's important for me to stay independent. It also provides a point of contact between Tildy and us since she has two kids."

He studied her a moment, a small smile pulling at his lips, the weight and warmth of his gaze only increasing the heat inside her, the whirlpool deep inside her.

"You have considered this," he murmured. "Still, why is your career on the upswing and not mine?"

"Because yours matters less. If I get pregnant, it wouldn't affect your day-to-day life as much as it would mine."

"For me, it would. No one says we have to be traditional. Perhaps I could work from home, be a—what is the term?—stay-at-home dad. Whatever you needed."

She narrowed her eyes on him, waited for the cold feeling on the back of her neck. Then blinked. "You're...not lying."

The image of a future together, a life together, flashed through her mind.

She swallowed, shook her head with a small laugh. "I should have known you'd be good. That's what you do best. Create illusions to fool people," she said, pretending to laugh it off. Certainly, he wasn't picturing the two of them together.

She opened her purse. "Come on. In you go," she said to Rojo.

"You know, if I have to live in the purse all the time, there should be snacks. Booze maybe?" Rojo hopped in.

Anna zipped up the purse almost fast enough to decapitate him before jumping out of the car. All without ever having the courage to look at Loki's reaction to her words. Her pulse beat too fast, and too much warmth tumbled through her, fizzing the clarity of her thoughts.

She started up the paved driveway, her shoes making sharp clicking sounds.

She didn't want a life with Loki. Would never have a traditional life. But if she found another War to rise, perhaps she could still have *a* life.

While someone else killed Loki.

Her chest squeezed.

Loki's sure footsteps were right behind her, and as he reached her side, he reached down, caught her fingers in his, intertwined his around hers.

She didn't flinch.

No, much worse than that.

Liquid heat coiled through her, her resolve steadied, and she felt better just being next to him. Felt too blasted much.

They walked up the sidewalk of the two-story brownstone and knocked on the door. Or rather, Mr. and Mrs. Farbautisson knocked. A small thrill went through her at the game. More danger.

"Why don't we use your real last name?" she asked as they waited.

"She may have heard of Laufeyjarson," he said quietly.

"Then I should hardly call you Loki."

A brow rose as he turned, captured her again in that pewter gaze. "What do you want to call me?"

Like his comment about staying home with the kids

while she worked, there was something too much about the real them in his question. As though he cared and would be whomever she wished.

She licked her lips.

His gaze darkened, tracking the action.

Loki would never be a common name. He'd certainly gone by others, yet the name was so intrinsically tied to who he was. Who he had been—which she should remember for her own good—and who he'd always been to her. Loki, her rescuer, the bad boy, the dark prince, the mastermind. Temptation.

"I'll, just, um, stick to pet names," she said.

Footsteps echoed inside.

"Of course…Baby Cakes."

She blinked, turned on him. Raised a brow in challenge. "Only if you're Big Daddy."

His lips twitched. "Dollface?"

"Boo Bear." She couldn't keep the grin from her lips.

Rojo made gagging noises inside the purse. "Stick with darling and sweetheart. Please!"

"Darling it is," Loki said, tugging her closer, his arm settling around her waist just before the door opened.

All amusement over their silliness vanished as every nerve ending fired at the close contact, her tongue too thick for words. Her breath rushed out, and she couldn't seem to look away from his lips, felt the burn of his fingers against her skin through her black flowered dress, the fabric again seemingly too fine, too small a barrier.

The itch flared up on her back, War abilities sparking and sizzling to life which, for once, seemed to focus on the woman at the door, smiling and inviting them in.

Matilda "Tildy" Cadman was of average height, brown hair pulled into a tidy chignon, makeup attractive if conservative. She wore a fitted suit jacket and pencil skirt, both dark red. Her brown gaze was pleasant, with sharp intelligence and watchfulness as she invited them in, said the usual things. It was unfurnished, leaving the house abandoned and somehow sad without the friendliness of furnishings and knickknacks.

Loki gave Anna a quick look but quickly became yet another character, this time the eager, unthreatening husband, asking questions, pointing out things to her as though she—or he—might actually care. This Loki was too tame, but he seemed to put Tildy at ease.

Anna occasionally murmured the correct sounds as Tildy led them through the empty house, pointing out period woodwork and the fireplace.

This was a War candidate?

Unlike with Wiebe, although Anna's back still itched—seemingly a reaction to any War or potential threat—Tildy didn't carry the same air of threat as she led them through the dining room, breakfast nook, and newly remodeled white kitchen.

Perhaps it was an act.

Anna frowned intently as they climbed the stairs to the second floor. Now, where had that thought come from? She shot Loki a dirty look as he followed the women up the stairs. Was he somehow biasing her against the other candidates?

He simply raised a brow, nonplussed.

She wouldn't give up on freedom so easily.

It would also be foolish to be too trusting.

While Tildy and Loki peeked into the main bath, Anna hung back, unzipping her purse. Now to add some stress to the situation, see how Tildy reacted.

On cue, Rojo flew out of the purse, flitting and flying about like a panicked bird.

Anna even managed a shocked cry—and to smother her gleeful smile.

Tildy cursed but efficiently opened a nearby window in one of the empty bedrooms and shooed Rojo outside. She turned, smoothing back her hair, but her smile seemed disappointingly calm. "I'm so sorry. I don't know how it could have gotten inside. Now, over here we have the master bedroom..."

Anna and Loki exchanged a look behind Tildy's back. Still inconclusive.

Equally so when Loki "accidentally" pulled one of the faucet's handles off in the bathroom, and Anna continually asked questions about whatever Tildy had just said, as though she hadn't been listening.

It was possible Tildy Cadman was the most even-tempered War in existence. Or excellent at her job.

Which made her ideal to rise as War. Even Loki couldn't argue that. She didn't have a temper, she was pleasant, and could get along with Anna's friends. Maybe she wasn't corrupted by War's ugliness, or maybe she had tight control over War's abilities and depravity.

Twenty minutes later, they headed back down the stairs—for the third time. Anna had insisted she didn't remember if the master was big enough, leading them back up there. Loki had led them up there the second time when he'd loudly wondered if there was a suitable nursery.

Tildy sent them a slightly frazzled but no less friendly smile. "So? What did you two think?"

Anna and Loki looked at each other, as though thinking.

Anna shrugged. "It was lovely. But...not the one."

"We'd need at least three bedrooms for the kids," Loki added.

Anna shot him a choreographed glare, the conversation entirely for Tildy's benefit. "Or one guest room and an office apiece."

His eyes sparkled with humor, and he wrapped an arm around her waist, as though it were natural and they'd done it thousands of times before.

She curved into him, her hands landing on his chest

like they belonged there, like she'd touched him much more intimately in private. Her throat thickened again.

"One nursery, one office, and a guest room, for when your friends visit. I can work from the sofa." He leaned closer, almost as though he'd kiss her with those teasing lips, but then didn't.

Her face burned, and she gently tugged away, attempted to get her scattered thoughts back into some order that didn't involve Loki, sex, kissing, or anything of similar topic.

He let her escape.

Tildy laughed and gave Anna what appeared to be a sincere smile. "They're always in such a hurry for children. We know the amount of work it really is!" She gave Anna a conspiratorial wink. "Well, no worries. If you'd care to drive down a few blocks, we'll still be in the Hemingway District, and there's a lovely house adaptable to both of your needs, a little larger than this one."

"You have kids?" Anna asked while they all made their way toward the front door. Honestly, she'd never considered the amount of work children required outside of library hours, where they were sticky, loud, and messy.

"Two," Tildy said with a smile, locking up the house and depositing the key back into the large gray realtor lockbox.

"If you'll pardon me, I have a call to take," Loki said, excusing himself and giving the women a chance to speak as he strode toward the rental car, making that tan pair of slacks look very nice from this angle.

Tildy leaned closer. "I was hesitant too. About kids," she said. Then laughed. "About marriage too."

Anna kept pace with the woman, prolonging the conversation. She tried not to notice the familiar pigeon perched on the hood of the rental car and hoped Tildy didn't either.

"Your career?"

The other woman looked thoughtful as she pulled her keys from her purse. "Not exactly. My...lifestyle, perhaps."

Perhaps the kind of lifestyle choices that led to a parole officer.

Anna calculated the odds and weighed her words, pretended she was confiding a deep secret and hoped it deepened the connection. Ginny always said sharing confidences helped people trust you. "The whole family thing, suburbia..." She shook her head. "It feels a bit...staid."

The other woman paused, turning, rotating her keys gently in her hand, as though considering. Finally, she said, "It doesn't have to be."

Sensation prickled low in Anna's back, that itch back again, her stomach tensed. Now they were getting somewhere. Just a little more, and the other woman would open up. "You mean kids soccer games, neighborhood block parties, and Tupperware?" She made a face. Goddess, please let other people actually live like those she'd read about.

"Not...exactly," Tildy said. She considered Anna, then shook her head. "Never mind." Her smile brightened with professional friendliness, and she started walking again. "Maybe exactly like that. It's a life that makes a lot of people happy. I can lead the way to the next property if you'd like to follow."

Well, damn. Another house she wasn't planning to buy was not on the schedule.

Anna leaned closer. "Not me." She shot a meaningful glance at Loki. "Not either of us. We're quite...adventurous."

Something sparked in Tildy's brown gaze. Her step slowed again. Maybe she recognized she was speaking to another War. She tapped her hand and her keys against her thigh a moment. She stopped, turned, and reached into her purse. It was one of her realty cards. She fished out a pen, and balancing it on her hand, scribbled something on the back.

Again, she hesitated as she turned toward Anna.

It took extreme self-control to not snatch the card out of the other woman's hand, or reach out and touch her, get a read off her. Ginny had given her the lecture on random touching and curiosity back when they were in kindergarten.

Finally, Tildy held out the card. "It's not for everyone," she said, relinquishing the card too quickly for their fingertips to brush, even for a moment.

Anna glanced down at the writing on the back in black ink: the address, a phone number, and time.

Tildy's professional smile was back in place. "In the meantime, shall we look at a few more properties?"

Anna mirrored the smile but could hardly wait to get back to the car and show Loki. They had a clue. Perhaps she'd just found the rightful War.

CHAPTER 14

That evening, after viewing three more properties they were never going to buy, then a quick dinner in their suite's dining room talking strategy, Loki strolled up the walk of an elegant historic property, Anna on his arm, ready to further assess the second War candidate. The house, at least as big as his, was all aglow, and he'd dressed carefully in fitted charcoal trousers, matching sports coat, and signature green silk shirt. Easy to move in, comfortable for a fight should they find one. Again.

Which was nothing compared to Anna on his arm, wearing a stunning red V-neck flare dress that did amazing things for her skin and curves…and terrible things to his imagination and ability to think straight. Either Trevor deserved a raise for selecting her wardrobe, or he deserved to be fired.

Rojo had gone ahead on reconnaissance, swooping around the property and ready to set off the alarm by pressing the car fob on his ankle that Loki had rigged to send a message to his cell. He remained unconvinced

Tildy Cadman could be a War, because of her even-tempered reactions this afternoon.

Anna seemed to believe this made her the perfect candidate.

No one was that perfect. Especially someone with a parole officer.

Anna leaned closer, her breast brushing his biceps. "You don't really think this will be a swingers party, do you?" she whispered, her face deepening to a shade almost as red as her dress. "I said we were adventurous, but it never occurred to me it could be interpreted in *that* way." Her face darkened further, visible even in the dim light.

Ah, Anna. Only she could be both so intelligent, strategic...and yet, so innocent, restrained.

He chuckled, and when she tried to pull away, he tugged her gently closer, her fingers twined once more with his. He was getting too used to that—her closeness, her hand in his, her charm. Pretending she was his.

He leaned closer, breathing in her lavender scent. "You have nothing to worry about. I don't want to share."

Her blue gaze flicked up to his, her lips parted.

By Ymir, it took sheer will and determination, plus a litany of reasons why he shouldn't, couldn't touch her and risk his plan when the temptation was so strong to bring his lips to hers, taste her, tease her, teach her.

He took a deep breath of warm evening air, not that it did a thing to clear his mind, to focus on his plan and the situation at hand.

Of all times for his mind to fail. He couldn't let it put Anna at risk. He already felt vulnerable, wearing his own face instead of another. It'd been years since he'd traveled in this, his normal form. Yet with Anna, it felt...right.

"It would be unusual for a War to organize that variety of event," he said, not even trusting himself to use the term, or any word related to sex. "Famine maybe,

Death possibly. War…"

"Doesn't like people," Anna finished, glancing at the other cars lining the driveway and up and down both sides of the street, everyone else seemingly already inside. "And yet…"

"Indeed," he murmured.

There were many peculiarities when it came to this War candidate, Tildy's friendliness and selected career among them. They were still missing the full story.

"Though, if she likes people, wouldn't that make her a better War? Less likely to want to cause harm." Anna sounded too hopeful by half.

"Unless it's a front." He led them to the double-wide carved wood door and pushed the bell. "Stay alert, don't let her deceive you." He paused. "If it is a swingers party, I promise the only one you'll be leaving with is me."

She turned to glare at him just as the door opened, Tildy Cadman herself standing there.

This Tildy was far different than realtor Tildy, wearing a sleek black cat-suit that plunged in the front and clung to all her curves. Her hair was pulled back in a ponytail, and her excitement and ability flowed off her in waves.

Tildy's ruby-red lips curved upward and her gaze did a slow once over of both of them. "I wasn't sure you two would show. Though I must say, I'm thrilled you did." There was husky invitation in her voice, in the way her gaze roved over them, first him, then Anna.

Maybe not swingers, but perhaps an orgy? Anna was unlikely to approve.

He'd prefer privacy with her. No further stimulation was necessary.

"Are we late?" Anna asked as Tildy led them inside an opulent but oddly quiet foyer.

"No, not at all," Tildy said, turning another red-lipped smile their way. "As first-timers, it's easier to arrive a bit after the preliminaries are underway."

Anna shot him an uneasy look.

He squeezed her fingers in comfort. Ah, Anna. An attack and fight in the middle of the night she was fine with, but any hint of orgy made her nervous. Oh, the things he could teach her…

There went a series of very distracting thoughts, not helped as Tildy turned back to them.

Seemingly sensing Anna's reticence, or perhaps because of the way her gaze lingered on the fit of Anna's gown, Tildy reached for Anna's free hand, leading her between them.

Blast, he needed to focus.

Tildy led them through the silent house. As they approached the stairwell leading downward, noise swelled up from below. Cheers and frenzied shouts. Guttural cries and grunts. The sound of flesh striking flesh.

His shoulders tightened. It didn't sound like an orgy. At least, not like any he'd ever attended.

Tildy turned toward them, light glowing in her eyes, an almost frenzied excitement in her expression. "It was difficult, building this here after leaving what I'd built in Houston." She seemed to focus her conversation more on Anna than on him, as though his invite had only been an afterthought.

Because she knew Anna was War, perhaps.

"It all felt so…sedate here for me when we first arrived."

Ah. Anna had mentioned the gist of their conversation. Evidently whatever happened below was far from sedate.

Tildy's hand caressed the railing as they slowly descended into the bowels of the house, down into a high-ceilinged cellar, the gypsum walls covered with plastic tarp, more plastic laid over the concrete floor.

In the center, as they moved through the wildly shouting crowd, two women, both somewhere between mid-twenties to early thirties, writhed in battle on the floor. They kicked each other, bit, punched, pulled hair, did all they seemingly could to destroy each other. The sounds they made were barely human. Rage reddened their faces, glazed their expressions, their lips drawn back in animalistic snarls.

One of them had a bleeding scratch down the center of her face.

The other held a clump of her combatant's blonde hair, her nose crushed and dripping blood.

Chills slid through him.

The fighters weren't the only women. Most of the audience was female, around the same age group, only a few men dotted here and there. They screamed and demanded blood, howled for violence with as much vehemence if not more than the men.

With unnatural thirst. It tingled against his skin, the ability used here, driving all of them mad.

"What…is this?" Anna rasped, no more able to look away than he.

Tildy's smile widened, and she hooted loudly, pounded her fist in the air before she swung back around. She had to shout to be heard over the crowd. "Fight club. For us, not them. Women only for the most part. Our escape, our adventure and call to the wild." She nodded at him. "Husbands aren't usually invited, but I could tell you two were special."

Ymir, one did wonder precisely what she'd thought. His gaze was drawn back to the fight. Found his hands drawn up in fists. An orgy would have been preferable.

Tildy whistled over the sound of the fight and cheers, and a teenager with a tray of champagne—a child who didn't belong here, of all places—wove his way toward them.

The other War candidate snagged one for both he and Anna, then another for herself.

"Settle in. Enjoy. First-timers are the only ones guaranteed not to fight. After that, well…" She winked. "That's half the fun, never knowing if tonight's your night." She pressed into the crowd, getting a front-row view of the fighters, shouting and urging them on.

The fight grew ever more frenzied, more desperate.

Anna reached for his hand again, squeezed his fingers, hard.

She must have felt it too. That this wasn't a natural violence, but spurred on by magic.

By War.

The blonde woman hit the other in the neck so hard, the other woman tried to rise, couldn't, slumped down onto the plastic-covered concrete. The winning blonde dragged the limp body of the loser toward Tildy.

Tildy patted the blonde on the back, leaned closer, and whispered in her ear.

The blonde's gaze cleared. She looked back numbly at the limp body of the other woman, others carrying it off.

Tildy lifted the blonde's arm and let out a triumphant shout. The crowd cheered. The blonde started to smile, bloody-toothed.

Loki's stomach twisted, and he struggled to keep the revulsion from his face. He set the untouched champagne on a passing tray. Another teenager. Ymir, were those her children, dragged into this ugliness?

Anna downed her champagne in one large gulp, fumbling with her glass as she refused to look away from the grotesque tableau.

He finally took the glass, set it on the tray.

"What is this?" Anna said again, this time to him.

Tildy Cadman's voice broke through the cheering, chanting crowd before he could answer. "Now that we've had that warm-up, let's see who tonight's fighters are."

More frenzied cheering. Did she have them all under her spell?

"Bring me the hat!" Tildy shouted.

❧

Anna's hold on Loki's hand seemed to be the only thing that was real, the only steadiness in the unreal insanity of the situation. She couldn't look away. The itch on her back was intense, as bad as it'd been around Wiebe. Nothing like the dizzying lightness of her head, the sickly-sweet taste on her tongue.

Tildy drew six names out of a battered top hat. Six names and six ordinary looking people stepped forward. Five women, one man. They could have been members of the PTA.

Or the knitting club.

Anna's stomach twisted.

They were stripped of anything that could be used as a weapon—shoes, belts, jewelry. The man lifted off his polo shirt, revealing a bony, hollow chest. Two of the women stripped down to sports bras and running shorts. One of the others just looked scared, face pale and vaguely green, as though she might be sick. Tears slid down the black-haired woman's face.

The situation was repulsive. Anna's insides churned, yet warmth radiated through her and adrenaline sped her pulse, left her head almost floating. That sickly sweet-sour taste was back on her tongue, anticipating the violence. Tildy began to speak to her six victims. Softly at first. She told them the rules, what few there were, mostly about stopping when someone was down and not moving, no head shots. Then she talked about their strengths and weaknesses as fighters.

The crying woman had never fought before.

The cadence of Tildy's voice changed as she encouraged them to win, spurred on their darker urges.

The sound made Anna's back sting and burn now, and her stomach tightened. The flame of War flared deep in her belly, writhed. Ready to fight. Hungry.

Tildy stepped back and shouted, "Fight!"

The frenzied combatants leaped at each other with snarls and guttural cries. Flesh struck flush, and the crowd chanted and jeered.

Something connected with those chants, those cheers, each strike of flesh. It sped her heartbeat, wet her tongue, coiled her muscles, shortened her breath. Every sense heightened, hot and writhing inside of her, making her head buoyant.

As though she were dizzy, drunk with it.

The realization sent bile climbing her throat. Still, the sensation grew, warm, inviting. Pleasurable.

Loki stepped closer. Wrapped his arm around her.

Most of the combatants converged on the crying woman. She was the weakest, War saw that, while Anna winced.

Yet the woman dropped down and gnawed on the ankle of one of the others, who screamed in pain. The skinny man was down on the floor, two women holding him down while another kicked him. Unresponsive, at Tildy's orders, he was quickly dragged off.

Still that hunger, that...excitement whirled through her. Goddess, part of her loved the violence, even more than she'd experienced last night at the bar. This was War's ultimate deception, adding appeal to its ugliness. This was the corruption that would destroy her even if the whispered truths didn't drive her insane first.

Tildy stood at the forefront, face in a fierce, wild smile. That smile grew as blood splattered her cheek. She howled like a wolf, cheered again.

Anna's eyes narrowed. Tildy was using War's abilities to incite others to fight. For her pleasure. Like Wiebe, corrupted and luxuriating in War's ugliness.

Another of the combatants had fallen and needed to be wrestled away from the others before being dragged away.

She wasn't even certain why, or what she'd do. Anna took one step toward the fight. Then another.

War's fire curled through her. Yes, it fed off this violence, like a vampire and blood. But it wasn't her; she could shove down the sensation if she tried.

The violence wasn't these people either. Tildy's victims.

"Anna, be careful," Loki said, an anchor against her forward progress.

She tugged.

He tugged back.

She stumbled against him, his arms coming up around her. She pushed hard against his chest. Then harder.

He didn't budge.

She leaned into his face. Heat from him, from War, all of it whirled and spiraled through her, overheated her brain, simply said she had to do something. She had to act. Had to win.

"This is unacceptable," she snarled.

He leaned closer, his lips brushing her ear as he whispered, "Then do something about it."

She wanted to growl at him. Some part of her whispered that he was manipulating her, getting his way somehow.

He smoothed his hands down her bare arms, setting off fireworks and electricity at his touch. It dimmed some of the wildness whirling through her until she could focus on him, see the wrongness of what was happening. He stepped back, released her.

She hardened her jaw, fisted her hands, then worked her way through the crowd toward Tildy. The fire burned low in her belly, and everyone else seemed slow-motion again, as they had back at the hotel when Wiebe attacked. It made it so much easier to slip between them, to make her way toward Tildy, also moving at full-speed.

As though she sensed her approach, Tildy turned, grinned, tugged her closer. Perhaps she didn't see the others in slow-motion, perhaps she didn't care.

Her touch, like it had when she'd taken Anna's hand earlier, was full of insatiable hunger, like a greedy wildfire. Hunger for the violence, for the power, her need for this violence with all the lure of an intoxicating drug overlay the fight and many of the images that flashed behind Anna's eyes.

Tildy's gaze was fevered, cheeks pink beneath the blood splatter. "God, it's never been this good!" she crowed.

Anna's lips trembled. Probably because there were two Wars here tonight. "You need to stop this."

Tildy cheered as one woman clobbered another and slammed the redhead into the floor. Then, as though realizing what Anna had said, blinked and turned. "What? No. There's no stopping it. Not until they're done. Besides, two more fights are scheduled for tonight."

"No."

The violence crawled through her, thick and oozing, sticky and cloying, but hot, so damned hot. Anna fought to shake it off.

Tildy snorted. "You're not up for it, that's your problem, not mine. Or…" She raised a brow and looked at Anna.

Anna's back itched and burned intensely.

Tildy leaned closer. "I'll make you and your husband fight. Each other."

Maybe it was the call of the surrounding violence. Or not getting enough sleep and being too far from home. Or the fact that children were being forced to endure this violence. Or maybe just the fact that this woman had the gall to threaten Anna and Loki with what she'd already done to her other victims.

Either way, Anna barely thought as she drew her arm back and punched Tildy in the face.

The room erupted into violence. Audience members turned on each other, began to scream and pummel each other.

Oops. Striking another War hadn't been wise.

And Tildy wasn't going down easily. She jabbed Anna in the stomach with an elbow.

Anna wheezed, the attack bringing black spots in front of her eyes. She grabbed for Tildy's arms. Twisted and jumped on top of her, trying to still the writhing, snarling woman with greater mass.

War's fire seethed within Anna, the hunger for violence as if she'd never eaten before—even worse than the craving for one of Ginny's muffins.

Which pissed her off more. How dare it try and control her.

Pinning down Tildy's arms, Anna took a breath. She shoved back the rage, the emotion. Reached for the cold that had become more familiar these past few months, the icy burn. It rolled through her, quenched the flame.

"Enough," she growled, power rolling through her, out through her voice.

Tildy went limp beneath her.

Fighting stopped. People blinked, as though waking up. Held their hands out to help whomever they'd moments ago been punching.

"Time to go home," Loki said, his low rumble and the authority in his voice leaving no doubt it was a command.

The crowd shuffled toward the stairs. The fallen combatants were carried off.

Anna levered herself up to glare at Tildy. "If I let you up, are you going to attack me?"

The other woman swallowed, shook her head.

No chill on Anna's neck. Not a lie. She climbed up, Loki offering her a hand. Once on her feet, she offered a hand to Tildy.

Tildy scrambled to her feet on her own, as though afraid to trust Anna. She tested her jaw, then glanced around the room with a scowl. "Damn. You know much planning goes into an event like this? The babysitters, the alibis, the right location that's empty, where I can guarantee no other viewings that night. You fucked it all up, just like that." She snapped her fingers in Anna's face.

Fire flared again inside Anna, and she took a step closer.

The other woman backed down.

Anna didn't. "You're making strangers fight. Someone could be killed."

Tildy looked at her a minute, then barked out a laugh. "*Making* them fight? You're kidding, right? They come to me, beg me to join. They *want* to fight. I don't make them do anything."

Anna opened her mouth to argue the point, closed it. There'd been no cold chill on her neck, no lie. Still, she had to be sure. "Your voice. You incite them to violence."

Tildy made a face. "How the hell would I do that? Like..." she laughed, "like magic or something?"

The way she said magic was so derisive. Still no lie. Surely...

"There's a prize for whoever is left standing, I suspect?" Loki said, tone weary.

The woman shrugged. "Naturally."

Loki and Anna exchanged a glance. People were stupid.

Still, she hesitated a moment more. "Where does your surname, Cadman, come from?"

"It's the only thing I have from my parents before the Moyers adopted me, then I married Fred. Seemed like the least I could do was keep it." Tildy narrowed her eyes. "What is it you two really want? Because it isn't this, and I'm fairly certain it's not a house with three bedrooms."

The fire drained out of Anna, leaving her aching and sore. "You know nothing about the War clan, do you?"

"The what?"

Anna sighed. No lie. No deception. "You can't continue these fights."

Tildy crossed her arms. "Says you."

Loki cleared his throat. "Also says the authorities I've informed. I also suspect your parole officer might have something to say about it."

Tildy cursed him out before she raced up the stairs.

Anna looked at Loki and sighed again. Gaia, she felt about a billion years old. "Did you really call the police?"

"Not yet. Though I could. Perhaps should. If this wasn't repulsive enough, those children shouldn't have been here." He held out a hand to her.

She hesitated only a moment before she placed her hand in his, let herself be surrounded by his warmth. "No. They shouldn't have been. Children don't belong anywhere near war." They'd only become casualties. Like she had. Perhaps like Tildy's children would.

Unless someone else rose, and Tildy's ability, along with any her children had inherited, was absorbed by the true War. Could she find someone who wasn't corrupted by War, who could use the abilities and not be devoured by them?

He pulled her closer, wrapped an arm around her waist, and helped her up the stairs, then through the empty house and out onto the street. Their rental was one of the few lone vehicles on the block. And obvious, with the pigeon perched on the roof.

"What happened? Everyone poured out of there so fast I thought there was a fire," Rojo said, waiting as Loki held the door open for Anna, and she lowered her aching body into the seat.

Rojo flew in just before Loki closed the door.

Anna sighed, let her head fall back against the seat. "She's holding fight club events for, from the looks of it, soccer moms. She has no idea she's even War clan, or that she's responsible for inciting people to violence."

Loki climbed in and started the car.

Rojo snorted. "You guys get all the fun while I'm on reconnaissance or purse duty. Think we should tell her? I could get used to fight clubs."

The lights of the passing streetlamps cast long shadows stretching over the ceiling of the car as Loki drove.

Tell Tildy. Share what War brought with it. It'd probably been responsible for taking her parents, the Cadmans, or at least a contributing factor. Besides which, Tildy seemed to be addicted to the high the violence brought. She couldn't be trusted with more ability than she already had.

Anna sighed. "No. I don't think so."

She turned to look out the side window to avoid both Loki and Rojo's gazes. "There are still two candidates left." Only two left. If the next two were as bad as the first two...

"Which means they have to be better. Buck up, Princess. We just found the crappy ones first," Rojo said, almost encouraging.

She couldn't convince herself there was hope left to even conjure enough for her voice. Goddess help her, escape seemed less likely all the time. *Alea iacta est.* Was the die cast? She might rise no matter how hard she fought. War would consume her...and Loki expected she could kill him.

CHAPTER 15

Yet again, his companions lapsed into silence for the drive back to the hotel. Loki tried to focus on the road, but his thoughts were distracted. It was becoming an unfortunate state of being. Tonight's events had been disturbing, although Anna had demonstrated increasing ability and control. She continued to grow in power, which meant tonight should count as a success.

But there'd been a text on his phone when they got back to the car from Trevor. The psychiatrist had seen Daphne today, and sedation was becoming increasingly ineffective, as though she'd somehow built up a tolerance. She was becoming more difficult to control, and his contact in Daimoleigh had backed out of taking custody of her. Likely thanks to rumors that an angel had roughed up one of the demon families in town who'd defied and spoken against the gods when Nia was arrested.

Demons in the mortal realm—refuges from their own world of Daimoleigh—should have been safe in Beckwell, but the angels clung to the old ways, before the veils, when they were the front guard of the gods. Worst of all, Heimdall had reached North America, was now tracking Anna and Loki, and could potentially show up any time. Just like that ass to ruin everything.

Not that he'd let anything happen to Anna. Heimdall or otherwise would have to go through him first. He slid a glance her way.

She sat perfectly still, rubbing her palm with her thumb as she'd long done whenever worried.

He parked the car in the hotel parking lot, frowning at himself. Perhaps he'd pushed too hard, encouraging her to stop the violence when it'd had an obvious effect on her. Yet…she needed to learn what she was capable of if she was ever to realize the truth.

Loki opened the rear window, cleared his throat. "Rojo, perhaps you'd like to head up to the room. I think Anna and I will investigate the atmosphere down in the hotel pub."

The flying rat snorted but flapped toward the window. "That's what you're calling it, huh? I saw a fine flock of pigeons in the park across the way. Thought I'd go make my acquaintance." He flapped away.

Loki got out of the car, then came around to hold Anna's door. He offered her a hand since she'd yet again almost beat him out of the car, as though to prove she didn't need him for anything.

She straightened and glanced down at her dress, her hand in his. "We probably shouldn't let him run around on his own. I look terrible. Maybe we should just go back to the room."

Their suite where they'd have privacy, a large bed, and the entire length of the night to themselves. His body hardened.

"You look lovely as ever. I think we could both use a change of environment. Somewhere that isn't plotting or planning our next move."

She smiled, her skirt brushing his trousers. "You're always plotting no matter where you are," she said, but there was no censure in her words.

He took a half-step closer. Because, clearly, he'd lost his mind. "So are you." It was one of the things he most appreciated about her. Her brilliant mind, equal at least to his own.

She ducked her head slightly, but that small smile still played on her lips, and she didn't move away as he placed his hand in the small of her back.

The two of them walked into the boutique historic hotel, then into the bar with its bright splashes of color on the walls and inviting candlelight at each table creating an intimate venue.

They were seated at one of the higher tables, their knees brushing beneath the table, perched on bar stools. She didn't move away, let her knee rest against his.

The faux-candlelight darkened the rest of her dress, highlighted the hollows of her cheekbones and the brush of her lashes. She'd pulled her hair back into what had been a severe bun, but the violence with Tildy had caused tendrils to escape. They brushed her neck, begged him to tuck them back, to follow their path with first his fingertips, then his lips.

The waitress came; he ordered only water, while Anna ordered a white wine.

He couldn't tear his gaze away from her. The way her blue gaze met his, tugged at something inside. She saw too much, knew too much. He couldn't afford entanglement. He was and always would be stronger alone.

But Anna... Ah, but then there was Anna.

The waitress brought their drinks, and Anna took a few sips before she spoke, twisting the wineglass around and around, her fingers on the stem.

"I just keep thinking about her kids. Tildy might not

know she's a War heir, but they may have inherited some of her abilities. It will affect their lives, as it has hers. As it does all of us."

"When War rises, those abilities will be stripped from them too," he couldn't help but say, earning only a minor glare at the reminder. "You could tell her. Explain."

Anna sniffed. "As though knowing would make it better." She took another few sips of wine.

Too much wine for what little she'd eaten at dinner.

He signaled the waitress and ordered them some variety of cheesy bread, good to fill the stomach and soak up alcohol. It was quick, too, arriving shortly after he ordered.

"Would you rather you hadn't known?" he asked quietly.

When he'd rescued her from the fire, she'd been vaguely aware of her heritage, but he and the Lacks had helped complete the history, placed the weight of that legacy on her narrow shoulders. He'd long wondered if he should have waited...or if it had been a form of cruelty bringing her to Beckwell as he had, making her part of his plan.

She pulled at the bread, pulling off a piece of cheese and putting it between her lips, licking the herbs and oil off her fingers.

His body tightened more. Ymir, she did it so innocently, as unaware of her power as Tildy with her ability to incite violence.

She had yet to answer his question. After she drank some more wine, he wondered if she'd decided not to reply when she spoke.

"No. I'd rather have known. To have some reason, no matter how horrible, for why my father murdered my mother, why he tried to kill me."

Loki's throat squeezed. "I don't think his actions were well thought out enough to consider what would happen to you." When he'd lit the fire that consumed his and his wife's bodies, he'd likely been too far gone to imagine how the fire would claw toward the bedroom door where his young daughter hid.

Her eyebrows twitched upward. "Maybe. Not with the rage I caused." She shook her head, lips tight a moment. "If I'd known more at the time, maybe I would have understood why it was better I didn't speak. Or have some idea what would happen when I did."

He'd known she was speech-delayed, attending even therapy to try and rectify the issue before he ever met her. He froze, sucked in a breath as the implications of what she said hit him like a broadsword to the belly.

He leaned forward, touched his fingers to hers where they rested on her wineglass. "Anna, what happened to your parents was *not* your fault."

She shrugged and wouldn't meet his gaze. "The psychologist said I was speech-delayed. I knew the words. I just wanted them to come out right before I spoke. But that day, *that day*, I finally tried to put my thoughts into words." Her lips trembled. "He became so angry, like nothing I'd ever seen before. If I hadn't said anything, or if I'd waited just a few minutes until he left for work—"

Loki shoved aside the appetizer, his water, even the wineglass, until there was nothing impeding his ability to clasp her hand in his. With his other hand, he gently nudged her chin up until she met his gaze. Their bodies angled toward each other, their thighs aligned.

"It was *not* your fault," he said again, holding her gaze with his. "They were passionate, their marriage volatile. That's…" He forced the words out. "That's why I found them. And you. Because of the complaints filed against them, calls reporting fights and potential domestic violence. Sweetheart, they were both War clan. The fact they stayed married and together as long as they did was probably because of you. The rest, their mistakes? Never.

You were not one of those mistakes, and you brought them joy and love. Nothing else."

Her fingers tightened around his, trembling. Her gaze shone and grew tremulous, but no tears fell. "You can't know that for certain," she whispered.

He leaned closer, inhaling the scent of her, the warmth, the irresistible charm. "Neither can you." Though he'd find a way to prove it to her. To prove she didn't need to carry this guilt.

He ached to make it better, to cut out the pain she'd so needlessly carried all these years. He may even have convinced himself getting closer to her made it easier to manipulate her toward his plan. But the naked truth, as he slid his fingers over the silken skin of her jaw, as he watched her eyes darken and dilate, as he brushed a fingertip over her lips... The truth was he wanted her and wanted her not to hurt anymore.

He brushed his lips over hers, lightly at first. Inhaled her soft gasp.

Her fingers squeezed his, her knees bumping his beneath the table.

He brushed his lips against hers again, deepened the kiss as she opened to him.

The cool tartness of the wine was on her tongue, her mouth soft, warm, and welcoming.

Suicidal. Dangerous to his plan, to his maneuvers, to his sanity.

He began to draw back.

She tugged her hand from his, cupped his jaw with one hand, the back of his neck with the other, and deepened the kiss.

She was naive but bold, fearless. Imitating his actions, she quickly grew more inventive, tasted him, tested him, kept him on his toes. She drew him in, drew him closer, made him want her more.

He slid his hand to her waist, pulled her closer,

partially off her stool, his other hand sliding over her back, wishing it touched bare skin.

Ymir, he'd never met another like her, and if he had his way, never would.

The first tap on his shoulder was irritating.

While taking small nips at her lips, he tried to slow their pace; they were in public, after all. For now.

The second tap came as Anna slid her hand down his shoulder, over his hard belly, hesitated, then landed on his thigh.

That second tap was aggravating.

The third tap was hard enough to hurt and came accompanied with equally irritating words. "Loki, old man, still doing stupid things after too much ale? Stop snogging with the wench and let's step outside so I can beat you properly and we can all go home."

Loki pulled away from Anna's lips, figurative ice water pouring through him, though not entirely damping his ardor the way it should have. He twisted, partially blocking Anna, giving her a moment to compose herself.

It had been foolish, not utilizing some kind of disguise. Sitting here in the open, kissing Anna while in his own form.

Trust family—even the adoptive kind—to sour his mood.

The broad, red-haired, blue-eyed bullocks grinned darkly, fingering his ornate, goat-headed cane.

Loki smothered a growl. "What are you doing here, Thor?"

CHAPTER 16

Anna blinked, tried desperately to bring order to her fevered brain and calm her still-tingling lips. The rest of her—tingling, aching, wanting—refused to see sense and obey any logic.

Did he just say *Thor*?

Faex!

Because, dear Gaia, she'd finally done it. Kissed Loki, object of her childish affections for too long, and the road to certain ruin and heartbreak.

Though, my, what a pleasurable and delicious road it would be...

Another blink, and she groped for her wineglass, gulped it down in a few sips. Or tried but ended up choking on it instead.

Which led to Loki patting her on the back and both men staring at her. Which only made her choke more.

Loki offered his water, and after a sip or two, at least she got her throat under control. Though her emotions and nerves jangled, and from the rising volume of voices and increasingly angry tones around them, she wasn't the only one losing control of her emotions. That sickly-sweet taste of violence tingled on her tongue.

Tossing some cash on the table, Loki placed his hand at her back, the touch singeing through her dress. "Let's continue this outside, shall we?" he said, shooting the gigantic stranger a dark look.

Loki was tall and muscular.

This red-haired man was bigger. The size of those superheroes in the movies Nia liked to borrow from the library. Even they might look puny next to this man.

Loki winced as he led her out, and she realized only belatedly he'd done whatever he did to absorb her ability, which seemed to pain him.

They'd already stepped outside, the night bringing a soothing chill to the air.

Whatever it did, Loki seemed already to be recovering. She knew nothing about the stranger so couldn't afford to reveal any potential weakness to him, especially if Loki was weakened.

Loki led them from the sidewalk outside the pub across the road, then a short distance until they entered a pleasant treed park. Still, he hurried her along until they were a distance in, a few joggers visible, a man walking a dog, the park otherwise quiet.

Anna pulled away and shot him a glare. She could have gained control of the situation; he needn't have hurt himself. She gave the stranger a similarly dark look. Not only had he interrupted their kiss, he'd upset Loki. She crossed her arms over her chest. Was Loki embarrassed to have been caught kissing her?

Loki paced a short distance away but stalked back, planted himself in front of the big stranger. He barely seemed to notice Anna's presence. "He sent you, didn't he?" Bitterness tinged his words.

The big guy shrugged, because Goddess, she

couldn't possibly call him by the name she suspected.

He crossed his arms. "Don't be difficult about this, Loki. Come home, listen to the lecture, promise to behave." He gestured toward Anna. "It's just a woman. There are others."

Anna's teeth clacked, and she fisted her hands. Her face burned, but at this point, she couldn't decide whether she was still embarrassed, angry, or both. Just some woman? How often had the stranger caught Loki this way? What exactly did the stranger think he'd seen?

Loki offered a dark smile. "I wonder what Sif would say if she heard you speak so disrespectfully about another woman."

The stranger—ugh, no almost certainly Thor, seeing as Sif was Thor's wife and not exactly a common name— dropped his arms and took a menacing step toward Loki. "You won't breathe a word."

Loki held his ground. "When would I be able to? I don't come to the family dinners. Haven't for nearly a century now. Honestly, Thor, I'm surprised at you. Here at Odin's bidding, still his errand boy after how many eons? Come to squash me to a pulp with your hammer, I expect."

Thor sighed, rubbed his tree-trunk neck, then headed for a nearby bench. He sat down heavily. "Nah, I don't do that anymore. Sif made me take anger management classes. I run my own construction company now in Braelyn. Building someone a house is pretty much as satisfying as smashing heads. Plus, afterward, you get paid *and* no one tries to kill you."

Thor sounded alarmingly surprised by the revelation. He also didn't look nearly as frightening sitting down.

"Good for you, Thor," Loki said and headed over.

She followed because she would not be kept out of the conversation. Not that either Loki or Thor seemed to notice her presence.

There was a flutter of wings, and a slight weight settled on her shoulder.

"Tell me that's *him*," Rojo said, voice awed and breathless.

"Shh. It's Thor. I'm trying to listen."

"*Thor*?" If a militant, chauvinistic pigeon could have squeed and gone fan-girl, Rojo would have. Instead, he fluttered and ruffled his feathers, then resettled them.

Anna glanced at her shoulder to make certain he hadn't squeed anything else.

Loki sat down next to Thor. "So why are you here then? You aren't Odin's errand boy."

Thor sighed, huge shoulders sagging. "Yes, but it makes everything awkward at family dinners. So I said I'd come get you and the female—" Here he finally acknowledged Anna with a nod. "Dad thinks we should just deal with this ourselves, keep your mistakes in the family."

"I'm sure he does," Loki said darkly. "But Odin is your father, not mine. Any brotherhood he and I may once have shared meant nothing to him. I owe him neither allegiance nor respect."

Thor growled and scrubbed his forehead. "Gods' teeth, you old asshole, why do you have to be so difficult? The girl isn't War yet. The other gods are getting pissy. Now you, Odin, and Heimdall drag me into it."

He shot a glare at both her and Loki. "You know what I could be doing? Building houses and playing with my grandbabies. Or great-great-grandbabies. I can't ever remember how many generations there are now." His expression suddenly brightened, and he banged Loki on the knee. "Did you know humans made new moving pictures about *me*? I'm a hero, all blond and pretty. You're kind of weaselly, and they somehow think you're my little brother, but have you seen them? Never has so genius a form of my legend existed. Plus, the renewed belief they've generated has me feeling like I'm barely a hundred."

"I've heard of them," Loki said dryly, clearly less appreciative of their virtues.

Though that was an interesting idea—how modern adaptation of myth had helped strengthen some of the gods. Perhaps that was why the Norse gods had never involved themselves as much in the pettier affairs of USED, the league of gods?

Anna made a mental note to borrow all the movies from the library or Nia when she returned home.

She frowned. When or *if* she returned home. What changes had occurred while she'd been away?

"You said something about Heimdall?" Loki prompted, nudging Thor back to the topic.

"Yeah, he's leading the hunt now. Came out of retirement for that fancy god spy agency, the Ukeleles or some such, just for this case. He really hates you. Both of you." Thor turned to her. "If you turn yourself in, they might kill you quickly."

Loki swore, deeply and fluently. She didn't even recognize some of the languages...or shouldn't have.

Yet she understood every word. A chill rippled through her. Her lips parted slightly. Another War ability.

"Can we just name him War and be done with it?" Rojo rhapsodized. "Now *that* is a warrior. Look at those biceps, those pectorals. The first War, Marius, he had that look about him too. It's what I've always known my War would look like."

She wiggled her shoulder and tried to dislodge him. "What, for the two seconds before you materialized in Beckwell and started a bar fight? You remember the other horses' memories. You didn't exist before."

He dug his claws in and held on tight. "Doesn't mean I don't know how to dream."

"She's not turning herself in," Loki bit off. He

shoved a hand through his hair and blew out a breath, his words still tight, but calmer. "Thank you for the information about Heimdall. It is troubling, USELESS having someone halfway competent working the case. But neither Anna nor I will be accompanying you home, so you may as well get back to your houses and grandchildren."

Thor was already shaking his head. "No can do. Do you know the lecture I'd get from Odin if I did that? If it's not those two damned ravens, he's figured out cell phones—mostly to annoy the rest of us, I'm sure, though everything else about the modern world is just 'passing fancy,'" Thor said, using air quotes. And, rather surprisingly, using them correctly.

"Then why don't you come with us?" Rojo said loudly.

"Shut up, Rojo," Anna said as both Thor and Loki looked at her and the bird, perhaps remembering her presence.

Thor stood, squinting as he lumbered forward. A grin split his face. "It's a talking parakeet."

"Pigeon," Rojo said. "But why not? That way you're almost following orders, if being a bit slow bringing Loki in. You can help us find the real War heir."

Thor's eyes widened, and a smile blossomed on his face in direct proportion to the growing scowl on Loki's face and the dread curdling in Anna's belly.

"You're going on a *quest*?" Thor said, practically whispering the last with awe.

There was a good chance he'd probably squee about it, too, if it'd occurred to him.

Anna's shoulders sank. "*Podex perfectus es,*" she said to Rojo.

Rojo was gleeful, chest feathers all puffed out. "I might be an asshole, but I just won this round, Princess."

She flicked the pigeon off her shoulder. "Terrific.

Enjoy your victory together. Out here in the park for the night. Hang out with him instead, if he's so perfect." Not that she cared if Rojo thought Thor made a better War. She didn't want to be War.

She forced herself to meet Loki's gaze. Tried not to flush as she again wondered why he'd been upset. Why had he kissed her in the first place if she was below him? Goddess, she never should have been so foolish.

Loki's kiss had been so distracting, Thor could have killed them both.

And if he hadn't arrived when he did...

Blast. Her face burned again. "I'm tired, and I suspect tomorrow will be even more trying." She glanced at Thor and Rojo, the bird now perched on the god's shoulder. "I'm going back to the room to call my friends and get some sleep."

Loki nodded. "I'll be up later, and I'll take the sofa." He reached into his pocket and lightly tossed her the keycard.

As though she were just some roommate. As though they hadn't almost made their way back to the room. Together.

She spun away and stalked back toward the hotel. She needed to regroup, focus on logic, not lust, not all the dangerous emotion that would only get her in trouble. Could get her killed. Tomorrow they headed for the third candidate, and Goddess help her if this one wasn't worlds better than the first two. She needed to find that incorruptible War horseman who could harness the abilities, someone as strong as her friends had been. Maybe Rojo was right. Maybe the real War was someone like Thor. Otherwise, Loki would get his way, and she might destroy everyone and everything she cared about.

CHAPTER 17

Anna got back to the hotel room and dug Ginny's phone from the bottom of her purse, discovered it'd been on airplane mode all day—or at least that long. By the time she plugged it in to charge, there were fifteen messages, twenty missed calls, and dozens of texts from her friends. She needed that connection with them, that hint of home, and she needed to know they were okay.

Her fingers shook, as, heart pounding, she pressed dial for Nia's number.

Nia picked up on the second ring. "Where the hell have you been?"

Tightness spread through Anna's neck. Her voice was clipped. "Getting chased out of Three Points by thugs, shopping for houses, attending fight clubs with my pretend husband, and meeting gods. You?"

There was a pause. Then the sound of whispered conversation, a brief scuffle, sounds of Nia swearing.

"Anna? Are you okay? What pretend husband? Why were you chased? Were you hurt? What gods?" Ginny's voice verged on panic on the other end.

More tightness. Anna sat slowly on the edge of the bed, massaged her aching neck. They were all together. Without her. "I'm fine. Why all the messages? What's wrong?"

Ginny laughed. "I'll let her tell you."

More noises as the phone was handed over, then it was Piper on the line.

They were all together. Happy together. The three.

"Hi, Anna," Piper said, slightly more nervous than the other two. "So, I didn't mean to, and it didn't feel right, you not being here but…" She half-laughed, half-cried. "Congratulations! You're an auntie."

For a moment, Anna froze. She couldn't breathe, blink, or move. Until the shaking grew so bad in her right hand holding the phone that she had to use her other hand to keep from dropping it. Her eyes stung, her throat burned, but she forced a smile to her face. "Piper! Congratulations! Are they both healthy? Are you?"

Another half-laugh from Piper. "Things went really well, actually. They're both fine. Daniel is going out of his mind. We named the boy Jonathan, and the girl June." Piper choked up. "I wish you could have been here. To see Daniel's face when I suggested it."

Daniel's aunt and surrogate mother, June Benoit, had sacrificed herself for Nia's daughter six months ago, leaving an aching hole that was still fresh.

"I wish I'd been there too," Anna said, voice barely above a whisper. She'd done all the research and reading about how to be an effective doula. Studied as many resources as she could about twins and their unique needs. All to be there for Piper, to take care of her, like she'd always taken care of all of them.

Yet here she was. Thousands of miles away, in an unfamiliar city with an ungrateful pigeon, a potentially unstable thunder god, and Loki, dear heavens, *Loki*.

Whom she'd kissed. All while they were no closer to finding another War.

She'd missed one of the most important moments in a friend's life. Because of War, stupid, goddamned War. The same reason she hadn't been there for Ginny's first, out-of-town wedding. Though, if she'd gone, she likely would have tried to stop it.

"Sweetie, are you sure you're okay?" Ginny had the phone again. Ginny, who had far too much sympathy in her voice.

Goddess knew what she could pick up, even over the phone line. Even without abilities, Ginny had usually been able to read Anna with the ease of a paperback novel, while Piper was empathic.

They were there, and she was here. Being useless.

Ugh. Too emotional. She looked upward, lowered the phone a moment and covered the speaker with one shaking hand as she inhaled and released a tremulous breath. The last thing they needed to worry about was her. She let cold soak through her. Logic. Goddess, she needed to be more logical. It was safer, especially with the Loki problem. It hurt less, with all the things this trip dredged up, with missing her friends.

Another calming breath and she lifted the phone back to her ear, hands almost steady. "There was just a setback today. Another War candidate who isn't a viable heir." She explained to Ginny in brief terms about Tildy and the fight club.

Nothing about pretending to be Loki's wife, the way he made her feel, the kiss. She couldn't seem to get the words out, as though she didn't deserve to.

As though maybe her friends wouldn't care anyway.

"Tomorrow we'll head to London to meet the third candidate. Third time lucky, perhaps. There are four. One of them will be suitable," she said, wishing she felt the same assurance she injected into her tone.

Answering silence crackled over the line for a moment or two.

Then Piper spoke, her voice a little tinny.

Anna winced. Oh Goddess. Speakerphone, they had her on speakerphone. Analyzing her, their socially inept friend.

"Have you considered maybe just coming home instead? You could meet the babies," Piper said.

Anna stood, walked to the window that overlooked the street. Piper, of all of them, should have understood. Though the first of them to rise, she hadn't wanted her abilities any more than Anna, had recognized how potentially dangerous they could be.

"There are two more viable candidates," Anna said stiffly.

Ginny again, clearing her throat and sounding uneasy. "That's true," she said slowly. "But Anna, have you heard the news? The gods are cracking down on all magic usage. They're sending angels into all the paranormal sanctuaries like Beckwell. Bringing what they call 'law and order.' Mal and the others have held them off so far. Anna, there are angels coming. *Here*. We need you and Loki back home."

Angels were the most brutal, feared creatures in the paranormal world, the gods' enforcers, cold and driven by their own twisted sense of justice.

Now they were threatening her town, her friends. A thin column of heat rose through her. Loki had to know. He always knew this kind of thing. His minions must keep him informed.

If she went back now, if she stood with her friends…was that it? A foregone conclusion, she'd rise. She'd be War.

"How is Loki and the fucktationship anyway?" Nia added, despite Ginny and Piper's shushing.

Anna rubbed her forehead and glanced up. Her gaze

fell on Loki's sleek black leather carry-on, pulled into the bedroom where he'd changed for the evening. Into her bedroom. Her head ached.

"Don't be crude, Nia." Her words lacked the usual heat.

Weighted silence from her friends suggested they'd noticed.

"He is pretty hot," Ginny started.

Nope, the pounding was behind her eyes now. "He's a mischief maker and a liar." With the most amazing eyes, a rock-hard body she'd felt for herself beneath his clothes, and an incredible mouth made for kissing. Not that she had a lot to compare to, but it seemed impossible anyone could. That'd always been the problem. Her problem.

"So...you have slept together?" Nia asked, voice more serious.

"He didn't change color, did he?" Piper added in, seeing as her fiancé had partially shifted form the first time they'd slept together.

Anna let her head drop into her hand. Goddess only knew what horrific consequences there'd be if she gave in and did anything more than share a kiss with Loki. What if he somehow called forth her abilities? She could lose control, somehow set the entire hotel ablaze.

What if she let him convince her to rise as War?

"Loki is helping me locate the candidates. Rojo, the pigeon, is helping me find the real War, the one more like the three of you. Oh, and now Thor is joining us, so that will be interesting." Although potentially would also mean less privacy with Loki.

She hardened herself against the brief pang of disappointment at the thought.

Ginny sighed. "Anna, look. We'll love you no matter what happens, what you decide...but we've always been the Four. It wouldn't be the same without you, with some other War. And"—her tone rose, as though selling the last bit—"if you do rise, the gods and the angels will stand no chance against us. You'll have that sword, the big powerful one, the one that can kill gods, right?"

Anna's jaw hardened. Powerful enough to kill Loki. She glared down at her black leather shoes. "The sword Hildebrand. I'm not like you, Ginny. I won't make things grow. I won't make people have an orgy or start a cupcake business. I'll be War. I will start violence, bring pain to my life and to others." Her reaction to the violence back at the fight club came back to her, twisted her stomach. She'd bring that violence…and like it.

Nia snorted. "I'm Death. Doesn't mean I have to start my own zombie army or practice necromancy and death-touch. That's a choice too."

Anna lifted her head from her hands, ground her teeth. They didn't understand. "It's not the same."

"It is," Nia said, sounding pissed. "You're just too damned stubborn to see it."

"Really? Because my War career will open with killing Loki if he has his way," she blurted.

They'd never understood. Even if what Loki said tonight was true, even if she hadn't caused her parents' murder-suicide, she had caused other violence. She wasn't so different than Wiebe or Tildy. She liked being in control, having the power like Wiebe. She felt that hunger for violence, the addictive potential of it as Tildy did. And, frankly, Tildy and Wiebe were both better with people. If Anna had all the War abilities, they'd change her, corrupt her until she became just like Wiebe or Tildy. Or worse. If she were capable of killing Loki, would she stop there? War was indiscriminate and brutal. She felt that truth every time her abilities soaked through her. She'd stop trying to prevent the destruction, just let it take over her, that feeling like at the fight club tonight.

More whispered argument over the line.

"He told you that?" Nia said, subdued.

Anna rubbed her forehead, blew out a breath. "It's what he wants. Why he wants me to rise."

"Well, of course, you couldn't do that," Piper said, as though it was impossible.

She hadn't seen Loki's steadfast belief. Hadn't spent enough time with him to understand he always seemed to get what he wanted. Eventually, you gave in. Through his persistence, his charm, a combination thereof.

"If you're War, think of what your companion abilities could mean? Real peace. The truth," Ginny said. "We'd be the Four."

"We don't even fully understand what that could mean, how dangerous it could be. People don't like the truth most of the time. Even you knew that and told me to stop telling them back in school. And peace at what cost? I just declare peace, great, but does that make all the past suffering, the pain, the reasons for war go away?" She shrugged. "Besides, I don't have any companion abilities."

"Anna, you're overthinking it." Piper sounded tired.

Exhaustion seemed to be catching. Anna wandered back to the bed, sank onto the end of it, the mattress dipping. The stress and surrealness of the past few days hit her with the weight of a toppling bookshelf.

"I'm sorry I wasn't there, Piper," she said quietly, her throat aching. *I wish you all understood why it's so important to me that I don't rise.* She pressed the button and ended the call before lowering her head to her chest.

She'd called for reassurance, some sense of normality to help her regain her focus. Well, maybe that's what she'd gotten, if not the way she'd hoped.

She took a deep breath. Two more candidates, two more changes for freedom. *Aut viam inveniam aut faciam.*

Either she would find a way, or she would make one.

∂੭

Loki unlocked the hotel room door and slipped

inside. Better he'd found a reason to stay away since the buffer he'd hoped for and dreaded—Thor and Rojo's presence—were currently drinking in the bar around the corner.

He locked the door behind him, toeing off his shoes and padding forward in the dark. Anna shouldn't be alone. Not with Tildy possibly being able to find them. Never mind Heimdall or any of his cronies. Loki's hands fisted, and his jaw tightened as he walked into the living room of the suite, toward the sofa, his undoubtedly lumpy bed for the night.

Heimdall was a problem. Ruthless, intelligent, he would never stop coming after Anna, possibly even after she rose. Worse, if anyone could find a way to harm War and foil Loki's plan, it was Heimdall. He seemed to make a hobby of it. Thor wasn't close to his brother Heimdall, either, so was unlikely to have spoken to him or reported Loki's location. Likely wouldn't think to in any case.

"Don't move, or you will be very sorry you did," the hard female voice said from behind him, out of the darkness.

He froze, cursing himself for his distraction. He held his hands up and visible, as though somehow more harmless while he calculated his odds. Funny, he didn't sense any unusual presence. "Perhaps we could come to some kind of agreement," he said softly.

"I don't…" The voice paused, softened into someone he recognized. "Loki? Is that you?"

He dared turn.

Anna stood behind him, a chair raised in her trembling arms, ready to bring it down on his head.

In a disturbing state of half-undress.

Well, fuck's sakes.

The fight club, Thor, Rojo, Heimdall, that kiss… Now her standing there, about to attack him, wearing some little scrap of nothing. It was too much.

"What are you wearing?" Or not wearing. Long, smooth bare legs, shapely and muscular were visible from mid-thigh down, and the pale, diaphanous gown floated around her, almost glowing in the faint moonlight through the window.

When he got home, Trevor was fired.

"Obviously, you need to better familiarize yourself with women's clothing and stop questioning mine." She reached over and flicked on a light.

The brightness blinded him momentarily, the soft thunk of the chair as it hit the ground theoretically meaning it wouldn't strike his head.

"It's a nightgown. A garment women wear for sleeping. Why are you sneaking around?"

"That is not a gown," he said, the better light showing him that not only was the heavenly creation short and white, but it had a deep V-neck and delicate lace straps. One of which was sliding down her shoulder.

She wasn't wearing a bra.

Tempting as it was to groan, he knew better than to show a War—especially Anna—any weakness. Everyone took advantage of weakness. They just needed an angle.

She scowled at him, crossing her arms over her chest, lifting her breasts.

The strap slid farther.

"Well, it's all I have. One of your minions took away my bunny pajamas at your house, and I didn't get them back before we went gallivanting away."

"Which you wanted to do," he pointed out tightly, shrugging his sports coat from his shoulders and folding it carefully over the back of the chair.

Down, down, down that blasted strap continued to slide. He couldn't seem to look away from the thing. From what it might reveal.

He looked up to find her studying him as he pulled at his tie. He froze. Better to leave as many clothes as possible between them.

"You'd rather go home? Forget this nonsense? Your…quest," he taunted, hoping it would distract her.

Her eyes narrowed. "Of course not. But…" She took a breath, glanced again at his shirt. Her hands dropped, one hand catching her arm.

The strap slipped a quarter-inch more, the lace edge of the nightgown drooping more, a hint of curved breast visible.

"We should talk about what happened. This"—she waved a hand between them—"nonsense between us."

Thor and Rojo were right now getting drunk and would cause Ymir knew what kind of trouble. The kind Loki would probably have to talk fast to get them out of, never mind the financial cost. Heimdall could be hunting them down this very minute. And if that strap slid half an inch more…

He crossed his arms, tried to focus only on the annoyed expression on Anna's face, the tightness around her lips, the way the wet tip of her tongue darted out…

He grabbed his coat, no care for its welfare, and strode off toward the bedroom and his suitcase. "Let's not," he said.

Anna was right behind him.

The welcoming king-size bed loomed in the room, covers pulled back. Waiting for them.

The bedroom had been a strategic error.

"This is about you being older and immortal, isn't it?" she said stiffly.

He turned to her, since it was either that or stare at the bed and imagine all the much more amusing things they could be enjoying instead of this conversation.

Ah. The strap had slipped another quarter inch.

His throat—among other anatomy—thickened.

"Why would my age have anything to do with anything?" he countered. "First, I'm not immortal." He strode toward her, since retreat was never an option, a counter-offensive always better. "I do age, particularly without Idunn's apples. I'm difficult to kill, as Piper kindly demonstrated when she ran me over with her truck. But I can die. Especially given a weapon like Hildebrand, a blow from which is always deadly."

Anna hadn't backed down, leaving them now toe-to-toe.

Close enough the drooping nightgown showed a hint of dusky nipple.

He met her eyes, kept his expression hard. "If my age is an excuse for why a relationship is impossible, it's equally unreasonable. Yes, I may have seen and done more, but whatever would be between us would be new, for both of us, as no relationship is ever like another."

He lifted his hand, trailed the back of his fingertips over her silken skin, up the length of her arm. The skin pebbled, her breath roughened. Neither of them backed down or stepped away.

His voice grew rougher. "If you're looking for some real reasons we can't and won't be together, let's start with the fact that the gods want to kill you. They've never liked me, but you? They fear you, fear what will happen when the Four rise. Fear how strong the Four will be because your power doesn't require faith or followers."

His fingers reached the delicate lace strap, and he slid it slowly upward, watched its progress and Anna's gaze, the rapid rise and fall of her chest. His body was hard, ready, and, Ymir, he wanted her. But still, he continued.

"Leading the gods' hunt is one of the most ruthless, all-seeing, backward gods I've ever known. Heimdall, the only Asgardian to ever work for the other gods, the one who can and will find us while you dither, still convinced someone else should rise when you are clearly the best, the only choice. To rise, to end me. Because I will die. I will make a difference, will prove them all wrong and choose my own ending so that humanity can rise again. I can hardly allow myself to be distracted by you."

Even if, gods curse him, he wanted to.

The strap in place, his body hard, raging with want, he slipped his finger free of the lace, turned on his heel, and strode for the bedroom door, closing her in the bedroom. Without him. He stretched out, fully clothed, on the sofa for a long night of not sleeping. To try to find a way to erase the feel of her skin from her mind, the hint of that nipple from his dreams, the taste of her lips from his soul.

CHAPTER 18

Neither she nor Loki said much the next morning as they checked out of the hotel and began the drive to O'Hare to meet their private jet and continue to London. Other than the snores from the back seat, Thor and Rojo didn't make much noise either.

When they reached the airport, Anna hopped out of the car before Loki could open her door and grabbed her bag from the back. After last night, she needed to replace the distance between them. Permanently.

Loki gave her a mild look, making her face burn as if she were a child, but he said nothing.

Between the two of them, they corralled Rojo into her purse and Thor through the private security screening before they boarded their jet. Once onboard, the two hungover fools curled up in two chairs near the rear of the plane, falling into snores and leaving she and Loki virtually alone. Again.

She pulled out a book before stowing her suitcase and buckling her seat belt. A distraction. That was all she needed. Something to stop thinking about everything that happened yesterday. Culminating in Loki's touch of her shoulder, the moment that stretched between them in the bedroom. The wild temptation to open the bedroom door and invite him back inside.

Loki settled into the chair next to her. Of all the seats on the plane, he took the one next to her.

She gritted her teeth.

Today he wore jeans that probably cost more than her car had, and a charcoal button-down shirt, black waistcoat, sleeves unbuttoned and rolled up to his elbows, displaying muscular forearms dusted with dark hair.

She opened her book and tried to focus on the jumping, bouncing words. *Faex*. The book began whispering its truths, revealing every dangling plot thread and unlikely characterization. The jet taxied out onto the runway, and her grip on the book tightened. Her breath shortened, and her ability to read did not improve.

Loki casually draped his arm over their shared armrest, the back of his hand grazing hers.

She tightened her lips but didn't shift away. Even though there were dozens of other seats on the plane he could have taken and still avoided Thor and Rojo. Even though thanks to him, she'd hardly slept last night, and the few times she had drifted off had been to dreams of him. A reimagining of last night. Her in that ridiculous white nightgown, Loki's hand against hers, their gazes locked.

In her dreams, he hadn't gently replaced the strap. He'd tugged it down, or it snapped in two, or he just pulled her into his arms for a kiss before they tumbled into bed together.

The jet picked up speed on the runway preparing for takeoff.

Anna fisted her toes inside her shoes and struggled to keep her breathing slow. Maybe one got used to it eventually, but she hated this part of the flight even more than landing. Mostly she pictured all the fiery crashes and horrible deaths they were certain to suffer.

"Interesting read?" Loki asked lightly, the back of his hand rubbing against hers where she clutched the paperback so hard the pages creased.

She blinked. Then tensed as they bumped. Once, twice, Goddess, they were going to die this time.

"Is this book from a new author to you, or an old favorite?" he asked, voice still calm.

She stared, mute. Another bump.

Oh, Gaia...

He gently disentangled her cold hand from the book, covered it with his own, drew her hand against his chest, against the warmth there. "Anna, you need to breathe. Come on, love. Breathe. It's a good pilot. We're in safe hands."

Ha. Maybe. But what if the pilot had taken up drinking? Or another plane hadn't contacted the tower and landed in front of them. Or there was a bird. Or—

Loki lifted their joined hands, pressed his lips first to the back of her hand. Then slowly pressed a heated kiss to each of her fingers.

Breath shuddered into her lungs, and she couldn't look away from his dark pewter gaze sprinkled with amber, the way he pressed kisses to seemingly every inch of her hand and fingers.

Lightness filled her chest, that peculiar lift as they rose, higher and higher into the clouds.

It was the sparks shooting through her that made her head light.

"This is a terrible idea," she said, her voice rough.

"Calming you down enough to breathe? Necessary to life. Your abilities could short-circuit the plane," he said, lowering their hands to the armrest, his fingers still tangled with hers.

"Us. This lust." The emotions…far too many, far too strong. "We need to stay focused. The gods are after us, Heimdall in the lead. And despite what you believe, there is still a better War out there. It isn't me. I won't let it be me."

He sighed, a brief, troubled look creasing his brow before his mask once more settled into place.

She'd started to recognize and resent the mask that hid the man she saw beneath. Not a kind man, maybe even a ruthless one, but honorable, caring, gentle.

"Consider what happened in Oak Park forgotten. It will be easier for both of us going forward if it is."

She nodded and lay her head back against the seat. Definitely.

Now if only forgetting that kiss, the way he made her feel, were so easily done.

❧

Midway through the flight, Anna fell asleep, her book folded and forgotten in her lap. When it started to slip, Loki caught it, leaned closer to her.

She sighed in her sleep, turning toward him, snuggled against his shoulder.

Loki glanced at the book. From the scantily clad man on the cover and the description on the back, a love story. A guaranteed happy ending. Perhaps that was what she wanted.

Anna's dark hair brushed his jaw.

Her lavender scent wafted over him, the memory of their kiss, Ymir, the temptation of that bloody nightgown last night. As though she trusted him. At least in her sleep.

He blew out a breath, slid down lower in the chair, so his shoulder was at a better level, then gently resettled her against him.

Her breath whispered against his neck.

He lay back against the chair, sliding off his shoes and stretching out his legs. Another erection made it unlikely he'd get more sleep than he had last night, lying on the sofa and wondering when he'd lost his edge.

She might recognize his lies, but becoming intimate with her could be an avenue to manipulate her into the plan of his choosing. As well as the obviously pleasurable side effects.

Yet she took his hand so freely in his. Leaned trustingly against him in sleep. Opened for him so sweetly beneath his mouth and wouldn't back down, bold and adventurous, open about her need. He couldn't take that innocence from her, that warmth, wouldn't.

He firmly closed his eyes. Tried to focus not on her soft breaths, her fingers clasped with his, but listened for the snores of the two buffoons in the back. Both of whom could slow progress toward his goals if this candidate wasn't as objectionable as the previous two.

His throat thickened and his chest squeezed. They were running out of time. Heimdall would be closing in. The gods would attack Beckwell. Despite her fears, he had to drive Anna to rise while he could.

Anything else, even that old foolish feeling that this time he wouldn't be left out in the cold, alone, all of it needed to step aside. Only his plan could matter.

ॐ

Daylight still gleamed off the undulating, ultra-modern roof of Farnsborough Airport when they landed, not far outside London. Anna again helped wrangle Rojo and Thor while Loki took care of their transportation, a waiting black Town Car more suitable for celebrities than their quiet arrival. This car came complete with a hired driver.

She couldn't help herself from ogling out at the sights as they entered London, and then central London, bursting with places she'd only read about. Even Rojo and Thor—conscious and not snoring—looked out the window.

This was London. *The* London. With red double-decker buses, black cabs. Traffic and lights were chaotic near Trafalgar Square, the sun glinting off the gray sheen of the Thames. There was Big Ben, the Houses of Parliament. She'd never thought to actually be here. Her pulse raced, lightness growing in her chest.

She glanced up and found Loki stared too. At her.

A small smile played over those supple lips, and shadows near his corner of the car deepened his cheekbones, made his eyes dark, enigmatic pools.

Heat coiled and twisted inside her.

She'd woken up on the plane to find her book carefully placed in an empty seat, bookmark in place, a blanket draped over her. Her head on his shoulder. Loki slept beside her, his chin lightly resting on her head, their hands still joined.

What if he was different than all the legends had portrayed him? Different, indeed, than she'd long imagined him. He'd spent likely thousands of dollars on this trip to find the other War candidates with no complaint, no word about the money, other than when he'd offered to give her more. He didn't even believe any of the candidates could or should rise but had accepted the quest for her sake. He could have found another way to manipulate her into rising, could have left her in Beckwell, homeless and desperate until she rose, never knowing there'd been any other possibility.

Never having seen Three Points, or bits of Chicago and Oak Park. Or London.

The idea of a happy ending like in one of her books had always seemed so far-fetched for her, a War heir. Because she'd never experienced anything remotely as intense, as exhilarating and tempting as she did when she was with Loki.

Loki, who wasn't immortal, but who would die like a mortal man. Who was sneaky about comforting her on the plane because he knew her pride would object. Loki, who wanted her to rise…and kill him.

CHAPTER 19

There was much to be said for the familiar comfort of luxury, Loki considered an hour or so after their arrival in London. He fastened the last button on his waistcoat and adjusted his black bow tie in front of the hall mirror in their hotel suite. He and Anna were sharing again, though this time he had a bed of his own, and Rojo and Thor were down the hall. While Anna and the pigeon appeared to be getting along, Rojo had glommed onto Thor, and Anna seemed grateful for the respite. Before they could rest, though, they would have to run the third War candidate through the gauntlet.

Trevor may have made some questionable decisions when it came to selecting Anna's delectable wardrobe—especially that nightgown—but the accommodations had been excellent, this one most of all, booking them at Loki's favorite London lodgings, Hotel 41. Located just behind Buckingham Palace, the small boutique hotel occupied the upper story of The Rubens at the Palace Hotel and was decorated with a dominant black-and-white theme, eclectic in taste, but perfect comfort and exceptional service. He attempted to lure away the staff each time he stayed here, but no luck yet.

He reached for his suit jacket, shrugging the fitted piece over his shoulders when the second bedroom door opened, and Anna walked out.

The rest of the world ceased to exist outside of Anna Fray in that gown.

She froze in the doorway, played with the shimmering crystal drop earrings. Her hair was pulled out of her face and to one side with a comb while the rest fell in soft waves around her shoulders. The sleek black gown—another vintage piece—floated over her curves, showed her as the goddess she was. Two sparkling rhinestone starbursts pulled and held the neckline of the gown open, revealing creamy, delicious flesh and collarbones before it dipped in a deep V to her breasts.

"Are you sure this is acceptable?" She touched one of the starbursts, drawing his gaze, hardening his body, making him wonder if there was a zipper he'd have to undo in the back...or if he could simply peel the gown down her shoulders.

What in the name of Ymir had Trevor been thinking with this gown?

Perhaps the same thing as with that white nightgown.

Even worse, he vaguely recalled granting permission to pull it out of storage, listened to the details that it had barely been worn, would likely fit Anna and suit the needs of a formal occasion.

Ah, yes. It hadn't mattered then, because he'd idiotically thought he was beyond the desire and need for Anna. His past self was an arrogant moron.

"Loki? I asked if maybe I should change. There's another black dress, though not as fancy as this one. Perhaps it would be better." She frowned, caught her lip between her teeth. Color stained her cheekbones as she studied the black-and-white tiled floor. She turned back toward the bedroom. "I don't know what I was thinking…"

He gently touched her shoulder. A zipper ran along her spine, the black crepe soft beneath his fingers, warmed by her skin. Her hair brushed over him.

"No," he said, voice rough.

She glanced at him over her shoulder, a dark brow rising, along with a spark of heat in that blue gaze. "No?"

"You look…" Delicious. Ravishing. Seductive. "…lovely." His usually agile brain was slow to offer up the necessary words. "Forgive me. It must be the jet lag." Which he'd never suffered from in his life. "Please, don't change. The gown is perfect on you."

Though damaging to his peace of mind. That likely had less to do with the gown and more to do with the woman herself.

He forced himself to back away, to keep his hands to himself and keep his distance. Though at the moment, all the reasons why they couldn't or shouldn't be intimate escaped him.

She turned slowly. Looked him up and down as he remembered the state of his poor jacket and pulled it on.

Anna studied him a moment before closing the distance between them. Her gaze never left his as she smoothed the jacket over his shoulders. Her hands on him, smoothing over tight muscle, burning through the fabric, focusing his mind on her touch, anticipating what she would do next.

At this rate, he'd soon be known as the god of slow wit.

"You look quite nice yourself," she rasped, her hands on him, deep blue gaze dark, inviting.

Through the door behind her, the luxurious and welcoming bed with its white duvet called to him, invited him to tear off the jacket he'd just put on. He'd push down her dress as he danced her back into the room. To hell with tonight's event, with the War candidate, with Rojo and Thor, with—

His plan.

The plan he'd carefully worked toward for more than a century.

The plan that would give humanity a fighting chance.

When he spoke, his voice was as stiff as his movements away from her, toward the door and entrance hall. "Rojo and Thor will be waiting. We certainly don't want to miss the event and Mr. Martin, do we? Or have you changed your mind about rising, Hadrianna?"

The broadside was clumsy, nearly spiteful.

But from the way her jaw hardened, her shoulders straightened, and her chin came up, eyes sparkling, he'd scored a direct hit.

A pity, really, to not get the smallest sense of satisfaction.

She swished past him and out into the hall.

Worse, a hollow ache bloomed in his chest while she knocked briskly on the door to Thor and Rojo's suite.

Better he pushed her away for the needs of the plan. Better to accustom himself to her not being there.

ೞ

Another sleek black Town Car and driver took Anna, Loki, Thor, and Rojo—the latter once more secured in her handbag, this a black sparkling one—from the hotel behind Buckingham Palace the relatively short distance to the other side of St. James's Park. She was careful to take a seat opposite Loki and place her purse on the seat, which left Loki and Thor seated next to each other. She couldn't afford the distraction. She needed to find this third candidate and assess his suitability.

Two gods, looking rather…godly in sophisticated black evening wear. Thor's red hair had been tamed and queued back, and Goddess knew where the tux had come from, never mind one large enough to cover his muscle-bound frame. Ha. Nia would have said he looked like a constipated penguin, though a relatively good-looking one.

Gaia, what she would have given to have them here with her. Helping her find the real War instead of insisting she come home and rise with them. Maybe she should have been more insistent, better explained how she felt. There was a reason War was the last to rise. She wasn't as strong as them, not able to access the good side of her abilities like they could.

Her gaze slid toward Loki. Maybe if they'd been here, she wouldn't have been so drawn to him, dapper and irresistible in his tux. The way the jacket accentuated his broad shoulders made him exceptionally debonair and mysterious. Nia would have said something caustic, forcing Anna to ignore him, suppress her reaction to him. Ginny and Piper would have been on the look-out for every shared glance, the way he lightly touched her, seemingly without clear intent.

They weren't here. There was no buffer.

Thanks to him, her stomach was in knots, and she could barely enjoy the short ride as they passed the likes of Westminster Abbey and Big Ben. All she could think of was the way he'd looked at her, the heat in his gaze that had lit an answering fire in her belly.

But when she'd dared touch him, he'd turned into master-manipulator Loki, pushing her away.

Which was for the best, considering her irrational and growing attraction for him. It was this candidate, Walter Martin, who mattered.

Their Town Car pulled into the queue to drop them alongside Banqueting House, an impressive edifice and part of the original Whitehall Palace. The classical, Palladian–style building with its uniform symmetrical windows, two stories of dignified columns and pilasters was another impressive edifice among the other sand-colored buildings surrounding it. Straight out of the history books despite the modern double-deckers, black cabs, and other cars driving the busy road in front of them.

Thor leaned forward. "So, we go in, cosh the bugger?" He rubbed the head of his goat-headed walking stick.

To her, the truth revealed itself, the faint, translucent image of Thor's blocky embellished hammer, not unlike a fancy toaster on a stick, overlaid the image of the walking stick, the lie of its disguise.

Rojo popped his head out of her purse. "Can we? Talk about a test of War abilities!"

Loki checked to ensure the driver couldn't hear them, the privacy window up. "There will be no coshing, bashing, or any violence not directed by Hadrianna or myself," Loki said, a mild edge to his voice.

Anna's lips tightened. Back to Hadrianna, were they?

"It is imperative we don't reveal our identities too soon," Loki continued. "The Martins are essentially royalty when it comes to the War clan. Other War clansmen may be present, never mind a good deal of British elite with requisite security. Moreover, our previous excursions and purpose may have preceded us. My staff was able to secure us tickets to this coveted social event, a charity event for War Widows and Children, hosted by the Martins. The names on the guest list are Luke Farbausson and Anne Fields." He turned his look on Thor. "Fortunately for you, even at the last minute we were able to secure an additional ticket for Theo Wilson."

Thor looked around the car, behind him, then pointed a sausage finger into his chest. "That's supposed to be me?"

Loki's smile was positively devious. "Unless you'd

prefer a gown and the name Theodora?"

Thor's face reddened and his hands fisted. "That was one time, one dress, and disguising myself as Freyja was *your* idea."

"Heimdall's, actually." Loki was still smiling as their car pulled in front of Banqueting House. The driver opened the door, and Loki climbed out first. He turned and held a hand out to Anna.

She pressed Rojo's head back into the purse and zipped it closed, grasping her long black skirts with one hand and Loki's warm fingers with the other. As much as she'd like to ignore his help, she'd probably only trip and fall on her face. Hardly a subtle entrance.

Loki pulled her aside to make room as Thor clambered out, pulled her closer to him.

A rush of heat flooded through her, more irritating for its growing familiarity.

"Are you ready?" Loki asked, his voice a low rumble through her, his thumb sliding over hers.

She pulled her hand from his, adjusted her purse, and smoothed her skirts. Enough of his rejections, of him pushing her away. Raising her chin, she met his pewter gaze that flashed with annoyed amber.

"Are you?" she challenged, then turned, offered a gracious smile to their driver, and headed toward the entrance.

Damn Loki and Thor anyway. Walter Martin was in there, was War royalty, and the suitable War heir she'd searched for.

Leaving the two Norse gods to follow, she entered the double doors beneath the bust of King Charles I and stepped into the cavernous golden-lit space of Banqueting House. Solicitous women in sleek black dresses checked guests' names against the list before guiding them down the stairs toward what they called the Undercroft.

Loki caught her arm, tucking her hand on his

muscular forearm as she started down the stairs. His grip was gentle but firm enough she'd make a scene by pulling away among the other glittering guests, most of the women in evening gowns and jewels.

"We need to stay together," Loki murmured.

"Do we, 'Luke'?" She batted her eyes at his glare and emphasized his pseudonym, though her voice was likewise pitched low. "I don't have the patience for your games, for the way you twist me around in circles. I need to find Walter Martin and hopefully the solution I've been looking for."

"I'm not playing games. I'm trying to keep you safe," he said tightly as they stepped down onto the polished stone floor of the Undercroft.

Warm up-lighting emulated candlelight and accentuated the broad, interconnected arches of the cavernous space, making the space at once airy and cryptlike. Well-dressed guests socialized on carefully placed cocktail tables or perched on low, black sofas and poufs.

"I can take care of myself," she said, tugging at her arm.

He gave her a dark look but relinquished his hold before he looked over her head at, she guessed from the shadow, was the looming form of Thor. "Keep an eye on her. I'll take the other side of the room, see if I can flush out our host." Despite his size, Loki seemed to melt easily into the crowd after one more dark, flashing glare.

Leaving Thor's bulk next to her. Two little fist fights, and what happened to her being able to take care of herself? She could take care of herself, thank you kindly.

"What does the guy look like?" Thor rumbled, walking stick/hammer still clutched in his right hand. He readjusted and tightened his grip on its handle.

"Tall, dark-haired. I couldn't tell height from the profiles on the charity page." Though there was a long list of businesses and charities associated with the good-looking man. Not Loki good-looking, but good lines, strong jaw, determined brown eyes.

"A quest," Thor breathed out with a smile. "Been ages since I was last on one. Sif forbids them. Says I drink too much, cause trouble, that it's not the same world it once was, nonsense like that." His blue gaze raked the crowd. His gaze went past, then quickly redirected back to the bar. "I'm supposed to stay here…"

This was almost too easy. If Loki thought he was the only one who could direct the plot, he was sorely mistaken. She kept her voice airy, as though she didn't care. "The hostesses said the drinks are free. Isn't that lovely?"

"Free?" Thor rumbled. "Well, one drink never has hurt anyone." He took a step toward the bar, then turned and stalked back with a dark glower. He wagged a warning finger. "Now you stay right here, see. I'll be right back."

Anna widened her eyes, as though she hadn't already plotted her escape route. "Of course." She patted his huge forearm. "You go get that drink. No harm in enjoying yourself a bit, is there?"

His expression brightened. "There's a bright woman. See why Loki likes you." He turned and happily strode through and over anyone unlucky enough to block his path to the open bar.

"That wasn't nice, lying like that," Rojo said from her purse. "Loki will be mad at him, and it'll be because of you."

Anna ducked through the crowd, looking for her quarry and watching out for Loki. She nodded her head in vague greeting at some of the guests she passed and searched for the brunets, a man likely about her height, trying to peer around the wide square base of the arching columns. The photo hadn't suggested much about

Martin's build either. He was either camera shy…or wary what was posted about him.

Unlike Thor, she slid through the crowd easily. They were growing in number, collected together in sparkling clutches. The whispers of their sins, their secrets brushed past her like doves' wings, just beneath the rumbling din of conversation.

"You're worried your hero can't handle himself with Loki?" she murmured quietly to the pigeon.

Rojo snorted. "Thor could wipe the ground with Loki." A pause. "He's just…not the sharpest sword on the rack. You might be shrewdest of any of the Wars I remember. For a woman. But it isn't fair, tricking Thor. Like fooling a child."

"A large, deadly child who's killed Goddess knows how many," she whispered back, pausing near one of the columns. That last chestnut-haired man hadn't looked like Martin either.

She chewed her lip. He was supposed to be hosting the event. He should be in the midst of a group. Yet every man she'd tracked down who fit the description hadn't been him.

The small of her back tingled, a small itch that wasn't from the silky gown. The back of her neck tightened. She paused, let awareness soak through her, let War's flames spark.

"Has no one offered you champagne or canapes? You're in the middle of one of the defining events of the season, yet here you, a beautiful woman, stands alone, hands empty, no company in sight," a masculine British voice said from behind her.

Her lower back burned now, but she forced herself to keep her expression neutral, to turn slowly. She already suspected who stood behind her, so it was no surprise to find the brown-haired, brown-eyed Walter Martin, War clan when she turned.

His profile photo hadn't done him justice. He was taller than her, not quite as broad as Loki, but trim, fit, and muscular. There was warmth in his gaze as it skimmed over her, a pleasant smile curving supple lips. In his fitted black tux and bow tie, he could have stepped out of one of her romance novels.

She stuck out her hand. She'd dispense of this quickly, read his truth, and decide how to proceed from there. "I don't drink, and I'm quite happy in my own company. Anne Fields. You are?"

Instead of shaking her hand as she'd hoped, he caught her hand and brought her knuckles briefly to his lips.

The action surprised a small gasp from her and made her want to pull her hand away, which jumbled the vision, garbled the truth.

Just a brief image of him emerging from the black, dapper and whistling, a red-stained, dripping sack slung over his shoulder.

The image vanished, replaced by a strong sense of peace, like a heavy, weighted blanket pulled over her head, smothering out the world.

War's fire lurched inside of her, incinerating the blanket. Leaving her staring at Martin, her expression tight.

The smile had similarly slipped from his lips. His brown gaze grew wary, though he was quick to set the smile back in place. "An American. How refreshing. I'm Walter Martin, host of this humble affair."

Her smile was knife-edged, her back itchy, that blanket of peace trying to sneak up on her again. "Canadian, actually. The event is hardly humble."

"Canadian? Even better." His smile broadened, and he leaned in conspiratorially. Charming dimples appeared on both cheeks, softening him. "No, it's hardly humble, is it?"

He took her hand and tucked it on his arm, much as Loki had done.

Honestly, did men think she'd turned into some helpless creature incapable of even directing her own arm's actions? Worse, too much fabric separated them. If he'd been a Normal, they'd have been plenty close enough to get a read, but for another War, she needed skin-to-skin contact.

"Come, let's stroll," he said, not waiting for an answer. "If I stay still too long, someone is sure to corner me in dull conversation." Martin smiled and exchanged brief conversation with some of those they passed.

"Seeing as you didn't wait for my answer one way or the other, I suppose let's," Anna said, a touch of acid in her words. That warning itch still tingled on her lower back.

Her words didn't slow Martin's step, nor the ease with which he greeted other guests, slipped them through the crowd.

"True. But then, you're hardly a common guest, are you?" he said lightly. "Your name isn't Anne Fields."

The itch on her back intensified.

"Are you threatening me?" she asked quietly.

He laughed, those dimples reappearing as he turned to her. "Not at all. We both know what a mistake that would be, one War threatening another, especially in such a dense crowd. All that unnecessary aggression, getting people worked up over nothing." He cocked his head, that smile still teasing.

Faint warmth pulsed through her, welcoming and bright. He was a rather charming scoundrel.

He raised a brow. "Though, I confess a great curiosity to know who you are. The other clans have that over us, don't they? How they mix and mingle without care. We're left quite to our own ingenuity."

He patted her hand quickly, and her shoulders eased.

It had always seemed unfair, how isolated the members of the War clan were. Even among her friends, marriage between clan families made logical sense, as it had for Ginny and James, both Famine clan.

Not so for the War clan.

"It is rather silly I've always thought," she confessed, her tongue seeming to loosen around him. A bit peculiar, really. Perhaps it was merely his open charm, so different than Loki's machinations. "And unfair. If the clans are immune to each other, shouldn't clansman and women be afforded the same?"

"My thought as well," Martin said, pulling her into a quiet alcove, away from the other guests.

Her pulse fluttered, and her muscles tightened.

Martin released his hold on her, leaned back against a column, one hand casually tucked in a pocket. There was a smile in his eyes, something in that sweet brown gaze that said she needn't be afraid, that he was no enemy. "Come then. Let's prove them wrong. I certainly feel no aggression toward you. Quite the opposite, I should say." His lips curved.

Nice lips. Kind lips.

"Confess. What's the harm in telling me your name? I already know you're War and that you came here likely looking for me. You even needed an extra invite for that extraordinarily large fellow at the bar drinking us out of stock."

"Perhaps this is all tactical strategy," she said, hesitant. The light was soft here, the temperature warm, comforting, yet there was something…peculiar. A strange peacefulness.

Martin chuckled, the sound making her want to smile, easing her concerns. "Spoken like a true War." He crossed his arms over that broad chest. "Fine then. I swear I will not attack you and that my curiosity is no play. Judge the truth of that."

Her neck remained warm, pleasantly so, like the rest of her body. There was no hint of deceit in his words. Furthermore, what advantage was there in knowing her name?

"Anna Fray," she said. "Well, technically Hadrianna."

Another warm chuckle. The warning itch on her back seemed to have gone away. Or at least, she didn't notice it now.

"Indeed. Gods forbid a War not have a suitably ferocious and storied name. Walter is old Germanic for 'ruler of the army.'"

Despite herself, the smile that spread her lips was genuine. "I'd expect nothing less for a Martin."

He laughed now, his entire expression lightening, answering warmth growing within her. This was quite lovely. Weightless pleasure suffused her.

"As though the Frays are a family to scoff at. One of the original twenty-five," he said, amusement still putting dancing light in his warm brown gaze.

She leaned against the other side of the broad, tapered column. Perhaps this was the way to have conducted their investigation from the start. Extremely un-War-like. Straight-forward, honest. Pleasant.

"Is it true what they say then? About your family?" she said.

He quirked a brow, and one corner of his lips rose higher than the other. "Pray tell, what do they say?" His look and the darkening of his gaze made her face heat at the unintended innuendo.

"Oh. I didn't mean—"

He reached forward, his fingers brushing her face as he tucked her hair behind her ear.

Her unease settled. Vanished. More warmth, leaving only the sense of how lovely it was to stay here, talking to him.

"Is what true? The abilities? We have some. Though it wasn't long ago the Frays were one of the few clan families to rival ours in that area." He took a small step closer, his voice dropping. "A shame, that we be rivals when one considers all we could accomplish together."

His eyes were the most amazing caramel shade. She'd never felt so…at peace with another person. No reason to object, no reason to fight.

"That is true," she said, a small flutter starting low in her belly.

"Anne. There you are," another male voice said, harder, darker. "I'd begun to worry."

There was a brief, cold tingle at her neck. The other man was lying. He'd already been worried. But Martin—no, Walter—had taken her hand and stared deeply into her eyes. The cold faded, along with any thought of the other man.

"I'm fine," she said, her voice soft.

"You sure about that, Princess?" This time the voice rose from her purse, sounding unconvinced and a little worried.

"Anna, together we could accomplish remarkable things," Walter said, his smile so warm, so welcoming. Safe.

She'd never have to hide her past with him, what she could or couldn't do. He was right. There wasn't the usual aggression between them. Perhaps that meant something.

"We really could, couldn't we?" she said, her voice breathless at the thought. All the other clans could safely intermarry. Perhaps she and Walter could show the others how it was done. Change their clan and their future for the better.

"Princess, I don't know what you were drinking, but you are seriously looped," the voice from her purse said. "Snap out of it. Get your game face on."

This time, though Walter's smile never dimmed, he

turned toward her purse with a quizzical look. "Did a voice just come from your handbag?"

She couldn't seem to look away from his eyes, how good just looking at him made her feel. "Hmm? Yes. That's…" She had to dredge through her mind for the name. "That's Rojo." She laughed. "Pardon me. Maximus Rojo. The War horse."

"Anna, you need to step away from him," that other man said, the one not in her purse.

She went to turn and frown at him, a faint tingle in her lower back.

Walter touched her jaw with a gentle hand, kept her focused on him. Melted away her thoughts until only he remained. "*The* War horse?" he asked, his voice still calm, still friendly.

"Yes. Isn't that crazy? Although…" She frowned, that strange tickle again on her lower back. She tried to ignore it. "Perhaps I should say your horse?"

More peace suffused her body, softened her shoulders, dulled that irritating itch.

Walter gave her a pleased smile.

Such lovely brown eyes he had.

"Anna. Please. Take my hand." That other man again.

"You'd like to give me that horse, wouldn't you, luv?" Walter's beautiful brown gaze seemed to see into her soul, saw exactly what she wanted.

Yet…not quite so gorgeous, as bewitching as another gaze.

A vague tingle in her back again.

She looked down, surprised to find her arm outstretched, offering her purse to Walter.

He took it from her with another smile.

"Anna!" That other man.

No…not man…

"Just a little longer, and you won't ever have to

worry again," Walter said, his hand on her face. "You won't ever be afraid again. Or alone. Or have to be brave."

The tingle was back, an itch, intense and burning on her back. That other voice cut through the softness of her thoughts. Familiar, maddening, alluring... Anything but peaceful.

"Anna, please. Take. My. Hand," that other man urged. He reached for her.

The touch of his fingertips on her elbow sent hint scorching through her. Desire.

Loki.

Fire flared through her. Burned away the sense of well-being, safety, and peace. The lies. Scoured away all but the truth.

Her fingers closed around Loki's, and she jerked away from Martin. From his brown gaze, his manipulation.

Her back burned, along with her face. What had Martin done to her? How could she have been so stupid? She let War's fire wash through her, sharpen her vision, her clarity.

"Are you okay?" Loki murmured, his hot, muscular chest behind her back.

She nodded, not daring to take her gaze off Martin, the little weasel. He was shorter than her when for some reason she'd thought him taller. Unlike Loki's light cedar scent, Martin smelled of overpowering cologne. His gaze was mud-colored, and there was a cruel twist to his lips. He'd manipulated her so easily. Gaia, what had he done to her?

What had she almost let him do? A chill chased down her spine.

"I'm okay," she said, but there was a tremor in her voice.

Martin held her classy little purse aloft, his smile still even. "Thank you, Anna. This has been a more successful evening than I could have dreamed." He unzipped the purse.

An enraged ball of gray and white feathers flew out of the purse and into his face. "Fight dirty, will you?"

Feathers scattered and swears filled the air as Rojo attacked Walter Martin. Going for the eyes, the nose. Biting and pulling at an ear, pecking his cheeks. Even grabbing Martin's lip and dragging the man to the ground. "Think you can attack my Princess, do you?"

Martin's cries for help as he attempted to crawl away from the pigeon drew guests toward them.

"It's her. Arrest her!" Martin tried to shout to his security team even as Rojo attempted to ram his feathered rear-end into the man's mouth.

The pigeon twisted, bit down hard onto Martin's bleeding nose.

Martin howled.

Muscular men in black suits rushed through the crowd of shocked onlookers.

They met the wall that was Thor.

Anna winced as the god—easily twice the size of most of the men—roared and bowled through the guards and security. It felt like she should do something...but Rojo and Thor did have things well in hand.

Plus, she'd made such an idiot of herself. Could she trust herself near Martin? Bile rose in her throat.

Martin had begun to cry, begging for quarter as Rojo pulled out beakfuls of hair.

A few of the male guests looked at each other, then moved toward Anna.

She tensed.

Loki wrapped an arm around her, placed himself slightly in front of her. "The only criminal in this room is on the floor, begging for your help. I suggest you more closely examine his so-called charities and their accounting practices. You'll likely see as I did the large discrepancies and funds disappearing into Mr. Martin's personal accounts. Now, if you'll excuse us." He bent and retrieved her purse, handed it to her wordlessly.

Then he led her through the still frozen guests, back up the stairs, and out onto the street.

A faint damp chill had settled in. Twilight had fallen, headlights glowing on the passing cars and buses, the classical buildings around them grayer in the deepening light.

She followed Loki as he led them back toward the busy road, then along the broad sidewalk beside the outside of Banqueting House, tall trees growing out of their small square of allotted earth.

Gaia, what had happened? She'd recognized Martin as a threat. Had noticed the first time that…peace blanket attempted to smother her. Yet somehow, he'd snuck beneath her defenses. Had her gazing up at him like his lapdog. She shivered, wrapping her arms around herself.

Loki slipped off his tux jacket and wrapped it around her shoulders, the soft fabric still warm from his body. "Just breathe. You're safe."

She'd let Martin touch her. Had been prepared to give him everything. *Would* have given him everything. She shivered again, the cold coming from inside. Safe now, but she'd been such a fool.

She glanced back at the grand old building as they continued down the road. "Should we wait for Thor and Rojo?"

"They're likely enjoying themselves." Loki reached into his pocket for his phone. "I'll text Thor to tell him to meet us if you like."

Loki texting Thor. The Asgardians had gone modern.

She nodded, then massaged her aching forehead. Trembles and nausea settled over her. She'd thought she'd been prepared. Then she'd barely felt Martin's attack, and he'd won. Oh Goddess, how easily he'd won.

How far would he have let it go? What else might she have given him? She swallowed back the rising bile.

"Try to think of something else." Loki pointed down the road they crossed.

Visible through the trees was the slowly turning, cantilevered Ferris wheel, like a huge thin-spoked bicycle wheel turning slowly from its island in the Thames.

"The London Eye," he said.

Lights illuminated the wheel, the round cars it carried and the safe, clueless tourists inside. Her gaze returned to him. His profile was strong and hard, nose almost hawk-like. When he appeared in books, he was more often the villain than the hero.

Perhaps she'd been reading the wrong books.

"When did you have time to examine his accounting practices?"

He didn't look at her, his brows furrowed, hands tucked in his tux pockets. "On the plane ride to Chicago."

Her breath hitched. Which meant he'd known long before today that Martin was unsuitable.

Images of his insistence to stay close, his careful layout of their plan, the tension riding him all evening. He'd been trying to protect her, while still allowing her the chance to discover Martin's character for herself.

Faex.

"Thank you. For back there...for everything," she said quietly.

He glanced at her, his white shirt still crisp, dark waistcoat flawless. An almost-frown creased his brow. He nodded, then turned back to the path ahead, pointing. "Unless you'd prefer to ride, it's a rather nice walk back. We can cut through St. James's Park if you're inclined."

She nodded because the only words circling through her head declared again and again what an idiot she'd been. The other two War candidates had been dangerous. She'd been stupid to underestimate this one. Especially a

Martin.

Loki, though, didn't lecture her on leaving him, or on ditching Thor. Didn't even go over the ways things could have gone worse or how easily they could have gone worse. Nor on how they should have gone differently. He just walked beside her, offered his coat, and tried to distract her. Her throat thickened.

"He's stronger than me," she said, voice barely above a whisper. "Charity conman or not, I don't even know what he did, nor did I realize in time to stop it."

They continued a few more steps before Loki answered, cars rushing past them, tourists snapping photos of some of the buildings they passed. Up ahead in the distance was a tall, Gothic tower that might have been part of Westminster Cathedral.

"He's not stronger, simply more practiced. The Martins may be an influential War family, but none of them has ever risen. Nor should they. The more influential clan families seem inclined to use their abilities for self-profit, as though whatever harm they cause doesn't matter. You have more ability than him, more than Wiebe and Tildy combined."

"If you knew this, why bring us here anyway? Why not tell me all this back home? It would have saved us both time, money, and effort."

He shrugged, his voice nonplussed. "You wouldn't have believed me."

They crossed the street, walking along past more regal stone buildings, the façade of white brick topped with columns and broad windows. Iconic red telephone booths dotted the street, while ahead was the dense greenery of St. James's Park.

"I also wanted you to see there is so much more to the world than Beckwell. To give you the freedom you haven't allowed yourself," he said.

This time when she looked up, she fell headlong into

his gaze. Then promptly tripped over her own feet.

He caught her, hesitated.

She captured his hand, tangled her fingers with his. She didn't have the words to say what she felt. Maybe she should have countered with the acerbic response that he was only willing to give her this taste of freedom before he saw her trapped as War. There was only one candidate remaining—and a disheartening likelihood the woman would be any better than the others.

Leaving Anna to rise as War. It seemed more likely all the time there was no freedom for her. War would win. She was just as susceptible to its corruption as the other candidates had been, but she seemed to resist more than the other candidates had. At least she tried.

She'd rise…and then Loki would insist she kill him. It seemed impossible to consider killing another human. Worse still if it was Loki.

She said none of that. Somehow, she couldn't, not with all this experience had shown her of the world. Of him.

Worse, though, was the rising warmth inside her, the muddled-up hot and cold, lust and fear, courage and cowardice whenever she was around Loki. There was none of the peace she'd felt with Walter. Just the peculiar rightness of her hand in Loki's that was no conman's trick.

Gaia help her if she was just fooling herself and Loki was the ultimate con.

CHAPTER 20

Anna was doing that thing where she scrambled his brain and made him consider impossible things. The worst of it, Loki decided as he took a sip of his water, perhaps an hour since leaving Banqueting House behind, was that she was unaware she was even doing it. She defeated him effortlessly. With the feelings aroused after seeing her at the mercy of Martin, the prospect of their shared hotel room seemed...dangerous, and the quick way she'd accepted the invitation for drinks suggested she felt the same.

Across the small round table, in the midst of the Cavalry Bar's cream walls, old-world elegance, and buttoned leather club chairs, she quizzed Thor on drinking a giant under the table. The dim golden light made her skin glow, picked up red highlights in her chestnut hair and glinted off the rhinestone decoration on her gown. His jacket remained draped around her shoulders. She laughed at something Thor said and challenged him on some small detail of history.

She knew a great deal about the Norse legends. His legends. Which was somewhat discomfiting. One hoped she knew better than to believe it all—good and bad.

Rojo dozed in her purse that sat open on the table. No one seemed concerned about the pigeon.

He and Anna had barely made it back to the hotel when Thor and Rojo arrived in a black cab, jubilant with their victory and battle. Ymir only knew which of them had had the wherewithal to summon the cab. Perhaps someone else had, in hopes of being rid of them. Still, no authorities followed them, nor an infuriated Martin clan, so that was something.

It was still tempting to return to Banqueting House and teach that cowardly whelp, Martin, a lesson or two on how one treated a lady, but that would have meant leaving her alone and vulnerable. When he'd found her entranced, alone, and glassy-eyed with that two-bit-lying sack of raven shit, he'd nearly gone berserk. Only the danger of the violence he could have unleashed, aggravating two Wars, had stilled his hand.

He sipped at his water. A pity it wasn't something stronger.

She downed the remainder of her amber-colored drink—at least her fourth by his count—a single-malt this time before she lowered it to join the other glasses that cluttered their table. Some of them were Rojo's, more of them were hers and Thor's. She appeared determined to outdrink Thor, who'd once almost drank the oceans dry on a bet. She flicked the god's hand away from her drink, seemingly fearless of him. Her lips on her new glass, her gaze met and lingered on Loki's across the table.

Lust seared through him. He tried to tamp it down with a sip of ice water, but he'd need to shower in it for it to help.

Thor laughed good-naturedly, his nose red with drink, but not enough to satiate him for the night. He pushed Anna's drink toward her with one large hand, but she didn't seem to care.

Seeing the two of them, comfortable with each other and his company, awakened that old ache. The one that watched his parents interact with his siblings in a far different way than they had he, the scrawny one. The one that reluctantly returned to Asgard with Odin, met new faces, found new hope that this time history would not repeat itself.

The foolish ache that never seemed to learn, never burned itself out. No matter the alcohol he'd once drowned it with.

It was worst around Anna. Renewed in strength.

He glanced down at his fingers on his glass. She took his hand so easily, seemed to change who and what he was with her touch. The same touch that awakened the familiar ache inside.

He could slow her drinks. Though she was an intelligent woman and would undoubtedly neither appreciate nor need his interference. She'd thanked him for interceding this evening with Martin, but she had to realize how things could have ended.

Perhaps it was the thought of Martin that made her hand tremble on her glass, the distant look in her eyes before she took a long draw of her scotch.

Loki ground his jaw. Modern woman that she was, she would not have appreciated him striking Martin either. Though it would have been immensely satisfying.

"Same old Loki," Thor was saying, the sound of his name sharpening Loki's focus.

Indeed, he found himself the focus of both Thor's amused, bloodshot gaze and Anna's more somber blue gaze.

Thor chuckled. "Plotting, plotting, always plotting, that Loki." He held up his empty glass, belching loud enough to make the glasses on the table tremble.

Loki grimaced.

Anna made a face.

Rojo snored on.

Thor held his glass out at Anna. "Gets himself in trouble, all that plotting." He tapped his forehead. "Too much in here." Then he banged his chest. "Not enough here."

Ah, another familiar feeling, the heat suffusing his body and curdling his stomach. Loki set down his glass before he crushed it and gave Thor a bland and warning look.

Thor either didn't notice, didn't care, or both, turning instead to Anna. "Caused his own grief in Asgard. Tricking everyone, playing his games, him and his plots."

Ymir, not this again.

Anna set down her glass, crossed her arms, and raised a brow. "Well, someone had to do the thinking. From the sounds of it, the rest of you were hardly doing much of it."

At least four drinks, but her voice was clear, steady, not a hint of inebriation.

That, and she'd just challenged, potentially insulted Thor, who'd killed men for less.

Loki shifted to the edge of his chair, ready to intercede if necessary. What was she thinking?

For him, no less. Defending him. No one defended him. Not even his own mother.

Thor stared at her a moment, his drink frozen midair partway to his lips. He sucked down the rest of his pint before plunking the empty glass down on the table and raising the waiting full one. He drank half of that down before he spoke, wiping beer suds from his beard with the back of a hand, gesturing with his pint.

"You know, it's lucky I like you. Or I might take offense to a comment like that," he said, wagging a finger.

Anna looked frighteningly unperturbed. And stone

sober. How could she be after matching Thor almost drink-for-drink? Though…her actions were not necessarily those of a sober woman.

"I know the myths aren't gospel, and certainly all of the Asgardians had some redeeming qualities. But can you truly be surprised Loki would eventually abandon you? You act like fools, blame and ridicule him for his intellect—and all he earned you."

Thor was open-mouthed.

Loki shared the sentiment. He really ought to interfere. That, and list all the reasons he needed to keep his distance from Anna. Only the plan mattered…

Thor plunked down his pint, placed both hands on the table, and leaned forward. "Are you daft, woman?"

"Are you? You've just spent the last hour or so regaling me with stories where somehow, you and your fellow gods are always the heroes, whereas Loki, who usually out-witted, out-planned, and out-manned all of you, is nothing but a sulking villain."

A fiery glow grew on Anna's cheekbones, a glint of heat shone in her gaze.

He stared at Anna and found only his War goddess, a creature of fire and heat, of beauty and justice. A woman who stirred something in him he'd thought unreachable. Who made lust and want crash through him with ferocious intensity.

Thor shoved back his chair with a crash, climbed to his feet, his walking stick clenched in his hand. "I would warn you to tread lightly, woman, lest you besmirch the honor of my family and make me break a promise to my wife."

Anna stood smoothly, leaned closer to Thor. "You owe him an apology," she said, her voice low, commanding as she nodded her head toward Loki without looking at him.

Thor's face turned a unique shade of purple. It was

several seconds before he could sputter out words. "I *what*?" He raised his walking stick, his hammer in disguise. "I ought to—"

Loki stood swiftly.

Not fast enough.

Anna grabbed the walking stick.

It shimmered and transformed in her hand. In War's hand. The walking stick handle thickened, grew an enormous wide square base until it appeared as the great hammer, Mjolnir, the weight of which no one other than Thor could bear alone.

Thor...and possibly Anna. She yanked Mjolnir right out of the god's hand. Then held it behind her back like an angry mother withholding a toy.

Thor's mouth fell open. His eyes widened. He stared from Anna to his empty hand. Waggled his fingers, as though to confirm they were indeed empty.

Power crackled through the room, tingled against Loki's skin like lightning, the scent of ozone in the air. A few bulbs in the fixtures above popped in a shower of sparks.

Even Rojo had stirred and stared at Anna, beak falling open. "Well...damn."

She was illuminated, fierce, and glorious in the flaring light.

Threatening Thor with his own hammer, as no other being had ever done before.

"Your. Apology," she enunciated.

Threatening Thor on Loki's behalf.

Something welled and grew in Loki's chest. A warmth that started out friendly but quickly grew hotter, fiercer. Hungrier.

At that moment, Anna wielded the power of War to use all weapons. A small push and she might have risen right then. Said thoughts flickered briefly through his mind but were eclipsed by the sheer magnificence of the woman before him.

Of Anna.

Thor slid a questioning glance toward Loki, then back to Anna. The god shuffled his huge feet, rubbed his hands down his tree-trunk thighs. "I, uh, sorry, Loki," he mumbled, then glanced at Anna. "Can I have my hammer back now?"

"Not until you apologize like you mean it. For all the times you assumed something was Loki's fault when it wasn't. For all the ways you were cruel and thoughtless, you and your fellow gods, excluding him, never letting him fully into your family. You should promise to try and improve that behavior. To treat him better," Anna said.

Another nervous glance from Thor, who massaged the back of his neck with a grimace. "We didn't, ah, think it mattered. I mean, Loki was never really one of us and—"

He swallowed at Anna's dark look.

"I mean, uh, sorry 'bout all that, Loki. Really sorry."

Once, it had mattered. When he'd first hoped to have found a surrogate family after his parents tossed him out like so much rubbish. Before hope had begun to fade and reality proved, again and again, he seemed to be the connecting factor in all the negative outcomes, all the betrayal. But now...

"And..." Anna prompted, balancing the massive hammer on her shoulder like it was a delicate parasol when it usually took two gods to heft it.

"And?" Thor looked hopelessly puzzled. Undoubtedly because until this moment, he'd always been the one to make the threats, not receive them. He frowned so hard in concentration, trying to figure out what Anna wanted, he was likely to strain something.

"Anna," Loki said softly.

"I'm going to get you the apology you deserve," she said, still glowering at Thor as though he weren't easily two feet taller than her. "I know you like to scheme. Hell, you're probably scheming right now. But you can also be incredibly kind and generous, and no one ever sees that. It's not right."

That's how she saw him?

"It doesn't matter to me," he said softly, moving closer to her. Not anymore. He was used to it for the most part. Unfortunately, Thor wasn't improving with apologies, and Sif would be upset if Anna killed her husband, particularly if she did so with Thor's own hammer.

Finally, Anna turned to him. Her gaze this close was remarkably clear and blue, more beautiful than all the lakes and rivers of Jotunheim. A tremor shook her free hand making her adjust her grip on the hammer. Gaping vulnerability shone in her gaze. She pulled him toward her, like the Earth orbiting the sun.

"Everyone thinks so lowly of you, and you don't deserve it. And if this is the last time I can leave Beckwell and tell them all, well, I think I ought to rectify the mistake, as it were."

The pain in her gaze, the heavy reality that she might have to rise as War scoured through him like a knife to the gut.

Because with her last freedom, she chose to defend him. When he was the one who wanted her to rise.

His fingers settled over hers where she clutched the hammer. "Anna, give Thor his hammer back. Please." His voice was rough, the heat and need burning through him too intense to conceal, what her actions meant to him too monumental to fully consider right now.

Perhaps he could show her. What she meant. How truly wondrous she was. Try to give her some tiny taste of the kindness she gave him. Tonight would be one night of temptation, one night to enjoy the luxury of belonging in Anna's arms.

Her gaze never left his as she lowered the hammer from her shoulder, and, letting it dangle lightly from her fingers, handed it back to Thor as carelessly as handing over a hairbrush.

She bit her lip a second, then lifted her chin, met Loki's gaze boldly. "I'd like to go back to the room now." She paused barely a moment, her voice raspy, eyes dilating. "With you."

She'd almost made the offer before. Still had the courage to make it again despite the many times he'd had to turn her down.

This time, he pulled her closer, wrapped an arm around her waist, and nodded. Then together, they headed for their suite and his bed.

CHAPTER 21

Had she just successfully propositioned Loki, Norse god of mischief and her childhood crush? Anna's pulse was in overdrive, Loki's hand on the small of her back as he led her inside the private wood-paneled entrance for Hotel 41, then into the elevator that would take them to the hotel's lobby.

Back to their suite.

This would have been easier if she'd been drunk, though irresponsible. For once, her War abilities had decided to prove useful. Heat coiled through her, desire unfurling and stealing through her limbs.

This was it. The night she'd planned, well, hoped for. No, not with the being-an-idiot part where she'd fallen for a dangerous con's schtick. But ending the night with incredible sex had to count for something. She'd decided not long after they returned to the bar that tonight she would retake her power, power Martin had tried to steal from her. Tonight, for perhaps the first time ever, she would ask for what she wanted, without fear.

Tonight, she wanted Loki.

Her gaze slid over Loki, who leaned back against the elevator wall, shirt sleeves unbuttoned and rolled up to his elbows, as usual. The charcoal vest only emphasized the breadth of his shoulders, flat belly, trim waist.

She forced her eyes upward. To meet his dark, heavy-lidded stare, shot with amber. His attention focused entirely on her.

A small shiver raced through her. Her nipples hardened under the intensity of Loki's gaze.

She and Loki were attracted to each other, unattached. Tonight would be mutually satisfying. Nothing to do with War, her plans, or his. *Carpe noctem.* Seize the night.

He raised a dark brow in that sexy way of his, that small hint of mustache curving with his lips. "We can go back to the room. Nothing needs to happen."

Kindly, thoughtfully providing an out, as though her plans were ill-conceived and spur of the moment.

As though she hadn't spent days, years, considering exactly how she planned to take advantage of the situation. How if they only had one night together, it would indeed be a night to remember.

She cocked her head. "I don't want to sleep."

His eyes focused on her lips before, seemingly with great effort, he met her gaze. "You've had a lot to drink."

"But I'm not drunk. The second Thor became my opponent, I was sober."

He frowned.

She could barely resist a smile. "You mean I know more about this War ability than you? A War is never drunk for a fight, even if drinking all night before a battle."

He turned her toward him with subtle pressure against her back, sent her pulse racing again. He caught the curtain of her hair with a finger, gently tucked it behind her ear, his lashes dark, shading his amber gaze from her as he studied her face. "Is this a battle?"

Martin had touched her similarly, but it didn't steal her breath the way Loki's touch did. Her every sense grew attuned to that fingertip trailing over her collarbone, tracing the outline of her neckline.

She couldn't look away, mesmerized for the second time that night. Loki's touch left her stronger. Not peaceful, on fire. Not without worry, but prickling with life.

It took her a moment to process his words, to form a response. "Not battle, no. Pleasure. Distraction. Sex," she said, her lips curving around the last as she watched the way it lit an amber flare in his gaze.

His fingertip continued its journey along the neckline of her gown, pausing before it dipped to follow the gown's deep V between her aching and heavy breasts. "I don't want this to be a drunken mistake you later regret. Our goals remain at odds—what happens tonight won't change that." His deep voice was rough, full of challenge that sparked rebellion.

She leaned closer, pressed her body against his, their hips aligned, her softness cradling his unmistakable hardness.

He hissed out a breath, and his hand tightened against her back, pulled her closer.

She cupped his jaw, brushed her thumb over his lips, over that thin mustache above his lips. They whiskers tickled her fingertips. "I'm not drunk. I won't regret this. I'm not talking marriage, a commitment, or any lies. I'm asking for one night where we can indulge in fantasy, where we can enjoy each other. Tomorrow we can go back to our plans and our fears. Not tonight."

Tonight, she could pretend she wasn't between either returning to her non-life in Beckwell or rising as War; either way, the Anna she had been slipping away. Loki saw *her*. Tonight, they'd indulge in each other and pleasure, and she'd feel something other than the cold or fear of tomorrow.

He cupped her face with his hand, his gaze studying hers, searching for something. Perhaps for sobriety or second-thoughts.

Oh, Gaia, please don't let him turn her away again tonight. On top of all the other humiliations of the day, she couldn't bear that. Ipso facto, she needed to be sure he had no excuse to run.

The most direct attack was to slide her hands up his chest, over his neck, and into the soft hair at the nape of his neck. She leaned forward and pressed her lips to his.

Her lips moved against his in a kiss that was perhaps not the most experienced, but she could taste her own yearning, the lonely nights and aching want. As he kissed her back, she tasted longing and frustrated hunger in the way he dueled with her, pulled her closer.

The elevator binged.

He pulled away, his arm around her, hand settled in the small of her back as he guided them through the dark-wood gentlemen's-club luxury of the hotel's "Living Room." Then down the hall toward their suite.

She let him lead, her thoughts still chaotic, her body and mind on fire. Loki. She was about to have sex with Loki.

About damned time.

ജ

Loki's hand was steady against the warmth of Anna's back, and his movements were smooth unlocking their suite. Unfortunately, he lacked Anna's ability to know if someone spoke the truth. Nor had he ever heard of the War ability to become sober on command. Yet Anna's kisses tasted of need and desire, no hesitation. He knew Anna. She wasn't a liar.

He closed and locked the door behind them, Anna

watching his every move. She still had his jacket draped over her shoulders, that sexy black gown whispering over her curves and telling all kinds of naughty stories— including how it would look better on his bedroom floor.

This was Anna. The only being who'd ever defended him, who'd taken on Thor, for Ymir's sake. Who hated her abilities and who, come tomorrow, he still needed to rise.

She closed the distance between him, slid her hands down his chest and made his breath roughen. Everything had been hard and wanting for some time.

Her fingertips were soft as she cupped his jaw, but faint vulnerability, an echo of what he'd seen earlier gleamed in her gaze.

Ah, Anna, if only I could protect you from all the ugliness of the world.

"This is a one-time offer," she said. "I want you. I'm fairly certain you want me. Just this once, instead of overthinking, instead of plotting, let's act. Just enjoy."

There was blatant challenge in her gaze as she stepped back, leaving his body chilled where he missed her.

Still watching him, she slipped his jacket off her shoulders. Let it slither to the floor. Then cocked an eyebrow, as though daring him to rescue the garment.

As though he cared or would look away from her for even one instant. He crossed his arms in answer to her challenge, waited for her next move.

She was incredible. Fierce, sexy, stating her demands despite the tiniest hesitation in her gaze. Never had he met a woman like her, who challenged him, spurred his desire on every level.

He wanted her mind. Her power. Her strength and challenge. Her naivete and innocence. Her hunger and daring.

Which was precisely the problem.

He couldn't let feelings—hers or his—get in the way.

She walked backward a few steps down the hall.

He followed, kept pace.

Never breaking eye contact, she reached behind her.

She soft zip of the dress's fastening focused his thoughts. The way it dipped around her shoulders before she turned and stepped into his bedroom pulled him like an invisible wire.

His footsteps were predatory, as he entered the bedroom, the black-and-white carpet cushioning his step, luxurious bedding pulled back and waiting.

Her lips curved up, gown drooping. He took a step toward her.

He should have known better than to believe his Anna was afraid. Or if she was, that she'd let it show.

Her gaze still on his, she let the gown drop, slide down her body to the floor.

He also never should have forgotten a War would never be prey. He was firmly captured and willing.

A small black lace bralette barely contained her beautiful breasts, their dusky nipples. Nor could the tiny scrap of lace covering the V between her legs possibly be considered underwear—and seemed unlikely wardrobe essentials for the librarian he'd known in Beckwell.

He approached slowly, taking his time, studying her. Deciding where he would touch first, how he could make this night worthy of her. "If I'd known that's what was under your clothes all these years, I confess I may have burned down your house myself."

Anna raised a brow. "If you mean the underwear, you'd have been disappointed. These were a gift with the suitcase, an early birthday present."

He stopped just in front of her, watched her as he reached for the comb in her hair and gently pulled it free. All that glorious dark hair flowed down her back and around her shoulders. He stepped closer, let his hands trail down her arms, watched as her eyes darkened with desire, the rapid rise and fall of her chest as her breath roughened.

"The lingerie is lovely. But I mean you, Anna. You are beyond compare." His voice rasped, something more burning through him beyond mere desire. Something too fragile, too dangerous to bear examination.

She closed the distance between them, pressed herself against him, and gave her mouth up to his. Her kiss was more aggressive than it'd been in the elevator, hungrier. It called to him, fired his responses, made his hands rove over her. Up and down her back, sliding over the slim lace bra band, down to the tiny slip of lace.

He grasped her bare, perfect ass in his hands. Could have roared as he pulled her against him. Her softness, her heat cupping his hardness.

She groaned against him, pressed herself against his erection, murmurs of pleasure from her throat.

He brought his hands up her body, around her front, until he cupped her breasts and that filmy excuse for a bra. Her nipples pebbled against his palms, and she moaned as he lightly pinched them.

He was just sliding his hand down toward her panties when, panting, she grabbed his hand. Danced away from him.

"Clothes. Off. Now," she said, putting her hands on her hips, licking her lips, bright red and bruised from his kisses. Her bra was askew, one nipple free of the cup, begging for his mouth.

He ripped off the waistcoat, then the shirt, no doubt tearing buttons in the process. To hell with them. He shuffled off shoes and shoved down trousers and underwear in one move, already stepping toward her. Grasping and pulling her closer. His erection bobbed between them. He lowered his mouth to that wanting, needy nipple.

She cried out, the sound half-triumphant as she clutched his head to her breast.

He scooped a hand behind her legs, lifting and carrying her to the bed.

She pulled his face to hers, captured his lips, her fingers digging into the muscle at his shoulders.

He teased her nipple with his fingers, tasted her, devoured her as his other hand found the lacy edge of her panties.

She arched against his touch, body molded to his as he slid a finger through slick folds and inside her. She moaned against him, reached down and grasped his erection.

Neither of them seemed capable of breath as she caressed his shaft. Her fingers wrapped around him, squeezing, while he slid his fingers along her seam, inside of her. Their kisses and touches grew more frenzied.

He should have slowed things down, given her pleasure first. But the intensity of the need driving him demanded more, stole all logical thought. Only her silken flesh beneath his fingertips mattered, the soft huff of breath as her head fell back, her small cry as she pressed herself against him, met him kiss for kiss. They descended into madness together.

She shoved at her panties, grasping, pulling him toward her.

He might have torn the flimsy panties, but he'd buy her more. Didn't matter. All that mattered were her fingers on him. His inside her.

She lay back against the mattress and gazed up at him. Passion sent a pink glow over her skin, sweat glistening at her hairline.

She was the most powerful, glorious, earth-shattering thing he had ever seen in all his many years. Fragile and strong, a natural leader and warrior, destined for so much more than she could know. Yet, somehow, she stared up at him. She defended him. She wanted *him*. After all he had done, all he had been, all he was.

Ymir, she deserved better.

Her breath still rough, she lifted her hand to cup his jaw. "What's wrong?" Doubt seemed to shimmer through her gaze, the blue almost black. "You don't...you want to stop?"

His body poised above her, so close to claiming the heaven he'd only dreamt of, he brushed the hair back from her face, searched her expression. "Are you sure?" He asked so much more than she could possibly understand, more than he could put into words. Asked why she could want him.

Her expression cleared, and her lips curved upward. "Loki? Don't be an idiot." She shifted, wrapped her thighs around his hips, lifting her body to caress his.

He couldn't stifle his groan as she cupped him, wrapped her fingers around his shaft and guided him toward her entrance.

His tip wet with her, he caught her hands with his, pressed their joined hands above her head. Kissed her, hard, before he surged into her.

The second he felt that small pressure against his tip, that delicate membrane, he wanted to freeze. To give her time, to let her adjust.

She wouldn't let him.

She squeezed his hips between her thighs, fingers dug into his shoulders, and arched upward, took him fully inside her.

"Please!" she begged, desire fogging her gaze, dark hair fanned behind her on the pillow.

Passion burned away all doubt. He lifted her thighs around him to shift his angle and reached down between their bodies, stroking her with both his fingers and his shaft.

Anna cried out, and her body tightened around him.

He slid into her again and again, faster and harder, keeping rhythm with his fingers. Maybe they didn't have forever, maybe she deserved better. But he'd give her all he had to give tonight.

Never let it be said he'd disappoint a lady.

ಐ

Sometime later—well, a few "times" later—the ability to think drifted back through Anna. Funny. She'd never considered something like thought so overrated before, but she needed to think, needed to absorb what she'd learned.

Her body was pleasantly relaxed and sated, Loki's nakedness against her back, his heavy arm slung over her waist. He held her in place, his shaft still twitching inside her after the last climax. He'd snuggled his chin into her shoulder, his murmur of satisfaction deeply masculine.

Her eyelids were heavy, but those pesky thoughts refused to stay quiet. She and Loki had indeed made the most of their night. His body moving against hers, in hers, creating a pleasure that still tingled over her skin, more intense than she could have imagined.

Much more treacherous than she could have anticipated.

Loki's hand slid to her hip, his breathing slowing with sleep. Only the sheet covered them, but heat came off him in waves. They wouldn't be cold.

Except on the inside.

She pulled the sheet around her breasts and frowned.

Each of her friends had experienced something unusual the first time they'd been intimate with their future partner. Piper's Daniel had partially shifted form, turning a metallic blue. Ginny and James had unintentionally created a wave of such heated desire, they'd ignited an orgy in the center of town. Nia and Mal had accidentally slipped through the veils that separated the world of man from those of the gods and the demons into the place between, the ether plain, the Gray.

Seeing as she'd warned each of her friends to beware of intimacy between powerful beings like themselves—advice which they'd ignored—she'd considered the potential consequences for she and Loki. Had planned for it during one lengthy trip claiming to go to the washroom while she'd slipped back up to the hotel's lobby and made her requests.

There'd been the possibility of spontaneous fire—good reason to wear only cotton and request extra fire extinguishers in the room, something the ever-attentive staff had seen to.

There'd been the possibility of conflict, so she'd warned the staff she had heard some fighting in rooms around her just so they were aware of it and ready to act should the need arise.

Back in the bar with Thor and Loki, she went over countless scenarios, countless counter-plans that she'd developed over years of fruitless fantasies.

All of them for nothing.

Instead, as Loki brought her to that first glorious climax, she'd seen the truth.

His truth.

A child who'd never been good enough for his parents. Too scrawny, too different, too clever, the hollow ache inside him to try harder to prove himself. Yet always inexplicably falling short.

Then after their disinterest and heartless banishment, a man who would try all over again with Odin and the Asgardians. Always with the faithful hope that this time, it would be different. Even as hope grew increasingly tarnished with each attempt, each rebuttal. Endless faces and countless, thoughtless pain. Leaving him, still alone, still reaching, still trying to prove himself.

The last part of the truth had been the image of him, as though she sat across the roughhewn table from him in some long-forgotten tavern. His face was gaunt, dark hair matted, the remains of fine clothing soiled and torn, so different from her Loki. He chuckled as, light-fingered, he stole money from a passing patron, used it to buy yet another mug of the strongest alcohol he could find. To lose himself to a drunken haze. A stupor the four large men found him in as they sat down at his table and proposed a bargain.

Four men. One a redhead in black armor, with a look of Ginny: Famine. Another thin and dark, wearing a dark gray hood and carrying a stave: Death. The third handsome and fair, a jagged scar down the one side of his face, his armor sickly green: Pestilence. The last, the broadest of the men, with chestnut-brown hair and beard, carried a sword with a ruby in the pommel: War. But Anna didn't see him. She *was* him. Sitting across from that vulnerable Loki, making him a bargain that promised him eternal glory, the chance to save the world, if he would be their catalyst. All while War considered how cheap and easy their bargain was, how perfect their dupe. Because Loki would die one day by War's hand and complete the plan.

A soft catch in her throat threatened to betray her. Anna ran her fingers over her lips. Couldn't do anything about the thickness in her throat, the ache inside.

That Loki, so broken, bleary-eyed, desperate for the respect and belonging he'd never had, agreed to their plan. The original Four. Masterminded by the largest one in the middle, brown-haired and clever, carrying a large blade with a ruby in the pommel. War. The first War.

She squeezed her eyes shut, a tremble sliding through her.

His truth.

War had tried to destroy him once, had promised him everything he longed for and left nothing but lies and the promise of destruction. Would destroy the loving, empathetic man inside who was as difficult to resist as she'd feared.

So far, she was the only War candidate who seemed able to resist the dangerous lure of War. Which meant there was a better chance every day she would be War. Loki would ask her to kill him. She could no more imagine ending his life than her own.

Yet, even now she sensed how hard she could fall for him, how she would sacrifice everything, do whatever he asked. He could erase her more completely than even War could. Because she'd let him.

CHAPTER 22

Loki woke as Anna slipped out of bed and tiptoed toward the door, leaving a cold spot where she'd been. For the briefest moment, before she tried to make her escape, her warm body curled in his, he'd experienced the closest to Valhalla he'd ever been. Well, without the constant battles and drinking.

He propped himself up on one arm, the sheet slipping well below his waist, to better watch as she tiptoed across the black-and-white carpet, dim morning light illuminating the room through curtains he'd left open. He could have let her sneak out, pretended he was asleep. She deserved more than that.

She deserved the truth. What little he knew of it.

What she'd given him.

"You don't have to leave. It's still early. I imagine Thor and Rojo won't be moving for at least another hour or so."

She froze in the act of bending to pick up her gown from the floor, creating quite the delectable tableau, the way she held her arms over herself doing little to conceal the curves he'd sampled and enjoyed. Wanted again.

His body stirred, and he scowled at himself for acting like a green youth.

Though a youth who'd just enjoyed the night of his life and was more than eager for a repeat performance.

Anna straightened, her tension drawing her muscles tight, making it ever clearer that somehow, his librarian had hidden a warrior's body beneath her frumpy closing. Not a scar to mar that creamy skin, but lithe muscles, strong, capable limbs, curves but no excess.

She turned, using her gown to shield the more interesting parts with, sadly, greater success than her bare hands. Tossing her hair over her shoulder, undoubtedly unaware of the way it only further piqued his interest, she raised a brow in challenge.

Ah, but now he was fully awake and more than engaged.

"Loki, we agreed. One night. This changes nothing."

Nor could it, despite the old familiar ache he shoved down.

He held out a hand, gave her a heated once-over for what little he could see, and planned his next salvo, what more he could teach her before they had to let reality intrude. He held out a hand. "Come back to bed, Anna," he said, voice raspy.

Her gaze was no less bold as it traced over his bare chest...then low enough she should have no doubt he wasn't suggesting a nap. "I'm not in the mood for games. We should get moving, get onto the fourth candidate."

He let his head drop back. "*That* sounds far less interesting."

"Not everything is about games or plots or strategy or, or...fun," she spat.

He lifted his gaze back to hers, those blue eyes livid. "Pleasure is not an abomination."

"No. But it can be a trick."

A chill settled over him, quieted his ardor, stoked old fires, and salted old wounds. They made his movements more precise, his jaw hard as he raised a brow at her before swinging his feet over the side of the bed and standing. Taller than her now, he crossed his arms over his chest. "Are you implying something, Hadrianna?" His voice had the warmth of a Greenland lake.

Color climbed her neck as she glared at him, pointedly never allowing her gaze to waver from his. "I might be."

Admittedly, at one point, for a brief instant, he'd considered and discarded the idea of using sex to alleviate his desire for her and manipulate her toward his aims. Yet to be accused of it?

A memory of Peter flashed to mind, the same accusation that Loki was merely toying with them, using them as pawns in his games. He and his friends overeager to enlist, to race off toward war no matter his insistence at caution, that they could accomplish greater things. Peter was convinced Loki used and lied to him. Convinced enough, he wouldn't listen to reason. War did indeed find him.

It was the last time Loki had seen him.

Alive.

He shoved down the raw emotion and focused on the words, the tone, how he could use this. He shouldn't be surprised. They never trusted him. They always expected his betrayal, whether it was ever delivered or not. Anna was no different.

He tried to ignore the small pang that last night, after her passionate defense of him, never mind her passionate response in bed, that this morning they were back to this.

"Are these uncertainties after experiencing your first time?"

"After—" She stared at him incredulously as still

more color flooded her face. This time, though, the way her eyes flared and how she clenched her hands in the fabric against her chest, it seemed unlikely to be embarrassment.

She strode up to him, as though suddenly unaffected by his nudity—a bit disappointing. "This is not the Dark Ages, and I am not some maiden whose worth has somehow been diminished for lack of a ridiculous membrane. I am a modern woman, fully aware of my own sexuality, and just because I hadn't exercised it before with anyone else shouldn't make any difference."

He lowered his gaze to her, his voice low and rough, muscles tight—whether for sex or a fight wasn't entirely clear. "I would be more than happy to indulge those desires—or watch you indulge them yourself. If you could trust it wasn't yet another ploy to manipulate you."

She stared at him a moment, perhaps evaluating the truth of his statement. Then she shook her head, brow still pinched, lips tight. "What do you want me to say? You as much told me you'd do whatever was necessary to ensure I rose as War. You're *Loki*. You are known throughout the world and legend as a master manipulator, a liar."

Last night you argued with Thor and said you saw someone else. Made me believe you might trust me. Yet here we are.

She shook her head, turning away. "I knew better. I *know* better. My apologies. Perhaps last night was a poor idea. Physical intimacy always tangles up emotions, whether deservedly or not, and both you and I know we're better served by a sharp mind not hindered by flighty emotion."

He'd thought that, too, for a long time. Before he'd learned there was no untangling the two, not without losing too much in the process. Though perhaps this was the best place for them—a reminder of where they stood. Where they had to stand. She would never accept him, and nor should she. His plan had to remain priority. Always.

"You gave me your word that if none of these candidates suffice, you will rise," he said.

She didn't turn. "I know. I will. If necessary. But there's still one more candidate." She reached the door, and this time, he let her go.

The room seemed cold and empty without her, despite the fine furnishings. The tangled sheets still echoed with their heated cries and frenzied love-making. She'd forgotten her panties, a tiny scrap of black lace peeking out from beneath the white duvet at the foot of the bed.

He should have known better than to give in to temptation when it came to Anna. It was dangerous. She was dangerous, and not just because she would be War.

The moment they'd reached climax that first time he came inside her, the stars exploding around them, she'd given him not just her virginity, but the ultimate gift.

Her truth.

He massaged his forehead then headed for the shower, turning the water on extra hot.

He'd seen the true Anna in her truth.

The tender woman who lived at the heart of an often-autocratic librarian and perfectionist. The child who dreamed of princes and castles, and whose favorite books among all her treasured belongings were the stories of love and romance, the ones with the happy ending she desperately craved. The happy ending she watched each of her friends achieve and enjoy but believed was impossible for herself.

The woman who, like him, peered, shivering, through the windows at the warm possibilities she saw inside, seemed to see everyone else achieve and enjoy—like love, experience, adventure—and then turn back to the cold, sterile existence she thought she deserved. Who, deep inside, was still that small child he'd rescued.

Shivering, soot-stained, and convinced she'd caused the death of her parents.

He braced his hands on the tile wall, let the water burn over him, soak into muscles that refused to relax. That didn't damn well deserve to relax.

She'd shown him a woman who deserved all those things and more, but who deprived herself of them to protect others. Because she believed her mere association with War, even the *possibility* of rising, would burn them all away, leave only the charred, smoking remains of anything good she touched.

And that was who he wanted to force her to become. Needed her to become.

Fuck.

ॐ

Goddess, sometimes she could be blindingly stupid. Which only made the stupidity more irritating. Anna flung items into her—or rather Ginny's—suitcase, replaying the argument with Loki and packing to find the last viable candidate. In her head, she replayed what she'd said to Loki.

Vincit qui se vincit indeed. She wasn't in control of herself, nor her own tongue, what with the horrible things she'd said.

All those beautiful clothes, balled up and abused. They weren't even hers. She shouldn't be so careless. She pulled them out again, her hands smoothing over the soft fabrics, folding them gently despite the urge to break something. They didn't deserve it. She didn't deserve them.

She'd lied last night. She'd told Loki nothing would change. She'd told herself sex was sex, no emotional strings. Then, because being manipulated and enthralled by Martin evidently hadn't been enough to assuage yesterday's bout of stupidity, she'd convinced herself that sleeping with Loki was somehow a good idea. That not getting married, not daring the emotional entanglement didn't preclude sex with the demigod she'd had a childish infatuation with for as long as she could remember.

She shook her head, grumbling as she folded the remainder of the clothes.

Well, she'd cured the childish infatuation. Now she had a devastatingly adult crush and lust for Loki Laufeyjarson. The way he looked at her, seemed to know exactly how she wanted to be touched, set her afire with a brief brush of his fingertips, made her spiral out of control with desire.

Faex. Then his truth. This was so much worse than a crush.

She sank down on the bed, the dress from last night pooling in her lap. She rubbed her forehead.

He seemed to read as easily as a children's bedtime story.

Worse, the emotions he unleashed inside her, the treacherous storm of them, all hurricanes and lightning bolts, they scrambled her thoughts and made her want impossible, ridiculous things.

Only one candidate remained. She had given her word. None of the others had been any more suitable than her. They were all corrupted by War. Martin could access the companion ability of peace but used it for destructive purposes. At least she'd never intentionally harm others. If she did rise, how could she possibly kill Loki?

There was a hard knock on her door.

She could feel that it was him, the hard strength of him. An able fighter.

A partner.

She stood, laying the dress absently on the suitcase as she headed for the door.

He leaned in the doorway, taking up the entire space, his green silk shirt unbuttoned down to his clavicle, his hair still curling and wet, eyes deep pewter sparkling with amber.

His gaze slipped over her, made her feel naked—or want to be. Heat spiraled through her.

"We need to leave," he said before abruptly turning and striding off.

She blinked a second and dashed after him. "Now?"

He paused just long enough to glance back, his expression hard. "Home. To Beckwell. Daphne has escaped. If she unleashes that destruction goddess, the world ends, War or not."

CHAPTER 23

Fifteen minutes later, rain spit down on Anna, who was flanked on one side by Loki and on the other by Thor as she attempted to get Rojo to see reason and into the black cab waiting at the curb to take them to the airport. Tourists crowded the broad sidewalk outside of the hotel next to stylish topiaries and snapped photos of Thor and the enormous chestnut horse standing beside the canopied entrance to The Rubens.

Faex.

This was what emotion, stupidity, and impulsiveness got you. Trouble.

And a large, literal apocalypse horse who mugged for the gathering crowd and pranced around on the sidewalk as the rain came down harder.

The hotel truly was worthy of that five-star ranking, as they'd been incredibly understanding and helpful when a horse had, inexplicably, appeared down in the Cavalry Bar. Either it happened more often than one might expect…or Loki was more generous with his recompense than she knew.

Anna was not so understanding about the matter.

Not the inconvenience it caused now. Nor the significance of the portent that made her hands tremble. They needed to get back to Beckwell. Now.

"Rojo, this isn't funny," she said through gritted teeth, rain soaking into her hair. She pitched her voice low; hopefully, she didn't start a riot among the tourists and make an even bigger scene. Fortunately, thus far, between the tourists' fascination with Rojo and Thor's enormity, and perhaps the heavy rain, the sound of her voice didn't seem to register. "Turn back into a pigeon."

"Princess, do you really think that will make them stare less?" said the now large, *talking* horse in the middle of London.

Goddess knew what the onlookers thought of that. A few started to push each other for a better view.

Anna compressed her lips together. A riot would not improve the day.

Rojo stood almost a hand taller than even Loki, around Thor's height, with a broad chest and deep, chestnut-red coat. He was so…so…*horse*-y. None of her friends' apocalypse horses had turned into actual horses. Skunks, pigs, owls…they were so much subtler.

Much more transportable.

The horse-who-used-to-be-a-pigeon tossed his mane and neighed, to the delight of the tourists and Thor, who laughed loudly. It was entirely possible the Norse god was attracting almost as much attention as the horse.

"If we'd wanted to find a way to broadcast our location to the world and the gods, this would have been beyond my dreams," Loki said, his tone dark.

She fisted her hands at her sides. Leaned closer to the horse to whisper furiously. "We need to get to the airport. We need to fly home. We had a deal. You help me find the real War. We can still do that. *After* we help

Beckwell."

Rojo's eyes narrowed, and his ears flicked back as he leaned down toward Anna, blew out a horse-y breath in her face. "Yeah. We *had* a deal. I help you find the real War because you didn't want the abilities, didn't want anything to do with it. Or me. You seem good with taking on all that power, don't you? So screw you. You want to go home and pretend you're not rising, you're not War, fine. But I'm staying here. I'll find the War who isn't ashamed of who and what we are. Who and what I am." He straightened, towering over her, and nodded his head at Thor. "Hey, Thor, want to come?"

Cold landed in the pit of Anna's stomach, icier than the rivulets of rain dripping down her neck, and the world blurred. What was Rojo saying? That now even he thought she was rising as War? Rojo had changed forms. Surely this wasn't it, rising. This couldn't be it. Horses had three forms. She wasn't War.

Yet…

Thor's booming laughter from beside her made her flinch, blink up at the massive god where he rested his hammer, disguised as an umbrella today, on his shoulder. A closed umbrella, despite the rain that plastered the god's red hair to his head. "*Two* quests in one century? Fortune smiles on me, and I thank you for the invitation, parrot friend."

Thor bumped her elbow. "However, I have decided to accompany Anna and Loki on their futile quest until Heimdall kills them. Since I found them, it's been the most fun I've had in ages." He looked down at her with a small grin. "You are a formidable warrior, worthy of the title of War. But Heimdall's success is as certain as the change of the seasons. He has long been prophesied to slay Loki, and you are merely a hindrance to his Unicorns or whatever they call themselves and his new employer. It's nothing personal, you understand."

"Of course," she murmured, her insides quivering still. "Why would I take someone trying to kill me personally?" Even Thor thought she was worthy of becoming War. There was a madwoman loose in Beckwell. Her friends needed her. The gods still wanted to kill her for power she'd never wanted, as greedy and out of control as small children let loose in her library after Halloween, all sticky hands, too much sugar, and chaos.

Thor nodded, pleased—and clearly immune to sarcasm. "Glad you understand. Now Loki? He takes it too personal. Doesn't even come for family dinners anymore because of it." He glanced at her again. "Wish you could have met my wife, Sif. Think you'd have liked her, and she you."

The tourists chattered excitedly around her like excited chipmunks. The whisper of their truths slid through her…in all different languages.

Languages she understood. Every one. Her breath stuttered. She could induce rage. Had nauseating reactions when it came to violence. Weapons sense, an ability to fight that certainly wasn't borne out of practice. She could control the fire that consumed her house. Couldn't affect peace like Martin could, but now she had an apocalypse horse that had grown into a literal damned horse.

Her hands started to shake. There was only one candidate remaining, but instead of heading toward her, they were heading home.

She was rising whether she liked it or not.

"Enough of this," Loki growled and stepped toward Rojo, grabbed him by the chin. "Here's what's going to happen, Rojo." His voice was as silky as a blade sliding through flesh. "Thor is going to create a distraction. I'm going to conceal you, and you're going to transform back into a pigeon. Then we're going to get in the cab, go to the airport, and fly home to deal with something that is immensely more important than your very existence. Do we have an understanding?"

Rojo put his muzzle directly in Loki's face. "You think you scare me?"

The rumble of aggression whirled through her like potent alcohol, the taste of it sweet on her tongue. Her hands fisted.

No. She wouldn't be War. Refused to accept the possibility. War needed to be able to control the abilities, not let them control her. War needed access to all the abilities, including peace, and all she seemed to have was a connection to violence.

If she rose as War, she might have to kill Loki.

She jumped forward, knocking into Loki, her gaze fixed on Rojo. "We don't have time for this," she said in a low growl.

Two tourists started fighting over whose photo was better.

Ignoring them, she focused on the horse, "We will discuss this later. Back in Beckwell. Now, are you coming, or are we leaving you behind?"

Rojo snorted at Loki once more before he slowly turned his deep brown gaze on her. "Who do you think you're talking to?"

She blinked. "What? You, *podex perfectus es*," she said through gritted teeth. "Turn. Into. A. Pigeon. Let's go."

He took a step closer to her, his hooves almost landing on her feet.

She refused to budge, even though now she was nose-to-nose with a horse.

"I'm the War horse, Princess. I don't know what you expected that to be, but I'll tell you who I am. I'm damn sure not some pushover like those other horses. I know the *truth*. I know your truth. Right now, that truth is that in front of me is a woman—" He snorted. "A flipping *woman* of all things, who is strong enough, capable enough to rise as War. A woman who'd rather remain intentionally blind and prejudiced against all War can and would be."

"B-but you didn't want me to rise. You said I couldn't be War." Desperation clawed at her insides, turning her stomach inside-out. "We'll find the real War. It can't be me. Right now, we have to get home."

Rojo stared at her for a long moment.

A few of the tourists had broken into a fistfight. More still visiting Buckingham Palace across the road were attracted by the action.

Finally, the horse shook his head, took a step back, and straightened. "No. *Aquila non capit muscas.* You're not War? Then there's no reason I should help you with something beneath me. Go on. I'll go find the real War on my own, find someone who needs, wants, and appreciates me being around."

Her nails dug into her trembling palms, heat flaring through her even as moisture pricked her eyes. "You want to play these games?" How could he? He'd been her one ally. The only other being who agreed she shouldn't and couldn't be War. Yet now... She blinked back the sting and lifted her chin. "Then you can play them on your own." Anna jabbed a hand toward the cab. "We're leaving. This is your chance. You come with us, we can be that team. Or...you stay here and look for your mythic War."

She turned on her heel. Rojo wanted to act like a child, she'd treat him like one. And if he didn't follow... Her stomach ached, her insides trembled, she could still hear all those voices, kept cataloging the War abilities she seemed to be accumulating. Rojo was supposed to help her.

Though why should he if she wasn't War? He was

right. Maybe she'd expected a horse like her friends had…and Rojo was nothing like them. He pushed and prodded her. Insisted she be more, be something she wasn't.

Loki's hand brushed her elbow as they headed for the waiting black cab.

Thor was a moment or two longer, and they all folded themselves inside.

The large chestnut horse stood resolutely on the sidewalk as the cab pulled away.

&

Maybe the trouble was that Rojo didn't understand authority. Specifically, *her* authority. Many hours later, after she survived the long flight back from Farnborough Airport outside London to the Edmonton International Airport, she considered the matter on what felt like the equally long drive from Edmonton to Beckwell. Anna stared out the passenger window of Loki's sleek car at the ribbons of fields and barbed wire, hemmed in by silhouetted walls of trees. No escape even as darkness began to fall, the hour late.

Thor snored from the back seat, contorted like a lumpy man-pretzel.

Loki was quiet as he drove, the quiet sound of classic jazz from the radio the only sound to accompany Thor's rumbling snores.

Rojo had just watched them leave. Said she could rise as War.

The War horse accepted she could be War.

Anna scowled out the window, lips tight, arms wrapped around her. It would serve the insufferably chauvinistic, juvenile idiot right if someone scooped him up and subjected him to scientific experimentation. He wasn't actually *her* horse.

Yet there'd been a growing ache, a space widening and pulling inside her with every mile that stretched between them. As though they were attached by some kind of elastic cord, the connection dragging within her, making her even want to hear his irritating voice and that belittling nickname.

They turned off the main highway onto the narrow, two-lane secondary highway that would lead them back into the heart of Beckwell. Back to a town who'd always feared her despite their own abilities. Back to where she was the spinster librarian with no house, no belongings. Back to her friends who still wanted her to rise and couldn't understand why it was so frightening to her, what it would mean.

The three candidates they'd met had been so blatantly terrible for War, yet she'd seen part of herself in every one of them, felt that affinity. Even if she could control her ability, War's corruption would always tempt her, threaten to swallow her. Unlike her friends, she still showed no sign of companion abilities, had found nothing redeemable about War in all her research, in any of the candidates, or within herself.

Loki expected that she'd rise. That she'd kill him.

What kind of person would she be if she could?

"Are you accompanying me back to the house, or shall I drop you at one of your friends'?" he asked, his voice shattering her thoughts, rolling over her like chocolate and cream.

Lupus in fabula.

Prickles of awareness cascaded through her, whispers of memory from last night, the way they'd touched, the taste of him. She frowned sternly at herself, but it did nothing to dispel the thoughts. "Your house, I suppose. We should convene with the others, determine the specifics of the situation."

"Good. I've arranged that they meet us there."

She turned a dark look on his profile, the hint of dark whiskers shadowing his jaw, the way a curl of dark hair hung over his ear. She'd run her fingers through his hair, their breaths mingled as he'd thrust into her.

Now she'd rather tweak that curl until he turned and looked at her. An impulsive, dangerous thought considering they were driving.

The heat curling through her called her lie, said she'd much rather be back in that hotel room, in his bed.

"Why bother to ask if you'd already decided?" she said tartly.

Thankfully, he wasn't looking to see the heat burning her face. She turned to similarly glare out the windshield, out into the gathering darkness where shadows crept toward the edges of the road.

"Because I value your opinion. Plans could be changed if necessary," he said, irritatingly reasonable and rational.

Was this because she was becoming more War-like, that it seemed to devour all her cool logic, turn her into this irrational being?

The weight of his gaze fell heavy on her, and she stared resolutely out the windshield until he turned away. He wasn't lying. Come to think of it, she couldn't think of the last time he'd lied to her. Not since before they left Beckwell.

His cologne, maybe just his scent, that musky spiciness, curled around her, reminded her of lying on his naked chest, the sound of his heart thrumming beneath her ear.

"Whatever else we are or could be, we could be an effective team." His tone seemed carefully neutral but still curled through her, filled her with warmth. "To succeed— if there's any chance of success—the town and our team are going to need effective leadership."

Our team. That's how it had felt while they'd been away, as though they were a team. Partners. She'd thought she and Rojo were a team. Or a kind of one, trying to find another War. That ally was gone. Could she and Loki maintain that partnership now that they were back in Beckwell, with the old expectations?

"Then you need to share your plans and let us work with you. We're not pawns, we're not game pieces."

He said nothing, his hands tightening on the wheel.

Anna laid her head back against the seat with a soft sigh. Had she been any better than Loki in the way she'd treated Rojo? What had she given him for their partnership? Goddess, if she trusted Loki, it could lead her toward heartbreak and destruction.

🍂

An hour later, Trevor gathered everyone in the wood-paneled dining room where there was room for everyone to sit with extra chairs, maps spread out on the polished walnut table, strategy to be discussed. They needed to plan the containment and destruction of the chaos goddess. Loki stood near the center of the table, leaned over the map of Beckwell, listening as the others' voices rippled around him, letting the facts filter through and plans formulate in his head.

His guests bickered at times, at least twenty people in the room, most of whom wouldn't have been able to agree on the color of grass. Anna's three friends were there, along with their respective husbands. Piper and Daniel each cradled a sleeping twin, quieter in their participation, and tired if the circles beneath their eyes were any indication. Mal was there as Police Chief, his daughter asleep upstairs in one of the rooms. Ginny's husband, James, seemed to have brought a contingent of his own people, para-military from the looks of them, but potentially useful. One of them, a large, dark-skinned fellow who smelled like a dragon, chatted with Thor over weapon choice. Trevor stood by the door though said little, while Old Henry was there to represent Beckwellians.

Anna stood near her friends, not beside him. With them, the Four together, their bonds stronger than even they yet realized. Which made the small ache in his chest ridiculous, especially when he needed Anna to realize the strength of those bonds and get on with rising. No matter how difficult it would be for her, no matter how much she feared the idea.

They'd been away nearly a week, yet it could have been yesterday that Old Henry and the knitting club gathered in his study to plead their case. His gaze slid over the War horsewoman's slim figure, in high-waisted, wide-legged trousers today that nipped in at the waist, a silk cream blouse, and a burgundy sweater that hugged her breasts, every button an invitation.

He'd had Trevor pull everything on her parents, their case, and the domestic situation before the murder-suicide. All the evidence necessary to prove she wasn't to blame for their deaths, to give her that freedom at least. Now he just needed to find a way to let her "discover" it herself so she wouldn't believe he'd somehow tainted it.

"Loki? You with us?" Mal asked from the other side of the table, where he'd been outlining the last known whereabouts of Daphne since her escape and the plan to make sure she didn't get out of Beckwell. So far, it'd been successful.

A pity they hadn't been more careful to make sure she didn't escape in the first place.

Mal's gaze narrowed, flicking from Loki to Anna, then back. Beckwell's new police chief was intelligent and sharp-eyed, which could at times be bothersome. He quirked a dark brow in surprise.

Which garnered his twin's attention, who likewise studied both Loki and Anna. Never had the empathic connection the Quilan twins shared been more irritating. Anna wouldn't appreciate anyone knowing anything had happened, and any suggestion thereof would be a distraction they couldn't afford.

Loki sent the Quilan men a subduing glare. "I'm focused on the issue at hand. Daphne must die violently for the chaos goddess to be released and capable of her full destructive ability. Which means we need to keep her alive, at all costs."

"No shit, Sherlock," Nia said, arms crossed over her narrow chest. "While you two have been off on holiday, we've kept her within the town borders, as well as kept the gods and those damned angels out of Beckwell. Daphne's batshit insane but clever. She'll chew off her own arm if necessary."

"Civilian patrols have scared her back from the Beckwell border wards twice now, but she's determined," Old Henry said. "If we carry through with Beckwell Days tomorrow, all of those unaware of her escape and threat will be out in the open, easy prey for her."

Making themselves potentially irresistible bait for one deranged would-be destruction and chaos goddess.

"She also uses her powers of Fate and the present to know where we'll be before we even get there," Mal said with a growl. "She sees us coming through the back door and goes out the front."

Ah, yes, always an issue when dealing with one of the Fates: they usually knew more than anyone else, even him. Daphne was, among other things, the representative of Clotho, youngest of the Fates, the spinner who knew and could influence the present. It was how she'd escaped in the first place. She'd realized he was away and after injuring herself to cause a panic, she'd stabbed one of the guards with a spike of wood she'd pried out of the floor with her fingernails, then taken the nurse hostage and gained her freedom.

"Keep her in the town and narrow the net. We need to get her back in custody. Do not, under any circumstance, let those trigger-happy USELESS agents shoot her, understood?" he said.

"Yes, but, if she does rise...we can stop her, can't we?" Ginny asked from where she stood next to Anna, distributing muffins and coffee to everyone.

He met Anna's gaze as he spoke. "If Anna rises and you become the Four officially in all powers, few forces in the world could stop the four of you then."

Pink stained Anna's face. "You don't know that," she said, her voice an angry rasp.

Which only started more bickering.

He didn't break away from her gaze. She knew as well as he did that it was only a partial lie. "It took almost twenty gods to trap and imprison the goddess before—three of which didn't survive. History remembers her last escape as in 536, considered the worst year in human history with global climate shift, volcanic eruptions, mysterious fog that brought endless dark and cold, drought and famine."

"Well, *we* didn't let her out, that time or this time. I thought you said she was secure?" Anna practically snarled.

He narrowed his eyes, a tic starting in his jaw.

Ginny cleared her throat, glanced from him to Anna's furious face. She clapped her hands. "You know what? It's late. Let's get some rest, huh?"

"Night watches need to be relieved in three hours," Mal said, slinging an arm around Nia as they headed out the door with everyone else.

Ginny whispered something to Anna, earning an angry glare herself as Anna jerked away. More rapid conversation he couldn't quite hear with the departing visitors and echoing voices. Whatever was said, Anna was having none of it, only eventually heading out of the room after her friends.

He considered the map a moment or two. And Anna, Thor's presence, Heimdall's inevitable arrival, the past few days, and every other reason he had a raging headache.

The sound of throat clearing made him look up to find Mal and Daniel Quilan standing in the doorway. Neither of whom looked especially comfortable, but there was a resolute way they stood that said they weren't budging.

His headache was about to get worse.

He turned, crossed his arms over his chest, and raised a brow. "You have something to say?"

Mal rubbed his chin, glanced at his brother, then back at Loki. "It's about Anna. Something going on with you two?"

Considering the history he had with the Quilans—not all of it positive, at least from their perspective and Daniel's continued cold fury—this was not a topic he'd expected. Yet again it appeared he was cast in the dubious role of would-be villain. "If it was, Anna is a grown woman and more than capable of making her own decisions."

"You're the master of lies, while she has no one else to speak up for her. You're supposed to be her guardian," Daniel said, his tone indicating his anger hadn't passed over what he saw as a betrayal—acting as his friend in the guise as Lou and possibly neglecting to explain Lou was also Loki. Every other aspect of their friendship had been sincere, including the pain of its ending.

It had been almost like losing Peter again. Perhaps, though, the pain of it ending had been more one-sided, the friendship he'd shared with Daniel clearly not strong enough to withstand greater openness. He'd been afraid Daniel wouldn't trust him if it were known Lou was Loki—and all evidence indicated he'd been right. He never learned. No one trusted him.

"I was never formerly her guardian, the Lacks were. And the master of lies is Satan. Different being, different abilities." Good to see the Quilan boys—or anyone—finally stand up for Anna. Though also annoying under the circumstances. He uncrossed his arms, held out his hands. "Your intentions are noble; I appreciate that. But we have far larger concerns."

"Yes, but… Look, she was hurt in January. Badly. That asshole god killed her during the attack at Nia's place, and all of us can see she hasn't been the same. The girls are worried. Trust me, that dying and coming back? That shit's tricky," Mal said, usually the hothead of the two, but more reasonable recently.

"Which means she doesn't need your BS," Daniel added, as though their message hadn't been clear.

The more things changed…

Loki opened his mouth to respond, but someone got there first.

"What's going on?" Anna said, coming in from the foyer, her eyes narrowing on each of the men, lingering on him as color climbed her neck.

It might have been amusing to throw the Quilans to her fury and see what happened…but their intentions were good. Besides, they were right. Anna deserved his protection, nothing else.

Especially with what he required of her.

"Daniel and Mal were simply acquainting me with further information I needed to know," he said, careful to tread the lines of truth. "They're worried." There, something completely true.

She studied him closely which, likely, did not have its intended effect since it only made him think of peeling those clothes down her shoulders and taking her back to his bed again. A thoroughly enjoyable but misguided plan.

Likely.

Daniel cleared his throat this time. "Yes. Just making sure Loki completely understood the situation."

"You do, right?" Mal said.

"Perfectly. Thank you and good night, gentlemen." He nodded, dismissing them.

Their gazes landed on Anna, and they hesitated when they should have been leaving.

Anna turned on them, raised a brow. "Good night. We'll catch up tomorrow."

They hesitated a moment longer, then nodded and both turned and left the room.

Leaving only he and Anna, who strode briskly across the room and scooped up her mug. "Forgot my coffee."

There was no smile, no hesitation as she turned and made her escape.

Loki rubbed his neck. Why he'd expected any different, that maybe she'd come down to see him, was obviously a sign of exhaustion. Forget anything else. He needed to do what he always did: focus on the plan, act carefully, never forget that he didn't belong and never would.

CHAPTER 24

After lying awake most of the night—hopefully, it was jetlag and nothing to do with Loki or a certain idiotic pigeon—even Anna would have described her mood as sour by the time she made her way down to Loki's kitchen in search of food.

Only to find the kitchens empty of all but Loki's lean, muscular figure, leaning against the counter and sipping from a steaming black mug. He wore his customary green silk shirt, revealing the smallest hint of his muscular physique over a pair of charcoal slacks. The green was the one part the movies had gotten right. They'd missed the full, overwhelmingly appealing package, the sheer power and rugged warrior. He was barefoot. Even his feet, long toes lightly dusted with dark hair, were masculine and sexy, damn him.

She froze in the doorway, hand on the frame, and her gaze locked with his. Heat whirled through her.

Last night she hadn't even made it to her room before she'd turned around and headed back to the dining room to find him. It had become a habit to end the day with him. To reflect on what had been. To ask what he thought of Rojo staying back in London. She wanted to hear his voice, watch the way his dark gaze flickered over her. Needed that assurance that despite the way everyone else acted, as though nothing had happened, nothing had changed, he knew that, like her, things *were* different.

She was different.

Coming home was like the moment after finishing a particularly enthralling book and returning to piles of laundry, unpaid bills, and pain. That's how their time together had been. An enchanting narrative that, if she were honest with herself, she hadn't been ready to let go, hadn't truly seen the value of until the plane had touched down.

Then she'd found him with Daniel and Mal, and though he'd denied it without lying, she'd felt their truth. The fact that they were worried about her was both touching and irritating. What business was it of theirs what she did or with whom? Something she'd similarly pointed out when Ginny had asked, Piper had implied, and Nia made crude hand gestures.

"Beckwell Days have proceeded as usual. Everyone is out watching for Daphne or sleeping. Coffee?" One side of his mouth turned upward, and his dark eyes glinted. "You can join me. You know I don't bite." His voice grew huskier, his gaze whisking over her figure. She wore another of the vintage outfits his minion had found for her, another pair of high-waisted slacks paired with a modern black tank top this time. "Unless you want me to," he said, eyes meeting hers.

Her throat thickened. Just like that, she had another reason to back out of the room, another reason to remember how he'd looked under those clothes, to make her escape while she could. To run.

He watched, his gaze patient, yet teasing.

Non desistas non exieris. Neither retreat nor surrender was in her DNA.

She strode into the room. Pretended she wasn't aware of every inch of him, the heat of him radiating outward as she plucked a clean mug from the old-fashioned dish rack then poured herself some coffee. She took the first sip and bit back a moan. Goddess above, Loki bought heavenly coffee, and he brewed it strong, just how she liked it.

She opened her eyes to find him watching her, unabashed hunger in his gaze that flared with amber. Amber when he was pissed…or aroused.

Not that it should matter. Or she should care. It'd been one night, one mistake.

"We should talk strategy," she said, huskiness roughening her voice.

"We should indeed," he purred, like some big, prowling cat. His gaze rested on her lips.

She took another sip of the divine brew, which probably only aroused her more. "Do you have an actual plan of how we're going to trap her or what we're going to do with Daphne when we have her?"

He sighed, his eyes losing some of the amber. "Daphne needs more permanent incarceration, somewhere her life can be extended until the goddess can be detached from her and imprisoned otherwise. I'm working on a solution." He took a sip of coffee, resting one hand casually back on the counter, mere millimeters from her hip. "There's something else you should know."

"About Heimdall's inexorable movement our way and his intention to kill me and destiny to kill you? Thor was most helpful."

He shifted closer. "I don't want you involved. Daphne's dangerous and reckless. Heimdall or some of his assassins are likely in town aiming for you. Until you rise as War, you're too vulnerable." He set down his coffee mug, lifted his hand to stroke his thumb over her cheek, his expression troubled.

She tried to keep her tone even, as though she wasn't calculating how long it would take them to reach his bedroom—or the likelihood they were alone in the house. That minion of his was probably lurking somewhere, watching. "Death happens to be one of my closest friends. I'm not concerned."

"You should be." His lips tightened a moment. "Anna, Death can be reversed, maybe once if, such as in your case, you happen to be around a particularly powerful entity who's capable of it, or if you have the power to regenerate. But when you die, the connection between your spiritual and physical forms becomes more tenuous. All that it means to be mortal, to be human, will have begun to drift away, become more distant, as I suspect you've already experienced to some small extent." Another small pause, his thumb stilling against her skin. "If you die a second time, even Nia couldn't bring you back. Your soul goes directly to the afterlife. Unless you rise. War is much harder to kill."

She pulled back, and he let her, the familiar chill more pronounced now that she understood its implications. Both the necessary distance from Loki, and the distant coldness she'd felt since January after Nia resurrected her.

"What about you? Whether Heimdall or the unlucky War heir kills you, do you regenerate? Can you be brought back?"

He considered her a moment before he spoke, his gaze steady. "No. I don't come back. The War sword Hildebrand sunders life instantly. If I die, humanity gets a new start, another chance. The Four said the world would be anew, humanity once more united, not warring with each other. There will be no great judgment, no suffering, and the stronger the world is, the more resistant it is to any other apocalyptic threat." He smiled, but there was only sadness in the gesture. "The one way I finally prove myself to everyone is by dying. I need your help to do that, which means I need you alive. I need *you*."

Her throat squeezed, and her stomach knotted. What could she say?

Worse though was the way something inside her shifted when he said he needed her.

Because he didn't need her the way she could only wish he did. He needed her to end his life. To become the kind of War she'd despised and feared all her life.

She closed her eyes a moment, her lips trembling.

She'd seen his truth. She'd seen how he'd been rejected over and over again. He'd finally revealed something of himself to her, the reason behind his plot— and it required sacrificing himself to save humanity, not harm it. To finally find a way to experience acceptance...though he had to die to get it. An ache opened up inside of her.

She opened her eyes, met his gaze.

He took her coffee mug from her numb fingers, set it on the counter.

If she rose as War, she could help ensure lasting peace. By sacrificing the one person she'd come to care about more than she dared put into words. She could give him everything he wanted...by killing him.

His hands cupped her face, and he smoothed his thumbs over her lips. "Anna, I—"

The shrill ring of his phone on the counter cut off his words.

He closed his eyes, stepped back, then grabbed the phone and answered.

Anna lifted a shaking hand to her lips. Emotion lied and deceived, better than the smoothest con. She needed to think this through, not be distracted by ephemeral and likely unreciprocated feelings. She was considering rising as War, embracing the full, dangerous possibility that could drive her mad, lead her to endless violence, and harm too many people. That needed more than just a decision based on the way his words made her feel.

"Understood. On my way." Loki ended the call, met her gaze again. "Daphne has shown up at the agricultural grounds for Beckwell Days. I'd prefer you stay here. Where you're safe."

Her smile was tight. "You can prefer it all you want. I'm coming. Carpe diem."

He said nothing further as they both ran for the door.

ॐ

When Loki, with Anna at his heels, arrived at the agricultural fairgrounds a few minutes later it looked like any other Beckwell Days event. No sign of the goddess. In the wide-open grassy square behind the library, the fuchsia Cow Palace making up one of the corners of the quad, Beckwellians out in short pants and T-shirts showed off horns, tails, and scaled skin without fear, without censure. Beckwell Days was about celebrating their oddities, their paranormal heritage, and this sanctuary. A place where they were safe from human censure, or whatever they'd faced in the other worlds of Braelyn or Daimoleigh. Beckwell was a place where everyone, no matter their species, no matter their faults, was welcomed and safe.

Or had been.

There were bouncy houses and inflatable slides set up for the children, along with a small petting zoo. The most popular animals, as usual, were the unicorns and dogs who could mimic the appearance of anything, leaving the poor old griffin, wings molting, lion-body boney, looking lonely, and a few mundane chickens and sheep looking nervous. Fortune tellers' booths featuring real psychics and face painting were set up in the tents ringing the large, open area, while near the Cow Palace there were races both on the ground and in the air, cheap gold-colored medals coveted each year.

For the first time in more than a decade, he attended as himself, rather than Lou. Hadn't even considered disguising his appearance before they raced out the door. Anna's doing, more of this honesty business.

Thus far, it was all merriment and fun, not the screams and horror he'd half expected. Mal's phone call had been short. Where was Daphne, and what was her play? Perhaps they already had her in custody. Though it seemed unlikely his luck could be that good, or that it would have gone so quickly and smoothly.

"Keep your eyes open, and please, be careful," he said, shooting Anna a hard look. He'd given away too much back in the kitchen, but when he'd told her his plan and the reasons, she'd almost seemed to care. Because she didn't want to rise and kill him probably, but it was nice to think she cared something for his personal well-being.

Nice, though foolish.

"Aren't I always careful?" she said, leaving her oblique response unclear as to whether she recalled the incidents where she'd been less than careful that had certainly taken decades off his life.

Like when she'd opened her door to let out a pigeon and let in an assassin. Or helped start fights in both Three Points *and* Chicago. Or wandering off on her own to confront a War heir and getting brainwashed in the process.

"I'll find the girls," she said, heading off toward the fortune tellers' tents.

He caught her hand, tugging her back toward him. "Careful. It means avoiding harm, staying out of trouble, not getting killed."

She pulled free of his grip. "I'm aware of its meaning. Let's just find her. Then we can go find the fourth candidate."

He contemplated staying close as she headed toward the tents and glanced at his cell. The service in this area was dodgy at the best of times, and with all the paranormal energy it was all but nonexistent, which may have contributed to Mal's short call. One last glance at Anna and Loki headed the other direction. She could take care of herself, and they'd cover more area apart. The sooner he found Mal or one of the others, the sooner he'd understand the situation and the degree of danger.

Beckwellians stopped and stared as he walked past, pointed him out to others as he did so. His impersonal, polite smiles didn't stop the stares, nor the way they tightened his shoulders. He should have transformed to Lou first, made himself less conspicuous. He was practically naked without a disguise. Honesty was overrated. Unless it came to Anna.

On the other hand, if Daphne needed a target, he'd make a convenient one.

Both Quilans were supposed to be here, along with Thor, and all of them were usually easy to spot in a crowd. Yet amid the complacent families enjoying a day out, idly keeping half an eye on their children, no Quilans, no Thor, no Daphne. Not near the inflatable slide, no sign near the concession, nor, indeed, the paranormal petting zoo, which, had he wanted to cause a scene, would have been a good target.

Plenty of people stared and whispered as he stalked past the first inflatable bouncy house, trying not to grit his teeth.

Behind the second, though, slightly around back, not far from the white fortune tellers' tents, was a tableau that froze his step and crashed his thoughts for a moment.

Daphne, a petite, buxom brunette who once might have been pretty, stood just outside the bouncy house entrance. Feverish madness glinted in her crazed crocodile smile. Her hair hung in dirty clumps around her face, and bloody scratches streaked up and down her arms. One of her pants legs was torn off near the knee, and her feet were bare and bleeding. Her eyes were bloodshot and wild, her thin arms grasping two crying children.

She held a revolver against the smallest one's temple.

The petite little redhead, two years if she was a day, sobbed quietly.

Ginny, Nia, and Mal—or maybe it was Daniel— were on the other side of the bouncy house, a hole sliced in the netting while they quickly and silently pulled the other children out to safety.

That had to be Mal then, creeping around the corner of one of the fortune tellers' tents, his gun drawn.

From the other side came two old men, wielding weapons that looked like they dated at least back to the second world war. Albert and Henry from the looks of it, part of the so-called "Beckwell Shades," a secretive group bent on protecting Beckwell and destroying Loki's peace of mind.

All that was missing was Thor swinging around that bloody hammer.

Loki clenched his fists. They couldn't kill Daphne. If they did, the goddess would be freed. He'd told them that. Had none of them listened?

The worst, though, was the slim figure, hands up, dressed in wide-legged trousers and a tank top, walking calmly and directly toward Daphne and the gun.

Anna. Ymir. This was not being careful. If her voice incited Daphne to even more violence…

He shifted quickly, whispering the spell that showered over him like a cloak, let him hide from the view of others temporarily. It was a trick; he wasn't invisible, and it wouldn't fool anyone who was looking more closely—or Anna—but with everyone distracted, it might be enough to bring down Daphne and not get her or anyone else killed.

He headed on an intersect course between Mal, Daphne, and the two senior citizens. Bedamned if he'd let any of this, any of them foul up his plans.

℣

What part of "don't kill the crazy woman" didn't anyone seem to understand? Anna tried to push the frustration out of her mind, as that almost certainly wasn't going to help, and continued to walk toward Daphne, her hands raised. She sent a quick prayer to Gaia and whoever else might have been listening to help her pull this off. She probably would be War. So…maybe it was about time she manifested some of those companion abilities which could help diffuse the situation instead of making it worse.

That con Martin had been able to use the powers of peace to manipulate people, so perhaps she could too. She was stronger than him. She'd felt the threat from the tickle on her back moments after she left Loki, the impending potential for violence in the sickly-sweet taste in her mouth and the surging euphoria.

Now two children depended on Anna to be able to use War abilities for good. In a way, she'd never practiced before but understood in theory.

"Hello, Daphne," Anna said, even attempting to add a smile. Ginny always said people responded to commands better if they came with a smile…or something like that.

She tried to focus on the peace, harmony, serenity Martin had used, first like a smothering blanket, then more effectively by layering it on slowly, the way he'd eventually gotten her. Of course, he'd succeeded in that because he was touching her, so the wet-blanket method might be the best bet for this situation, at least until Anna could get closer. She dug deep, deep beneath the heat and flames of War until she touched something different, let it flow out of her like cold mountain air. Or at least, that's what she pictured, but the flames were so prominent, so powerful.

"Oh, good. You're finally here. I was starting to think I was crazy or something and you weren't coming," Daphne said before erupting into demented cackles.

The third and youngest of the Fates, Daphne Spinner, looked even worse than she had back in January. Any semblance of pretty—or sane—was long gone in the tangles of dark hair around her face, the scratches that looked like self-harm on her arms. Six months ago, she'd attacked Nia's house after going on a murder spree, only to be shot by the middle Fate. Unfortunately, seeing as her body was a vessel for a deranged chaos-destruction goddess, Loki hadn't let her stay dead, Nia had brought her back to life, and now here they all were, dealing with the damned woman. Again.

Her anticipation of Anna's arrival was unlikely to be good. Daphne was the incarnation of Clotho, the youngest Fate, who could spin major decisions into life and knew all things present. Which meant she probably knew more about how this day was likely to end than the rest of them. The key word being "likely." From Anna's research, the Fates weren't always right. Which meant it didn't have to play out the way Daphne wanted.

"Isn't that nice. Why don't you put down the gun and we can go chat? Get a hotdog perhaps?" Because what could be better than chatting with a psychopath over mystery meat.

A flicker from her periphery saw that Loki had shown up. What was he thinking, just walking right through the middle of the scene like that? Oh, wait. Perhaps he was headed toward Mal and the old men with guns. From where Anna stood, she could see them, whereas the tent largely concealed them from Daphne.

The madwoman cackled again, the most grating kind of sound. "Ooh, you're trying to be nice to me, aren't you? I wondered if you'd try that." She gestured with the gun. "Come on. Try again. Something nice. Tell me how sweet I am or how pretty I look." Her tone turned darker, and she pressed the gun against the frightened child's temple again. "Try!"

A baby. The little girl with the red hair, sobbing, was barely more than a baby. Not even as old as Anna had been when her parents died. Nia was on the other side of the tent, but how would this child's life be altered if she died, even for a moment?

The peaceful feelings started to shudder and shake, calm breaking as fire threatened to burst through. Children, trapped in violence that wasn't their fault, who would suffer nonetheless.

Anna clenched her fists. She took two more steps toward Daphne, closing the distance between them, hoping the psycho-bitch would aim the gun at Anna, not that child.

"Let the children go. I know your truth. You don't want to kill them. You want us to kill you. You think you'll be stronger as the goddess, but do you know what you'll really be? Dead. You're a vessel, another prison cell to her, and she longs for you to scream in pain and die so she'll finally be free."

A few things happened in the next few moments, which made it fortunate how time slowed and distilled with crystal clarity.

First, Daphne seemed to notice the approach of Mal and the others.

Then her truth shifted. She did want to kill Anna. The itch increased in intensity on Anna's lower back. Daphne wanted vengeance on the other Fates who'd wanted the Four to rise, who'd betrayed her with the goddess and the ensuing insanity. She wanted vengeance on Loki, for ensuring she was well-cared for and healthy. And she wanted to make Beckwell suffer, all the paranormals who'd never quite accepted her before she'd absorbed the goddess, the Fates who hadn't listened to her, the town that defeated her again and again.

She was going to kill the children.

Faex.

Daphne's finger tightened in slow-motion on the trigger.

Anna's lips curled back in a snarl, and she dove toward Daphne. Grabbed Daphne's wrist and jerked it upright. The bullet exploded from the gun in a slow puff of smoke and a small black projectile.

Mal reached Daphne's side, wrapping his hands around the children and pulling them away, all in slow-motion still.

Loki intercepted the two old men, jerked the guns from their hands. Turned and looked toward her, moved toward Daphne.

Daphne twisted, jerking free, aiming the gun at Mal and the children, her motions not as quick as Anna's but not as slow as they could be, as a human would be.

The goddess was cheating.

Anna's mouth tasted of sickly-sweet violence. She grabbed for Daphne's wrist and wrenched it down, blocking the hit that would have struck Mal or the kids.

Daphne turned on her with a snarl, and with inhuman strength, twisted the gun toward Anna's face. Her truths screamed through Anna. How she'd threatened and wanted to have Piper murder Daniel. How she'd helped almost destroy Ginny by whispering lies of power and greatness to Ginny's false brother. Her memories of slaughtering that young family, the pleasure she'd taken killing the small boy even as the mother screamed and he wept. That weeping little boy, who'd had nothing to do with violence, who hadn't deserved that pain, who should have grown up. Destroyed by calculating, sadistic evil.

War's fire evaporated any hint of the cool, calm beneath.

The universe demanded justice.

Dark fury unlike anything Anna had ever experienced swept through her, burning away everything but clarity and the truth of what she needed to do next. She grabbed Daphne's wrist, the two of them locked in a perverse dance. Anna shoved aside the first shot that went off over her shoulder. She twisted Daphne's hand. Pressed the weapon into Daphne's chest. Wrapped her hand around Daphne's fingers.

Daphne grinned at Anna. "*Tu futueo et caballum tuum,*" the goddess said through Daphne's lips.

Detached peace settled over her—the peace she could have made more use of a few moments earlier to calm Daphne down, damn it. War's fire and strength burned through her. This was War. This was what everyone wanted her to be anyway.

"You first," Anna whispered.

Her hand on Daphne's, together they squeezed the trigger.

The next three things happened almost simultaneously.

The gun fired with a bang that jerked it toward Anna's chest, the sound echoed by two more weapons.

Anna was knocked away from Daphne by a horse.

Another weapon fired, and Daphne flinched. The gun tumbled from her hand.

Time resumed at normal speed with all the friendliness of a speeding locomotive. Anna's head throbbed, her vision went blurry for a second as she tried to scramble out from beneath the large and immovable horse. Every part of her felt that he'd definitely been running when he hit her, and damn was he big. Whispers of truth echoed around her.

"Did that woman tell me to fuck off? That's rather uncalled for, seeing as I haven't even met her." Rojo leaned his long neck down to look at her, where she crawled out from beneath him. "You don't look so good. Don't barf on my hooves. Hey, any idea how long it takes for horses to heal from bullet wounds?"

"She said screw you and the horse you rode in on. I didn't ride you. I don't know how long horses take to heal, but you're not a real horse anyway," she murmured, the words tripping and sticking to her tongue. "Who shot you?"

"Some of those old guys. They were aiming at Daphne, but you were in the way." He swung his head toward his flank and the slowly oozing wound. "It kind of stings."

She struggled to stand, but her knees kept giving out beneath her, and the ground swayed and undulated beneath her, all of which made her stomach lurch.

She squinted, tried to focus on the four Lokis who knelt beside Daphne. Truths whispered through her, one louder than all the others.

Daphne Spinner was dead.

Nausea rocketed through her.

Oh Goddess. She'd *killed* Daphne.

Another three figures stopped near Loki. Or maybe it was only one. The double vision made it hard to tell for sure. This new figure was as big as Loki, dark and cloaked. His truth said he believed he'd killed Daphne.

"Come on, you've got to get out of here," someone said, maybe Mal or Daniel, one of them. Whoever it was dragged her to her feet, but her knees wouldn't hold her.

Her mind whirled in as many circles as her vision. She'd pulled the trigger. She'd killed someone. Goddess, she'd *killed* someone.

Mal or Daniel half threw her over the giant whirling horse. "Get her somewhere safe. Meet us in an hour, the library." They weren't talking to her, but to Rojo.

"Roger that."

Blackness crept in at the edges of her vision, warring with nausea for supremacy. There was a loud crack of thunder, the sky broke open, and it began to rain. It might have been the double vision talking, but it looked like it was raining blood.

CHAPTER 25

Loki watched the large chestnut horse carry a limp Anna out of view and recited the Norse Prose Edda backward and then forward before he finally cast a cold look over first Thor, then the one being he could have done without seeing for at least another few days. Or ever.

"Look who I found. Can you believe it?" Thor said with a big grin, blood-red rain dripping down his face and making his sodden hair where it stuck to his big moronic head even redder. He still held Mjolnir in umbrella form in one hand, and clamped the newcomer, of similar size and build, on the shoulder. "I told them you'd just keep coming, that you'd be here. I told them. Here you are. Loki, can you believe it?"

"Unfortunately," Loki said, moving his gaze to the other man, dark where Thor was light, hiding behind his mirrored sunglasses. Thor had barely shifted him with the blow to the shoulders that would have flattened others. "Heimdall," he said, voice cool, tone hovering on the edge of polite and infuriated.

Heimdall removed his glasses, his eyes a shimmering mercury like the cut edge of an obsidian blade. His face and nose grew in blunt, hard angles, skin dark, hair black and cropped short. No softness anywhere on him, other than the long dark duster jacket that almost brushed the ground and the battered fedora that now kept some of the blood rain from his face.

"Where is she?" Heimdall said, voice gravelly.

Loki wiped the blood rain out of his face, shoved back his hair, and glanced around at the rapidly clearing fairgrounds.

Few Beckwellians remained after the first gunshot. Even less after the second. The bouncy houses sagged as the motors were shut off and the air drained out, and the unicorn neighed wildly as someone tried to load it into the trailer, the scent of blood likely driving the poor animal mad.

"The unicorn?" he asked, turning slowly to look back at Thor's infuriating brother.

The way Heimdall ground his jaw and tightened his grip on his service weapon said Loki had his usual effect on him. The Verdict, a peculiar cross between firearm and wand, was Heimdall's invention, including the pompous name. Carried by all USELESS agents, it was just like the one the agent had tried to use to kill Anna.

"The War woman. You've crossed the line for the last time, Loki. We both knew this day would come, but it's a pity you dragged those girls into it, filled their heads with tales of power and glory. You'll all face execution."

He'd screwed up. Let Anna get into the line of fire. Let himself get distracted by the hopeless desire someone actually saw and accepted him without his dying to earn redemption. He should have found a way to make her rise sooner. Should have dealt with and kept Daphne properly contained. Should have better protected his town.

Now, the only chance of defeating the goddess was

in the Four rising, the only beings more powerful than one enraged goddess determined to have her vengeance on the gods by destroying what they considered their playground, the mortal realm.

Now Anna had blood on her hands.

Loki squeezed his fingers into fists until his nails cut into his palms. The fact that Anna had anything to do with Daphne's death would bring trouble of its own. He needed allies, and he couldn't afford to be choosy.

"They're not 'girls.' They've never been interested in either power or glory—and despite what you may have been told, they are strong." He leaned closer. "Right now, though, I think you'd be a little more concerned with what's going to happen to you. The gods and the angels want blood."

Heimdall's changeable eyes narrowed, whirled slightly silver for a moment, as though he peered into whatever past or present he could see. As irritating as a bloody Fate.

His brow furrowed, just a little. He glanced down at the empty body of Daphne Spinner, laying in the rain and pooling red puddles. "She can be brought back," he said gruffly.

"Not a second time." Loki leaned closer. "Maybe you should be figuring out how you're going to stop—and explain—the chaos-destruction goddess *you* just let loose." Let Heimdall believe his second shot with the Verdict killed Daphne. The two had been almost simultaneous, and if Anna's bullet hadn't struck first, Heimdall would have been responsible for the death. He pounded Heimdall on the shoulder, hard, gave him a tight smile, then turned on his heel.

"This is your fault, Loki. Not mine," Heimdall called after him.

But he wasn't chasing. More, there was the barest note of uncertainty in his voice.

Loki kept walking. He had to find Anna.

೫

Anna opened her eyes to a horse leaning and dripping over her, his coat chestnut red. *Dear Goddess, please let that be rain that's dripping on me.* She groaned and flapped her hands to shoo him away, tried to find some part of her that didn't hurt and figure out where she lay. Everything was blurry, the world from a merry-go-round.

Memory rushed through her with the speed of rapidly flipping pages. Beckwell Days. Daphne. The truths. Oh, Gaia, *the truths*.

She'd held Daphne's fingers on the trigger and pulled it.

Anna's eyes stung, and her stomach flipped.

"Oh, good. You're not dead," Rojo said, giving his head a shake.

Blood-red water droplets rained all over the library. Over the shelves of books, the new beanbag chairs, the DVDs. Well, it didn't matter so much about the DVDs.

She rolled into a sitting position, clutching her still-aching, spinning head. Rojo. He'd been there. Knocked her clear. "You're not in London where I left you. Did you do this?"

"Your head? No. That's from staying in fight mode too long, Princess." He snorted, trotting over to the sink and small kitchenette area, using his teeth on the tap and turning it until water sprayed out before slurping some. Splashing a lot more.

"Stop that, you're making a mess. Transform back into a pigeon. Can't you do that? Nia's horse could switch forms easily."

"I am definitely smarter than some Death horse," Rojo said, splashing a bit more before turning off the water and turning to face her, upsetting a book cart of returns and scattering all the material in the process. "But why would I be a pigeon when I could be this?"

He struck a pose, chest out, head held high.

Her headache was taking on new, Rojo-sized proportions. She massaged her eyes, not that it helped. "Because pigeons fit better inside buildings. Like libraries. What are you doing here? I thought you were going to find the real War?" She struggled to stand again, but her knees were still dangerously soft. She crumpled back down, grit her teeth, and tried again.

Rojo bumped against her, lowering himself down onto his forelocks. "Grab on. I'll help you up. Damned women, always all weak and fainting." His voice was gruff, with a note of softness she hadn't heard before.

She scowled at him but reached one arm over his broad back and another around his neck.

This time when she forced herself upright, Rojo rose beneath her, and she stayed upright. Mostly. While leaning heavily and panting a moment against the horse.

It was better standing near Rojo. Touching him. The dizziness was passing. Vision almost single again.

Plus, that ache she'd had for the past two days, that elastic cord stretching inside her, was eased.

"About that…turns out it hurts like hell to be far from a certain pain-in-the-ass librarian."

Anna sniffed, but her thoughts spiraled in other directions. She'd still killed Daphne. The violent need to do so had risen in her so sharply it had barely been a choice. Just certainty. Was it another War ability, or just part of the inheritance? That certainty that made her able to kill someone because the truth told her to. Bile burned the back of her throat.

She'd taken a step closer to killing Loki by taking one life already. If she'd seen his truth, had he seen this truth, that she was so much closer to becoming the killer she feared than she realized?

"You should have listened back in London. We

could have used your help. Now there's probably a chaos goddess on the loose, and that's going to slow progress finding candidate four and the real War."

Could there be another viable candidate out there still? She'd denied what now seemed inevitable.

She wasn't even officially War yet, and she'd already killed someone.

Was this how she'd somehow be able to kill Loki? More bile. She swallowed back with difficulty.

The horse studied her with those big brown eyes. "Yeah, well, I had to fly back here on my own, and not only is that grueling when you have a narrow wingspan, but there are also a lot of things that like to eat pigeons. Those predators ate up a lot of time."

All her friends' horses had died at least once, and they'd always come back to life. But…this was Rojo.

She sighed, almost grateful for the distraction he provided. Better than thinking about killing. "Because you had to stop and beat them up?"

He widened his eyes, lifted his brows…if horses had brows. "Of course. I owe it to my pigeon brethren."

She didn't want to, she didn't even want to like him, but her lips twitched upward. *"Podex perfectus es,"* she said, but it was said with fondness. She pushed off from him, wobbly a second, but waved him off when he shuffled closer.

He snorted. "You're still a useless woman, Princess." Again, there was a hint of fondness in his words, even in that horrible nickname. "So, about that finding another War…"

She made it to the scarred conference table near the front of the library and was about to lower herself into her usual chair at the head of the table when the door flew open, and Loki stormed in.

His hair was plastered to his head, clothing to his body, and he looked ready to fight legions. That, or a lot like Mr. Darcy rising from the lake, shirt plastered to his muscular chest.

Her breath wheezed out, and her knees lost all strength as she sagged down into the chair, heat whirling through her.

His dark gaze shot with amber fixed on her, and he took a step forward. "Anna—"

"Anna! Thank gods," Ginny said, spilling into the room just ahead of Nia and Piper. Ginny dashed forward and gave Anna a warm hug. "I was so afraid for you, sweetie."

They were followed closely by Mal, Daniel, James, and the two older men who'd almost shot Daphne. All the children were safely ensconced in the Senior Center.

"You didn't look so good for a minute there," Nia said, coming in and giving Anna a warm squeeze on the shoulder.

Did they know what she'd done? That she'd pulled the trigger?

"Yes, but the way you moved? It was like a blur, some kind of superhero zipping from one place to the next," Piper said, leaning down to give Anna a one-armed hug.

All of them settled in around the table, even the old men pulling up chairs and settling in.

Only Loki still stood near the door, looking like he wanted to say something or possibly make his excuses and leave.

Like he felt as though he didn't belong.

Anna took a breath and held out her hand, met his gaze. "Come on over." A small smile tickled her lips. "I don't bite."

Humor sparked in his eyes. He hesitated a moment longer before his shoulders rolled as he made his way to her side.

"Someone, grab another chair, will you?" she said.

"On it," Rojo said, his mouth around the back of a chair. He dropped it next to Loki, gave it a small kick, and sent it sailing toward the table.

Loki caught it before it collided or tipped, gave the horse a small nod, then pulled the chair up beside her and took a seat. Not close enough to imply they were together, the way some of the others were clustered, but close enough his knee bumped hers, his foot nudged against hers.

She slid her sodden shoe closer to his until their feet touched. Together, she and Loki made a good team, he'd said so himself. This was about logic and strategy, not emotion.

She took a deep breath and faced her friends. They deserved this truth, to understand her part in it. "It appears we have a chaos goddess to stop. Because of me."

❧

Anna was doing it again. Bringing him into her circle, connecting him. Making him less alone. Loki shifted slightly, bringing his leg against hers more. Tempting though it was to reach for her hand, lay his fingers over her knee, there were too many witnesses. The action would raise too many questions—and complications.

"You were trying to save those kids," Mal said gruffly.

"This better not mean everyone is going to die. There are only so many people I can bring back to life in a day," Nia said, sarcastic as ever, though there was underlying fear beneath her sarcasm and in the way she reached for Mal's hand, squeezing his fingers.

"I'm sure that's appreciated, Petunia—" Loki started.

Anna cleared her throat, interrupting him, and leaned closer to whisper. "She prefers 'Nia.'" The look in her blue gaze was significant, a reminder of the discussion they'd had on the drive back to town, her accusation of treating everyone like pawns.

Which was much easier than knowing each of these people. Their lives, their successes, and knowing if some of them didn't make it, it'd leave another hole carved out of his soul. It was a test of his resolve to push aside emotion and continue with his plans.

He raised a brow but continued as though not interrupted. "*Nia*, I'm certain your actions would be appreciated, but better we avoid the need for resurrection, wouldn't you agree?"

"This goddess is old, entitled, and out for blood. She also needs life energy to create her physical form. She'll be looking for easy prey to start," Old Henry said, his face longer and grayer than it'd ever been, as though he too felt the weight and failure of letting the goddess escape. He rubbed a hand over his mostly bald head. He'd been helping protect Beckwell since before most of the other occupants of the room had been born.

Piper paled and turned to Daniel, her hand coming to his chest. "The Senior Center. Where most of the children are. Where *our* children are."

Daniel snorted and wrapped an arm around her. "Watched over and under the protection of three apocalypse horses, a dragon, and a lot of residents. The children might be easy targets, but have you *been* to the Senior Center? I pity the idiot who believes anyone in there is 'easy prey.'" He exchanged a wry look with Old Henry and the other man, a quiet fellow by the name of Albert.

Both the older men looked at Daniel, looked at each other, then started to chuckle.

Albert turned to Loki. "It won't be the Senior Center."

"Then perhaps after lone individuals. Like prey animals pick off the stragglers in a herd," James, Ginny's husband suggested, competence in his British accented voice. "I have my team doing a door-to-door at Mal's suggestion, getting people grouped together, better able to protect themselves."

James had combatted famine in Third World countries before marrying Ginny, and his settling here had brought the strength of his team with him. A quasi-military team with skills in engineering and various paranormal abilities, they included a former USELESS tech, a male siren, a dragon, fraternal nymph twins, and James and his brother, both Famine clan.

"Excellent. Thank you, James, Malc—"

Anna stepped on his toe and gave him a look.

"Mal," Loki finished, meeting her eyes.

She gave him a small smile.

Very tempting to kiss that smug look off her face, but that would definitely attract some questions.

"We have another problem. Not only do we need to deal with the goddess, but Heimdall has reached Beckwell," Loki said, his gaze not leaving Anna. "The only advantage we have is that I convinced him he was responsible for Daphne's death, which may give us both some leeway and a potential ally, in stopping the goddess at least."

"Why is Heimdall after you?" Ginny glanced at Loki. "Aren't you a Norse god too?"

"Heimdall founded USELESS. He wants to see me dead, and according to Thor, he usually succeeds," Anna said, sounding more irritated than concerned.

"Indeed. Heimdall is…rather pedantic, and like some of the other gods, refuses to see that change has and must come to the modern world for all, paranormal or otherwise. However, he is honorable and will want to see his mistake rectified, if only to maintain his perfect record. Releasing a chaos-destruction goddess in the gods' favorite playground will not be looked at favorably, even if he could succeed in harming Anna." Heimdall wouldn't get near Anna.

"So, just to keep this straight, we have to get rid of two gods? My to-do list is getting all confused here," Nia said.

"Heimdall is a threat to Anna, and possibly the rest of you if he wishes to fully eliminate the threat of the Four. He isn't a threat in general."

"So…is that a 'no, don't hurt Heimdall'?" Piper asked.

"You'd be hard-pressed to," Old Henry chimed in. "He's trained centuries of USELESS agents and assassins. Came out of retirement specifically for this case from what I hear."

Interesting. Henry was clearly more connected to the network of spies and gossip than Loki had realized, something that could come in handy.

"Something for which I'm probably supposed to feel flattered. We need to focus here. The goddess. She's spirit, not flesh, correct?" Anna got up, her expression distracted as she headed for the circulation desk and some of the older books behind. She quickly skimmed through them, pulling out a volume and flipping through the pages, frowning as she returned to the table with the book. Her gaze met his, and she retook her seat, shifting in position until their knees once more touched. "That means we have a chance while she creates—or steals—a body for herself, doesn't it?"

"Or an opportunity to attack while she's at her most vulnerable," Mal said, bringing an arm around Nia.

"Amazingly, I agree with cop-boy. Let's smash her while we have a chance," Rojo said with a neigh, coming up and leaning over Anna's shoulder.

She flicked her hand at the horse, who backed off with a horsey snort.

"If it were that easy, I would have suggested it to

start. We can look for her, but there's a good chance she isn't even in the same dimension, or she's using a kind of bubble dimension while she grows stronger," Loki said.

Nia sat back with a sniff. "Well, that's just cheating."

"She's going to use whatever cheats she can," Anna said. She sighed, rubbing her eyes. "I suspect she played me, convinced me to help Daphne die. I screwed up, and she's fast, smart, and deadly. We need to find out more about her to even know how—or if—she can be killed. The gods didn't kill her before, but destroyed her physical form and imprisoned her spiritual one. We may need to do the same. Which means research. I can handle that. We also need to get Beckwell prepared for attack, whether she's looking for a body, victims, or just target practice."

Ah, there it was. Anna taking charge, handing out assignments, beginning to lead her troops. Getting closer to rising as War. Loki sat back and let her work.

"We can get on that," Daniel said, looking to his brother, then the two older men, all of whom nodded.

"Good. We also need methods of containment. James, your team has some experience with rogue gods, don't they? Why don't you and Ginny lead the task force on putting together some options for us if we need to try and trap her. I'll get back to you as I know more about how she was trapped before and the requirements."

"We're on it," Ginny said, giving James's arm a squeeze when he nodded.

Next Anna turned to Nia. "We need patrols and advance fieldwork. Use your ghosts, reapers, whatever you've got for patrol work. We need to know where the goddess is. Observation only, do not engage."

"Maybe a little?" Nia held up her fingers, almost pinched together.

"No engagement. Not until we know what we're dealing with." She turned to Piper. "That leaves you, Heimdall, and Thor. You're running distraction and keeping him off us. I don't think he should be a threat to you?" She turned to Loki for confirmation.

Damn, she was sexy.

He shook his head, forcing his gaze off her and to Piper. "No, she should be fine. We're his targets. He'll want to deviate course as little as possible, even concerning the goddess."

"Daniel, Mal, gentlemen, while you're getting town defenses ready, do a weapon hunt, will you?" Anna continued. "We should know what we have at our disposal, and I have a strong suspicion there may be a few interesting and unusual choices among the population."

A throat cleared, and everyone turned to the door where Deirdre Boniface, the eldest of the Fates stood, ramrod straight, steel-gray hair and gaze, lips pinched.

Anna and most of the others jumped to their feet. Which was natural perhaps, considering she'd tried to kill or use them all in some way.

Loki just turned his chair for a better view.

Deirdre Boniface, Beckwell's school principal, was the last remaining Fate, the eldest and most feared of them, the incarnation of Atropos, the crone who could cut the thread of fate and saw the future. She'd plotted to have them rise and help her end the world. He'd been complicit in the plot, as it suited his purposes and provided a cover for his own plans, but animosity remained on all sides other than his own. If he took it personally every time someone tried to kill him, he'd have ulcers and spend all his time plotting vengeance rather than anything more interesting.

"What do you want?" Anna said, her voice glacial, the expressions on the faces of the other three horsewomen just as friendly.

Deirdre pushed back the wet hood of her rain jacket, then held her hands together in front of her. They trembled slightly. "I come to offer assistance. And if you're collecting weapons of import, I suggest you also consider those stored in the school."

James, the only one who hadn't been born and raised in Beckwell, turned to his wife and whispered softly. "There are weapons in the school? The *children's* school?"

Ginny shrugged, not taking her eyes off Deirdre. "Not for them to play with. They're in a case. It's not locked, but they're really dangerous, so everyone pretty much knows not to touch them."

James's eyes were wide, and he appeared quite alarmed.

Anna shot them a quelling look, making Ginny's face color.

The War horsewoman turned back to Deirdre. "Is that all?"

Faint color climbed the older woman's cheeks. "No." She paused, as though considering Anna, her fingers massaging her knuckles. Perhaps recalling the times she'd tried to harm the Four. "I realize we haven't always seen eye-to-eye, but our aims are, I believe, similar. I don't want our town harmed. I knew Daphne, and through her, the goddess. Daphne grew increasingly unstable as the goddess exerted greater influence. I could be useful. If the end must come for humanity, I'd rather it be quick and painless. Humane. I foresaw this possible future, you realize, along with countless others, some that may still be. This is why I tried to recruit you. If you'd gone along with our plan, done a small cull of humanity, a reset as it were, this might not have come to pass."

"Wait. Why are we listening to this bitch? She hates us," Nia practically snarled.

"She kidnapped me and threatened Daniel's life," Piper said, gaze dark.

"She tried to kill me and give my dead twin—or a version of my dead twin—my abilities," Ginny growled.

Anna, though, remained silent, arms crossed over her chest as she studied the older woman.

Rojo leaned down over her shoulder. "Should I throw her out?"

Anna's considering continued a beat or two longer. Before, finally, she dropped her arms, voice calm. "No." She walked closer to Deirdre, still studying her, staring so hard the other woman looked away, tried to avoid Anna's gaze.

"I see her truth. She does want to help. She could be useful." Anna pointed to the table. "You let Mal and the others into the school, giving them explicit locations and directions concerning all of the weapons there. Then you come back here, and you start writing. I want to know everything you do about the goddess, her personality, her triggers. Then I want everything you know about the future and possible futures. Which plans succeed, which fail, how this might all play out. Regarding both Heimdall and the goddess."

"But—that's countless possibilities. I could write until next year and still not see all of them," Deirdre sputtered.

Anna's smile thinned, and she raised a brow. "Then you'd better get started. Despite the evidence, you're an intelligent woman. Sort through and give me the most likely and best options. If the goddess is going to cheat, so are we." She turned her back on Deirdre, as though dismissing her, turning to the others. "Off you go. Stay in touch, keep communicating. We reconvene tomorrow morning at Loki's house if the goddess hasn't made her presence known. If we're still alive. Good luck."

Chairs and bodies shifted as everyone moved toward the door. Deirdre grumbled something as she pulled up her hood and headed back outside, but Anna was right: the woman could prove useful. Plans were murmured. Rojo backed up to go stand in the children's section, and

Loki stood, leaning against the circulation desk, arms crossed so he could best observe Anna in her habitat.

She directed each of the groups, even as the four women all gradually moved closer to one another, convening as though partially by chance, partially drawn together like the forces of nature they were.

Their voices were quiet, too low for him to hear what they said. Promises maybe, the way Anna nodded in response, the way they all embraced, said their farewells.

The Four as women interacted differently than they had as men, but the connection was the same. War was always their leader, while they remained equals. Perhaps because they were women, these four had overcome greater challenges, refused the status quo, and found unique ways to use and enhance their abilities. Their compassion combined with intellect made them stronger than Peter and his friends had ever been, with youthful arrogance and certainty of their privilege. Anna didn't realize it yet, but when she rose, their bond would be even stronger in ways even he didn't fully understand. Some secrets of the horsemen were never written down, only experienced.

He just needed to push her that last step further to rise.

Gradually, the library emptied until it was only he, Anna, and the damned horse. He chose to pretend it wasn't there—as it appeared to be reading and chuckling over a children's book anyway. Perhaps it'd spent too much time with Thor and dimmed its intellect.

Anna turned to him, straightened, almost as though bracing against their next encounter.

Or perhaps resisting, as he was, the distraction their relationship could prove. A most seductive, warm distraction.

He tucked his hands in his trouser pockets, his clothing still damp from the blood rain, just as Anna's were. Though, at least the black tank hadn't clung to her every curve as silk would have done. She was already far too attractive for his peace of mind.

"I thought I might assist with research. Share what I know," he said.

Her brows flicked upward momentarily, surprise at either his offer to help or share, he couldn't be certain. "I... Well... Of course." She headed back to behind her circulation desk, her brow creasing. "Though I'm afraid what I have on ancient chaos and destruction goddesses may be insufficient."

He closed the distance between them again until he was close enough to catch her scent, the floral fragrance of her hair. "Which is why I suggest an alternate library. Mine." Bringing her back to his house, back to his territory.

Where she belonged.

He tried to keep his face smooth over the latter, seemingly random thought. If she picked up anything, she didn't say so. Just went through her books, selected about four and put them in a bag over her shoulder, then turned back to him.

"Let's get to it, then."

CHAPTER 26

After a brief argument with Rojo involving the spacial realities of Loki's car versus a horse and Rojo's continued refusal to transform, she and Loki set off for Loki's house while Rojo made his way on foot through the blood rain.

On the way, they passed carloads of Beckwellians, packed and taking to the roads. Taking them anywhere but Beckwell.

Anna frowned at them, sensing their passing truths, their certainty of doom. "They're running."

"That's what most people do when they believe they might die," Loki said mildly.

She turned, falling into his dark gaze, the flare of amber there.

She licked her lips.

Amber began to blot out the pewter.

"I'm afraid too," she said. She had to say it to someone. She'd sent her friends in all directions, initiated a plan that delayed any attack on the goddess, pretended she was somehow their leader. Maybe it was the wrong plan. Maybe she'd sent some of them to their deaths. She'd have to live with herself afterward.

"I said most people." Loki turned back to the road, speeding up as traffic thinned. "You, though, run toward the battle, toward your fear. To make a difference, to win."

No, she didn't. She stared down at her lap, her hands twisting together. She'd been running a long time from her past, from what had happened to her parents. The tragedy she'd been certain she caused. She'd spent even more time cultivating a safe, dull life to protect her from things that she only feared might happen. Fear had stolen moments, like being there for Ginny at her first wedding—and possibly stopping it. The opportunity to attend University in person. Even being there for the birth of Piper's twins, because Anna had been so afraid of rising, she'd been in another country instead.

"If that was true, wouldn't I want to be War? That's what I most fear."

Although, increasingly, she was more afraid of rising and having to make the choice between staying true to herself or fulfilling Loki's wish and killing him. Ending a life that had become more precious to her than her own.

He was silent as he turned down his long driveway, only the shush of the windshield wipers providing a counterpoint.

He didn't speak until they stopped in front of the house and he shut off the car. Undoing his seat belt, he turned to her. "You say you want to avoid rising, but you've used your abilities. Learned them, embraced them, found ways to use them to help people rather than for your own gain. It only confirms to me why you are the only person who should rise as War. Who needs to."

She didn't want to hear his words, tried to block them out as she opened the door, stepped out into the rain. How much did he remember of the Four manipulating him?

Making him the catalyst in their plan. Part of War's plan. That was part of who she was too—the need to win and plot, like the original War. Only it was her who'd have to act.

Loki raced to meet her around her side of the car, lifting his arm over her head with his shirt to try and shelter her from the blood rain as they ran up the front steps.

His minion opened the door as they arrived and dashed in, shaking off the wet.

"We need to focus on research," she said grouchily, struggling to kick off her shoes, the leather swollen around her feet. She looked down at the once classic pair of trousers, now probably ruined forever with ground-in mud, water stains, and wrinkles. Because that was what happened around a War: things were ruined.

"You don't want to change first?" Loki asked, barefoot again, equally sodden, though he made it look attractive, rather than the drowned-rat look she sported.

"No. We can't waste time." She'd rather be wet and miserable. Deserved to be if she was anything like the War who'd plotted to kill him. She'd never considered her strategy and intelligence were connected to her War ability, nor dangerous, but perhaps that had been a mistake.

His brows raised in defeat, he gestured down the hall.

She followed him but already knew the way to the room she and Rojo had discovered. Less than a week ago. A veritable lifetime ago.

When he slid open the doors, the luxuriously magical room was revealed again. This time, a fire roared in the fireplace with a crackle and snap, and the faint scent of wood smoke covered the smell of the books.

Loki, muscles rippling and making it look easy, briskly climbed the narrow, winding staircase to the second level, retrieving his book from the secret hideaway. He disappeared in the upper gallery a moment before he leaned over the railing, holding the book, then strode back down toward her, flipping through it already.

His version of the Bigass Book of Research. "She's gone by the name Sekhmet, an Egyptian goddess of death and destruction, but it's believed she's much older. Potentially disguised and inserted herself into the Egyptian pantheon. Some of the old ones did that, found a way to extend their existence by creating fresh believers."

Had a man reading through a book of his own creation, his own intense research, ever looked sexier?

No. Only Loki could look that good.

He looked up, and she tried to pretend she hadn't been thinking dirty thoughts and drooling. The whisper of a smile over his lips, the flicker of amber in his gaze said perhaps this time, he knew she was the one lying.

He cleared his throat, frowned, and looked back at the book. "The trouble is we don't know her name. We'll need that if we have to imprison her."

"Won't Sekhmet be enough?"

"Partially. But if we want to trap her in the vessel, we need the older name."

"So, we start looking up goddesses, see who fits the description. I'll take Cycladic, you look at Mesopotamian. Maybe an early creation goddess?"

"Or an older Egyptian goddess even," he said, coming down the stairwell.

She glanced around the room, recalled the careful organization, took a moment to calculate, then pointed toward the lower right. "Somewhere over there I'm guessing?"

Another almost-smile as he reached her side, the look of it sending a warm glow through her. "Yes. I've gone through all of those. She's not in them." He took her arm and led her toward what appeared to be another wall of books, this section mostly fiction. He reached up and pulled down one paperback until it rested on its spine, then lifted another partially upward. There was a small click.

He pushed gently, and the entire shelf swung inward. He held out his hand for her, his voice hushed. "We'll have to be quick and quiet, but this should help. Don't let go of me."

She reached out and placed her fingers in his, his grip firm on hers as he tugged her toward the opening. She peered inside, unable to prevent the small gasp as she gazed into the bright, enormous space, rows and rows of shelves that soared up beyond view. "What is this?" she whispered.

"A back door that's not supposed to exist into Braelyn and the library of the gods. Every book that ever was, some that have yet to be." He pulled her closer. "All for you, Anna. Whenever you want it."

The library was beyond her dreams: enormous, classical, enough to keep anyone more than occupied for centuries.

Yet, she was drawn to something better. The warmth of the man beside her, the awe and appreciation in his gaze that matched to hers, his thirst for knowledge and intellect unparalleled. Other men might have given her flowers or chocolates. Maybe *a* book if they were clever.

Loki had given her the library of the gods.

There was no one like him, nor would there ever be. It was dangerous, it was foolish, it was terrifying. It wasn't necessarily even what she'd have wanted if given a choice. She had little choice in this matter. Indeed, perhaps it was even logical. She was in love with Loki Laufeyjarson.

ॐ

Hours later, she and Loki emerged back into Loki's library. The advantage of working in a library that was technically located in Braelyn, home of the gods—besides its sheer grandeur and breadth—was that thanks to the gods' eccentricities, time worked differently there, even though it and all its structures and people—as with Daimoleigh—existed in a parallel world that existed within the same physical laws. Rumor was that long ago, Daimoleigh, Braelyn, and the mortal realm had all been one world...before fighting between the species had become so brutal, the mortal world had been torn apart and the veils created to separate them.

Still, in this case, the closeness and peculiarities of Braelyn had worked to their advantage. She and Loki worked the entire night, until their vision was blurry, and she could barely read over the raucous chatter of truths from all the surrounding books. Yet only a few minutes had passed back home by the time they stumbled through the secret door back into Loki's library.

Anna rubbed her eyes and stifled a yawn, trying to focus on her phone as it connected and she could check for messages then send texts out to her friends and tell them what she and Loki had uncovered. The disadvantage of working in Braelyn, besides that the gods already wanted them dead and were unlikely to be lenient should they discover she and Loki, was the terrible cell reception. Seeing as it was a different world and all. Almost as bad as some areas of Beckwell, which meant she'd had to wait until they got home to check.

She frowned. Home. To Beckwell. That's all she'd meant, wasn't it?

Loki closed and secured the door, once more hidden by the bookshelf. He had two books under his arm.

"You didn't sign those out properly." A smile touched her lips.

He glanced down at the books, then back. "It's possible I might return them. And there might be further information on how—or if—we can kill her in these."

She should have scolded him but laughed instead. Or, the tired version of a laugh. "Just so long as you return them."

"Almost likely, I promise. Come. We should get some sleep. No news, I take it?" He gestured toward her phone.

She shook her head, walking with him out of the library and toward the stairs. "No news is good news, I hope?"

He glanced at the grandfather clock in the foyer. "They've barely had time to start work yet."

Loki's minion emerged from one of the hallways. "Sir, Miss Fray's, er, horse arrived. I've seen him comfortably installed in one of the garages, along with the food and beverage he requested. I hope that was suitable?"

Loki nodded with a smile. "Perfectly. No horses in horse form in the house." He placed his hand in the small of her back. "We're going to get some sleep, Trevor. Please wake us if there's any news or anyone needs us."

His fingers burned through the soft fabric of the tank top, but she didn't move away, and he left his hand where it was. How oddly normal to climb the stairs together, as though she belonged here. With him. Which was dangerous thinking, likely befuddled thinking from too much research and too little sleep.

"Did you tell them what we found?" he said as they reached the top of the stairs, their footfalls quiet in the plush, patterned green carpet.

"Her name is Tukmis. Imprisoned in 526 after being charged with causing the Antioch earthquake, she escaped and is believed to be responsible for the worst year of human history in 536 and was subsequently imprisoned by twenty gods. Hobbies include maiming, raining fire from the sky, triggering earthquakes and volcanic eruptions, and occasional human torture." Because of

Anna, she was free. A chill went through her, that sluggish twisting of her stomach again.

She shook her head, tried to focus on Loki, not the memory of the triumphant look in Daphne's eyes when the gun went off. Nor the certainty Anna had felt just before, that what she was doing was right. The certainty that Daphne needed to die. "I only gave them the highlights. We'll have to see what Deirdre has to add, if anything. And what's in those books you're going to return." A thought managed to make its way up through the tired mire of her thoughts. "If you had this back door, why didn't we use it to help free Nia when the gods arrested her and took her to Braelyn?"

"Because I didn't have it then. It's a recent addition after it became clear it could prove helpful. Nia and Mal also needed to see to their own problems. They needed to grow. If we'd just rescued them, they wouldn't have."

She growled low in her throat. "Because you needed Nia to rise."

He glanced at her, expression unperturbed. "That, too."

Anna massaged her forehead, sighing. She was too tired for this argument or trying to outthink Loki. Besides which, he might have been right. As much as she'd wanted to rush in and rescue her friends, they grew more when she couldn't. Didn't mean she liked it. Or Loki manipulating them as he had. Asking him to act in a straightforward, honest manner was probably like asking a fish to tap dance.

They stopped at the place between the two sets of facing double doors, one leading to his suite, the others to hers.

His hand dropped from her back, and he took a step toward his room. "Get some sleep, Anna." He turned and reached for the door handle.

She rubbed her temples, though it didn't diminish the

growing ache behind her eyes. They knew the goddess's name, but she could still do things like rain fire from the sky. Anna had ordered her friends into tasks that could bring them to danger. She still hadn't met the fourth candidate, and it seemed less likely all the time there'd ever be a chance to meet that candidate. She'd given Loki her word. She had no idea if their semblance of a plan would work or if tomorrow they'd all die. Perhaps as troubling as those other realizations was that she'd finally realized—or perhaps admitted—she had feelings for Loki. Irresponsible, reckless, dangerous feelings.

She was also rising. Everyone believed it now, even Rojo. Which meant Loki would expect her to kill him, help fulfill his apocalyptic vision.

Her chest grew heavy, and the back of her throat ached. She couldn't spend tonight tossing and turning, alone.

"Loki?"

He paused in the doorway, turned slowly back to her.

The two steps to reach him were some of the hardest she'd ever taken, never breaking her gaze from his. His eyes smoldered dark pewter, shimmering to amber. She could barely resist looking away but didn't want to miss his expression, his truth.

"May I…join you?" she said, voice quiet.

He pushed open the door farther, gaze hot and gone completely amber.

Her shoulders sagged in relief even as heat coiled through her, and she walked through the door into his room.

He followed her inside, his presence at her back heightening her awareness. Her skin tingled, the brush of her clothing over her almost erotic, the sound of the door closing behind him loud.

Anna swallowed, tried to consider the room and the situation objectively. They'd slept together before. They were good together, whether conducting research, leading their team, or physically. Sex in his bed should make little difference.

The layout of the room was a mirror to hers, the large canopied bed dominating the space—bed hangings deep olive green of course—the wood furniture dark and strong, as male as their owner. Bookshelves gathered in the corner beside two worn, tobacco-colored leather chairs, the shelves crammed with books, as though even with the massive library he still didn't have enough shelf space. There was something comfortable in the quiet luxury and masculine sanctuary.

This wasn't the same as the night in the hotel.

This was his room, his territory.

This was what she'd dreamed of too many foolish nights.

Her stomach squeezed, and she turned, found him standing near the door, all that masculine grace, her warrior…simply watching her as she invaded his space, waiting to see perhaps if she'd changed her mind. Patient, surprisingly gentle, sexy as hell.

Something inside her bloomed and expanded, warmed her hotter than War's fire, settled her doubts, made her step sure as she approached him. Some of that heat whirled low in her belly and made her anticipate his touch, but it was more than mere desire.

This was Loki. *Her* Loki.

She stopped just in front of him.

Still, he only watched her, even as she settled her hands on his chest, the heat of him burning through his silk shirt, his muscles tightening beneath her touch. He'd rolled up the sleeves of the battered green shirt during research, his hair ruffled from the way he'd push his hands through it while studying the pages of the book. She let her fingertips caress his jaw, the faint prickle of whiskers beneath her touch. Leaning forward, she pressed a kiss to his lips.

His mouth moved beneath hers, heated, opening to her touch. His arms came around her. He slid his hands up her arms, but he let her take the lead, didn't accelerate the kiss, didn't move his hands from where they caressed her.

She pulled back to consider his gaze, the steadiness that waited there. A thrill of excitement chased through her, tinged with fear. He had much more experience. She was making this up as she went. Her hands trembled as she reached for his shirt, her fingers slipping on the small buttons.

This had been a mistake. Being here with him, in his space, was too much. She started to pull away. "Maybe I should go. I…I'm just me, no more experienced than I was the first time. While you… You have several lifetimes of experience under your belt." She turned away.

He caught her hand, tugged her gently toward him before she'd taken more than a step away. Another tug before he caught her other hand and brought her against him, lifting their joined hands against his chest. He lowered his head to hers, their foreheads almost touching.

"Please. Stay," he said, his voice rough, as though he had to force himself to say the words.

It was enough to lift her gaze to his.

He lifted a dark brow, a small smile curving his lips. "I think you assume I've spent a lot more of my existence in bed than I have. When would I have any time for plotting?"

She couldn't quite smile at the attempted humor. "If I stay, we do this together. I…I need help."

Loki pressed a kiss to her forehead. "Anna, you are capable of anything. You seduce me with your smile, with a look, with your courage. Ymir help me if you did have more experience. It takes immense restraint to not grab you now and show you all the ways I've thought of enjoying you in my bed. But I want more. I want to know what *you* want and how you want it."

That curious warmth ballooned inside her again, thickened her throat, made the moment more precious, made her more daring. He did that. His faith in her, the way he looked at her, the things he said made her braver, stronger than she was.

Yet could she trust those feelings? A tiny chill chased through her. Gaia, he'd asked her to *kill* him. He needed her to become War. She couldn't trust her emotions when it came to him any more than she could indulge in fantasies of a happy ending for herself.

She shoved the chill away, let it harden her resolve, heat her passion as she pulled her hands free before sliding them down past the buttons until her fingers landed on his belt buckle and the zipper to his fly. Tonight was about passion, nothing further. She was too weak when it came to him as it was. She wouldn't give him more power over her than he already had.

So much more than he knew.

"What I want is you naked and inside me," she said.

One of his brows rose and his gaze darkened.

Ha! Take that, too many years of keeping her thoughts to herself. Her fingers found the small zipper pull and lowered it. He swelled beneath the fabric. "I want you to lose control." The way he stole all logic, all her intentions with just a touch. She slipped her hand through the opening of his fly and grasped his length, hot, hard, naked flesh. He still didn't care for underwear, evidently.

He groaned low in his throat, his hands finding her shoulders and pulling her closer. He pressed a hot kiss to her lips, his mouth opening beneath hers. He slid his hand beneath her panties and a long finger inside her.

She gasped, pulling back from him, watched a different kind of amusement glint in his expression, along with triumph. Considering the rapidly spiraling pleasure tightening within her, she couldn't complain.

"I love it when we have the same plans," he rasped. A second finger joined the first, and he slid slowly in and out of her.

"That's not fair," she said, or at least tried to as she grasped his shoulders and her breath came in shorter bursts. Her body focused on his touch, those magic fingers and the pleasure building within her.

"I play to win." His mouth found hers and his fingers delivered lightning.

Pleasure shattered Anna, and she cried out as her knees went weak.

But Loki was there. Loki was always there.

He caught her in his arms, held her as climax shuddered through her and until her vision cleared.

Well. He'd done it again. Left her shattered while he remained immaculate.

Maybe it was that War combativeness that needled her, maybe it was the reality that tomorrow this—he—could be gone.

Whatever it was, as her legs found strength again, pleasure still echoing through her, her hands settled on his chest, and she worked open the buttons of his shirt.

"I think you cheated," she said, her voice still rough.

He helped with the buttons from the bottom and shrugged the shirt off those magnificent shoulders, the defined muscles of his flat belly, the jut of his shaft from his charcoal pants. "I merely sought to fulfill your wish list." His eyes crinkled with a smile that faltered as she stepped out of his reach.

She kept her gaze on his, her pulse still fast, fire still whirling through her, that heady fullness of all he made her feel expanding her chest, making her daring. "Umhmm. Is that what that was?"

She grasped the hem of the tank top and lifted the soft fabric up and over her head, dropping it on the ground.

His gaze tracked the movement, roved over her, but he stood where she'd left him.

"I told you. I can take care of myself." She reached next for the button and zipper of her fly before pushing her slacks and panties down and stepping out of them.

"It doesn't mean I don't want to help," he said, his voice gravelly, his breathing more rapid.

His reaction made her braver, made her more daring.

She reached behind her, unclasped her bra, then slid the straps down her shoulders.

His hands clenched and unclenched at his side, but still, he didn't move. Still, he let her lead.

Her gaze connected with his as she pulled the bra away, let it dangle from a fingertip before she let it drop to the ground.

"Help is fine. But I've decided to cheat," she said, her hair sliding over her bare shoulders, the cool air hardening her nipples as she stepped toward him. Heat spilled through her as his hungry gaze roved over her appreciatively.

His gaze once more met hers, and he raised a dark brow. "Cheat?"

His patience emboldened her. With anyone else, she couldn't have been so daring. Only he made her feel as strong, as capable, as sexy. She could be someone she could only otherwise be in her fantasies. If this was their last time together, she would live with no regrets.

She loved him, and though she didn't dare say the words, didn't dare give him more power, she could show him with her body.

She let the smile slowly spread across her face as she stood before him, reached for the waistband of his pants. "You cheated. Why shouldn't I?" Stepping closer, his shaft brushed against her, sent prickles of anticipation shivering through her veins. She pushed the waistband

and belt of his pants down until it slid past his hips and to the floor, hitting the carpet with a soft clink of the belt buckle.

"You realize this is a game we can both win," he said.

"I'm counting on it," she said and encircled his shaft with her fingers, squeezing gently until he hissed out a breath. "Because I've decided to add to my list. I want to see you lose control."

He choked out a half-chuckle that turned to a groan as she slid her hand down his length.

Before she knelt and took him in her mouth.

He half-swore, half-groaned her name, and his hands tangled in her hair.

She got her wish. He did lose control, and they did end up in the bed together...eventually, leaving her body blissfully exhausted.

Even while his truths haunted her. The echoing emptiness and loneliness that mirrored her own. Then Loki with the dark-haired, handsome young man pictured in the library, Loki's arm around the other man's shoulders. And the love, Gaia, the intensity of Loki's feelings made Anna's eyes sting. The love he felt then. The love he still felt.

For someone else.

CHAPTER 27

Hours later, staring up at the gathered silk canopy of his bed, Loki wasn't sure whether he'd slept. She was doing it again. Making him feel. Cracking open that door inside where the lonely child peered out wondering if this time, with this woman, things could be different. He lay on his back, Anna asleep and draped over him, the sheet covering more of her than him, her breasts pillowed against his chest.

Last night he'd seen more of her truths. Seen the way she wasn't even fully able to be herself with her friends. The hurts they'd unintentionally caused her that made her retreat further into herself when they mocked her wardrobe, her brilliant mind that was more often lost in thought than engaged with the present. They called her socially inept when she easily saw through the games and pretenses of others, especially men. The sense of abandonment she felt when they'd all moved onto different lives, and she'd been left behind.

Left her only with thoughts and fantasies about him.

Dreams in which he was so much better, more worthy than the reality. A good man. A hero. Someone she could love.

He smoothed his fingers through her silken tresses, scented with his shampoo after their shower and with him after their lovemaking.

It was all too easy to picture days, years, decades like this with her. Challenging his mind, satisfying his body, making his soul new again.

His hand stilled. His eyes narrowed.

That was how the best tricks worked. They created the illusion of something desirable, something almost within reach while stealing what was actually important.

He was so close. He could feel it, the growing power in her, her desire to protect her friends and her town, that small step away from finally rising, finally becoming who she was meant to be and what he needed. Decades of work for this plan to succeed. He was too close to give it up, smart enough to spot a trick when he saw it. Anna was special. But the plan had to take priority.

His shaft was half-hard, ready to lose himself inside Anna again, but he'd let temptation get the better of him too long already. He shifted, partially lifting her off him as he slid toward the edge of the bed.

She grumbled in her sleep, which, despite himself, made him smile.

Ah, Anna. If only in another lifetime.

He climbed to his feet and was pulling on a clean pair of trousers when there was more mumbling from the bed, and Anna propped herself up.

She shoved a hand through her hair, pushing it back from her eyes, and glared through slit eyes around the room until she found him. "Did they call? Is it morning?"

He glanced at the clock, pulling a shirt on over his shoulders and buttoning it. "Technically. It's five a.m. Go back to sleep. I'll wake you later."

Still grumbling, she dragged herself toward the edge of the bed, threw her legs over, and pushed herself upright. "No. I'm up. I should be up. We should finish that research. Check in with everyone. Up is good." Said while, he was certain, her eyes remained closed.

It was too tempting to step closer, to gently tumble her back into bed, follow her down and give them both a few more hours of pleasure. Instead, he headed for the door, foregoing the buttons on his sleeves and rolling them up to his elbows. "Go back to bed. You don't need to be awake yet."

He snagged his phone off the dresser and escaped out the door, clicking it softly closed behind him. He headed down the stairs, checking messages. Two from Mal, reporting in on progress moving and collecting townspeople and weapons cache, and one from Nia with locations on Heimdall and potentials for the goddess.

Trevor cleared his throat.

Loki stopped and turned to find the man behind him, having gotten there soundlessly. "Trevor, you have bright a future in assassination or espionage if you have the stomach for it."

"Thank you, sir, but I prefer working for you. As well as games where no one dies. I've had food sent out to the horse, I'll have a tray made up for Ms. Anna, and would you like me to pull out the weapons for today's battle?"

Loki just looked at the man a moment. Sometimes he'd swear that Trevor was one step ahead of him.

A shame that he'd be unemployed soon. If the plan succeeded as it should. While Daphne's death was unfortunate considering the goddess, it meant Anna was capable of killing him.

"You are a wonder," Loki murmured, continuing down the stairs and not entirely certain whether the words were complimentary. Other than Anna, it was rare for anyone to get the better of him.

"I try," Trevor murmured. "Your...well, sir, he claims to be your nephew is in the kitchen. I've removed most of the alcohol—what was left after the horse had his share—but I'm not certain Mrs. Greaves will be pleased with the depleted state of her pantry."

Nephew today, hmm? Surely, he wouldn't have been stupid enough to bring Heimdall.

"I'll see to him. Thank you." He headed toward the kitchen.

A pity it was no surprise who waited at the table, making a clear attempt to eat him out of house and home.

Thor drank what looked to be orange juice out of a jug gripped in one massive hand while he shoveled cookies, bread, and whatever else he'd found in the fridge and pantry into his open mouth. Crumbs clung to his red beard, but when he spotted Loki his blue eyes brightened, and his lips curved into a smile around his latest mouthful.

Loki leaned against the opposite counter and crossed his arms. "Thor. You're not my nephew, and that isn't your food. What are you doing here?"

Thor finished chewing, swallowed, belched as he pounded his chest, then shoved back from the table—or shoved the table back from him—and leaned back in the groaning chair. "You mean you were going to go hunt down that goddess without me?"

It was difficult to refrain from rolling his eyes, but Loki managed it. Barely. "No. You can help if you wish. Where's Heimdall?"

This soured even Thor's expression. He waved his hand vaguely in the air. "Hunting your woman. Complaining about how this is all your fault, how the gods are giving him grief because of this mess, which they say wouldn't have happened if the woman had been killed sooner. You know Heimdall. Fun when he's drinking but dull as troll droppings otherwise."

The woman in question strode down the hall toward the kitchen. Her hair still hung in loose, dark waves around her shoulders, and when she stretched before stepping into the kitchen, her black tank top with a plunging V-neck pulled against her breasts, breasts he'd paid loving attention to a short while ago. Fortunate that Thor's back was to her and he hadn't been able to enjoy the view.

"Of course," Thor was saying, as though maybe he'd been speaking for a while and no one had been listening. "Heimdall says this plan of yours is brilliant. You kept the parts that worked, like the ward thing. But sleeping with the woman to keep her close? Even he admits that was a stroke of genius. That maybe there's a chance this time your plan could work if he doesn't stop you."

Loki identified the instant Thor's words registered, and Anna's eyes flared with blue heat, her chin coming up.

Ymir, he should have told her. Had half forgotten that part of the truth.

His chest tightened. "Thor, shut up," he said, voice rough.

"No, Thor. I'm very intrigued." Anna jerked out a chair from the table and sat across from Thor, flashing a challenging smile.

It was like Thor never even heard him, too distracted by Anna's smile likely.

Thor shoved a handful of lunch meat in his mouth and took another swill of orange juice. "What about?"

"You said this time Loki's plan would work. What did you mean?" Her fiery-blue gaze met Loki's above Thor's head.

Loki's lips tightened. Damn the bloody idiot anyway. "It was a long time ago, Anna."

"If it involves you treating people like pawns, not long enough. Thor?"

Even Thor was smart enough to sense the tension around him. He tossed back the rest of the orange juice then plonked the empty jug on the table and shoved to his feet. "I should go. Is the parrot-horse here?"

"Rojo's out back," Anna said, her gaze never breaking from Loki's.

Thor ducked his head and scuttled past them, then out the rear door.

"Explain," she demanded, her jaw tight, eyes flashing, barely noting Thor's departure. "What's different this time?"

Loki kept his movements slow, deliberate, despite the tension riding his shoulders, the urge to batter Thor or tell Anna he didn't damn well owe her answers. Because he did, if there was any small chance of salvaging his plan. He came around the table, pulled out a chair, and set it down beside her, facing her.

"It was more than six decades ago. It was different. It isn't about you, doesn't affect you," he said, his stomach roiling, neck tight.

She slammed her hand into the table with a bang. "Don't. Lie. To. Me!"

He leaned back in the chair, a tic starting in his jaw. He crossed his arms. "Fine. You want to know the truth? I tried before. With a different set of horsemen. I told you, the Four have risen before, and they will again at times whenever the world is in grave danger. From paranormal threat, war, disease, or all of the above as it is this time. Those Four started to rise in 1939."

"War was your ward?"

"Yes."

"You loved him?"

"Yes."

She flinched at his response, looked down at the table where she pressed her hands so hard into the wood the tips of her fingers turned white.

327

"Anna, we have bigger concerns to deal with right now. We can come back to this. *After* the goddess is dealt with."

Her gaze came up to meet his, burning with the blue heat of something inhuman. With War's fire. "We deal with this now. Did you sleep with him too? Or was that how your strategy changed?" she said, bitterness in her voice.

Maybe it was her tone, maybe it was the fact he hadn't slept—because he'd been too busy enjoying her body—and that he'd worked so hard toward this plan, toward what should have worked for too long to just let it be ruined by one moronic god or destructive goddess. His jaw hardened, and his words came out tight and harsh. "You mean a history of my sexual preference? Love is love, whatever the combination, and I'm open to all of them. But I didn't sleep with Peter. He was my ward. He was—"

Like a son. The last time he'd been idiotic enough to think that just once he might be deserving of love. That it wouldn't be thrown back in his face.

He bit back the words at the emotion roiling just beneath them. The pain.

"He was young and foolish."

The memory of Peter accusing him of manipulation flashed through his mind. Telling Loki he was tired of the games, that he wouldn't be part of a plot for Loki's advancement. Throwing everything back in Loki's face just as Anna did now. Peter hadn't listened; none of them would listen. Loki hadn't been able to stop the four of them from heading out the door down to the recruitment offices and then overseas. To return in four caskets.

"They joined the madness threatening the world," he said, voice rasping. "They were impulsive, hot-headed, and didn't see the bigger picture. As I do. They could have changed history, but instead, they were swallowed by it."

"How noble," she said, voice biting. Then, as though the thought had occurred to her, her breath caught a moment, and her gaze sharpened. "So, did it have to be any War? Why me in particular?"

His stomach muscles clenched over the truth, what had once seemed perfectly logical. Moral even. "You were the closest geographically. There was a history of domestic violence and a high chance you'd be seized by social services."

She swallowed a moment, as though over a thick lump, and her gaze fell. "My friends? Did you manipulate all of us?"

A muscle worked in his jaw, but he smothered the resentful growl that tried to rise from his throat. This time, only the truth would do.

"It isn't common knowledge that rising is a choice. I sent invitations to Ginny's, Nia's, and Piper's parents that painted Beckwell as the ideal sanctuary. Just having the three of the horsemen clan families in one town was enough to start the rumors that they were destined to rise, that they'd been brought together by fate. But they were otherwise no more likely to rise than any of the other heirs."

Color stained her cheekbones. Her voice was hollow. "Then all you needed was that one last chess piece. Me."

He wanted to reach out, to hold her until she damn well listened and didn't run, didn't do this. Didn't lead them down this road.

"You're also the best option. The only one who can control the abilities, who I'd trust with that much power. When the Four rise, you will be immeasurably more powerful, all of you. You'll be able to communicate without words, combine your abilities, manifest armor, weapons, and your horses will take whatever form is most suitable for the battle."

Her words, when she spoke again, were soft, edged

with desperation, her gaze bright as it met his. "Does it always have to come back to that? To the power? For what? Why do we need it? Why is all of this worth the risk?"

"I told you. Because if the world is going to end, it needs to be the right ending. I can help ensure one."

"Because of a drunken agreement with the original Four?" Bitterness rubbed the words like salt into a cut.

"Because I give a shit! Because I don't want everything to end in pain and flames, because that's what it does over and over, humans finding new and more creative ways to destroy each other and this planet they live on."

He scrubbed a hand over his face, focused on her gaze, tried to get her to understand. "I was promised a way to prevent that. For the world to rise anew and replenished, humanity more connected and stronger than ever, better able to face whatever challenges come for them. So, yes, I needed you and your friends to do that. I needed you as a distraction while I completed the details of the plan. I worked with the Fates to convince everyone, including you, your friends, and the gods, that you were destined to rise, leaving me to my own plans. I need you for the final part. To kill me so humanity can survive. So the alternate version of Ragnarök, the End of Days, all the other horrific visions of apocalypse don't come to pass. With humanity stronger, their eventual destruction becomes less of a certainty."

"You don't even know that for sure. The Four manipulated you."

"But they're not wrong. This is the right answer. Why can't you accept it?"

"What, that this is more about you getting the recognition you want than about saving anyone?" She shot to her feet, hands fisting and opening at her sides. "I don't even know what to believe. I don't know what the truth is or what was you manipulating me however you could so you could achieve this. So this time this War would rise, and you could—" Her words broke off, and she shook her head.

He stood, too, urged her with his eyes and his being to look up at him, to see the truth. That he hadn't wanted to hurt her. That it wasn't supposed to be this way. That *this* was why he'd tried to keep his distance. To spare her this pain if nothing else.

He waited what seemed like forever, but still, she wouldn't look at him.

Maybe couldn't look at him.

Ice broke and cracked inside him, the old wound torn open again.

"So that this time, I die," he rasped. "You need to rise. Whether it's for you or me or your friends. You are supposed to be War. There is no one better suited. It may be the only chance we have of defeating the goddess. When you and your friends stand together."

Slowly, she raised her gaze until it met his, her lips a thin line. The fire flared again in her eyes and seemed to give her strength as she straightened, raised her chin. "Because I've already killed Daphne, it shouldn't be too hard to kill you, right? You think that's all I am. A War. A killer." Her eyes shone over-bright, and she shook her head with quick, jerky movements. "No. I won't do it. I won't be what you want me to be, what everyone expects me to be. I can't."

She turned, spun on her heel, and headed for the foyer.

Head lowered, he followed her. Trying to think of the words, any words that would make her turn around. That would convince her she was wrong.

"Anna. Please…"

For the second time in his life because of Anna, he who was known for his quick tongue had nothing to say.

Leaving him only watching as she grabbed the keys off the front foyer tallboy, shoved on her shoes, then flung open the front door and pounded down the front steps.

It wasn't toward the recruitment offices this time. This War didn't want to fight as she jumped into his sleek dark car, revved the engine, and peeled out of the driveway.

Resentment, rage, pain simmered inside of him as Loki watched the remnants of his plan, his hope for redemption, littered like broken glass around him.

ஐ

Anna peeled out of Loki's driveway, leaving him a long silhouette in the rearview mirror. Her eyes burned, her throat ached. She couldn't head for the open road and questionable freedom, where she might just cause more unintentional harm as War. Nor the library, where everyone was sure to find her. Loki's car bumped into the rutted grass driveway, the burned-out shell that used to be her house before her. The walls were closing in on her, War demanding more blood, demanding all of her. Everyone demanding so much.

She shut off the car and sat there, staring at what remained through the windshield, the blackened pile of rubble. It was somehow smaller than she remembered, so insignificant.

Climbing out of the car, she closed the door and wandered closer to the ruins.

There was almost nothing about it to suggest it'd even been a house. *This* was what War created. This was what it cost. Lured you in with all that power until the truth, the rage, the destruction burned you out, left you nothing but ashes and the remains of the person and life you used to have. This was why it was so important she get ahold of herself and stick to logic, stick to cold reason and control and not let herself be carried away by emotion and frivolous, dangerous feeling. They were too easily manipulated, left her vulnerable.

The few pieces of charred timber that remained were just broken sticks, could have been part of a bonfire. Her boots crunched over scorched remains and broken glass as she walked in what had been the front door, or thereabouts. The lingering scent of smoke burned her nostrils. The springs from the sofa were still visible, like a ghostly skeleton.

In the kitchen, the blackened hulk of the fridge and a twisted stainless-steel sink were all that defined the space. That might have been a chair over there.

She wandered toward the bedroom, crouching to pick at the glimmer of something under what might have been part of the wall. She wiped it off, the glass cracked and blackened. The photo inside was still just visible.

A cheap snapshot in the backyard. Her face so young, so innocent, big smiles on Mom and Dad's faces. The perfect family captured on film. How long before the fire had the photo been taken? How many more days had they lived before War took them too?

Maybe this was what Mom and Dad's house had looked like. After the flames had been doused, the embers cold. After the bodies had burned away. She'd been hundreds of miles away by that point, here, in Beckwell, under Loki's and then the Lacks' protection.

He must have gone back. She rubbed her thumb over the ridges of the frame, exposing more silver. This photo had survived two fires now. He'd found and brought it to her, some small reminder of the life she'd had, the life she could have had. With Loki, how could she tell if it'd been kindness that made him give it to her, or some greater plan and manipulation?

She stood, turning and looking at the blackened desolation surrounding her. Her house.

Her home.

Her throat squeezed. She pressed her lips tight

together, but moisture pinched her eyes.

It hadn't been much. What she'd had hadn't been much. Most of it hadn't meant anything. But it'd been hers. It'd been all she had. Every penny saved and scrounged, always logical, never guided by an urge, frivolous desire, any dangerous emotion. She'd worn cheap clothes no one else wanted. She'd stayed near home to ensure she didn't endanger anyone else. She'd avoided most relationships just to make sure it didn't end in tragedy like her parents' had. Her life, the one she'd built without War, without help, a place where she could be who and what she wanted. Here. In this one place, she'd been able to be her, had been safe to be her.

She dropped her gaze back to the photo, the image of that happy family blurring as her throat thickened.

Hadn't mattered, though, had it? She'd ended up right back where she started. Back in the destruction. Back in the fire and the death and the pain. There was no light, no good side to War. There was only wrestling with it and trying to control it before it controlled her.

A sob broke from her lips.

War and what it meant had hunted her for so long. Taken so much. All that she'd had left, that tiny sliver of self that she'd carved out, it wanted that too. Would drive her mad with its truths. And Loki wanted her to lose herself too. Made her care for him yet demanded his death.

Loki, who'd claimed to save her from that first fire. Who'd tried to save her from this one. Who'd almost, it had seemed, for a few brief moments, helped save that sliver of self.

Because he wanted it for his plans. Because War needed it. Because it was only important if she could give it up.

Her shoulders slumped, and she fell onto her knees in the ash and the char. She let her chin fall forward and hit her chest.

Another sob tore from her throat. She lifted trembling fingers to her lips, as though to hold it in. Another escaped. Then another. Tears streamed from her eyes, and Anna wept.

CHAPTER 28

Anna wasn't sure how much time had passed when the sound of hoof-steps and someone clearing their throat in an obvious way to catch her attention made her start and scrub at her eyes. She glanced back to find a large chestnut horse standing near Loki's car.

If she wasn't already at rock bottom, evidently the War horse was here to make things worse.

"What do you want? To gloat?"

Rojo hesitated near the car, pawed at the ground. Finally, he tossed his head with a neigh and took a few steps toward her. The outline of his body shimmered as he neared the ruins, then he flapped his wings and flew in pigeon form toward her.

He landed lightly on a piece of charred wood and cocked his head. "Wondered where you'd gone."

She snorted, avoiding his gaze, although he'd have to be an idiot not to have noticed she'd been crying. Rojo was many things, but not an idiot. In front of her was the charred ruins of what being War meant. "I wanted to be left alone."

"Wasn't sure you should be," he said gruffly.

She flashed a glare in his direction. "What do you know? What do you even care? Yes, I'd make a terrible War. Yes, I know that just as well as you do, but everyone seems convinced otherwise. Because me becoming War fits better with their plans. Their ideas." She shook her head, her lip curled. "It's never mattered what I wanted. What I need, though I don't know why I'm surprised."

Rojo remained uncharacteristically silent for a moment or two. No needling comments on what a "real" War horseman would or should be doing in that moment. Not even support for her statement that she shouldn't rise, that she'd be terrible at it.

It was enough to make her look at him, but he was looking around with some curiosity, his movements quick and jerky in pigeon form, beady black eyes taking in everything. He made a little hop down from his charred perch and into the thicker ash and rubble.

"This was your home," he said slowly.

She sniffed. "What gave it away? Or do you suppose I enjoy rooting through the ashes of other people's homes?"

"I can…feel it. Feel how you felt about it," he said, as though still processing. He turned to her. Hopped a little closer. "This burned down a week ago. Why cry now?"

"Perhaps I'm homesick," she lied. She'd rather be able to deny she'd been crying whatsoever. Weak, useless tears and letting emotion guide her. Again.

He fluttered up and leaned closer, peered into her face. "It's because of Loki, isn't it?"

"Ha! You want to blame this on me being female." She jumped to her feet, photo still in her hands, and stalked out of the ruins, taking the same route out the front door and around the roof beam of the house, though it was completely mad, considering there was no house. "Just…be quiet until the rest of them get here. Then you can argue with them about how they're wrong, and I'd make a terrible War but that the world needs someone to rise and what a glorious history I'm sullying."

"I told you I was going to find the real War. Find the person who appreciated the abilities and me."

"Which isn't me. Yes, you made that clear."

She felt the flash of energy rippled across her skin, then the trot of hooves as Rojo transformed back into a horse and followed after her.

She turned on him. Almost caught him on the nose she swung around so fast. "What do you want?" she shouted at him. "Leave me be. Just…leave me alone."

She stalked farther into the yard, the long grass catching at her legs, her arms wrapped around herself. She clenched her jaw and blew out a breath through her nose. So much for not allowing herself to be controlled by emotion. She had to get herself under control. She was calm. She was calm. She was…

"I didn't tell anyone where you were. Or that I was coming here," Rojo said from behind her.

Her eyes opened. Ridiculous damned horse. A *literal* horse. Because not only did War want to take everything, it wanted to rub her nose in it too.

Slow hoof-steps toward her. "I felt… You needed me."

She sniffed. "I don't want to be War. Can you at least understand that?"

"Why?" he asked, his voice quieter and more somber than she could remember hearing. None of the arrogance or outrage, just the quietly worded intensity of his question.

It was enough to make her turn to him, to find him still a good horse's length away from her.

"Why? Why what?"

"Why don't you want to rise? Why not become War?"

"Because of this." She gestured toward the burned remains of the house. "*This* is what War brings to my life. It destroys everything I've ever wanted, everything I might have dreamed of, and devours me whole to make of me what it wants. You said yourself: it's destroyed lesser men with the abilities, with the truths, with all that it demands."

"Your War abilities started the fire?" His dark-brown horsey gaze remained steady. He took a few steps toward her.

"What? No."

"War didn't literally burn things down."

She threw her hands in the air. "Does it matter? War ruins everything. It makes me dangerous. Makes all Wars dangerous. Exhibit A. Our first candidate, Chief Donovan Wiebe. War abilities corrupted him, made him cause violence in his town, made him power hungry."

"Meh… Nope. He used his abilities that way. You used yours to see his truth, to see his corruption."

Her eyes narrowed. "Candidate two, Tildy Cadman with her fight club. War makes us crave that violence, hungry for it. Able to bring ordinary people to blows just by speaking."

"Yeah, but you made them stop. And even if you liked it, you didn't let it control you."

She glared. "Walter Martin was better at his abilities. He saw the truth, he used war—and peace—to, again, control and manipulate people."

"You broke free. Then went and threatened Thor with his own hammer because you thought he might have hurt Loki's feelings."

"Stop it," she ground out, stalking away through the grass as it tangled around her legs, sticky in the growing heat. Stupid grass. Stupid horse.

He followed her. "Stop what? Knowing everything you do? Seeing the truth you refuse to see?"

She turned on him. "Stop justifying how War is anything good. How it can possibly cause anything but chaos and destruction. Even the gods are afraid of me. If I rise, that will mean the Four have risen. I will be responsible for whatever chaos we cause."

"Or whatever good you do."

"Stop it! Stop being so…so…"

"Rational?" If the horse could have smirked, it would have. Instead, it twitched its ears and pressed on, following her as she tried to stalk away. "War is not what kept you here. *You* kept you here. In the library, in the little house, in your little life. Your fear keeps you here. Your War bloodlines will not be what destroys you. That'll be on you."

She rounded on him again and tried to remind herself why punching a horse was not the answer. "Now you're my therapist?"

His big brown eyes were clear, honest, not all that horse-like. "No, I'm your partner. And clearly, the more rational one, though we knew that, didn't we? You're sitting here, terrified what rising as War will mean, afraid of what might happen. While out there? There's a goddess who wants to kill and destroy everything while we, the only ones who could stop her, sit here. But, hey, you want to let her destroy the world because your feelings are hurt."

She stopped, pivoted, and stuck her face even with the horse's. "Don't. You. Dare."

He kept his gaze even with her. "Tell you the truth? What, is that one more thing to be afraid of? 'Cause here's the thing, Princess. I'm the War horse, and I don't lie. All this comes down to you being scared."

"I'm not—"

He shoved his face closer until his soft muzzle and

her nose touched. "For someone so hungry for knowledge, why have you never asked me what I know? I bear the memory of every War horse there's ever been. I remember each War's abilities, their strengths, their weaknesses."

She swallowed, struck. "I...I—"

"Didn't think I knew shit because of your own preconceived ideas about who—and what—War is?" He pulled back, flicked his ears. "I remember the Wars. Including the first one. You know what his name was?"

"Marius." She'd seen him, been in his head as he'd entrapped Loki.

"Yep. Marius *Fray*."

She could only blink. The first War had been a Fray? There was no time to process, though, as Rojo continued, relentless.

"I know War's abilities better than you do. Yeah, there's the easy ones, like making people fight with the sound of your voice like you've done as long as you can remember. An affinity for fire." He tossed his head back meaningfully at the house, or what was left of it.

He swung his head back. "Then there's the subtler ones. The truth. The voices. Not all the Wars can cut it. Some of them lose their minds, unable to block it out, but it barely slows you down. The ability to wield any weapon, like picking up Thor's hammer, a weapon that can only be wielded by him, and that you treated like it was no more than a freakin' feather duster. Always battle ready, sobering up after drinking me and almost Thor under the table, and doing battle to save your town with speed greater than almost any other War before."

She shook her head, jaw tight. "Don't talk to me about emotion. I have a temper. I lose it all the time. That makes me dangerous."

"And more powerful. Yeah, you get mad, but you never lose control. Emotion is what lets you access your abilities. Whether you're protecting Loki and stealing magic hammers, stopping fight clubs and rescuing kids from psycho-bitches. You get pissed, you get stronger. You get closer to rising."

"I…I killed Daphne."

"You saved those kids and yourself."

"If I at least understood how to use peace…"

"Maybe you will. Someday. For now? Meh. Maybe it's just not your style." He lowered his head, stared into her eyes. "You might hear everyone else's truth, Princess, but I hear yours. I stayed in London because I could see exactly who you were. You weren't who or what I expected, no. You were more. You didn't want to hear it, don't want to see it. I've watched you grow in strength, watched you acquire and master every ability. I've recognized my true partner. You *are* War."

"No. I won't be. I can't be."

"Just because you don't want to see it—"

"War killed my parents! Made *me* kill my parents." She screamed it at him, the words torn from her throat. Despite what her friends had told her, despite what Loki had told her. They didn't know. They weren't there. She had been. They'd been a family, they'd all been there, then she'd spoken, and it was gone. All of it was gone. Her eyes burned, and she swiped at them angrily, her voice low and rough. "I will not become that. Not now. Not ever."

Rojo watched her silently a few moments. Then blew out a noisy breath through his nostrils. "Loki was looking into it. I might have seen it on his desk when I went looking for booze last night. He had his minion dig it up. Police reports for domestic violence, repeated calls out to the house. Princess, they had issues."

Loki had investigated it? Why? He'd told her they were volatile, told her what he knew. Why would he bother? "Which they wouldn't have had if they weren't

War."

"Holy shit. Would you get over that already? Wars have issues, yeah, but it's not a death sentence. They could have separated, lived apart, found another solution like other Wars have—Marius Fray spent most of his time away and made lots of kids when he was at home. Loved his wives, found other solutions. Your parents didn't want to." Rojo grumbled something uncomplimentary beneath his breath, trotted away a few steps, then back. "Look, Child Services was involved. There are documents. Recommendations for counseling for your parents, concerns about domestic violence…and the recommendation to remove you."

Her breath whooshed out, and she tried to think of all the memories she had of them. The times she remembered. She shook her head, backed away, stumbling in the grass. "What? No. No, that can't be. They were good parents. They fought sometimes, sure, but…but that's because they were War. Because they were passionate." Her shoulders slumped. "It was me. I was the one who made it worse. Because I spoke."

"Princess, they probably knew Child Services was coming to get you. They heard the recommendation. The day before the fire. I'm betting they were itching for a fight, but anything you said or did was unlikely to have changed what happened."

She stared down at the tangled, long green grass beneath her feet, tried to focus on it as it blurred in and out of focus. Tried to slow her breathing, the tremor in her shoulders. *I'm calm, I'm calm, I'm calm…*

She could still remember that day. Rubbery eggs for supper, the smell of grease in the kitchen. The way the argument started about money, about the eggs, and escalated when she spoke. When Daddy said they were wasting all that money on the therapist for her because she wouldn't speak. She'd been practicing, though. She'd wanted to be worthy of being his little Princess; she'd wanted to be perfect. She'd had no idea the better reason she shouldn't speak was because her voice was dangerous. Then she was shuffled off to bed to hide in the nest of stuffed animals in her closet with her books while the real shouting started, doors slamming. Then the acrid smell of smoke waking her. And the footsteps as someone came to find her. To pull her from those flames.

The horse nudged her shoulder with her head. "I'm sorry. What happened to them sucks. But I don't think it was War's fault. Or yours."

Her knees softened, and she dropped down into the grass. Covered her face with eyes with her hands a moment, her breath still raspy, still rough, vision still blurry.

All these years. Imagining them, that day in the back garden. Swinging around in Dad's arms, the sound of his laughter and hers and Mom's. The dreams she'd had of more days like that. The time she should have had with them. The normal family things they should have had. Child Services. Papers. Removal from the house. She would have been removed from their house?

"I...I wouldn't have grown up with them anyway." Her voice was rough, quivery.

"Probably not. They didn't want to change. They didn't want other options."

She forced herself to swallow past the hard, sore lump in her throat. "I-I'll want to see that evidence, you know."

"Sure. Happy to steal it. But I'm pretty sure Loki collected it for you. Might even have left it on his desk for me to find to give you. He can be a schmuck sometimes, but I have never, in all the memories of those before me, seen someone look at another the way he looks at you."

She closed her eyes, still hot and sore, stinging. Pictured catching Loki watching her, the amber-shot softness in his pewter gaze, that slow smile on his lips. Loki, rising above her in bed, bringing her to unimaginable pleasure before he found his own.

Loki, who'd pulled her from that burning house and brought her here.

So she could complete the plot the first War had engineered. To finally give Loki the belonging and accolades he wanted.

Loki, who wanted her to kill him.

Gaia, she ached inside, like she'd been burned and left charred and empty as the house. All the truths, her parents, Loki, the possible futures she'd once imagined flickering and blackening in the flames.

"You going to barf?"

She inhaled slowly. One breath. Two. Opened her eyes to see horse's hooves in the grass beside her. "Loki…"

Rojo blew out a breath. "Is Loki. Yeah, he's tried this before. Yeah, he's probably done lots of things you wouldn't approve of. Doesn't make him a bad guy." He stuck his face down beside hers. "Come on. Get up. It's weird staring down at your hair."

She looked up to glare at him.

"Better. Okay, so Peter? I remember Peter through Reginald. Remember Loki too. Don't you start with me knowing and not telling you either. You didn't ask, you didn't want my knowledge. But now you are listening, and I assure you their relationship wasn't anything like you and Loki. Peter was younger, impulsive, a bit of a hothead, opinionated—"

"Male."

"Well, yeah. Not my point. He was Loki's son. When war broke out, Loki argued with him, tried to keep him here, to keep him safe. Peter wouldn't listen. Got the other three to enlist, too, and all of them shipped out, were determined to win the war together. You know what that

War found? The most violent battles. The ugliest encounters. Eventually, the path of a howitzer. All four of them wiped off the Earth."

She swallowed, the truth she'd seen making more sense. If Peter had been like a son…of course, Loki had loved him. She'd misunderstood. "They could have made a difference."

"Maybe. If they'd practiced more. If they knew better how to work together, how their abilities complemented each other, what they were willing to risk for their relationships. When all four rise, we horses will manifest into whatever form you need for battle, including weapons and armor. We don't know how to work together without the human element."

"Did the horses die at the same time?"

Rojo seemed to be avoiding her eyes, pawing the grass again. "Most of them. We can survive a while after our horseman dies, but usually not long. Reginald survived the attack, badly injured, but damned determined to make it back here. To tell Loki the things Peter had wanted to. That he was sorry. That Loki had been right."

"Did he?"

"No."

War hadn't killed her parents. The phrases "Child's Services" and the smell of overcooked eggs seemed to circle and cling inside her head. The images of her friends. That blood rain. The battles they'd fought before. And always Loki, that smile of his. Loki, hurt so often by those he cared about.

The way he'd just watched as she drove off in his car. Almost as though he'd expected it. Something thick and burning roiled in her stomach.

"So now you think I should rise too." Slowly, she raised her eyes to the horse. To the one creature who, up until now, had agreed she shouldn't be War.

Who'd brought her the truth. An ugly truth that

soured the images of her parents. Made the shouts of that day echo and bleed into other memories, other fights.

The horse looked away a moment, back at her house. Then back at her. His gaze was steady, a long pause before he finally spoke. "No. Not if you truly believe it will destroy you. I mean, I don't believe it will, but I'm not you. I don't feel the fear that gives you nightmares at night. Yeah, I know we could take charge and kick both this goddess and those gods' asses, rule the world even. But if you don't see it, it ain't happening."

He sat on his haunches. Like a dog. "Rise or don't rise. I'm not going anywhere. Hurts too damned much when you get too far anyway."

She stared at him a moment, slightly afraid her mouth could be hanging open. She said the only clear thought in her head. "Ordinary horses don't usually sit that way, you know."

He snorted. "As though either of us could ever be ordinary, Toots."

"That's not better than Princess."

Rojo cocked his head, ears flicking, appearing genuinely surprised. "It's not? I was sure it was."

"Definitely not." Oh, dear Gaia, she had to be careful to look him in the eye and not confirm he was indeed male.

He shrugged, closed his eyes as though he didn't have a care in the world. As though he wasn't an apocalypse horse sitting as though he were a dog. "Princess it is."

"You're wrong about ordinary too." Certainty was slipping away like sand through her fingers. If she convinced him of the truth, maybe she'd believe it herself. "Ordinary is safer. Ordinary doesn't get us noticed, doesn't get us in trouble."

"Maybe. But everyone else will be weaker without our extraordinary selves." He opened his eyes a slit, looked at her. "Loki included."

I have never seen someone look at another the way he looks at you.

She swallowed past the thickness in her throat. Loki had told her from the start he wanted her to rise. He'd never hidden it. It wasn't him who'd seduced her—well, not intentionally—either the first or second time. He'd tried to keep his distance. He'd been respectful. He'd flown her around the world to meet other candidates he'd never believed were viable. Yes, there'd been manipulation. But nothing she hadn't realized, no truth she hadn't seen.

Including his sincere belief that dying was what he needed to do. That he needed her. He believed the world would be better, that he could save humanity.

"He's spent his entire life plotting. It must have taken him a while to figure out how to manipulate which Four rose, but he's spent over a hundred years working toward his goals between you and Peter. He won't stop now," Rojo said quietly. "Though I think you were an unexpected complication."

Complication. She snorted. She pictured Loki's smile, felt the memory of his hand stroking her face, his hand curved around hers on the plane when she'd been afraid.

No, he wouldn't stop. She didn't want to kill him; she wasn't like her parents. She and Loki weren't her parents.

Further, if this was what he really wanted, wouldn't it be better if the last thing he saw was the face of someone who loved him?

"If he dies, will it save humanity? Will it prevent apocalypse?"

"The horses were outside when the original deal was made, but yeah, the Four believed Loki was the key. He was too stubborn and alienated from any of the magical species to align with any of them. He was naturally tough and long-lived and already had a prophecy about him that said his death would cause Ragnarök, a different kind of apocalypse. Maybe they also saw some of what you do, including his intellect. He'd rather save humanity than destroy it."

There was a rumble off to the south, the clouds splintering with lightning and thunder though the sky was pink and orange. Unnatural.

Loki, her friends, the rest of the town would be headed that direction to try to stop the goddess. The rumble of coming violence circled in her stomach, created the lightness of euphoria despite her thoughts and reality, brought the sweet-sour taste to her tongue. She could go and try to help as she was. Yesterday proved she was far from powerless. But if she closed her eyes, if she listened to the wind, felt the earth beneath her feet, the faint hint of water in the air, the truth whispered to her.

Had been whispering to her all along.

Her insides shivered. She wanted to be a bit sick, and, dammit, she was scared.

She couldn't let that stop her.

She blew out a breath, put her hands on her hips, and looked at Rojo, who watched her almost patiently.

"All right, Mr. Smarty-pants," she said, her throat thick with what she was about to do, what she had to do. "What do I have to do to rise?"

CHAPTER 29

Anna had driven off without ever once turning to look back. Without any sign of regret, damn her. Did nothing they'd been through matter? How genuine could her emotions have been if she could walk away so easily?

Loki rubbed a hand over his face. He shouldn't be surprised. All of them did that. Said they felt one way. Promised they'd be there, in their words, their actions. But they all left or made him leave. Which was just as well. He was stronger without them. Didn't have to worry about them. He had other things to worry about. A blasted goddess to stop, if that wasn't enough, let alone the need to protect his town and citizens.

Because his day wasn't bad or busy enough... walking up his driveway, so recently vacated by Anna and his car, was yet another problem. Evidently guided by whatever bloodhound heritage the bloody Asgardian must have, Heimdall, still in the large gray trench, sunglasses, and fedora strolled up to the front porch.

Well, fuck.

No one particularly liked him—even his family. Not with the way he always knew more than any of them did, was happy to lord it over them and use it however he could. Word was he visited Asgard about as often as Loki. A shame he was such an ass, really. Maybe they could have been friends.

Loki stared off toward the tree line. Recited the entire Prose Edda *and* the Poetic Edda backward. Still wanted to rip out someone's spine.

Fine. He was better off without her and without the car. It didn't fit in around here. Never had. Wouldn't be much help fighting the goddess or Heimdall. Maybe she'd taken it and driven as fast and as far from here as she could.

Maybe she'd drive until she was finally free, or her definition of it. He closed his eyes. If nothing else, he'd pushed her out of the prison she'd built herself. Not toward his plan—quite the opposite, it would seem. Yet…he tested the wound, like tonguing a missing tooth. He was less infuriated or disappointed she'd refused to go through with it than expected.

It dimmed compared to her leaving.

Loki counted to seven before slowly turning, his expression carefully neutral, betraying none of the seething emotion. He'd played this game too long to ever let anyone see a weakness in his armor. All the better for them to jab something sharp and poisonous.

Heimdall jerked a thumb back toward the road, like the know-it-all ass he'd always been. "That was the War woman. In your car, driving recklessly down the road."

"I suspect even you've seen enough of Ms. Fray to know there's no making her do anything she doesn't want to," he said mildly.

Anna had known what she wanted right from the start. It wasn't power. It wasn't him. She'd made no secret of it. He should have known better.

He'd known what he wanted, too, what was realistic. He'd known it was safer to keep his distance. Had tried.

He'd failed at that too.

"What do you want, Heimdall?"

"I have…a proposal, Laufeyjarson," the god said, stiffness and a hint of hesitation in his words, as though even calling Loki by his first name implied too much connection. A sign the other god was uneasy.

Loki raised a brow, crossed his arms, and waited.

Tried not to think of Anna, facing him down in the car and telling him she didn't mind her name Hadrianna. Anna in the library, interrupting him and making him call Nia by her preferred name, doing the same with Mal.

Rather like Heimdall.

He shifted, struggled to maintain a blank expression.

"You have a rogue goddess wreaking havoc in your town, in your world," Heimdall said. As though perhaps Loki hadn't noticed.

"Because you let her loose."

Heimdall studied the carving on the porch step so closely he should have been able to replicate it. "Yes, well, allegedly. Perhaps, before we attend to other business, I could assist with that issue."

Loki let a smile curve over his lips at the god's discomfit. It was rare and deserved savoring, no matter the other feelings and aching hole. "The gods are pissed, I take it."

Heimdall seared Loki with a glare.

Loki simply looked at him. The sound of a fight was appealing. He'd considered going after the goddess himself even before Heimdall's arrival. Better he take out his frustrations on her. If she noticed. But the others might try to do the same thing. Beckwellians. Anna's friends. The Four. They could be hurt, if not worse.

Contemplating the odds while formulating a quick

plan, still, he only looked at Heimdall. Waited long enough until even Heimdall looked ready to squirm.

Served the ass right. Anna would have understood if she'd been here. The hollowness inside threatened to swallow him. Like it had tried before. He'd survived before. The empty halls. The seemingly endless circuit of funerals. The echo of their voices in the rooms before he entered. Now it would be her scent lingering on his sheets, a quick step he'd swear was her, thinking of something she'd have appreciated as no one else did.

It was Anna. There was no one, nothing like her.

Better to get in a rousing, bloodying fight then. Maybe shake him up so he couldn't think for a while.

He shoved off from the porch, clapping a hand on Heimdall's shoulder as he passed, headed for the garage and Thor. They'd need him and his hammer. Besides, it made the idiot so happy to hit things. "Good thing you didn't get around to killing me yet, isn't it? Prophecy aside. All right. Come along. Let's call it one for old time's sake."

Heimdall's teeth flashed in a small, tight smile. "It would be acceptable."

❧

Perhaps two hours had passed. Maybe it was longer, maybe it was shorter. Always hard to say when fighting for one's life...and having one's ass handed to you.

Loki lay in the crumpled, splayed position the goddess had thrown him in.

He was now down two cars, counting the one Anna had taken, and the one the goddess had picked up and thrown at them. After going through some trees, it was now lodged in the side of the Cow Palace.

It hadn't taken him, Thor, and Heimdall long to find the goddess, seeing as she'd created a physical form for herself using natural elements and life energy from those she'd already killed. He hadn't considered she'd be able to use the very land against them to form her body. She was easy to spot, towering around five stories high, and she seemed inclined to stay close to Beckwell and crush it to dust before she wreaked havoc elsewhere. Hard to say whether it was because of her fury at all things paranormal or for some other reason.

He had to get up. He wasn't going to die and couldn't let her hurt anyone else. Every part of his body ached like she'd chewed him up and spat him out like bad meat. Their defense was paltry. She'd flicked him and Heimdall aside like irksome flies. Perhaps it had been longer since he'd seen battle than he remembered. He forced himself upright to a sitting position.

The view was no better.

A large swath of devastated blackened destruction nearly half a mile wide and endlessly long swept the horizon and the next hill from the Beckwell agricultural grounds. What had been trees breaking up farmland were flattened and marked the path of the goddess. One he, Thor, and Heimdall hadn't been able to even slow, let alone stop.

Of the goddess, he could see only the bare bit of her head as she vanished over the next hill, off to wreak more mayhem, more death and destruction within his town. If her monstrous size wasn't enough, she also opened her hands and rained down foot-soldiers formed of her own flesh, extensions of herself to fight hand-to-hand and exact more personal revenge than a large, heavy foot. This was the kind of suffering and destruction he'd wanted to prevent with his death. The first Four had promised the world would be as it was, humanity united.

Now that wouldn't happen.

To his right, Thor pulled himself out from beneath the overturned car that'd been thrown on him and straightened his back with a crack. "I don't think that plan was very good," he said, yanking his hammer free from where it'd become embedded in the side of a truck abandoned by fleeing Beckwellians.

"You may be correct," Loki agreed. Yet his mind seemed curiously uncooperative when it came to developing a new one. Usually, plans sprang to mind as easily as the ability to breathe. Not right now, though, which could prove problematic.

When that monstrous entity had turned her attention on him, formed like a gigantic woman but with the ability to shift her physical form to any element she pleased, make weapons from her limbs, breathe fire, and spit lava, he'd indeed contemplated the "demi" portion of his mortality. His blades, of the sharpest steel and obsidian, shattered against her skin. His illusions made no difference, didn't slow down her inexorable path forward. This was far different than getting run over by Piper's truck or surviving minor explosions. There was every chance he could be killed, and not even for his plot.

It wasn't regret for lost plans that entered his mind. Nor a lament that he'd never prove everyone wrong about his worthiness.

His last thought, the image his mind produced, was Anna.

Anna, the way she'd looked that morning in his bed, her naked body against his, the dusky brush of her lashes against her soft cheek, the deep blue of her eyes when she slowly opened them and looked at him. The way she bit her lip but never once broke her gaze from his even after the night they'd shared and despite the color that stained her cheeks. It was Anna, color high in her face, eyes flashing as she demanded he tell her the truth and stop telling lies, stop plotting. Dragging her into her circle of friends. Making him forget any pleasure of tricking others with disguises and lies. Anna. *His* Anna.

Who, despite what she said, despite what perhaps everyone believed—perhaps even what he'd tried to convince himself of—was so much more important than any plan. She made him stronger. She saw through every lie, demanded the truths he couldn't admit to anyone else. Demanded he become part of her army, one of her friends, and brought him greater welcome in Beckwell than he'd ever experienced. With his own face, with his own history, welcomed at their table.

Anna didn't want to rise as War. She wouldn't help him with this plan. So...he'd either figure out how to handle the goddess and achieve his means another way. Or let them die. She would be free. At least he could give her that.

Forcing his bruised and aching body onto his knees, then testing his legs and demanding they hold his weight, Loki made it to one knee. Almost up...back down to a knee again.

A shadow blocked the sun, and someone extended a dark, gloved hand to him. Heimdall.

Loki lifted his gaze warily.

Heimdall had lost both his fedora and mirrored sunglasses. The hair was singed off the left side of his head, and most of that side of the trench coat was burned away. He leaned wearily on his sword like a cane, but his outstretched hand didn't waver.

Hesitating a moment, Loki reached out and grasped Heimdall's hand.

The other demigod hauled, and they both ended up wobbling but on their feet.

"That...did not go according to plan," Heimdall said, as though just realizing the fact.

Loki snorted. "You'll find that's quite common in the mortal world."

He rolled his shoulders, cracked his neck. Winced. Ouch, that shouldn't have hurt that much. Okay. New plan. Anna had his car, the fastest around here, and she'd be as far away from here as possible. Which was good, seeing as the goddess seemed determined to grind whatever remained of Beckwell into pea gravel.

"But we can't defeat her. I've already let the Fray woman temporarily escape." Heimdall gestured at Loki. "I should have killed you both days ago. The gods will be most displeased if that goddess continues to wreak any more damage." He looked up, as though puzzled. "You just let her go. The Fray woman. She was part of your plan. Could have delivered us victory and you vengeance, power, and destruction. Yet you...let her go." He scowled. "*I* let her go. Should have just beheaded her when I had the chance. Going soft, that's what it is. Too many years behind a desk, not enough time in the field. They're just pawns, all of them. It's up to us to get things done."

Icy rivulets of shock dripped through him as Loki regarded the other demigod. It was tempting to cut him down for speaking so lightly about beheading Anna, but that was neither here nor there.

The trouble was that he'd heard those words before, or thereabouts. The reminder that they were all just pawns. That it was only the plot that mattered. The end result.

He'd heard the words when he'd told himself the same thing dozens of times over the years, over the decades. With the others, with Peter...with Anna. How many times had he tried to remind himself of that just the past few days? When Anna started to matter more. When it became clear as the rivers of Jotunheim she *did* mean something.

Although she left believing his plot was all that mattered to him. Believed maybe just as Heimdall did that it was only the plot that mattered. The quest for power, for vengeance.

By Ymir, he wasn't as much of a dolt as Heimdall, was he?

Loki sighed. "Come on, Heimdall. We're going to need help. I think I know who might be able to provide some."

CHAPTER 30

Being honest with people was, frankly, a lot more trouble than lying. Loki stood quietly, arms crossed near Anna's desk in the Beckwell library, and let the group hash things out, as was their wont. No sense noticing the hole where Anna should have been—the empty chair at the head of the table no one else would sit in, including him.

"You should have called us earlier," Daniel said, shooting Loki a look and leaning over the map of the Beckwell spread out on the conference table.

They were joined by the other three horsewomen, Mal, and James. Nia's owl perched on the corner of the table, Piper's skunk sat in her lap, and Ginny's pig squealed and attempted to lift his porcine behind into a chair so he could see, earning a resigned look from James before helping him.

"I called when I understood the situation," Loki said mildly.

Heimdall and Thor were out scouting and keeping an eye on the goddess. Hopefully not getting themselves prematurely killed.

While these six lives were his responsibility and would weigh heavily on Loki's conscience were they harmed.

"What? Like the part where we're all probably going to die?" Nia said sourly. "Where the hell is Anna anyway?"

Hopefully as far from here as she could be. An uncomfortable ache panged in his chest, and Loki shifted his arms. "She won't be joining us. You don't have to either, Nia. Your involvement is voluntary."

The Death horsewoman's dark gaze stayed on him a moment or two, considering.

Calling her by her name personalized their connection, forced him to remember her journey, her struggles. Made it harder to see them as mere soldiers but as people he'd watched over all their lives. Cared about. She and Mal had left their daughter in the care of the Senior Center, as had Daniel and Piper, along with many other Beckwellians. Those who hadn't fled. Some children could be orphans by the end of the day.

Nia snorted and shrugged. "Yeah, well, someone has to resurrect your sorry asses when things go badly. As they will. Anna should be here."

"She would be if she could," Ginny said, voice quiet, not looking up from where she frowned down at the map, their sticky notes marking out battle plans. "Maybe we asked too much. Pushed too hard."

Ymir, hadn't they all.

"Bullshit," Piper said, scowling. "She's the one who insisted we train and understand our abilities. She's seen us all rise. She knows we can handle it, so why not her?"

"She wasn't ready, or she'd be here. Anna is one of the smartest, fiercest people I know. If she's not here, it's for good reason," Mal said, giving Loki a nod. Tension bracketed his lips as he moved and changed the positioning of one of the stickies. "Now, let's focus on the plan and go over this one more time."

He pointed at the large red children's building block which represented the goddess, spotted in the northern sector of Beckwell.

Once Beckwell was destroyed, she'd head for neighboring Buttercreek, and from there the cities of Spruce Grove, Stony Plain, and Edmonton. All of which were primarily settled by Normals who wouldn't stand a chance against her and whose dense populations guaranteed casualties.

Mal turned to his brother. "Daniel and I will come in from the air, keep her distracted and disoriented, hopefully, make her mad enough to follow us. James, we need you as bait-like as possible. Shout at her, piss her off."

"Perhaps a bell?" James said dryly. He looked down at the map, pointed out the tree line. "I can have some of my team concealed back here. We'll be down Maddox, who'll be at the Senior Center, but that still leaves six of us with my brother and me, and we've got experience corralling troublesome deities."

"Good. Piper, Ginny, it's up to you to drive her back toward us and Old Man Gilford's field. It's level, flat, nothing to obstruct our view but some shelter with the old troll stones." Mal pointed out the blue sticky note on the map, marking the unnatural formation where three trolls had gotten into a drunken brawl over a century ago and been turned to stone when the sun rose.

"We need to get her back there before we engage. It's deep earth for Ginny to hold her. We need to destroy the body she's formed, then trap her spirit in a solid, warded vessel," Daniel said, taking up the plan. "Nia, your spirits are going to help drive her back." He paused before, for perhaps the first time in a year, meeting Loki's gaze without blatant animosity. "Loki, you and the other gods—if they haven't decided to turn on us—need to help driving her back."

Loki nodded. "We'll be there. James, you and your team have the vessels warded? This will be more difficult than containing a rogue demon."

Ginny's husband nodded, his jaw hard. "My tech expert has warded several different options, and we'll have them spread out among all of you. We may not have dealt with a goddess this big, but this can be done. After her physical form is killed, she'll still be dangerous, trying to use a body as her vessel as she did Daphne. We need to be sure everyone is clear so she can't take over another human."

"Shouldn't we have more backup?" Ginny asked. "I mean, if we're bringing her back around toward Beckwell, if we fail, she's going to go for the Senior Center."

"We're not going to fail," Loki said.

"If we fail, we're all dead anyway. Better others are at the Senior Center to mount a defense." Daniel glanced back at Loki. "Can we trust you in this?"

Loki's throat thickened, but he kept his expression carefully neutral. "Yes. This is my town too."

Daniel studied him a moment longer, then finally nodded, gave him a look that might have been something like forgiveness.

Mal nodded grimly, pointing out the yellow sticky note. "Try to hold her here, Ginny. Open the earth to swallow her if possible. We need to hold her long enough to trap her."

"Then we behead her," Loki added, making everyone look at him. He shrugged. "It's the most likely way to kill her physical form, and we need to do that before we can try to trap her." The trick was which of their gathered weapons would be strong enough to pierce her when his blades hadn't. There was only one weapon guaranteed that deadly, and without a War to wield it, they didn't have the sword Hildebrand. "Besides trying to take over someone else, she'll try to slip between dimensions or into one of the other worlds, like Braelyn or Daimoleigh."

"Seriously? How the hell are we supposed to do that? In case you didn't notice, we're not giant, and we don't have giant swords," Nia said.

"We have Heimdall and Thor. They'll have to do," he replied.

Another snort. "Which worked awesome when you tried to take her on before. We're so screwed."

"Maybe. But we have to try," said Piper. "We're the best chance of stopping her."

Nia sighed. "Yep. Screwed."

ॐ

Loki ducked and rolled, narrowly avoiding the car-sized fireball thrown his way that exploded in a shower of sparks as it struck the troll stones. He ducked behind one, where James and Piper took shelter before rushing out again. The first part of the plan went well. Between Ginny, Nia, and Piper, along with the men's aerial attacks, the team was able to get the goddess turned away from the cities and headed back toward central Beckwell, the field, and the troll stones.

Unfortunately, holding the goddess still long enough to stop her—let alone kill her physical form—was proving impossible.

"Mal's down!" James shouted.

Loki dove out from behind the rocks, running. Bedamned if he'd let one of the Quilans die, especially when he might finally have earned their forgiveness.

Mal in Fomorian winged form and blue skin plummeted in a downward spiral out of the sky near the goddess's head.

Nia was already running to meet him. "Piper, I need

you!" she screamed, calling for the Pestilence horsewoman's healing ability.

A gray owl swept toward the falling Mal, while Daniel, his skin bronzed and wings golden, spiraled and dove after his brother.

The goddess turned to watch. Smiled as her enormous black eyes narrowed on Nia running from one direction, Piper from the other, the small skunk struggling to follow.

The goddess formed another fireball in her hand.

Loki pushed his body harder to reach them in time. Ymir, he wasn't going to make it.

The fireball arched toward Nia and Ginny.

The fireball would incinerate them all—

The blood-red horse and rider seemed to emerge from nowhere, racing out of the trees so fast they were barely a red blur.

The horse leaped. It and the rider inserted themselves between the horsewomen and the fireball.

Daniel, his dark wings almost slicked back to his spine, dove down through the sky after his brother.

Loki skidded to a stop. Could barely breathe.

The fireball exploded over the horse and rider, eclipsing them in flames.

Then, as though it'd been placed in reverse, the fire pulled away, reformed a ball, and raced back toward the goddess. The ball struck her side in a blinding splash of flames.

She roared in fury, her monstrous hand going to the spot, her dark gaze zeroing in on the red horse and rider.

Daniel caught and hauled his brother off toward safety.

Loki started moving again, broke into a run.

The red horseman. Not horseman. Horse*woman*. Anna.

Anna was on the ground, speaking to Nia and Piper

at her side. Ginny raced toward them, followed by her scrambling black pig.

None of them looked up. None of them seemed to see the goddess.

Who'd formed another fireball and flung it toward them.

"Anna!" he shouted, pointed. "Move!"

She turned toward him, the moment stretching, her long dark hair rippling out behind her.

Neither she nor her friends moved. Only joined hands and turned to face the goddess and the approaching fireball.

"What is she doing?" a sweaty, sooty Thor said, panting as he ran up to Loki.

He stopped. Felt the echo of power in the air, like the gathering power of a summer storm, crackling and feral.

Unstoppable.

"Down!" he shouted to the other men, tackling Thor and throwing him to the ground.

The smell of dry dirt, sweet grass, and sweaty god was strong in his nose as they hit the ground.

The explosion made the ground shake.

He rolled over to watch as the fireball shattered around the four women. Their figures shimmered, until standing behind them was not just the red horse, but three others: Pestilence's white horse, Famine's black horse, and Death's ashen-gray horse. Actual horses, ready to ride into battle.

The Four had risen.

ॐ

Anna's pulse thrummed with excitement, and the sickly-sweet taste of violence filled her mouth. Nia's cool fingers tangled with her right hand, Ginny's warm one in the left. Their abilities rippled through the four of them, the elements swelling against each other, tangling and combining into something new, something powerful. The potential stages of the battle flicked through her mind like an old-fashioned card catalog.

As she'd ridden through town on Rojo's back, they'd seen swathes of blackened trees and farmland, some of it flattened, others razed by fire. Deep cracks gouged the earth, and an overturned car smoldered. What had happened in Beckwell seemed reflected into the outside the world, which meant the world was in trouble.

The goddess Tukmis leaned back, as though eyeing distasteful insects on the ground. Which made it likely there'd be another fireball, or maybe a well-placed foot coming next.

For the first time, Anna felt comfortable in this role. With Rojo's help and experience, she was the best leader. They might not fully understand the true implications of what all four of them rising meant, but they needed to survive today first before they'd have time to analyze.

"Woohoo! Now, this is what I'm talking about," Ginny's horse, Roger, crowed from behind them, prancing around in his new horse form.

"Shut up and focus, you idiot," Rojo said, voice cold.

"Loki and the others are fine?" Anna asked, refusing to take her eyes off the enemy.

Ginny glanced back, a shudder going through her. "Yes. They must have gotten down in time. What was that…I mean, that ripple?"

Tukmis inspected the blackened mark on her side where Anna's reflected fireball had struck, like a mountain examining the effects of an avalanche. Her face contorted in rage as her massive fingers found singed skin.

Good. About time the bitch took a hit too.

"That was us. Our combined abilities. Just a taste of what we can do. Together, we control the four elements. We can influence thoughts, and we have telepathy and empathy to communicate. We can foresee death, influence desires, heal, and hurt as needed. I look forward to exploring it, but right now, we need to mount up." Anna turned and headed for Rojo, who now stood beside three other saddled and armored horses.

Rojo was still the largest of them, lowering his head and allowing Anna to step into the stirrup and throw her knee over, straightening as she took her seat and the reins.

"That puts you in charge then?" Nia asked, only a touch of her usual cynicism as she turned toward her gray mare.

This time, for the first time, the hesitation that stuck Anna's tongue lasted barely a few seconds. "Yes. I'm War, and this is a battle. We can't let any of our troops doubt our victory. Piper, send them the encouraging vibes they need. Ginny, make them hunger for it. Or you're going to have a lot of deaths on your hands, Nia."

"Luv, I don't know about this," Roger, now a black horse, muttered to Ginny, who looked equally uncertain.

"It's not practice; it's instinct," the whispery feminine voice of Nia's horse said, even as Nia settled herself aboard the gray mare, armored in dark gray. As she did so, cloudy black-gray smoke settled over them, both cloak and armor.

Piper similarly had managed to mount her yellow-green mare, who was armored in forest-green leather. "I've never been good at horseback riding. But this…is different," she said, her armor a shining yellow-green metal.

"It is different. This is the fourth form we can take: battle-ready as needed," Rojo said. "We carry your weapons, your armor, and you, and foster the connection between the Four."

It took Roger and Ginny a few more moments before Ginny was mounted on the dancing black horse, their matching armor a gleaming black leather embossed with vines.

Nia shifted next to her, her energy as icy and flowing as Anna's was hot. "I get that you want to make a grand entrance and all, but isn't this the part where we should be attacking?"

"No," Anna said. "Wait for it."

Her mind was cool, while emotion roiled like flames just beneath the surface, infuriated with the destruction she'd already found back in town, what the others had only told her about. Part of the school crumbled to bricks and mortar. Fields of cattle now charred carcasses. The goddess Tukmis could divide herself into troops who swarmed in all directions while she remained here, focused on pounding Beckwell into powder.

Worse was what would follow. What Rojo and the truth whispered she had to do.

"Wait for what?" Piper asked, a small dark cloud seeming to surround her and her horse.

"Reinforcements," Anna said grimly.

"Here they come," Rojo said, his tone matching hers, his head turned toward the goddess, never looking away.

The others turned to look.

Anna didn't need to. She could see it reflected in the goddess's expression, feel the echo of the truth as the goddess prepared to focus not only on crushing the Four, but destroying all the others.

Tukmis probably saw mere peons, insects raging out with shouts and roars as they poured from the tree line.

Anna knew better. These were warriors. The disenfranchised, the disinherited, the unwanted, and the irregular. These were the paranormals and demons and minor deities who didn't belong to the human world but were equally unwanted by the demon world Daimoleigh or the gods' Braelyn. Now their sanctuary was under attack, and they'd had enough threats, enough browbeating, enough rejection, and enough abuse.

"Holy shit," Nia breathed. "It's...the entire town.

But how? Why?"

"I asked for one favor after they burned down my house. This is what I asked for."

Old Henry, it appeared, had friends. A secretive group who called themselves the Shades—mostly old men, but that couldn't be helped. When she'd asked her favor, they'd been quick to round up any and all troops they could muster and armed them with the collected strangeness Beckwell could offer.

Now they came by air on feathered and leathery wings to join Mal and Daniel as air support. They raced forward on foot—whether it was two or more—bearing the weapons of their ancestors. The old swords and battleaxes, the teeth and the claws, the spells and the curses. They would fight for their home and for survival, certain of their victory.

Because she'd convinced them of it. Shown them that "truth" and burned away doubt.

The ripple of uncertainty shivered through her, but she let the fire of War burn it aside. She couldn't afford to think of it right now. They needed Beckwell. As a distraction, and to help bring Tukmis down. Even Gulliver hadn't been able to resist the Lilliputians.

"It's not all of them. A guard of mostly seniors has been left at the fallback position of the Senior Center. Asha and the twins are safe. This is the rest of them. Deirdre has done her work. I've seen the path to victory. We just need to follow it."

A path slicked with blood, but the only possible future where they won. As the last Fate, Deirdre Boniface, once their enemy and with the powers of Atropos—the ability to see what would be—she'd always been the most feared Fate for a reason. This time, as Beckwell and the world faced annihilation, she was on their side. She'd proved her remorse as she'd passed out in the Senior Center, nose and ears bleeding after forecasting and detailing the twenty most likely scenarios for success.

Anna firmed her grip on the reins. She'd tried to choose the one that required the least blood as payment for that success. Had tried to ignore the sacrifices that had yet to come.

"Get ready. When I give the word, we're going to attack at the same time. Piper, you and Nia see to Mal. Get he and Daniel back up in the sky, leading our air support. Nia and I are going to make it rain—Piper, an assist with the air if possible—and we'll slick the ground beneath her. Ginny, I want you to make the earth swallow her, slow her down. Nia, you and I need to throw back whatever that bitch tosses out, run interference with the ghosts. Piper, stop any projectiles in the air if you can, try to give our people some cover. Then you and Nia turn that air cold as possible. Freeze her down, keep her still."

"Got it," Piper said, her amber gaze hard, a spear shimmering into reality in her hand.

"Oh, I am so on this," Nia agreed with a feral smile, Death's scythe already in her grip.

"Yeah, sure, great," Ginny mumbled, Famine's scales dangling from her belt. "Where exactly does that leave you?"

The weight of War's sword, Hildebrand, formed in her hand, the leather-wrapped hilt warm, worn from the grip of all the Wars before, a blood-red ruby in the pommel.

Anna let the abilities of the others, their joined and greater powers flow through her. Let War take her. Let herself join that line, to stand with them on her own terms.

Her voice when she spoke was steady, calm. "I'm going for the head."

CHAPTER 31

He'd seen Freyja, shield maidens, and the legendary Valkyries in battle. Anna was all of them and more. Fierce, beautiful, deadly as she raced toward the goddess Tukmis and defended her town.

To hell with being left behind or not running defense for her. Loki disguised groups of Beckwellians sneaking up behind the goddess and her many troops. He mirrored Nia's appearance, making it seem as though they attacked from the west as she came around from the east.

His muscles burned as he continually shifted position or thrust his daggers into Tukmis's foot soldiers. Irritating that when you killed them they just dissolved into dust and reformed somewhere else, merely an extension of her. But each one down gave Anna and the Beckwellians a moment longer.

He added his weight, shouted to Thor as a group of Beckwellians got the rope wrapped around Tukmis's ankles, and they pulled.

"Harder! Get her down!" Anna shouted, racing,

sword in hand, toward a group of Beckwellians surrounded by Tukmis's foot soldiers, spotted by a slowly smiling goddess.

Anna disintegrated the soldiers with the blurred movement of her blade. Rojo ran in beside her, and together they sheltered the Beckwellians as Tukmis aimed another fireball at their heads.

"You heard her. Pull!" He and the others heaved on the ropes binding Tukmis's ankles, tighter and tighter.

Heimdall grabbed a section near Loki, gave one mercury-colored look before he, too, leaned into the fight and pulled.

Tukmis bellowed and glared down at them as though finally noticing their presence.

Her foot soldiers raced toward them. .

Thor, hammer swinging, raced into action, soldiers bursting into dust on the left and right.

Nia led a screaming group of spirits who clambered up Tukmis's body like ants.

The goddess grabbed at them, tried to get them off her.

Ginny, standing directly in front of her, clenched her fists at her side. The earth shuddered and cracked open.

Tukmis began to wobble.

"Once more!" Loki shouted. He and the others pulled again. The ropes tightened.

One of her massive, sandaled feet slipped into the gaping hole Ginny had created.

Tukmis's red gaze widened as she began to topple.

"Clear!" he shouted.

A group over near the goddess's thighs weren't going to make it clear in time.

Dropping the rope, he raced toward them with everything he had, threw himself into the group of four shaggy-headed boys, shoving them aside before the ground shuddered and Tukmis struck the earth with another enraged bellow.

Beckwellians swarmed now that she was off her feet, pinning her to the ground with more ropes, stakes, and whatever they had to try and tie her down.

He stood, ensured those he'd pushed out of safety were unharmed. Ymir, just kids from the looks of it, some of Sheila Dryad's kids, not even out of high school.

Not much younger than Peter and the boys when they'd gone off to die in war.

He glowered at them, one of the boys clutching his hooved foot. Loki jerked a finger toward the troll stones. "You take rear, you hear? Your mother doesn't want to lose you today."

"She'd want us to fight," the other satyr boy snarled back, moisture sheening his eyes.

Shit. Past tense.

Loki softened his voice, gripped the boy by the shoulder, met the gazes of the others. "Then survive. For her. Fall back to the Senior Center. Make sure our second wall of defense is secure. Please."

The tallest of the satyrs grabbed his younger brother—who looked ready to mouth off—nodded, and collected their friends.

Boys clear, he turned. Sucked in a breath.

Anna, sans Rojo, clambered onto Tukmis's body, her sword clutched in her hand.

On the other side, Thor leaped onto the goddess's left shoulder.

They were going for the head.

Tukmis must have sensed the threat. Her remaining troops turned and raced toward Thor. Toward Anna.

Loki broke into a run, gripping a sword in one hand, a handful of daggers in the other.

Tukmis, teeth gritted, pulled on her arm. Ropes began to snap. Beckwellians cried out as that massive hand freed itself.

Dodging the snapping ropes, Loki threw daggers into the soldiers going after Anna, behind her while she sliced through them from the front. Where the hell was the damned horse?

Thor smashed through the soldiers that surrounded him. Got in one good blow to Tukmis's cheekbone.

Before Tukmis grabbed him.

She bellowed in rage, the earth rumbling, cracking, and shuddering beneath Loki's feet. More ropes snapped as she reached up. She grabbed Thor like a toy, then flung him away from her.

Thank Ymir the fool had a hard skull.

Loki ducked and dodged the snapping ropes. Went under her arm as she reached for her face, for Thor.

Now she groped for Anna.

Loki jumped and slid. Rammed his sword into a section of the goddess's upper tunic. Pinning her temporarily to the ground.

Another enraged, earth-shuddering bellow.

The sword shuddered.

"Now!" Anna roared and drove for the goddess's exposed throat with Hildebrand in hand.

The blade sliced through throat without resistance. Flames and blood poured from the wound.

Tukmis jerked her arm free, reached for the wound with bulging-eyed horror and gurgles. Blood spilled between her massive fingers.

Her foot soldiers turned to dust. All energy diverted back to her, back to protection of her body.

It was already too late for her.

"Get clear!" he shouted to everyone else. "Anna. Clear!"

Anna turned to look at him.

Tukmis gurgled her last.

The enormous body heaved.

Anna had only a moment to leap off the body before

it caved in on itself, flesh into flesh.

The flesh of the body turned to fire, a massive, distorted face leaping out of the flames and heated magma to bellow in rage.

The four horsewomen each took a place on a side of the body. Beckwellians surrounded the other sides. A bright, glowing essence escaped from the body, flickered.

Piper and Nia lifted their arms, creating a whirling wind that encircled the essence.

Ginny's red curls blew around her face as she lifted her arms in sync with Anna. Anna, who stood resolute, hair pulled from her face.

Magma cooled, what had been the body becoming blackened stone.

Earth and fire coalesced, gripped the now screaming and inhuman figure that emerged from the glowing magma that used to be the massive body. It tried to dodge toward the nearest Beckwellian.

The four women closed around the struggling figure.

It twisted and howled, sprang up, taller than them. Recoiled like a spring, into that small figure. Couldn't break their line.

The Four continued closing the distance, stepping onto the cooled magma. Stepped closer, until they joined hands around the writhing, glowing blue figure.

There was one last, ear-shattering shriek.

Then silence.

People picked their way over the charred landscape, over the cooled rock that had once been the goddess Tukmis. Some helped friends up from the ground or knelt beside those who could no longer rise. There would be loss today.

Loki helped people up, who stared at him with surprise. All the while, his gaze remained steady on Anna. He had to reach her side.

"You two see who can be helped," she said to Nia

and Ginny when he was close enough to hear her. "Piper, you're welcome to head back to the Senior Center. They'll be setting up triage. You can see for yourself that the twins are safe."

Piper shook her head. "I'll help from this end. The twins already told me they're fine. Don't tell Daniel, but I'm pretty sure they're telepathic…among other things."

Anna nodded, kneeling and picking up what appeared to be an empty squeeze ketchup bottle, the contents now black and smoky, writhing, flashing with red.

He approached more slowly now. This wasn't the same Anna who'd been in his bed last night, who'd shouted at him in his kitchen. This Anna was now War. Were she still angry, there was every chance she might not be done with her god-smiting for the day.

The other women stepped away, and Anna straightened. Her gaze snapped to him. She put on hand on her hip and color climbed her neck. Her hair was only in a ponytail, not a braid, and tangled around her shoulders. Moisture glinted at her temples, and there was a tear in her once stylish slacks, dirt smeared on her tank top and arm.

She had never looked more beautiful. Or more dangerous.

His throat grew thick, the echo of what they'd said to each other in his ears. "A ketchup bottle is an interesting choice for a prison," he said, then cursed himself for sounding like a fool.

She glanced down at the bottle in her hand, shrugged. "We went with the closest vessel at the time. Besides, one of James's friends is convinced ketchup is holy."

He took a few more steps toward her, resisting the urge to close the distance and pull her against him, reassure himself she was unharmed, beg her forgiveness.

It wasn't his right. He didn't deserve it.

He glanced around. "Where's the damned horse?"

A ghost of a smile crossed her lips. "He stepped between a sword and me, if you'd believe it. Ginny's horse is carrying him around now that Rojo has temporarily transformed back into pigeon form with an injured wing. He and Roger might become friends if they don't kill each other first."

Rojo, Roger, and all the other apocalypse horses able to take horse form now that the Four had risen.

Because Anna had risen. Something she'd never wanted to do. Something he'd pressured her into.

His chest ached. He stepped closer still, close enough to touch her, though he kept his hands at his side. He wasn't certain he had the right to say how he felt, what he needed to say.

"Anna, I—" His throat thickened, cutting off his words for a moment. He forced himself to meet her blue gaze. "I'm sorry," he said quietly. "For trying to manipulate you. For concealing parts of the truth. For forcing you to become something you didn't want."

She cocked her head. "You didn't force me to rise."

He blinked. "I—"

She closed the distance between them. Hesitated the smallest moment before she cupped his jaw with her hand, offered him a small, crooked smile. "You helped me become…me."

His hands rose to settle on her waist, to assure him of her solidity, that this wasn't just a dream. He stroked her hair back from her face.

She dropped her gaze for a moment. "I won't be the War you want, or maybe the War anyone else wants. Because I'm going to be the War I am. Not like the first, not like the candidates we met." The smallest tremor crept into her voice. "Not like my parents."

His grip on her tightened, and pride suffused him with warmth. For her. For rising to become the woman he'd always known she could be. Powerful. Without equal.

"You and your friends have proven your abilities will not define you. You refuse to accept the status quo, have proven time and again why the four horse*women* are uniquely more powerful than any four men ever could have been."

Pleasure glowed in her expression, warmed her gaze. "Now you're being too nice," she teased, her voice raspy.

He brought his hand to her face, smoothed his thumb over her cheekbones, his voice rough. "Never. Not about this. You are the most incredible being I have ever had the pleasure of meeting, ever had the joy of knowing."

Inexplicably, her expression crumpled, her lips trembled, and moisture filled her eyes.

How had he so completely lost his touch and ability with words?

A man cleared his throat behind him. Heimdall. Bloody Heimdall.

Loki clenched his teeth a moment then dropped his hold on Anna and turned, placing her behind him.

Heimdall walked slowly, his beloved long trench gone, fabric wrapped around an injury on his left biceps. Behind him came Thor, limping, most of his shirt burned away, red beard singed, and a large lump on his head. But he'd live to go home, get a lecture from Sif, and watch silly, highly inaccurate movies with his grandchildren.

Anna moved to stand beside him. Where she belonged. She met Heimdall's whirling mercury gaze with an unhappy glower.

His ally. His partner. His equal.

"It's too late. Neither you nor your cronies can stop the Four now. Perhaps you might consider some groveling apologies to ensure the gods don't execute you instead," Loki said, voice dark.

From his periphery, he saw the other three

horsewomen return to Anna's side, flank her.

Heimdall, too, noted the return of the other women with a small flick of his gaze, a tic in his jaw. He lifted his chin, gaze landing heavily on Loki. "Arresting any of the Four would be counterproductive. At least not until I've built a solid case against all of them."

Loki wanted to swear at the stubborn, immovable ass.

Heimdall spoke first. "However, I can place you, Loki Laufeyjarson, under arrest for the willful manipulation of fate, and treason against the United Supernatural Exalted Deities."

Loki gave the other god a flat look. He shouldn't have been surprised. Indeed, most of the other gods, especially Odin, had been looking for a reason to lock him up for centuries now. This was his big play, and he'd failed. Better he went quietly than cause any further problems for Beckwell.

He took a step toward Heimdall.

Anna stopped him with a hand on his arm.

Ginny's hand touched his left.

He turned, finding the Four arranged around him. Behind them, Daniel and Mal Quilan. James, standing with his brother and the two warrior women and men that formed his team. The four horses. Old Henry, wobbly but standing. Deirdre Boniface, gray with ash but as unyielding as ever. The other citizens of Beckwell, battered, bloodied, but victorious. Resolute.

"You're not taking him anywhere," Anna said, voice hard. She slid her hand down, tangled her fingers with his.

"Nope. He's our asshole," Nia said, shooting him a wink.

"He's our town protector," Piper said, both she and Daniel giving him a nod, forgiveness and protectiveness in their eyes.

"He's our friend and one of us," Ginny said,

squeezing his arm and giving him a sweet smile. All the sweetness drained out as she turned back to Heimdall, fierce and ready to fight.

For him, it would appear.

"Which leaves it up to you," Anna said, voice dangerously even, expression fiery. She held up the ketchup bottle in one hand. "We take the protection of our town seriously."

Loki could only stare at all these people, risking their safety for him. Claiming him.

Accepting him.

It was either a credit to Heimdall's courage, or a mark of blinding stupidity when fury contorted his features and he took a step toward Loki.

The Four and all of those defending him closed around Loki. Became an immoveable human wall.

"Step aside. You do not want to test the patience of the gods," Heimdall said, head not visible above the protective human wall.

Anna tugged him backward, through the crowd. "Come," she whispered. "This is the only way we'll get privacy with Heimdall out of the way. And…it needs to be now."

Loki barely cared about Heimdall's continued bluster, captivated by Anna's hand in his, pulling him toward the shelter of the troll stones. More baffling still was the broken expression on her face.

Once among the stones, he tugged her close, brushed away her tears. "Don't cry. It's just Heimdall and his usual posturing."

She shook her head, stared downward a few moments before meeting his gaze. "I need to do this now. Before I'm scared again, before I can't. The world…I can hear their pain." She covered her lips, choked back a sob before she looked up. "I can hear their truths. All of them, if I allow it. You said yourself the Four only rise when the world nears apocalypse."

"Sweetheart, we can train you to keep the voices out, to—"

"Do you still want it to end? Do you still—" Her voice broke, and she looked away and swallowed before she once more met his gaze, her eyes wet cobalt, her voice a whisper. "Do you still want me to kill you?"

He'd sacrificed so much to reach this point. Yet now, staring down into Anna's face, with that crowd of wonderful people back there defending him as no one other than Anna had, it would have been easier to tell her he'd changed his mind. Ymir, he wished he could change his mind. That he could take her home, clean her up, make love to her, and build a life with her. The life he'd always wanted.

But he couldn't lie to her. Not to his Anna, his beautiful Anna.

He smoothed her hair back from her face, slid the back of his knuckles along her silky skin. "I have spent a third of my life working toward this moment. Researching every angle, every possibility. I have spoken to Fates and psychics, cast the runes, and consulted the oracles. Humanity will destroy itself if something doesn't change, doesn't interrupt that inevitable march. I may not be human, but I will not see an entire species destroy itself. I want to help. I need to do something, and this is what I can do." The hope promised to him by the original Four. By the prophecy of Ragnarök. A reason for all he'd endured. Recompense to the world for his sins.

"What if they're wrong? What if you're wrong?"

He quirked a brow, memorized the feel of her cheekbones beneath his thumbs. "You truly think I wouldn't have considered the angles?"

She made a sound somewhere between sob and laugh.

He dropped his face to hers, his forehead against

hers, and dropped his voice. "The world will be new, humanity will unite, it will be another chance to get it right. This is the future I want. For you, if for no one else."

"The right apocalypse," she said hollowly.

"I won't ask you to do this."

Her gaze met his, and she attempted a weak smile. "I know. It's always had to be me. I feel that truth as well as the certainty that it needs to happen."

His heart banged in his chest. So many years, to finally reach this point. Yet...to lose her. He'd save humanity but lose Anna. His gaze ranged over her features to memorize them, to take some small part of her with him to whatever came next, if there was a next.

Anna shifted back, and the long, silvery blade of the sword Hildebrand shimmered into existence, the hilt grasped in her hand. The blade could change length and breadth as needed, and there was no weapon as deadly. She glanced at the blade and shuddered, the sword trembling in her grip.

Her gaze met his. "I...I don't think I can do this," she said, voice cracking.

He closed the distance between them, placed his fingers over hers on the hilt and moved the blade between them, settled the tip just under his breastbone until its razor-sharp blade cut through his shirt and pressed into his flesh.

"You're not killing me, you're setting me free. You're helping me achieve something I've only dreamed of until now." Until her. Until he'd started to have different dreams.

Anna choked on a sob.

He kept his voice quiet and steady. "Do it quickly, before I can expect it. Aim for the heart, and Hildebrand won't miss. You're not a killer. You're saving me. You're going to change the world."

"I don't know how I'm going to do any of it without

you," she said, meeting his gaze.

"Because you're the most extraordinary warrior I've ever met. And you won't be alone." He lifted his hand from the hilt, cupping her face. "I love you," he said, for the first and last time of his life, the words so simple yet filling him with a kind of euphoric lightness.

Tears streamed down her face as she pressed against him, pressed her lips to his. The kiss was both tender and scorching, salty with her tears. A series of small kisses, then one long, lingering kiss before she pulled back.

She pressed her forehead to his, her breath brushing his face. "I love you. So much more than I could have believed possible. I will always love you. Don't forget that. I love you."

"I—"

The slide of the blade up between his ribs and into his heart was so quick, so smooth, he barely had time to suck in one last breath. Anna's face was the last thing he saw before the world cracked open in blinding light and everything burned away.

CHAPTER 32

Loki's eyes widened in surprise the second War's blade, *her* blade, Hildebrand, found its mark. It slid so smoothly into him, then dissolved at her command, as painless as she could make it. Anna choked back a sob as she clutched him against her, his weight growing against hers as his body went limp.

She could barely breathe, didn't want to breathe as she lowered them both to the ground, cradled his head in her lap. "I love you, I love you, I love you," she whispered again and again as she pressed her forehead to his. As his last breath left his body.

She shuddered against him, wouldn't let go as the warmth of his body, as his blood soaked into her.

Oh, Gaia, what had she done? She'd given him what he wanted, but she'd lost everything in the process.

"Shit. You...you did it," Rojo said, hopping closer, his one wing bandaged.

They were all approaching. She could feel them. The other horsewomen, her friends, the town.

She forced herself to gently close Loki's eyes. Her hands were shaking so hard, and another broken sob tore from her throat as she leaned over him again, struggled to catch her breath. To try to remember why she needed to breathe. Truth said this had to happen. He said this needed to happen. But dear Gaia, it hurt. Oh, it hurt.

"Oh, Anna," Ginny said, dropping down beside her, wrapping her arms around Anna.

Ginny's hug was warm, strong, but like someone else received it. It was as though someone else smoothed their fingers over Loki's beautiful face, willed him to breathe, to open his eyes. All the dreams of waking up beside him, that teasing glint in his eyes, the amber heat in his eyes…all of it flickered through her. While his skin grew gray and cold. While his blood soaked the earth.

Daniel knelt and checked for a pulse. Rocked back on his heels with a troubled expression.

"But he… He'll be okay, right?" Piper said. "We ran him over, and he was fine. Or…or Nia, you can bring him back. Or we can do it together."

Nia's shoulders slumped, and she pressed a trembling hand to Anna's shoulder. "He's not there. I've looked. I…can't find him."

Mal wrapped an arm around Nia's shoulders.

Rojo broke into loud, ugly sobs.

Thor came closer, stopped, then hung his head, shoulders slumped. "There is no bringing him back if he was killed by the sword Hildebrand. There is no recovery from its bite."

Their conversation drifted around Anna, but all she saw was Loki. Images in her mind of how worried he'd look that morning when he'd raced to her burning house. The tenderness in his dark eyes, in his touch the first time they made love. The way humor glowed in his gaze even when he otherwise kept his expression even. The naked surprise in his expression when she and the other

Beckwellians claimed and protected him, as he'd done for them so many times.

As he'd done for her.

A broad shadow blocked out the light. "Why did you do this?" Heimdall asked, voice still like a rake over sheet metal. "I thought you wanted to save him. Cared for him even."

She smoothed her hand along Loki's jaw. "He wanted me to. Needed me to. It was part of an agreement with the original Four. He said…" She paused to steady her voice. "He said this was the option that saved humanity." Her smile was bittersweet, recalling his impassioned explanation. "This is the only way to save us all. Ragnarök. A new beginning from which the world can rise anew and fertile."

"Oh, child. What have you done?" Heimdall said on an exhale, the horror in his voice enough to make Anna look up.

Thor stood behind Heimdall. The warrior god leaned his bloodied hammer on his shoulder and scratched his head. "You're not sore because she killed him and you didn't, are you?" he asked Heimdall.

Heimdall rubbed a hand down his face, staring down at Loki. His gaze lifted to meet hers. "I wouldn't have dared fulfill that prophecy."

A chill settled over her. "Because you aren't as brave as him."

"Or not as reckless," Heimdall said, tone even.

"Hey. Back off, motherfucker," Rojo said, growling and hopping threateningly closer, still nursing his injured wing.

Heimdall opened his mouth, might have replied.

The winds picked up. First, a breeze, then faster and harder, howling and tearing around them. Next came the rumble beneath their feet as the earth shook and trembled. People cried out, clung to each other.

Anna held on tighter to Loki. He seemed to be slipping, growing less solid. She grasped at him, but his form grew lighter and lighter, more insubstantial. "No. Please, please, no." She wasn't ready. Couldn't lose him so completely. She grabbed for him, let War's abilities rush through her.

His hands slipped through hers. His body grew more and more translucent. Her fingers gripped only air. Loki slipped into the trembling earth and vanished.

"No!" she cried, the sound covered by the cracking thunder, the howling wind ripping away her tears.

The skies opened, their color shifting from gray to pink to red to black and green, shot with red fire. The ground shook harder. Rain poured over all of them.

There was a brief flash of light. Fire roared across the sky, illuminated everything in red. Anna looked up with a gasp. Fire, the sky was on fire, the world shaking, water pouring out from the clouds. Then the world went black.

ဢ

Anna groaned, her face pressed down into gritty earth, damp grass sticking to her hands. She levered herself upright. Daniel was helping Piper up, her knees seemingly unable to hold her. Mal and Nia just held each other, helped each other up from the ground. Ginny rested her head on James's shoulder while he stroked her back. Heimdall and Thor similarly shook their heads, rubbed their eyes as they climbed to their feet. So, too, the rest of those who'd followed them here. Helping each other up, trying to make sense of what happened.

She was alone.

She lifted her hands, dusted with small bits of grass and gravel, smeared red with dried blood. He was gone. Loki was gone. Her lungs seemed reluctant to fill, a heaviness keeping her on her knees even while the others staggered to their feet. Helped each other.

Rojo, still in pigeon form, hobbled toward her,

favoring his wing. The other horses were still in horse form and went to seek her friends. Her friends and their husbands, their other halves.

She didn't even have his body. He was gone. Vanished. Turned to air and swallowed. He should have been here. With her.

A dark hand reached out toward her.

She looked up to find Heimdall, his mercury-metallic gaze unnerving, his expression grim but somehow sympathetic. He gave her a small nod, and she touched her hand to his, let him help her to her feet, moving away from his touch as soon as she stood.

His truth was complicated, something she didn't have the faculties to analyze right now other than the simplest part: he was sincere, he was sorry, and he wished this hadn't happened.

"I, um, guys?" Piper said, the first to speak. She pointed a shaky hand. "What the hell is that? Where did they come from?"

Anna forced herself to look up. To see, as they all did, the large, imposing stone fortress now plunked down in the center of the previously empty field one over from where they'd fought the goddess. A huge, medieval looking fortress that looked as though it'd been there forever.

Nearer the road was a tall, almost Disney-esque tower, all pale ivory. A door opened near the base, and a beautiful woman in white stumbled out the door, gazing around her in wonderment.

"They're scared. They're all so..." Ginny covered her ears and winced, and James wrapped an arm around her. "*Frosted jellyrolls*, I can hear them. Feel them. All over the world. Terrified to see things they've never seen before." She gulped and looked up. "To see people and beings they've never seen before. Humans are all seeing the paranormal world."

The sky crashed with pink again.

All of them flinched, afraid the fire would return, but all seemed calm. Serenity after the storm.

"They should be scared," Nia whispered. She stood beside Mal and her horse, surrounded by legions of the wispy dead. They all looked around like the woman in the tower, pulled on Nia's clothing despite her swatting them away. "The Gray is still there, the ether plain, and the place for the dead in the beyond. But..." She shook her head. "Something's wrong. The dead are seriously freaking out."

Anna's shoulders squeezed. She forced herself to close her eyes. Rojo leaned against her leg. She listened to the air, to the earth, to the water from the rain, and the fire burned them all to their base, to the essence of their truth. She listened and opened herself to the truths all around her. Her breath accelerating, shoulders shuddering as it crashed over her. All those truths, some of them shattering with this new reality.

The world was anew. Humans were indeed uniting.

Because they had something non-human to unite against.

She opened her eyes to find everyone staring at her. Waiting for the answer. She turned to her friends and saw in their grim expressions they already understood, at least partially.

"Well? What is it?" Thor asked.

"It's...the veils. The dividers between the worlds of man, god, and demon." She took a deep, steadying breath. The words of Loki's prophecy washing through her. The specificity of the words the Four had used. The world anew, humanity united. A new world, as the old had been.

Dear Gaia, nothing would ever be the same.

She forced herself to speak the truth. "The veils are gone. There are no barriers. The worlds of the gods, the demons, and us... We're all one now. There is no sanctuary. Normals will see us as we do. Magic is free in the world again."

CHAPTER 33

Hours later, Anna stood on the front porch of Loki's house, Rojo perched on her shoulder, but she couldn't seem to bring herself to knock on the door. Her body was exhausted from the task of cleaning up some of the mess Tukmis had left behind. Her mind and head were weary of the arguments that insisted the veils couldn't really be gone, the realities of the new Beckwell, with houses and castles no one had ever seen before, the gods and demons who lived in them. The worlds of the gods, the demons, and the mortal realm had all become merged as they once were. The world as it was and humanity united…against the newly exposed magical community. Beckwell was at least three times the size. Though there still wasn't a traffic light.

Her heart…

She swallowed, hard.

Ginny and James had tried to insist she and Rojo stay with them. While she'd accepted their ride, she'd known she had to come back here.

There was one person who didn't yet know what she'd done. That Loki was gone.

She squeezed her hands together, took a deep breath, and forced herself to lift her hand to the door.

It opened before she could touch it, Loki's minion standing there, immaculate as ever in his blue suit, gray eyes sharp. "I was hoping you'd be ready to come inside now, Miss Fray." He stepped back, sweeping her a partial bow and indicating she enter.

Into Loki's warm wood foyer with the polished floors and expensive carpet dirtied by her grubby shoes as she stepped on it. She stared down at the dirt, as though seeing it for the first time. Somehow, ridiculously, she'd had this thought it would be Loki who opened the door. Loki, warm and smiling that sexy smile of his, somehow alive, as though none of this had happened.

But it wasn't. It never would be again. Because she'd done what he wanted. She'd killed him. She and the first War, with machinations and twisted truths. Her throat thickened, and nausea rose in her throat. And this man, his min— Gaia, that was a terrible thing to call him. Selfish and rude of her not to even know his name as he stood there patiently, waiting for her to say something.

"What—" Her throat was parched, voice rough and broken. She swallowed, tried again, forced herself to meet that even gray gaze. "What is your name?"

His smile was gentle, no judgment at her filthy, torn clothes, nor the pigeon on her shoulder. Or even the fact even after he'd given her all those beautiful clothes, she didn't know his name. "Trevor, Miss. Trevor Edwards. Now, would you prefer a warm bath or something to drink first?"

She just shook her head, fisted and unfisted her hands at her side, tried to come up with the right words. Tremors started to slide through her, building in intensity, her knees shivering. "I… He…"

Trevor just nodded a little nod then moved toward one of the closets built into the wood paneling and withdrew a black sweater. He walked back. "Mr. Rojo, if I may?" He offered his arm to the pigeon, who stepped onto his wrist before Trevor carefully lowered him to the floor.

"We could...we could use a stiff drink," Rojo said, his voice gravelly. He sniffled a few times.

"Certainly." Straightening, Trevor draped the soft sweater over her quaking shoulders before indicating the parlor.

The sweater was silky soft, and... Her eyes pinched. Her throat thickened, and no matter how hard she squeezed her lips together, they trembled. She pressed her fingers to her lips.

The sweater smelled of *him*. Of Loki.

A sob choked out of her chest, escaping past her lips. Tears burned down her face, tears she'd thought all dried up by now. Her knees weakened.

Trevor wrapped an arm around her and helped her toward the parlor. "This way, Miss. We're almost there. Just a little farther," he said in soothing murmurs as he practically carried her into the parlor with its masculine leather club chairs pulled up near a roaring fire.

Loki's chairs. The room was soaked in memories of him. His bringing her here the first time, kneeling in front of her and promising she'd be safe now, that he'd keep her safe. All her friends gathered around the fire after the gods first attacked them, and Loki helping them develop a plan despite their distrust of him.

More wretched, broken sobs tore from her throat, blinding her to the room, to all but the look in Loki's eyes as the blade had slipped between his ribs, his body falling against hers then vanishing, turning as insubstantial as air and just as hard to touch. Gone, so truly gone, beyond anywhere she or her friends could heal him from.

The storm of sobs passed, and she found Rojo seated beside her, staring limp-winged into the fire. Trevor bustled around, pouring amber liquid into two narrow-mouthed short glasses before he returned from the sideboard to her and Rojo.

He gave her another gentle smile before he balanced the short glass on the chair next to Rojo.

Rojo shoved his head into the glass, guzzling, the odd stifled sob now and then.

Anna pressed her hand to her throat, as though she could feel the lump of pain lodged there. As though maybe she could keep it down.

Trevor turned to her. He cocked his head. "Still nauseous? Shall I fetch a bucket, or shall you have a drink yet?"

Something about his words was enough to penetrate, and she slowly raised her eyes to him. "How do you know how I feel?"

He just smiled and offered the short glass with amber liquid. "I know a good deal about you, Miss Fray."

"Whether I'm nauseous or not?"

"Oh. Well, that's because I'm not human, but you've already figured that out." He nodded at the glass still in his hand. "A small drink first. Then we talk."

She considered him, that face good-looking in an ordinary, unassuming way. The way one might want to look if they didn't want to be especially memorable. Reaching out, she took the glass, caught the sweater as it tried to slip from her shoulders, the cedar scent of Loki rolling over her again. She curled the glass close to her and shuddered.

"Loki is…" She'd said the words dozens of times in her head but couldn't seem to let them pass her lips. As though somehow, by not saying them, they were less true.

Trevor crouched down in front of her. Much as Loki had done, so many years ago. But this bland, gray-eyed man was no Loki. "It's all right, Miss Fray. I know. Mr. Laufeyjarson is dead."

She squeezed her eyes shut again, a tremor going through her, eyes burning again. "Do you know I killed him?" Her voice quivered. "Because the original Four tricked him. Because they wanted him to end the world."

"Please, Miss Fray, take at least a small sip of the alcohol. It will help. Yes, I know what happened. The Four didn't want to end the world, no more than you or Mr. Laufeyjarson."

This was enough to make her look at him.

He raised a brow, indicated the glass. "Drink first. Then answers."

Her eyes narrowed. "You won't get me drunk if that's what you're hoping for." He didn't seem the sort to want to take advantage of her. And yet... She frowned. "I can't read your truth."

"Because it's too complicated right now, and because I don't want to overwhelm you. I remember well drinking with Marius and the others. Marius was particularly fond of a particular sweet mead."

Drinking with the first War?

Anna tossed back the contents of the glass, swallowed, and shuddered as it burned all the way down. Then held out the empty glass. "Now answers. Who and what are you? Why do you know anything about me? Can you help Loki?"

Trevor took the glass from her over to the sideboard and raised the bottle, but when she shook her head, he nodded and returned. He considered the chair, where Rojo glared out at him, then pulled up a footstool and perched on it near Anna.

"Answers. My name is Trevor Edwards. Or at least, that's the name I've chosen for this form. I'm a Watcher, a species charged with, as one might surmise, watching. I have accompanied Mr. Laufeyjarson for some time on his journey, and by connection, you. No, I offer no judgment about you running your blade through Mr. Laufeyjarson. It was what he wanted, what needed to happen. Yes, I can read your mind. Are you certain you wouldn't prefer another drink? Humans, even gifted humans, tend to react quite strongly to this sort of information."

She shook her head. "Get out of my head. Why was it meant to be? Because of the Four?"

Trevor folded his hands in his lap, cocked his head, considering her. Probably reading her mind, the jerk, but his gaze wasn't cruel. "Are you satisfied being War?"

She leaned back in the chair, pulled the sweater more tightly around herself despite the fire and the fact it was July. "It's what I am now. That isn't an answer, it's a question."

"In time. Are you your parents?"

She shifted. Recalled Loki telling her they were passionate and volatile. Rojo's words about the police reports, Child Services. Her own memories, less rose-colored now. Of the fights, how many times she'd retreat to her nest in the closet, to her books and fantasy.

"No," she said, voice rough. "I won't be them."

"Are you the first War, Marius Fray? The one who involved Mr. Laufeyjarson to begin with?"

"He lived thousands of years ago."

"Yes, but he, too, was War, and you share that part. Are you he?"

"No."

"Why not?"

She blinked. "Besides the obvious?" She gestured at her form. "I'm a horse*woman*, not a man."

"You saw the moment through his eyes when they selected Mr. Laufeyjarson for the plan. When the Four determined he, part-giant, part-god but with allegiances to neither, nor ties to man or demon, would be the perfect catalyst for their plan. During the great wars when man, god, and demon tried to destroy one another, the Four determined a way to ensure survival. An extended time-out, if you will, separating them with the veils."

She swallowed. "Loki, Ragnarök…that was their way to make sure the 'time-out' ended?"

Trevor nodded and smiled like a proud teacher. "Precisely. You saw him at that low point. Hurting. Alcohol soaked. Broken. Desperate for acceptance. If you were Marius, would you have made the same choice? Are you he? Would you and your friends have made the same choice?"

She was tired, hurting, just wanted to get to the part where he told her if they could somehow save Loki. But the question had all the earmarks of a test. She'd always been an A student. She closed her eyes. Considered Loki as he'd been. A situation where the species of the world were locked in war that could destroy them all. A solution had to be found. Creating the veils made sense. Using Loki…

Marius, like her, would have seen Loki's truth. He'd exploited it cheerfully, he and the others. Depended on someone else to clean up after their solution somewhere down the line. Didn't care what happened to Loki as a person.

"No," she said.

"Why not?"

"Because if it was their solution, then they should have taken care of it themselves. Immortality was possible; with their combined abilities they could resurrect each other if need be. It didn't have to be Loki. Or at least if it had been, he should have been properly informed. He didn't deserve what they did to him. They used his pain and vulnerability. They could have made better use of their companion abilities. They could have fought harder."

As Piper had done, to control disease but also learn

to heal. As Ginny had done, able to destroy food but so much better at creating it, at feeding rather than starving the world. As Nia had done, defying even the gods and the nature of death to fight for her daughter's life.

"Anna would never sacrifice someone else, let someone else do her fighting when she could do it herself," Rojo said from the chair, using her name for the first time. When she met his gaze, he gave her a small supportive nod.

Trevor studied her still, a small smile growing on his lips.

Her head pounded, she still hurt, and she was getting really tired of games. "Fine. You're the Watcher, spying on both Loki and me. How are you going to bring him back?"

"One last question, Miss Fray," Trevor said, steepling his fingers. "Do you trust your emotions? Do you trust your love for Mr. Laufeyjarson?"

She rubbed her hands down the dirty legs of her slacks, her mouth gone dry. She'd spent so long avoiding emotion, trying to remain only logical. She'd spent most of her life convincing herself trusting Loki would be the height of stupidity.

She thought, too, of the way Loki had held her hand on the plane, and somehow, she'd believed him when he'd told her they'd be safe. She'd fallen asleep on his shoulder, unafraid as ever that he would ever do her harm. This morning she'd run from him, certain he'd manipulated and tried to trick her into becoming War, yet he'd never denied his intent to see her rise. He'd helped her see the truth she'd been afraid to see, to see that so much of her was War, but that didn't mean she had to hide that part of herself, nor be afraid of it. He made her stronger, not only because she'd risen, but because she'd stopped feeling so alone and afraid, so much so she couldn't even reveal the full truth to her closest friends.

He made her strong enough to do the most awful, terrifying thing she'd ever done because she believed him when he said that he needed to die, that it was what needed to happen. She loved him so much that she was willing to give up everything—including a life with him—to give him what he wanted, what he needed.

"Yes," she whispered. "I love him, and I trust him. More than I ever have anyone else. *Please*, can you save him?"

"No," Trevor said.

"What?" Rojo burst out. "Why you perverted *ophidia in herba*—"

Trevor held up a hand, and Rojo was silenced. Which only made the pigeon hop up and down in fury then hop off the chair, brandishing his one good wing.

Trevor didn't seem to notice. Only met her gaze. "I have spent my existence following the rules of my people. Watching without interference. Well, without *much* interference. Perhaps I should have intervened earlier. Or perhaps now is exactly the right moment. For you see, Miss Fray, you, too, have experienced death. Which presents us with a unique opportunity."

Her chest tightened, and lightness suffused her body. She spread her fingers out over her knees, dug them into her pants. "You can bring him back," she breathed.

Trevor shook his head. "No. But if you're brave enough to trust your emotion, to trust him, trust your love, there is a chance."

❧

Valhalla was not living up to the hype. One hoped it was possible to put in a request for a different afterlife. Loki pushed his flagon of ale away from him—again. Someone continually kept giving him another. Rambunctious warriors on either side of him bumped shoulders with him as they jostled with each other like rowdy children. It was possible to leave the large keep for short periods, to fight in endless battles outside. Always it returned him here, an endless loop.

At first, there'd been bright light. Nothing for a little while, like a dreamless sleep, then he woke up here, laying on the rush-strewn floor of the monstrously huge keep, staring up at the ceiling covered with golden shields. Ymir knew the last time the rushes had been changed—this crowd seemed unlikely to care.

A huge cheer went up.

Loki ducked his head into his shoulders. Ah, hell. Not again. The great warrior hero had made his return, eliciting the cheers. What he wouldn't give for invisibility, but here, few of his abilities seemed to have effect. Perhaps they'd died with him.

The other warriors all cheered and clamored around him. Time was funny here, drifting from one drunken feast or brawl into another. And each blurred into another, punctuated by these visits from the warriors' greatest hero, Odin.

Asshole had to be lapping this up, as he always had. Though from his time on Asgard, Loki knew Odin didn't come every day, not since Frigg had insisted the dead warriors had to live in a different castle from hers.

The hollowness that gnawed inside of him was enough to make Loki eye the bottomless flagon of ale. He could lose himself in there, as he had before. Until he didn't picture her face every time he closed his eyes, imagine he caught a faint hint of lavender, of Anna, on the air. Remember that broken sob tearing from her throat as he floated high above his body.

It wasn't that he regretted dying and the change the act would bring—or had brought. He regretted she'd had to be part of it. That somewhere, she ached and bled inside as he did because they weren't together.

Because his plan had succeeded. He'd won. He'd gotten her to kill him.

He scowled at the flagon. The afterlife was not going to get easier if he continued to grow this maudlin. Ymir save him.

A hard hand clamped down on his shoulder.

He turned, a snarl on his lips. It quickly hardened and turned more cynical as he saw the large man with dark auburn hair and beard shot with silver, an older, crustier version of Thor. His leather armor was worn with use, the black leather eye patch oddly humble—likely an affectation.

"Go away, Odin," Loki said, turning away and again considering the flagon.

Odin leaned down, voice pitched low. "Is that any way to greet your brother?"

Loki shook off the other man's grip. "You made it clear I was never your kin—blood oath or otherwise." He reached for the flagon. If he had to spend the remainder of his existence here, he might as well be drunk.

Odin knocked it out of his hand. "Leave us!" he bellowed.

Ah, yes, because why say something when you could bellow it.

Despite a few grumbles, the large hall and the long tables cleared quickly. Without looking up, Loki knew only he and Odin remained.

He stifled a sigh. He must have incorrectly filed his afterlife papers. Because this felt more and more like the Christian hell.

He took his time climbing out from the bench, inspected the room and saw, indeed, they were alone. Only then did he cross his arms and reluctantly face Odin. A man who'd once been like a brother, enough so after many adventures together Loki had accepted the offer to return to Asgard. Only to have Odin's kindness wither and his jealousy grow when he was no longer the only voice of intelligence and reason in Asgard, when Loki would question his decisions or make better ones. Odin had given up his eye for all the knowledge of the world, and yet sometimes Loki still outwitted him, which infuriated and embittered the other god. Made him blind to all he had until he begrudged Loki even a small bit of happiness.

Loki kept his mouth closed. Odin could do the talking. Ymir knew the god never listened anyway.

Odin looked Loki up and down, took in the charcoal trousers and button-down shirt, quite different than the other armored warriors. "You look well," he said gruffly. Then his bushy eyebrows lowered, and he wagged a finger. "And young. Did you steal Idunn's apples again?"

"I'm dead, not well. Get to the point, Odin. You're disrupting my rampant pleasure."

Odin snorted. "Still think you're better than us, I see."

"Still pretending it's the ninth century, I see."

Silence crowded with their history, and rancor thickened and held court.

Damn the idiot anyway. Loki owed him nothing. Didn't have to pretend to tolerate his idiosyncrasies.

Odin, at long last, cleared his throat, smoothed down his bushy red-and-gray beard. "Heimdall told me I might find you here. And Thor. I sent him to straighten you out, make sure our gods didn't get mixed up with the rest of those powerless fools, but instead he tries to *help* you. Bugger gave me a long lecture about being more respectful and thinking about other peoples' feelings and a lot of nonsense, damn you."

Loki allowed himself the smallest of smiles. If only Odin knew it was likely Anna's influence on Thor that had caused the lecture. She did that. Lectured with love, pulled you closer if only to make certain you heard the lecture.

Shared her love with abandon, with all the heat and fury of fire.

"Word is you're responsible for this mess we're all in. The whole lot of us." Odin shuddered. "Mingling. With mortals again." He shook another meaty finger. "It's your fault we had visitors. First visitors from the human realm in, well, I don't rightly remember how long it's been."

Loki's brow lowered. "Mingling?" The horsemen and the prophecy of Ragnarök had promised a new beginning. A fresh start.

Odin scowled, the effect still potent even with only the one blue eye. "The veils, you idiot. You died, and the veils went with you. Chaos ever since. The world is like it was before the great wars, all the species mixing and mingling, humans terrified of the lot of us." A small smile twitched his bushy beard. "Those fools and their table of gods—the Uptights or some such—they're shitting themselves. I don't know what Heimdall was thinking, involving himself with them. Afraid of the Four, of the humans and the demons."

Loki couldn't share the smile. The world anew. Shit. He'd thought it meant renewed and healthy, but the Four had twisted the words. Had put the world back together as it had been: the gods, the demons, the humans, and all the paranormal species sharing the same earth. All of whom were about as happy sharing as a three-year-old on their birthday.

Furthermore, if the gods were unhappy, they might blame Beckwell. Blame the Four. He dropped his crossed arms and rubbed a hand back through his hair. "If they're scared, it could mean war. We all barely survived the last one." He paused. "Although the Four could stop it. Anna could bring peace."

Odin cocked a brow. "Yes, well, there's something else Heimdall wanted you to know."

A small chill slid through Loki. He'd lay odds it had to do with Anna.

Odin shook his head, looked up from beneath bushy brows. "She's calling for you. Won't take dead for an answer."

CHAPTER 34

"Anna, I don't know how many times we can keep doing this," Nia said, her expression troubled as she stood beside the filled clawfoot tub in the center of the large, white-tiled bathroom. Loki's bathroom.

Ginny and Piper, on the other side of the bathtub, looked equally concerned.

In a black tank top and panties, Anna stepped into the clawfoot tub, the water warm for now, though by the end it would be icy. The water helped bring her closer to the Gray and to the door of the afterlife. By the end, her limbs would be numb, teeth chattering as her friends dragged her from the tub.

She studied her friends' expressions. They'd helped her up to this point for weeks now. She needed them if there was any chance of success, small though it was. She had to try and reach him. Had to try and find a way to save Loki—if he'd allow himself to be saved.

"Is it hurting you?" she asked.

"Well, stopping your heart again and again isn't

exactly fun," Piper said quietly.

"It's not hurting me. Not hurting any of us—other than maybe you," Nia started then growled and looked desperately to Ginny for support.

Anna speared her oldest and dearest friend with a look and a raised brow.

The old Ginny might have quailed, blushed, and looked away. New Ginny, now that she'd married, risen, and come into herself, put her hands on her hips and glared right back. "She means we're tired of helping you kill yourself and only 'mostly' die every night. So far, you've brought back a demon, one horny Persian god, and I don't even want to know how many satyrs and leprechauns."

"Ugh. *So* many leprechauns," Piper said, shaking her head, eyes wide.

Ginny's voice softened, and she stepped forward, placed her hand on Anna's shoulder. "It's been two months, sweetie. Either he can't hear you, or…"

"Or he doesn't want to come back," Anna finished for her, forcing the words out through the thickness in her throat. She rubbed her eyes, sore and gritty from lack of sleep.

She and her friends had been trying to reach Loki in the afterlife since that first night Trevor had proposed the possibility and explained the idea.

Anna had died before, which meant if she died again, her soul wanted to head straight for the afterlife. With her friends' help, and because of the Four's strong connection, Nia and the others acted like an elongated diving cord. Anna could travel partway through the light, or doorway to the afterlife. From there, she called to Loki using not words, but her feelings.

Sometimes it was her aching grief, memories of their time together, the hopes and dreams that had died with him. Sometimes it was her anger over his decision, the

Four's part in it. Often it was just how much she hurt without him there, the cold emptiness of his bed without him, the hopelessness inside. Always it was her love in all forms, calling to him, begging him to come back to her.

So far, he hadn't answered.

She considered her friends. How much they meant to her, how willing they'd been to help her with this, to try and ease her pain. Goddess, she'd wasted so much time not trusting them fully. There was a chance this put them in danger. They had their own families, their own lives. She couldn't ask them to do this forever.

"We've done what we can to fix the damage from the goddess. Heimdall has also been surprisingly helpful with negotiations between the species."

She hesitated then met each of her friends' eyes in turn. Women she'd known since she first arrived in Beckwell, a scared and lonely child. Other than Loki, these three were the only ones she'd ever shared herself with, ever trusted.

"If tonight doesn't work, I won't put your lives at risk. I want…I want you to let me go," she said. "If I can go deeper, go farther, I can find him. We won't be here, but we'll be together."

Piper twisted her hands together, her face pale.

Ginny's eyes widened.

"Fuck that," Nia said.

Anna glared at her. "It's my choice. Wouldn't you do the same for Mal if you were in my place?" She turned to Piper, who reluctantly met her gaze. "Or Daniel?" Then Ginny. "For James?"

Nia growled. "They'd want us to live. He'd want you to live. You're asking us to kill you. So, I repeat: fuck that. If the asshole doesn't want to listen, he sure the hell isn't worth your life."

"We try again," Piper said.

Ginny nodded, squaring her shoulders. "Tonight, and

for as long as it takes. But you come back—every time. You hear me? That's the deal. No DIY routes to the afterlife either."

"Or we'll come in after you, and then you know you're up shit creek," Nia added. Her voice softened. "We need you, Anna. We'll help you, but we're not letting you go."

Anna's eyes stung, and warmth suffused her. She could feel them, all three of them, their truths, their dedication. "Thank you," she said, voice rough. "You are the most wonderful friends, the strongest women, and the fiercest fighters I've ever known—real or fictional."

"Yeah, yeah, don't start crying. Or I'll cry, and it makes it harder for me to focus. It'd really suck if I accidentally dropped you," Nia said, stepping forward. There was a wet shine in her dark gaze, and she squeezed Anna's left hand.

"Be careful down there. Just say 'no' to leprechauns," Ginny said, giving Anna's left shoulder a squeeze. "You get back here, you hear me?"

"Yes, ma'am," Anna said softly.

"We've got you," Piper said with a fierce smile. She placed her hand on Anna's right shoulder. "Tonight will be the night. I can feel it. You ready?" She and Ginny joined hands across the tub.

Anna took a deep breath, preparing herself. "Ready." She slid lower down in the water. Focused on Loki. His slow smile. The way he touched her face. The way just thinking about him sent warmth flooding through her body. She had to find him. Get an answer one way or the other.

Piper stopped her heart.

I love you. Come back to me. Please, come back to me.

⁊

"You're certain I'll hear her from here?" Loki asked

Odin for possibly the third time. Which annoyed both of them, but he couldn't help himself. Apparently, he'd been dead nearly two months—those drunken feasts did drag—and Anna had been trying to reach him ever since. Causing herself pain, endangering her soul as she stretched out into the afterlife for him.

Maybe she'd given up. Maybe she'd accepted his death and moved on.

He allowed himself a wry smile. Indeed. War had given up fighting? Unlikely.

He couldn't let her endanger herself either. She had so much to live for. So much of her life remaining.

He blew out a quick breath and shot Hel—beautiful on one side and decayed and decomposed on the other—the Queen of the Norse underworld a nervous smile.

Her irritated expression didn't shift. "If she calls you, you'll hear her here. As we all have. Night after night after night." She rolled her eyes. "Mortals."

Maybe it was a Death thing. Nia seemed to prefer resting bitch face herself.

Or maybe it was all those rumors that Hel was one of his monstrous children—the association never one she'd appreciated. Which at the time had made the rumors all the more amusing to spread.

Odin stood beside him, the first time in centuries they'd been in the same room for this long without fighting.

"It's fine. You can go," Loki said. Ymir knew why the other god had stuck around as long as he had.

"I'm curious to see how it works. What happens, really," Odin said, clasping his hands, stretching them out in front of him and rising on his toes, watching the movement.

More silence.

How long did they have to wait before it was clear Anna had given up?

Loki glanced at the black castle around them, the stones glistening with condensation, the walls bare and unwelcoming as Hel herself, though she treated her charges with great respect—the "unheroic dead," or all those who hadn't died in battle. The quiet keep was a welcome reprieve from the rowdy noise of Valhalla.

He could stay here. Wait forever for Anna's call if need be. Or until the day she finally passed, hopefully many, many years from now.

Hel stared at him like he was something nasty and slimy she'd found on the bottom of her shoe.

Many long, long years from now.

Odin cleared his throat but avoided Loki's gaze. "If this works and you're not dead, well, Frigg would like to see you at the family dinners. You know, once a year or decade or so."

"Did you know I founded Beckwell on the vortex at the precise farthest point from Asgard possible?" Loki said. "Frigg and I talk, we see each other. Video chat usually."

"Video chat? What in Ymir's name is that? Troll magic of some kind? Pornography?" Odin blustered, hands clenched and rising.

Silence a moment or two.

Odin sighed gustily, shuffled his feet. "*I'd* like to see you at the dinners. Not all of them, mind...but sometimes."

Loki, brow raised, turned to the red-faced Odin.

The big man shrugged, studied his gnarled fingers. "No one knows the old stories as you do, or all the adventures we had. No one tells them better either."

"I won't tolerate your abuse, not even for Frigg's sake," Loki said, hardly sure why he said it, what he was considering. All he could picture was Anna there with him, her reaction as he showed her around Asgard, perhaps Jotunheim, too, to see if any of the lakes or rivers truly could compare to her eyes.

Odin grumbled something unflattering beneath his breath but blew out a beard-ruffling sigh before that blue eye of his met Loki's gaze. "I've made mistakes. We both have. Maybe…we can try again."

There was sincerity in that one-eyed gaze. Maybe even regret and a touch of apology.

Well, damn.

"If you two are done with this slop then kiss, make up, and listen. This is usually about when you'll hear it. If she calls. If she hasn't regained her senses," Hel said sourly, crossing her black-clad arms over her narrow chest.

"It would be lovely to see you at the dinners too, Hel." Loki couldn't resist.

Her eyes narrowed to slits.

He was about to ask what he was listening for when he heard her.

Anna's voice. Or something like a voice…or a song.

Without thought, he started moving toward it.

No, not a song, at least, not a song with words. It was pain and frustration and joy and laughter and sex and fear and hope and comfort and home all balled up together. All of that and so much more.

He started to run. Out of Hel's black hall. Down through the darkness. Following Anna. Her voice, her song.

Her love.

He ran until he couldn't run, until his lungs ached. Which seemed strange, seeing as he was dead. He ran through darkness, through light. Through strange worlds of jewels and pleasure, through hellish, fiery worlds. Even worse than Valhalla.

He ran until he reached a sturdy, paneled walnut door that looked suspiciously like the one that led to his bathroom.

He opened the door, and, sure enough, he stepped into his bright, white-tiled bathroom.

The tub in the center was full. Anna, wearing a black tank top and panties, was helped out of the tub by her three friends.

She dripped from head to toe, shivering, her friends practically dragging her limp body from the tub, supporting most of her weight.

Her anguished sobs broke through between the shaking fingers she used to try and hold them back. The sobs tore at him, made his throat ache, his eyes sting.

When she sank to her knees, her friends clustered around her. He could barely hear their comforting words and murmurs.

Only Anna's broken cries, torn from her throat, from her heart, raw and bleeding.

He took a step forward. He had to find some way to help her. To make this better.

A warm hand on his elbow stopped him.

He turned.

Trevor stood there. Yet...not. This Trevor was a creature clearly not of this world, judging from his faintly glowing aura. That, and his ability to touch the dead.

"Good to see you back, sir," Trevor said, a small smile touching his lips.

Along with filing different afterlife papers, he needed to review Trevor's resume and application again. He was quite sure the "god-like powers" box had not been checked.

"I'm still dead, I take it," Loki said, then turned back to Anna, whose broken sobs had become a low, keening moan. "Can you help her?"

"I'm trying," Trevor said pleasantly. "What can I help you with today, sir?" He moved his hand to Loki's shoulder.

Perhaps he should also ensure Anna had mental

health checks done on all her employees too.

Trevor smiled. "I'm perfectly sane…I think. I want to help. But you need to ask for it. You need to make the choices, choose the path. I can't do it for you."

"The path—" Loki broke off, his mind flicking through the possibilities, what this could mean. He kept coming back to Anna, her low, keening moan. The ache to feel her in his arms. The way he couldn't quite remember the last time he'd lied. "I want to be able to comfort her, to ease her pain. I want to take her to my bed, make love to her all night and again in the morning, day after day, night after night. The afterlife will provide time enough to sleep."

His throat thickened as he studied her dark head. His thoughts flooded with images of her smile, the way she'd looked in that ridiculous white nightgown, the trusting way she reached for his hand.

"I want to feel the softness of her skin again, taste the sweetness of her kisses. I want to show her Asgard and Jotunheim and all the corners of the globe. I want to curl up together, her head on my shoulder, our fingers twined. I want to introduce her to my family. More than that, I want to make a family with her. Our family, here in our town. Whatever form it takes, however long we have, just with her. I want her."

His voice broke off. He turned to Trevor. Anna's weeping had stopped, but for how long? She'd suffered because of him.

Trevor's smile broadened. He nodded then turned toward the Four. "What do you think, Miss Fray? Is that satisfactory?"

Loki blinked. Warmth raced through his body, and his heart drummed in his chest. He turned to face Anna.

Who stared at him. Who climbed to her feet, took two slow steps forward, then closed the rest of the distance at a run. She flung herself into his arms with a

413

small cry.

He closed his arms around her wet, shivering body, squeezing harder than he should have. But Anna was in his arms, and bedamned if he would ever let her go again. No moment, beginning or end, had ever been so perfect.

CHAPTER 35

The paranormal world called the day the veils came down the Awakening.

Humans were more likely to call it the apocalypse.

The day all the worlds came back together as they'd once been—demons, gods, humans, and every paranormal in between once more sharing one small planet. Humanity was united. United in their fear of this "new" world they'd convinced themselves didn't exist. Squabbles between species broke out every day, land disputes where castles and homes had appeared on once seemingly empty land, pollution controls from the magical species who didn't approve of the destruction humans spread. It wouldn't be easy, keeping the peace in this new reality. But it *was* a new world. The truth said they would all learn to live peaceably. The Four had been right about that at least: another apocalypse had been averted. For now.

Whatever the case, it hadn't disrupted the plans pulled together quickly for a triple wedding, the grandest and likely strangest Western Canada had ever seen, held that warm autumn day in Loki's beautiful gardens, nearly a year since Ginny's wedding.

Even the knitting club had been invited.

Anna stood, arms crossed, a small smile tipping her lips as she considered the collected wedding guests. Her town.

Odin, Thor, and their wives had staked a position near the bar, the male gods' glares daring anyone to try and partake of the open bar. Heimdall, too, stood near them, caught her glare above the mingling crowd, and saluted her with his red punch cup.

She nodded at the other two gods.

Heimdall considered them, assessed the situation in that efficient, cold way of his. Then he moved to, hopefully, rectify the situation and not cause a new one. He wasn't as bad as Loki claimed, though she was still working on getting Loki to admit it. Indeed, the former USED leader had been instrumental in helping smooth the situation since the Awakening and this new world they all lived in. Turned out he didn't want war any more than she did.

Piper looked radiant in her yellow wedding gown, and she and Daniel slow-danced together over on the temporary dance floor set up by the rose garden. They each held one of their twins and were from all appearances the perfect, normal family.

Just wait until they discovered the truth about the twins. You couldn't combine the Pestilence horsewoman and a Fomorian without getting something entirely new, powers that would ripple through history.

Mal and Nia slow-danced together. Nia's concession to a wedding gown was a short, lacy, black cocktail dress. She'd foregone walking down the aisle with her scythe, but it'd been a close thing. Their daughter, Asha, ran up to them before she raced off with a group of combined ghost, god, and demon children.

It was one of the things that made Beckwell unique—and a new paranormal hotspot since the Awakening, too unruly even for the angels to try and impose justice. It was one of the few places worldwide where all the paranormal species lived together in relative peace. Well...most of the time. Sometimes they needed a bit of encouragement.

James and Ginny stepped onto the dance floor, Ginny in another bright, cheery dress, this one with cherries. Unfortunately, it wasn't long before she turned a peculiar shade of green—again—and raced for the rosebushes. James held back her hair, murmuring comforting things. Those poor rosebushes. Anna made a note to see what she could find about morning-sickness relief...and how one washed off rosebushes.

Otherwise, the rest of the yard was alive with guests. The entirety of Beckwell almost certainly. They'd all been invited, and those numbers had swollen in recent months. The magical vortex the town was built around seemingly had existed in all three of the worlds—mortal, god, and demon—which meant each had settled it, and Beckwell was a good deal larger than anyone had realized. Including a demon castle and some god estates. They'd all been invited, too, since it was always best to understand the battlefield.

Plenty of Loki's family from Asgard had come, though she'd been cool in her reception of them and made it clear she would protect Loki if necessary. He'd put up with enough abuse for ten lifetimes, and he'd never have to again on her watch.

The large black pig that was Roger, along with Rojo in horse form, had secured a place for themselves near the back porch with their own bowls of punch thanks to Trevor. She'd lay odds they weren't alcohol-free if Rojo had his way. Her lips tightened. Perhaps she and her friends shouldn't meet so frequently at Loki's bar, leaving the four horses outside. Roger's black ice cream truck parked beside Queenie's snot-green Port-A-Potty, Esther's gray chopper motorcycle, and the newest, Rojo's entirely impractical cherry red Humvee.

Piper's skunk, Queenie, was curled up near the corner of the porch in a sunny spot, paying more attention to Nia's large gray owl, Esther, so at least those two might be a settling influence on Rojo and Roger. Might.

Although, what scene they could cause that could top Rojo's horse-of-honor speech she didn't want to imagine. He'd promised to help kill Loki and hide the body if Loki wasn't good to her. Then sobbed about what a beautiful bride she made.

Warm, strong arms wrapped around her waist and pulled her against an equally muscular body.

Lupus in fabula…

She leaned back into his embrace, wrapped her arms around his. "There you are."

He wore another tux that she looked forward to removing at the earliest opportunity. She'd researched the shortest possible time they were expected to entertain their guests, and even if she did get Trevor to compress the schedule, there was likely still an hour before they could disappear.

Loki settled his chin on her shoulder, his chin brushing her ear. "The bride isn't supposed to be worried about the guests. She should be enjoying herself, not strategizing."

"That is enjoying myself," she murmured. "Besides which, I suspect you've been off pulling strings yourself."

There was movement against her, suggesting an answering smile before he swayed them gently to the slower tempo music that came on.

"Have I told you today how gorgeous you look, and how much I look forward to pulling that dress off your body?"

Her lips curled upward, and she turned, her cheek brushing his. "Only every time you see me. But you're not allowed to tear it. It's vintage. I won't, however, make any promises about your tux's survival. You can buy a new one."

He chuckled, the low rumble rolling through her, warming her in a way nothing, not even War's fire truly could. "Trevor is turning you into a clothing snob."

"This gown was made by a bride out of the silk parachute that saved her groom's life."

"Parachutes contained a lot of silk. She could have made more than one dress."

She turned in his arms, mock outrage on her face, but didn't get to use her snappy comeback. There was only time to glimpse the teasing sparkle in his pewter eyes, the flash of amber before his lips settled over hers in a breath-stealing, soul-surrendering kiss.

Anna clutched at his lapels and plotted how to shorten the event's schedule into ten more minutes by the time he pulled away.

There were loud hoots and whistles from the crowd. Who'd evidently become their audience.

Her face heated. There were disadvantages to no longer lurking on the edges.

Loki secured her to his side with an arm.

As though on cue, Trevor appeared at Loki's elbow with champagne flutes.

"A toast," Loki called to the crowd.

Trevor winked at her as she took her flute while he watched over the rest of the staff circulating with champagne for the other guests.

He'd given Loki part of his immortality so Loki could live again, and Trevor would live out this life as his last. More peculiarly, he'd opted to remain with them as their butler, valet, and personal minor-deity or whatever the Watchers were. She hadn't tracked them down yet, but her next stop was Braelyn's library. The veils had come down, but Loki's secret entrance still granted them access.

When she'd asked Trevor why he'd stayed, he'd just shrugged. He said Beckwell had become more interesting again. That, and he'd watched her and Loki for so long he was curious to see how the rest of the story played out.

She chose to take it as sweet, even if it was a touch creepy.

"A toast," Loki said, raising his voice and his champagne glass, his gaze lingering on her. "To the three most beautiful brides." He leaned closer, dropping his voice. "The loveliest of them being mine."

While heat flushed through her, he raised his voice again.

"Here's to new beginnings, new understanding, new worlds. *Amor vincit omnia*. To love conquering all, even death. To which I mean no offense, Nia," he teased.

"Sure you don't," Nia shouted back, her voice laced with humor, Mal's arm around her.

The crowd laughed.

"Here's to the four horsewomen, the sisters of the apocalypse. To the new roads they've forged, to the future they ensure ahead. To Beckwell's future."

There were here-heres from the crowd as they all drank to the toast.

Trevor was back at their side to scoop up the flutes the second they finished. A quick hand signal from him and the music resumed while he went out to encourage movement toward the dance floor.

"Come," Loki said, his breath brushing the curls beside her ear, his fingers stroking the inside of her wrist, stoking the rising heat within her. "I have a wedding present for you."

She raised a brow but tangled her fingers with his and let him lead her into the house and back to the conservatory with its lacy cast iron garden furniture and lush greenery.

He smiled as he led them to what looked like a fern near one wall. When he pressed his foot against the fern's pot and touched a place on the wall, the wall swung open to reveal another room.

At his gesture, she stepped through first.

The room was circular, walls and a domed roof all of glass. There was only one plant. A large, canopied apple tree in the center, growing from a circle of soil dug out from the rest of the tiled floor. The tree possessed the most perfect red-hued apples, all of them evenly shaped and identical, weighing down the branches.

She turned, glanced back to the door they'd entered from. It appeared to be the only door. Yet…the room was entirely glass.

"This must be visible from outside."

"Not when you pay for the best concealment spells and upgrade yearly," he said, once more taking her hand and leading her toward the tree.

His expression turned serious. "No one else knows of this tree, grown from one of Idunn's apples. You know what the apples do, I presume."

She blinked, studying the impossibly perfect, identical apples again. "The Norse gods consume them to regain their youth and strength."

"They allow us to live forever young if we wish," he said.

She met his gaze and raised a brow. "You stole one of the apples."

The corner of his lips rose. "Not this time. Frigg sent an apple pie the first year I declined the invitation to family dinner. 'A taste of home,' her note said. Only, she 'forgot' to cook or slice the apple. Just a pie crust with an apple sitting in it."

"Odin would be pissed if he ever found out."

"Which is why I stole it if he ever does."

She reached for his face, smoothed her fingers over his jaw and the faint stubble there. "Still trying to protect everyone. Trevor probably knows about it."

Loki's eyes narrowed. "He's either the most ideal or the most terrifying employee possible."

"Definitely both."

He chuckled, but as he stroked her face, his expression turned serious again.

"So…you want us to eat an apple?" she said slowly, both curious and a bit terrified at the idea of staying forever young.

"That's not up to me."

She made a show of looking around the room before leaning closer. "We're not leaving that up to Trevor."

"No." He blew out a breath, rubbed the back of his neck before brushing back his hair.

Her eyes widened. He was *nervous*. Goddess help them all. She cupped his jaw. "Loki, whatever it is, we can handle it together."

He took her hands, clasped them in his. "I know. Anna, I have spent most of my life plotting, striving to be one step ahead of everyone else. I try to outmaneuver and out-plot everyone, position everyone to my advantage." He smoothed his fingers over hers, glanced down at their joined hands before returning his gaze to hers.

"Which is why I'm giving you the tree. Giving you the power over this choice, about the rest of our lives together. I love you more than I imagined possible. You gave me a second chance, a family. So I give you this. The choice to grow old together or stay as we are. The power to be the one who plots our course."

At first, she didn't have words to answer him, especially as his words sank in. Goddess, no wonder he was nervous. To him, this was like giving her everything. She could barely imagine what it cost him to say it.

Because truth echoed through every word.

She tugged her hands free, put them on his shoulders, and pulled him closer. She pressed her lips to his and their breaths mingled. There was no taste of champagne on his tongue, only apple juice.

She pulled back before they got carried away and she forgot what she wanted to say. They'd spent enough time with their guests today, hadn't they?

She held him close. "I love you. And thank you. This is immensely generous. I've found the best plans are the ones we make together." Her smile turned mischievous. "Although…"

Loki's answering smile was full of love, as it would be whatever she chose.

Anna reached for an apple.

Dear Reader,

Thank you for reading and I hope you enjoyed Anna and Loki's story as much as I did – they waited a long time for their HEA (not so patiently I might add!)

I love hearing from readers, and if you want to keep up with what I'm writing or just need some good news in your inbox, sign up for my newsletter (www.shellychalmers.com/newsletter-sign-up/) where I bring you Five Magical Things no more than once a month. I try to look for the magic in the ordinary world, especially on the hard days, and these are things that made me happy that month. Plus, we can talk sneak-peeks about what I'm working on, along with goodies.

You can also find me over on Facebook, (https://facebook.com/shellyc.chalmers/) where I have a readers group called the Brazen Librarians, because librarians are my superheroes. It's where you can find out what I'm working on next, like the spin-off series, Shades of Beckwell, which is centered on the Beckwell Senior Center and a group of retired heroes out to find their replacements and play matchmaker (coming Fall 2019).

If you enjoyed the book, I'd greatly appreciate you leaving a review on the retailer of your choice. Otherwise, thank you again for reading, and wishing you both joy and magic in your life.

Sincerely,

Shelly

LATIN PHRASES USED IN MUST LOVE WAR:

(In case you too want to swear in Latin.)

Adolebitque illud	Let it burn
Alea iacta est	The die is cast
Amor vincit omnia	love conquers all
Aquila non capit muscas	an eagle does not catch flies; ie: an important person doesn't deal with the insignificant
Aut viam inveniam aut faciam	Either I will find a way, or I will make one
Carpe noctum	Seize the night
Culus	Asshole
Faex	Shit
Lupus in fabula	Speak of the devil
Non desistas non exieris	Never give up, never surrender
Ophidia in herba	Snake in the grass
Podex perfectus es	You're a complete asshole
Puto vos esse molestissimos	I think that you are very annoying
Statum tuo neque testimonio	State your evidence
Tu futueo et caballum tuum	Screw you and the horse you rode in on
Vinait qui se vincit	He conquers who conquers himself

COMING SOON...

The residents of Beckwell are up for new adventures in a world where magic is free...

Meet the **Shades of Beckwell** – a brand new series featuring some of the characters you've met already, along with many new ones as some of Beckwell's seniors and aging heroes look for replacements... and find a whole lot of trouble, romance, and fun.

Coming Fall 2019

ABOUT THE AUTHOR

Shelly Chalmers' first favorite book was Cinderella, so once she could form letters, naturally she turned to romance where everyone "loved" each other—though mostly because she didn't yet know how to spell "like."

A 2014 Golden Heart® finalist, she has a bachelor's degree in English and French, and has never lost her love of romances and their happily-ever-afters. Her stories run the gamut from Regency shifters to space opera. All include a touch of magic, a sense of humor, and a dab of geek. She makes her home in Western Canada, where when not reading, writing, crafting, or hunting unusual treasures and teapots, she wrangles a husband, two daughters, and two nutball cats.

She loves hearing from readers and chatting! You can find her at:

Website: shellychalmers.com
Email: shellychalmers@scchalmers.com
Twitter: @scchalmers
Facebook: https://www.facebook.com/ShellyC.Chalmers

Plus, if you'd like to be the first to know about Shelly's new releases, giveaways, and other goings-on, sign up for her newsletter, and get Five Magical Things in your inbox once a month. shellychalmers.com

MUST LOVE WAR